'Rachael Johns writes with warmth and heart, her easy, fluent style revealing an emotional intelligence and firm embrace of the things in life that matter, like female friendship.' —*The Age* on *Lost Without You*

'Heart-warming and compassionate ... Any book lover interested in life's emotional complexities and in the events that define and alter us, will be engrossed in *Lost Without You*.' —*Better Reading* on *Lost Without You*

'Full of heartache and joy with a twist that keeps the pages turning ... *The Greatest Gift* will appeal to fans of Jojo Moyes and Monica McInerney.' —*Australian Books + Publishing* on *The Greatest Gift*

'Rachael Johns has done it again, writing a book that you want to devour in one sitting, and then turn back to the first page to savour it all over again. I loved the characters of Harper and Jasper; their stories made me laugh and cry, and ache and cheer and ultimately reflect on all the many facets of that extraordinary journey called motherhood.' —Natasha Lester, author of *The Paris Secret*, on *The Greatest Gift*

'The bond between Flick, Neve, and Emma blossomed as their sons grew up, but even best friends keep secrets from one another ... Fans of emotional, issue driven women's fiction will welcome Johns' US women's fiction debut.' —*Booklist* on *The Art of Keeping Secrets*

'... a compelling and poignant story of dark secrets and turbulent relationships ... I fell completely in love with the well-drawn characters of Flick, Emma and Neve. They were funny and flawed and filled with the kind of raw vulnerability that makes your heart ache for them.' —Nicola Moriarty, bestselling author of *The Fifth Letter*, on *The Art of Keeping Secrets*

'Written with compassion and real insight, *The Art of Keeping Secrets* peeks inside the lives of three ordinary women and the surprising secrets they live with. Utterly absorbing and wonderfully written, Johns explores what secrets can do to a relationship, and pulls apart the notion that some secrets are best kept. It is that gripping novel that, once started, will not allow you to do anything else until the final secret has been revealed.' —Sally Hepworth, bestselling author of *The Secrets of Midwives*, on *The Art of Keeping Secrets*

'A fascinating and deeply moving tale of friendship, family and of course—secrets. These characters will latch onto your heart and refuse to let it go.' —USA Today bestselling author Kelly Rimmer on *The Art of Keeping Secrets*

'Packed with Johns's signature style: modern issues, relatable characters, wit, intelligence and so much warmth—an absolutely putdownable story.' —*Better Reading* on *The Work Wives*

Rachael Johns is an English teacher by trade, a mum 24/7, a Diet Coke addict, a cat lover and chronic arachnophobe. She is also the bestselling, ABIA-winning author of *The Patterson Girls* and a number of other romance and women's fiction books including *The Art of Keeping Secrets*, *The Greatest Gift*, *Lost Without You*, *Just One Wish*, *Something to Talk About*, *Flying the Nest* and *The Work Wives*. Rachael rarely sleeps, never irons and loves nothing more than sitting in bed with her laptop and imagining her own stories. She is currently Australia's leading writer of contemporary relationship stories around women's issues, a genre she has coined 'life-lit'.

Rachael lives in the Swan Valley with her hyperactive husband, three mostly gorgeous heroes-in-training, two ravenous cats, a cantankerous bird and a very badly behaved dog.

Rachael loves to hear from readers and can be contacted via her website rachaeljohns.com. She is also on Facebook and Instagram.

Rachael Johns

How to Mend a Broken Heart

FICTION
HQ

First Published 2021
Second Australian Paperback Edition 2023
ISBN 9781867255895

HOW TO MEND A BROKEN HEART
© 2021 by Rachael Johns
Australian Copyright 2021
New Zealand Copyright 2021

This is a work of fiction. Names, characters, places, and incidents are either the product of the author's imagination or are used fictitiously, and any resemblance to actual persons, living or dead, business establishments, events, or locales is entirely coincidental.

Published by
HQ Fiction
An imprint of Harlequin Enterprises (Australia) Pty Limited (ABN 47 001 180 918), a subsidiary of HarperCollins Publishers Australia Pty Limited (ABN 36 009 913 517)
Level 19, 201 Elizabeth St
SYDNEY NSW 2000
AUSTRALIA

® and TM (apart from those relating to FSC®) are trademarks of Harlequin Enterprises (Australia) Pty Limited or its corporate affiliates. Trademarks indicated with ® are registered in Australia, New Zealand and in other countries.

A catalogue record for this book is available from the National Library of Australia
www.librariesaustralia.nla.gov.au

Printed and bound in Australia by McPherson's Printing Group

MIX
Paper | Supporting
responsible forestry
FSC
www.fsc.org   FSC® C001695

To my writing buddies Maisey Yates, Megan Crane, Jaime Collins and Anthea Hodgson—thanks for the adventures we've shared in New Orleans

1

Felicity

Felicity Bell took a rather large sip of her champagne, slipped off her uncomfortable high heels and flopped back in her seat. All around people were dancing, drinking and laughing, but Flick simply wanted to go home. She was happy that her friends Emma and Patrick had finally tied the knot, but all the dressing up, trailing around the city for photos and then dancing the night away had been exhausting.

When were the jubilant bride and groom going to leave anyway? It was almost midnight—didn't they want to jump into the limo, head to their flash hotel in the city and make mad passionate love all night long like newlyweds were supposed to? Someone really ought to give them the memo.

'You looked whacked,' said Sofia as she lowered herself into the neighbouring seat and put her champagne glass down on the table.

'I am.' Flick smiled at the woman who used to be her husband. Out of a misguided sense of solidarity, Emma had worried about inviting Sofia but Flick hadn't wanted her to feel excluded. It was bad enough the looks and comments she sometimes got from strangers without her closest friends making her feel like an outsider as well.

'Nice frock.' Sofia nodded towards Flick's pink bridesmaid dress and smiled in a way that once upon a time would have sent her heart soaring.

She took in Sofia's black wrap gown with bright red flowers splashed across it. 'I could say the same about yours. It looked like you were having fun out there on the dance floor.'

'You know I love a good party.'

And wasn't that the truth. Sofia had always been the life of the party, so much better at socialising than Flick. Her friends had often admitted jealousy—*I wish my husband was more like him.* Well, she bet they weren't jealous of her now.

'It's been a great wedding,' Sofia added. 'Emma's dress is gorgeous. What about you? Having fun?'

Flick swallowed. She'd always been a hopeless liar.

'Yeah,' she said, cringing at her squeaky voice. It wasn't that she wasn't happy, not exactly, but being single at a wedding simply rammed home how alone she was these days. 'I'm so happy for Emma.'

They both looked over to the dance floor where Emma and her brand-new husband were locked in a passionate embrace. They'd been dating for almost four years—pretty much as long as Flick had been single—but Emma had wanted to wait to get married until all her kids were grown.

Not too far from the newlyweds was Flick's other best friend, Neve, pressed up close and personal with her handsome boyfriend James. She doubted they'd ever make their relationship 'official' but they were shacked up and committed in every sense of the word. Dotted around the dance floor were dozens of other loved-up couples, including Flick and Sofia's daughter Zoe and her husband Beau.

She couldn't believe Zoe's wedding had been four years ago now. So much had changed since. When Zoe had come home and announced her engagement to her high school sweetheart, Flick believed the biggest concern in her life was her daughter getting married too young. How naive she'd been back then.

As if Sofia could still read her mind, she said, 'So what are we going to get Zoe and Beau's baby to call us?'

'What?' Flick almost choked on the mouthful she'd just taken. 'She's *pregnant*?'

'No.' Sofia chuckled. 'But as they're about to start trying I thought maybe it was something we should discuss.'

'Oh right.' *Phew.* For a moment there she thought she'd missed a very important announcement, but she knew that babies were on the agenda asap—Zoe could barely talk about anything else of late. It made Flick feel old. Surely forty-nine was too young to be a grandma? 'How do you feel about becoming a grand … parent?'

'You were about to say "grandfather", weren't you?'

'No!'

'It's okay.' Sofia squeezed Flick's hand. 'You've been so great and so supportive, but I don't expect you not to slip up occasionally, and we have plenty of time to decide what Zoe and Beau's baby will call us.'

Slip up? Flick *never* slipped up. As hard as the last four years had been, she'd done everything she could to be there for Sofia and that meant working hard to use the right pronouns and call her by her new name. Not wanting to get into an argument right now, she took another sip of her drink only to discover it was empty. 'So what are our options?'

'Granny? Nanna? Nonna?'

'I'll be Granny.' Who'd ever have thought she'd be fighting over the terms 'Granny' and 'Nanna' with her former husband?

'I guess that leaves me with Nanna? Nonna would probably be a little weird, considering I haven't got an ounce of Italian blood in my body.'

Flick laughed. 'So, what's new in your world?'

'Um … nothing much.' Sofia's eyebrows twitched.

'Really?' Flick hadn't been married to her for almost twenty-two years not to be able to tell when she was holding back. She raised one of her own less tidy eyebrows. 'What's going on?'

Sofia sighed and reached for her drink. 'It's … look, I'm not sure now's the right time to tell you, but there is something I need to talk to you about. Are you busy tomorrow? Maybe we could catch up for a coffee?'

Flick frowned. 'Why can't you tell me now?'

'I-It's just …' Sofia's voice trailed off.

God, don't tell me she's decided to transition back to …

Don't be stupid!

How could she even think such a thought after all they'd been through these past four years? This wasn't like putting on one outfit and deciding you'd rather wear something else. She *knew* that … at least intellectually, but sometimes, deep down in her heart, Flick couldn't help wishing she could go back to easier times.

Maybe she'd been too quick to end things between them? Maybe she simply needed more time to wrap her head around a new way of being married? It wasn't like they'd completely been banished from each other's lives. Even after being separated for so long, they saw each other frequently and Sofia was still her closest friend.

'Well, out with it then,' Flick said. 'Seriously, there's nothing you can say that would shock me anymore.'

'Okay.' Sofia took a quick sip of her champagne. 'I've started seeing someone.'

Except. Maybe. That.

'That's ... *Wow*.' Flick glanced longingly at her glass. 'What's her ... name?'

'Actually ... *his* name is Mike. We work together.'

Flick opened her mouth, but no words came out.

'Are you okay?'

'I ...'

'Ladies and gentlemen,' boomed the DJ. 'It's time to send our stunning bride and handsome groom off into the night.'

Whoops and cheers erupted all around and Flick shot up from her seat, welcoming the excuse to get away from Sofia.

'However, before that, there's just one final thing we have to do. It's time for Emma to throw her bouquet. Everyone except the unmarried gals off the dance floor, please,' the DJ motioned with his hands, 'so we can get this game started.'

It's not a game. It's a stupid outdated tradition.

Saying that, at least it gave her an excuse to leave before Sofia said anything more about her new man. As the young single women formed a group in the middle of the dance floor, Flick pressed a hand against her stomach to stop the queasy feeling. Thank God the evening was almost over.

'Is that everyone?' called the DJ.

'No!' Zoe shrieked from across the other side of the room. 'What about you, Mum?'

Flick shook her head as her daughter made a beeline for her, arms outstretched.

'Come on, you're single,' she said, grabbing hold of Flick's hand and tugging her towards the gaggle of women. At the same time,

Beau—clearly finding this whole situation hilarious—made a big show of pushing Sofia onto the dance floor as well.

Were they for real? Did they think this was funny?

'No no no no no no no,' Flick protested loudly, but her friends and family refused to accept her resistance. Her protests were only prolonging the agony, so she gave a reluctant nod and stood among the other women, willing this stupidity, this whole damn day to be over.

'Okay, could I ask our lovely bride to join me,' requested the DJ.

Emma, glowing as all brides should, made her way to the front, the diamantes on the bodice of her sleek gown glittering under the lights. Following the DJ's instructions, she turned her back to the group of single women, slowly raised her bouquet of beautiful fresh frangipanis and hurled it over her head. Mayhem erupted and Flick jumped out of the way as the scrum of bodies scrambled for the bouquet. Due to Emma's terrible throw, it landed wide of the young women, right in front of Sofia. She blinked as if bemused, then stooped to pick it up as everyone around her began to shriek with delight.

Everyone except Flick.

'Congratulations,' Emma said, glancing nervously at her as she kissed Sofia's cheek.

'Looks like you'll be next.' The DJ winked. 'I wonder who the lucky guy will be?'

Oh my God! As an image of Sofia's wedding landed in Flick's head, all the hurt and shock she'd been desperately trying to hide since her ex's declaration erupted within her.

Tears cascaded down her cheeks and sobs heaved in her throat as she turned and fled towards the bathroom. She'd barely been there ten seconds, hadn't even had the chance to lock herself in a cubicle, when the door flung open and in rushed Emma and Neve, just in time to see her vomit the expensive dinner and champagne into the toilet bowl.

'Oh my God!' they exclaimed in unison.

'Please don't tell me it's the catering?' Emma said. 'I recently read this book where all the wedding guests got food poisoning!'

'Not. The. Food,' Flick tried to reassure her, but she wasn't sure her words were decipherable.

While she heaved into the bowl, Neve held back her hair, rubbed her back, and made sympathetic noises.

'I'm sorry,' Flick said, when she was finally done. She emerged into the main bathroom area, took the proffered paper towel from Emma and dabbed it against her eyes.

The blushing bride, her dress swishing all around, closed the distance between them and pulled Flick into a hug. 'Don't be ridiculous, you've got nothing to apologise for. I didn't think ... When the DJ pushed me to do the bouquet toss, I didn't—'

'It's fine, it's not you, it's ...' She sighed. 'Sofia told me she's seeing someone.'

Their mouths dropped open.

'A man called Mike.'

This new snippet of information did nothing to ease their shock. While Neve and Emma digested what she'd said, Flick tried to wipe the mascara streaks from her face.

'It was just a shock. I know it's been nearly four years but ...' She couldn't bring herself to say the rest.

'Is Mike a ... a serious prospect or merely a ... date kind of thing?' Emma asked.

Thank God she didn't say 'hook up'.

'Does Mike know Sofia ...?'

Neve didn't finish her question, but Flick knew what she meant. 'I don't know. I didn't get the chance to ask any questions before the bouquet toss. But I guess she's serious enough that she thought she should tell me.'

'And how do you feel about this?' asked Emma.

'How do you think she feels?' Neve snapped. 'I think the fact she exorcised her dinner gives us a pretty good idea.'

'You know, Flick,' Emma said, 'maybe this is a sign that it's finally time for you to start dating again too.'

Neve nodded encouragingly. 'Now Emma and I are shackled, we can live vicariously through your sexual escapades.'

This wasn't the first time her friends had suggested this. A mere six months after their separation, Neve had recommended Tinder as a good place to start. Emma, a little more conservative, had suggested she join some groups, things like ballroom dancing, tennis, gardening clubs.

You want her to meet people with one foot in the grave? had been Neve's response to these suggestions, but Flick hadn't been ready for *any* kind of interactions with the opposite sex.

Even almost four years later, she still wasn't.

Before she could comment, the door flew open again. Flick puffed out a breath of relief that it was her daughter rather than one of the other guests, or worse, Sofia.

Zoe rushed over to her. 'What's wrong? Are you sick? You look terrible!'

'Thank you, darling, that's kind of you to say. I think I just had a little too much to drink.' Utter lie. She probably *had* drunk too much, but that was not the reason for her falling apart. She looked to Emma. 'You should get back out there, but do you mind if I sneak off?'

The bride squeezed her hand. 'Of course not. I'll call you tomorrow, okay?'

'Don't be silly. Tomorrow you'll be too busy with your new husband to worry about me, and that's how it should be.'

'Beau and I will take you home,' Zoe offered.

'No, it's fine,' Flick said. 'I'll get an Uber. I don't want to make a scene.'

Five minutes later, she slipped into the back of an Uber and rested her head against the seat. Silent tears streamed down her cheeks all the way home.

2

Felicity

Flick's border collie cross labrador—aptly named Dog—greeted her when she let herself into the unit that, even after two and a half years, still didn't feel like home. Her old house, where they'd raised both their children and stayed living in for over a year after Sofia came out, had happy memories all around. There'd been family photos on the wall hanging alongside her animal mountings and framed artwork of Zoe's, shoes that she complained about constantly littering the floor, unwashed dishes left on the bench right above the dishwasher, the TV often playing in the background, and an aroma she associated with all the people she loved best in the world.

But they'd sold that house when they'd divorced. When she and Sofia had finally stopped living together, this poky two-bedroom unit was all Flick had been able to afford with her part of the settlement and her inconsistent income. Although a sought-after taxidermy artist, commissions could never be relied on in the same way a regular wage could be. She shouldn't complain, Sofia's new place was even smaller because so much of *her* money had gone towards her transition. Even with the assistance Medicare offered, the hormone treatments, surgery and everything else involved didn't come cheap.

As a result, they'd had to sell a lot of their furniture, and most of Flick's personal belongings were stuck in storage. Tonight, this fact seemed even more depressing than normal and she headed straight down the short hallway into the kitchen, where she immediately took a bottle of wine from the fridge.

A little voice in her head told her she was in danger of becoming an alcoholic, but she told it to bugger off. If there was any time to drink away her sorrows … this was it.

She couldn't believe what Sofia had told her. Mike. Mike. *Mike?* A name that had always seemed unassuming and slightly boring suddenly made her want to scream and punch something. Sofia was seeing a man. Flick sloshed wine into her glass and guzzled half of it. What did this mean? Had her husband been attracted to men all along? Had Sofia ever really been attracted to her? Enjoyed their intimacy? She wasn't sure she wanted the answers to these questions—just thinking about it made her feel sick.

Or maybe that was the wine? Refilling the glass, but vowing to slow down a little, she gave Dog a treat and then headed into the adjacent dining room. It was equally as poky as the rest of the place, but Dog—munching loudly—followed her in and found a small space to slump at her feet as she put the glass on the table. Hopefully she'd be able to distract herself with work.

'You're really letting yourself go, aren't you, Felicity?' she said to herself as she slipped her dark green apron over her head, no motivation to take off her pretty silver gown before getting started.

At their old house she'd had a studio outside, keeping the mess of her taxidermy business separate to her family, but also providing a place to escape when needed. Oh, how many times she'd retreated to her workshop, seeking solitude when it felt like her house was jam-packed with people or everyone in her life just wanted a piece of her. Now, no one wanted a piece of her. Her kids had both flown the nest and, with no one but Dog for company, Flick didn't need peace, thus she hadn't got around to setting up the spare room as a studio just yet.

These days her work was her life and her work bench the kitchen table. On the rare occasion she had visitors, they sat around the coffee table in front of the TV. Zoe had been appalled the first year or so, but even she'd stopped complaining about the mess now.

As Flick surveyed the landscape of the table, she smiled at her scalpel blades, surgical gloves, fishing line, borax, insect pins, rubber bands, critter clay, modelling tools, tongue presses, superglue, plyers, staple gun, tweezers in various sizes, cotton balls, and the dozens of different-sized eyes in tiny boxes. In a bar fridge plugged into the wall nearby, she kept everything else she needed—water bottles, chemicals in tubs such as tanning solution, pickling agents, luminal and bactericide. These were the tools of her trade, and while everything else in her life might have changed, taxidermy never failed her.

Flick moved her glass off to the side of the table and slipped on some gloves. She'd taken the Willy Wagtail out of the freezer earlier that day before heading over to Emma's place to get ready, and she couldn't wait to get stuck into it. Birds were a little fiddlier, but she still enjoyed them more than almost any other kind of animal. It was a grouse claw belonging to her mother that had first fascinated and inspired her when she was a little girl to think about taxidermy. Her dad thought it was something she'd grow out of, but the desire to preserve beauty after it had passed had only become stronger. It had taken years of perfecting her craft, learning from other artists and mentors, but she couldn't imagine ever wanting to do anything else.

This Willy Wagtail, however, was for her. It was a passion project, not something anyone was paying her to do, which meant she could really let her creativity run wild. Flick had found it newly deceased in the front garden when she was coming back from taking Dog for a walk a couple of months ago, but she'd been so busy with commissions and the lead-up to Emma's wedding that she hadn't had a chance to get to it yet.

Her phone pinged from somewhere in the kitchen, but she ignored it. It would be Neve, or Zoe, or Sofia, or even Emma, calling to see if she was okay. As much as she loved them all, she felt like a burden now. All getting on with their lives, they didn't need her sadness dragging them down.

As she worked, Flick tried to banish thoughts of Sofia (and Mike) from her mind, but it was easier said than done. She shouldn't be so shocked. What did she think? Sofia was going to remain celibate forever? That's what happened when people got divorced—they moved on. She could hardly begrudge Sofia finding someone else when Flick had been the one to break things off.

And she didn't begrudge her friends' happiness either, but once upon a time she'd been the one trying to squeeze Emma and Neve in around work, her family and a husband, and now they were the ones making time for her. Then there were her children—Zoe was all grown up and wanting to start a family of her own, and Toby was living across the other side of the country in Queensland, having joined the air force to pursue his dreams of becoming a pilot after finishing school. He dutifully called his mum once a week, but he didn't need her now either.

She felt obsolete. Her life lacked something.

Were Neve and Emma right? Was it time to finally consider entering the terrifying world of dating again?

Merely the thought gave her the heebie-jeebies. Dating would lead to getting up close and personal with someone, and that would involve exposing herself in a way she hadn't done to anyone except her husband in decades. Besides, at almost fifty she felt set in her ways and the prospect of having to get used to another partner's little quirks and annoying habits didn't appeal in the slightest.

She took another gulp of wine. There had to be *something* she could do to rejuvenate her life, but if not dating, what?

She glanced around the room. Stuck sometime in the late eighties, the unit could do with a facelift. Nah, interior design didn't interest her. Never mind watching paint dry, she'd be bored before she pried the lid off the tin. She could start baking more, but with no one to eat her cakes, she'd simply end up eating them herself, putting on weight and getting even more depressed.

Her phone pinged again in the distance, only this time it wasn't for a text message, but a notification from Facebook or Instagram or something. She glanced at her glass, now empty. Removing her gloves, she decided to risk a look at her phone while she went into the kitchen for more wine. In addition to messages from Zoe and Emma, she had a notification from a taxidermy group she was a member of on Facebook. Mindlessly, she swiped it open as she refilled her glass.

Flick's eyes widened and something fluttered inside her as she read the post from a member of the group who lived all the way across the other side of the world.

Admin, please remove if this is not within group guidelines. I have a taxidermy business in the French Quarter (New Orleans) and am looking for a fellow taxidermist to take care of my business while I am in Florida for a few months caring for my ill sister. This will mostly involve looking after my shop/gallery on Bourbon Street. You will not be required to take on commissions, I will pay you a reasonable wage and you will also be able to live in my flat above at no cost. If this sounds like something you may be interested in, please contact me via Messenger to discuss further. Kind regards, Harvey Nedderman.

Flick only realised she hadn't stopped filling the glass when wine spilled onto her fingers. She slammed the bottle down on the bench and read the message one more time.

New Orleans? She didn't know much about the place, not even exactly where it was located. American geography had not been something she'd paid much attention to at school but she put it in the southern states, at a guess.

Abandoning the poor bird on the table and the mess of wine in the kitchen, she grabbed her laptop and collapsed onto her bed to research.

One website called it 'America's Most Unique City'. Situated on the famous Mississippi River, the French Quarter was New Orleans' most historic neighbourhood, boasting a fascinating chequered past. It was described as an eclectic destination with bohemian charm, offering something for every kind of traveller, from jazz clubs and art galleries to delicious Cajun and Creole cuisines, specialist boutiques and voodoo, not to mention the most magical architecture Flick had ever seen. It was impossible not to smile at the photos of the brightly coloured French and Spanish inspired buildings and, Lord knew, she needed a genuine reason to smile. The streets were so picturesque they looked like something out of a fairy tale.

And, in contrast to these quaint, cheery houses, the dark undertones of the place also intrigued her. Some people might be put off by the fact it was apparently America's most haunted city.

Not Flick. She didn't think she believed in ghosts, but she had a fascination for the macabre that unnerved most people, and she would *like* to believe. New Orleans looked to contain everything she loved in one spot—beautiful art, creepy cemeteries, markets, a fascinating history of witchcraft, delicious food ... the list went on.

The more she read the more she fell in love with this place she'd barely spared a thought for until this evening. And here was a lovely sounding old man in need of a taxidermist. It had to be a sign.

Flick couldn't remember the last time she'd done anything without carefully thinking it through, but suddenly living across the other side of the world, far away from everyone who knew her and her past—far away from Sofia and *Mike*—felt exactly what the doctor ordered.

Feeling more enthused about anything than she had in a long time, Flick crossed her fingers and sent a message to Harvey Nedderman.

3

Zoe

As Zoe put a freshly made lasagne into the oven, she felt a warm glow—and it wasn't due to the hot air that gushed out. With dinner safely inside, she wiped her brow and glanced at the time on her phone. Only half an hour until Beau was due home and her schedule was running right on time. The oven was set to switch itself off after forty-five minutes, which meant she didn't have to worry about getting distracted and burning the dinner.

She'd left the gallery a couple of hours early after giving her boss—the terrifying Gretchen—an excuse about having an appointment, rushed home, made the lasagne, showered, shaved pretty much every surface of her body, lathered herself in luxurious coconut body cream and then slipped on the sexy lingerie Beau had given her for her twenty-fourth birthday. A red and black lacy see-through bra and thong set, which left little to the imagination. Even better than the actual present was the blissed-out, slightly bamboozled expression on his face whenever she wore it, which hadn't been for a few weeks, when she thought about it.

She'd been very busy with work, but all that was about to change. Tonight it was time to prioritise Beau and their family.

She'd sent him a text midmorning while she was scheduling Instagram posts for the gallery.

Don't be late home, I have a surprise for you.

What is it? You know I hate surprises.

She'd smiled in anticipation as she replied: *I promise you'll like this one.*

Technically, it wasn't actually a surprise. They'd been talking about the family they were one day going to have since they were in high school. They wanted to raise their children while they had energy and could be young 'cool parents'. Back then they'd joked about having six—enough for two teams of four (including Zoe and Beau), which made a nice number for family basketball (Beau's fave sport), but as adults they'd decided that two was perhaps more sensible. Kids, as their parents often said, were expensive and time-consuming, and while Zoe couldn't wait to be a mum, she didn't want to sacrifice her own dreams because of it. In fact, she was hoping that having a baby might even give her the chance to spend *more* time pursuing her passion in the hope of turning it into a career.

However many children eventuated, they'd agreed at the beginning of the year that they'd actively start pursuing Project Baby. In preparation, the last few months she'd been taking folic acid tablets, eating all the foods the books recommended, exercising regularly, and had also bought an ovulation prediction kit, which had told her this morning that today was the perfect time to set their future in motion.

She could hardly wait.

Next step, ambience. Just because they were planning sex according to her cycle, didn't mean it couldn't be romantic. She'd read that children conceived in comfort, fun and relaxation were much more likely to grow up into well-rounded, stable individuals.

First off: rose petals. She'd raided the garden of her mum's friend Emma this afternoon and had two big bags full of pink and red petals, which she now scattered through the house from the front door, down the hallway to the bedroom where she'd be waiting. Feeling like Hansel and Gretel as she laid her trail, she then moved on to candles, dotting little tea lights throughout the house and closing the blinds in their bedroom where she lit even more.

Tonight's scent—vanilla and spiced cinnamon—had been chosen specifically because it was infused with an oil that apparently encouraged fertility. Once the candles were lit, she chose a playful but romantic playlist on Spotify and commanded Alexa to play it throughout the house.

'You really are a pro, Zoe Thompson,' she congratulated herself when she'd set everything up to perfection and there was still fifteen minutes until Beau was due home.

She glanced into the living room where her easel and paints were set up in one corner. She was currently working on a piece for her in-laws' thirtieth wedding anniversary—a colourful depiction of the house they'd lived in since they were married. Although she was itching to get back to it, it wasn't worth getting started for only fifteen minutes, so she decided to read another couple of chapters of her current novel instead. Said novel happened to be a sexy romance by her favourite Aussie author—perfect for getting her in the mood. Not that Zoe really needed any encouragement. Since the moment she'd first laid eyes on Beau—looking all surfer-boy cute with scruffy golden hair and big brown eyes in his school uniform—she'd had a real problem keeping her knickers on around him. It was a miracle she hadn't got pregnant in her teens!

All these years later, although they weren't quite as rabid as they'd once been, their sex life was still more satisfying and creative than many of her friends reported, despite the fact most of them were still single and fancy-free and often indulged in one-night stands with strangers.

Zoe shuddered at the thought.

When six o'clock rolled around—almost an hour after Beau was supposed to be home—she started to twitch. The lasagne had long finished cooking and the book was no longer holding her attention. Frustrating, because she could have spent the time painting after all. She knew Beau had a staff meeting this afternoon, but seriously, how long could that take? When they were at school—and that wasn't *that* long ago—the teachers couldn't get away from the place quick enough, but Beau often stayed late planning lessons and coaching teams, unless they had something on. He'd even done extra swimming coaching at school in the recent holidays!

'Well dammit, Beau, we *do* have something else on tonight.'

What could be more important than making a baby?

She'd texted him twice already and all she'd received was radio silence.

Hurling the saucy novel onto her bedside table, she picked up her phone once again, positioned herself seductively on the bed, pouted and snapped a photo to send him. She didn't add a caption; the image spoke volumes.

Sure enough, twenty seconds later, her phone pinged with a message: *I'm almost home. What's for dinner?*

Was he for real? Not even one word about her underwear?

Her mouth gaped, but before irritation could turn into anger, she started to laugh. He was clearly messing with her. Knowing Beau, by the time he walked in the door, his work shirt would already have been discarded and he'd be unbuckling his pants as he stomped over the roses to get to her.

I am. And I'm feeling very tasty, she texted back as she heard the front door open.

'Come and get me, baby!'

The door slammed. Beau's keys landed with a clang on the hall table and seconds later she heard the fridge opening. Next came the twist and fizz of a bottle of beer being opened.

Zoe frowned. Although she hadn't expected him to stop drinking while they were trying to get pregnant like she had, she didn't think it was a good idea to have alcohol immediately before conception. And what about that *selfie*? Maybe he needed a cold drink to cool him down? She chuckled. Well, too bad, pausing to quench thirst was not on the schedule.

She was about to get up and go see what the hold-up was, when he stalked into the bedroom.

'What's with the roses and the candles?' He took a long gulp, barely glancing at her as he went into the ensuite.

Someone must have had a really bad day!

Luckily Zoe wasn't one to offend easily and she had a good idea how to draw her husband out of his funk. As she heard the shower turn on, she rolled out of bed and went to join him.

'Are you okay?' she asked, standing there in her see-through lacy bra and matching thong. Beau, already stripping off his clothes, didn't even acknowledge her.

Drastic times called for drastic measures. As he stepped into the shower, she reached around and yanked off her bra, then wriggled out of her knickers, letting them fall onto the floor next to his clothes.

'What are you doing?' Beau scowled as she stepped into the shower.

'What does it look like?' She smiled seductively, reaching for the shower gel and squeezing some onto the palm of her hand. Not quite the chocolate-scented massage oil she had next to the bed, but Zoe was nothing if not flexible.

Beau stepped back, almost crashing into the tiles as her hand landed on his chest. 'Not now, Zoe. I'm not in the mood.'

What? Since when did a healthy twenty-four-year-old man have to be in the mood to have sex with his wife?

'Must have been a really bad day,' she said, trying to rein in her impatience and be compassionate instead. 'Do you want to talk about it?'

Beau shook his head, running his hands through his hair, his eyes closed as he let the hot water pummel his skin.

'Okay then. You get cleaned up, and I'll be waiting for you in bed. We'll work on making you forget about it instead.'

His eyes snapped open and he glared at her. 'What part of "I'm not in the mood" don't you understand?'

Zoe recoiled. Beau very rarely raised his voice, and he'd never looked at her like that before.

Tears rushing to her eyes, she stepped out of the shower and yanked a towel from the rail, wrapping it around her naked body.

'Sorry,' she said, more sarcastically than she meant to, as she hurried out of the bathroom, letting the door slam shut behind her.

Still slightly wet, she discarded the towel and climbed into bed, pulling the doona up to her chin. What the hell could have happened to make Beau act so out of character? It wasn't only that he'd rejected her advances, but the way he'd done it. As if the thought of her touching him repulsed her. Tears dripped down her cheeks and she tried to stop them with the towel. So much for conceiving in an environment of bliss and peace, now she wasn't even sure *she* was in the mood, but she didn't want to waste this perfect timing.

It was a good fifteen minutes before he emerged, a towel wrapped around his waist. He crossed to the dresser, pulled out a pair of boxers and tugged them on.

'Are you going to tell me what's wrong?' Zoe asked as he reached for a T-shirt.

He sighed and finally looked at her. 'I just had a busy day. I wanted five minutes peace. Is that too much to ask?'

He looked calmer now, but his voice still had an edge she didn't like.

'Okay.' She bit her lip, paused a moment. 'How are you feeling now? Do you want to eat dinner or do you want to join me? Maybe I can give you a massage?'

'What's got you in such a horny mood?'

She let the sheet fall, exposing her bare breasts—let him try and resist her now. 'Well, you know that ovulation prediction kit we bought?'

'Uh huh.'

She grinned. 'It told me this morning that I'm gonna pop an egg any minute. It's time for your kick-arse sperm to strut its stuff.'

Beau grimaced. 'Right.'

'What's that supposed to mean?'

He sighed and leaned back against the dresser. 'I'm wondering if maybe we should postpone this baby thing?'

'What?' Her hands squeezed the edge of the doona. 'You mean like a few hours? Till tomorrow morning?' As a health and phys. ed. teacher, Beau also taught sex education, therefore understood enough about the female reproductive system to know the window of opportunity lasted a couple of days at most. 'We can't just do it once; we need to have sex every day while I'm ovulating to increase our chances.'

He didn't reply, just stood there as if he'd rather be anywhere else.

Zoe's heart quaked. 'Don't you want a baby?'

'It's not that. It's just …' Beau crossed the room and sat down on the edge of the bed. 'I'm wondering if, like, maybe we're rushing into things?'

'*Rushing into things?*' The tight hold she'd been managing to keep on her anger crumbled. 'We've been together almost ten years and talking about getting pregnant since long before we got married—we both agreed we wanted to be young parents.'

'Yes, but there's young and there's … young.'

'Fifteen is actually physically the perfect time to have a baby for women, and I'm already well past that.'

Beau looked horrified. 'I think you've got a bit of time before you need to worry, but what are we gonna do about income if we have a baby? We can't both work with a newborn. Maybe we should save a bit first. Get more established. We rent a two-bedroom unit—not exactly a great family home.'

Zoe forced a smile and shuffled closer to him on the bed. She took his hand and tried to rein in her annoyance that he hadn't raised any of these concerns over the last few months.

'Babies don't need a lot of stuff,' said Zoe. 'All they need is love, and you and I have love to give in spades. Besides you'll still work, and I'll hopefully be able to devote more time to my art and maybe even start selling some pieces, when I'm not tied down to Gretchen's demands. I really think if I give it a good chance, I can make my painting pay, but if not, I can look for a part-time job. Mum loves babies; I'm sure she'd be happy to look after ours for a day or two a week.'

'Isn't your mum moving overseas?'

'She's not moving, it's only for three months max. She'll be back long before the baby's born.'

When he didn't say anything more, Zoe took it as a good sign.

Leaning in close, she whispered, 'Don't stress so much. I love you, and together we can achieve anything. Besides, who knows how long it'll take to get pregnant, but at least we'll have fun trying.'

With that she let go of his hand and placed hers between his legs. He groaned. She wasn't entirely sure whether it was a sound of pleasure or something else, but she leaned forward and put her mouth to his neck as she slipped her hand inside his boxers. Her fingers closed around his silky length as she began to move her hand up and down.

After about a minute, when Beau's cock was still limp, she looked searchingly into his eyes. Not once had she ever failed to turn him on.

'Is there something *else* bothering you?'

He shook his head. 'I'm sorry. I just can't.' Then he shot to his feet and fled the bedroom.

Zoe had never felt so confused and rejected in her life.

4

Felicity

'Take two,' Neve said as she reversed into a parking space at Perth airport.

If Flick believed in signs, having her plane from Sydney to Dallas cancelled yesterday might have been one. She'd been all packed and taking Dog for one final walk around the block before dropping him round to Sofia's when she'd received the news that she wasn't going anywhere after all. The woman she'd spoken to at the airline had apologised profusely, trying to get her on an earlier flight—*Hmm, maybe we could send you via San Francisco?*—but in the end, despite her best attempts, she hadn't been able to make it work. As a result, Flick had spent last night on the couch at Zoe and Beau's because her house-sitters—two middle-aged women travelling Australia—had already arrived.

'Have you got your passport?' Neve asked. 'What about condoms?'

'I'm going to *work*!' Flick glared at her friend as Zoe giggled and Emma chuckled from the back seat.

Sometimes Flick felt like her loved-up friends never thought about anything but sex. You'd think Emma and Neve were in their early twenties, not their late-forties. At their age, they should be buying control undies and worrying about hairs sprouting from their chins, not Brazilian waxes and getting it on.

'No messages from Qantas today, Mum?' Zoe asked.

Flick glanced at her phone, tightly gripped in her hand. 'Nope, thank God.'

Although she almost wished there was. The extra twenty-four hours had given her time to second-guess her spur-of-the-moment decision. The three weeks since she'd accepted Harvey Nedderman's offer to take care of his shop had been a whirlwind of organisation—making sure her passport was still valid (check), organising her rushed work Visa (check), advertising her own house on a housesitting website (check), booking flights (check), finishing her current commission and passing on the next couple to other taxidermists (check).

She was one hundred per cent prepared—so why did she feel so damn nervous?

'Did you pack earplugs?' asked Neve as they got Flick's suitcases and her overnight bag out of the boot while Zoe went to fetch a trolley. 'Remember how noisy and difficult it was to sleep when we were in New York all those years ago?'

'It'll be even worse in New Orleans,' Emma said, 'especially where you're staying in the French Quarter.'

'Harvey said it was the quiet end of Bourbon Street.'

Emma, a travel agent, laughed as Zoe returned with the trolley. 'From what I recall, there's no quiet end of Bourbon Street—maybe the old man's deaf? You might even need *two* pairs of earplugs,' she joked, 'if you want any chance of getting any sleep for the next few months.'

'You won't have a chance to sleep, will you, Mum?' Zoe gave Flick a cheeky wink as the four of them started towards the terminal, the heavily laden trolley making loud clunking noises as it went over potholes in the bitumen. 'You'll be too busy partying.'

Flick gave her daughter a look; the only party happening right now was in her stomach where a flock of butterflies appeared to have taken up residence. What if this was an absolutely crazy decision? And what if she *had* forgotten something important?

She patted the handbag hanging over her shoulder. 'I've got earplugs, lip balm, hand cream, painkillers, sleeping tablets, a change of undies, my credit cards, US dollars, and everything else I packed when we all went to New York. I have travelled before, you know?'

And although this was the truth, she'd never actually travelled alone—as a kid she'd always holidayed with her parents, and then when her mum died, with her dad. She'd gone on school camps of course, but those didn't count as solo voyaging, and neither did that Contiki trip she'd taken to Europe before she was married. All of the vacations she'd taken in the last twenty-four years had been as a family, except for a trip to New York, but even then she'd been with her friends.

Now, she was not only travelling halfway across the world alone, but also planning to stay there on her lonesome for up to three months.

What was I thinking?

Hadn't she always told her kids not to make major life decisions when under the influence? And the night of Emma's wedding, when she'd reached out to Harvey Nedderman, she'd most definitely been under the influence—of alcohol, yes, but also shock, sadness and a cocktail of other dangerous emotions. The thought of Sofia and Mike had seeped into her brain and affected her sensibilities.

'Have we got time for a wine?' Neve glanced upstairs to the bar the moment they entered the terminal.

'It's ten o'clock in the morning,' Emma chastised.

Neve winked. 'Don't you know that once you step into an airport all rules about drinking disappear? It's like a parallel universe with no time zones. Besides, it's the weekend—live a little.'

Flick looked up at the departures board. Her flight to Sydney was due to take off in an hour and a half—plenty of time for a quick drink, and if she had to wait out that hour with Neve, Emma and Zoe, then she probably needed one. She was beginning to regret accepting their offer to escort her to the airport. Ever since Neve and Emma had picked her and Zoe up, the three of them had been talking nonstop like nervous parents seeing their child off on a school trip.

One minute they were excited for her: *Oh my God, I'm so jealous, you're going to have the time of your life!*

The next they were trying to scare her to death: *Isn't New Orleans the murder capital of America?!*

A topic they'd debated back and forth between themselves— eventually deciding she wasn't at risk because most murders were to do with domestic violence or gang wars, not random acts on tourists—before finally threatening tears because they were going to miss her so damn much.

As if she didn't have enough mixed emotions going on inside *herself* already.

'Let me check in first,' Flick said, wrenching the luggage trolley from Zoe and starting towards the queue for international departures.

While waiting in line, she double-checked she did have her passport, her ticket, and her Valium. It wasn't that Flick was a nervous traveller, she'd been on plenty of planes in her life, but ever since her marriage break-up she'd been having trouble sleeping, even at night when she was tucked up in her comfy bed.

So, the Valium was a precaution. She wanted to be as fresh as absolutely possible when she landed on the other side, especially now she was going to have to make her way to the taxidermy shop on her own. Harvey had planned to meet her at the airport and give her a grand tour of the French Quarter before leaving for Florida the following day, but thanks to her cancelled flight, he'd already be gone by the time she arrived.

'Next please,' called a neatly presented woman at the desk.

'Hi,' Flick said brightly as she handed over her passport.

'Where are you off to?' the woman asked with barely a smile in reply.

'New Orleans.'

'Are you flying alone?'

When Flick nodded, the woman asked her a few more security questions, before snaking luggage labels through the handles of her cases, then handing back the passport, her paperwork and three boarding passes.

'This one's for your flight to Sydney, then you have to change terminals. I've also checked you in for your flight from Sydney to Dallas, which is where you'll go through customs. Pick up your luggage, go through security and then make your way to the next terminal for your flight to Louis Armstrong.'

'Louis who?'

The woman actually rolled her eyes. 'Louis Armstrong is the New Orleans International airport.'

'Ah right, thanks.' Of course, Flick knew that—it was just nerves messing with her mind. She'd barely turned to leave when the woman called 'Next please' again and an eager couple almost rammed into her with a trolley in their haste to get to the desk.

Great start. Pasting another smile on her face, she made her way to where the others were waiting off to one side.

'All ready for that wine? My shout,' Neve offered.

Flick wasn't sure she should really be drinking at this time of the morning before a long-haul flight across the world, but maybe it would help calm her anxiety.

Once upstairs, they headed for the bar and found a table.

Neve reached into her bag for her purse. 'What's everyone having?'

'Shall we buy a bottle of bubbly to toast Flick's big adventure?' Emma, suddenly on board with the whole morning drinking thing, suggested.

'Great idea,' exclaimed Neve and Zoe in unison.

'Sounds good.' Flick nodded. Who was she to argue with champagne?

'I'll help you carry the glasses,' said Emma, leaving Flick and Zoe alone.

'Will you be drinking champagne?' she asked, although she assumed Zoe would have said if she and Beau had already hit the jackpot.

Zoe's smile faltered. 'Why wouldn't I be?'

And there was her answer. Flick thought she'd been a little highly strung the last few days and now it suddenly made sense.

She reached across the table and squeezed Zoe's hand. 'It'll happen, honey.'

Zoe scoffed. 'We have to be actually having sex for that.'

Flick blinked, blindsided by the notion that there may be trouble in paradise. Was that why Beau had made himself scarce last night? She'd assumed he was giving Flick and Zoe a chance to spend some time together before her trip, but maybe not.

'Are you guys fighting?'

'Your guess is as good as mine. *Something* is going on with him, but he won't tell me what it is. He's so stressed he's barely talking to me. I think it's got to do with work, but he doesn't even want to … you know?'

Flick could tell Zoe was close to tears. For as long as Flick could remember, Zoe and Beau had struggled to keep their hands off each other. They were one of those couples who were always touching, his hand on her back, hers on his knee when they were sitting at dinner, one of them brushing the other's hair off their forehead as they exchanged a tender look.

Before she could pry further, Emma and Neve returned with an expensive bottle of champagne.

'I know I said it was my shout …' Neve waved the bottle around. 'But this is actually on James. He said to wish you a fantastic trip.'

'Thanks.' Flick flashed her a grateful smile as Neve began to pour the bubbly into flutes, before looking back to Zoe. Concern for her daughter and son-in-law had replaced her own nerves.

After Neve filled each glass, Zoe perked up and made a toast. 'To Mum and her crazy adventure!'

Crazy? Flick's stomach twisted as she lifted her glass.

'To Flick,' echoed the others.

'Although,' added Neve, 'I can't help being jealous. I wish we were going with you.'

'I doubt James or Patrick would support the idea of either of you coming away with me for three months,' Flick said. 'And don't even pretend you'd be able to part with them either.'

Neve and Emma exchanged soppy smiles. They'd both been very lucky in love after years of putting up with bad dates and a selfish, cheating scumbag of a husband respectively.

'Well, maybe the four of us could come visit you?' Emma suggested.

'Ooh, what a fabulous idea,' said Neve, her perfectly made-up eyes sparkling. 'I've always wanted to go to New Orleans and James has been talking about us going back to New York for a holiday and catching some Broadway shows. We could come see you on our way?'

'Sounds great.' Flick tried to show a little enthusiasm but the idea of being the fifth wheel on their happy couples holiday didn't really fill her with excitement. She wanted this sabbatical to be completely about her. She loved her friends and family dearly but was in dire need of a break and some time alone to work out who she was. The last four years had been so much about supporting Sofia through the mental, emotional and physical components of her transition that she hadn't had time to think much about herself. Her own life had been sort of on hold.

Neve winked. 'Maybe you'll have met some spunky American by then and we can go on triple dates.'

Zoe remained quiet.

'Sorry,' Emma said. 'The last thing you probably want to be talking about is your mother's love life, but now that Sofia has found someone—'

'I don't *want* a love life. I'm hoping that in New Orleans I get to experience some new things, explore all the unique history and hopefully try some taxidermy on animals we're not so familiar with here.'

As if none of them had even heard her, or possibly they just didn't want to talk about dead animals, Zoe said, 'Honestly, I'm fine with Mum dating. I'd love her to meet someone new, but I'm not sure about an American. She might never come home.'

'Not going to happen,' Flick promised, much more worried about Zoe. In the hope of getting her alone, she pushed back her seat. 'I'm just going to go to the bathroom. Do you need to go too, Zoe?'

'She's not five,' Neve exclaimed with a chuckle.

'I'm fine,' Zoe said with an expression that suggested she'd guessed her mother's sneaky plan, so Flick marched off to the bathroom alone.

When she returned, conversation had moved on to Zoe's job at a boutique art gallery in the city.

'I love being surrounded by such amazing pieces all day every day, and meeting *most* of the clients is fun too, but Gretchen can be hard work,' Zoe said, twirling her champagne flute between her fingers. 'Sometimes I feel like I can't do anything right. The other day she actually praised me when a post I put on Instagram resulted in an inquiry from a rich overseas collector—I almost fainted.'

'She sounds like a nightmare if you ask me,' Emma said.

'She's dedicated,' Zoe said kindly, 'and maybe a little eccentric, but she's good at her job and so knowledgeable about the art world. There's so much I can learn from her.'

'Have you been painting much yourself lately?' Neve asked.

Zoe sighed. 'When I can find the time, which isn't as often as I'd like. I'm working on something for Beau's parents at the moment.'

'Show them your work-in-progress shots,' Flick said, unable to keep the pride out of her voice.

'Mum.' Zoe's cheeks turned crimson, but Flick could tell she was delighted when her friends begged her to see the photos on her phone, which they then oohed and aahed over.

'You have such a creative family,' Emma said as a voice overhead announced it was time for Flick's flight to board.

'This is it,' she said, trying to swallow the lump that had sprouted in her throat. Goodbyes were always hard and she didn't want to cry for fear she might never stop.

Zoe picked up her mother's travel bag from the floor and they all escorted Flick towards the gate.

'Don't forget to send us lots of messages and photos,' Emma instructed.

'Of all the hot men you have sordid affairs with,' added Neve.

Flick rolled her eyes as her friends stepped back to give Zoe a chance to say goodbye. She pulled her daughter into a hug and held tightly.

'Mum, you're hurting me.' Zoe extracted herself from Flick's embrace but squeezed her hand.

'I love you, Zo-Zo,' Flick said, losing her battle against tears.

Zoe's eyes were also misty. 'Love you too.'

Flick glanced towards the gate. 'Maybe I shouldn't—'

'Don't even think about not getting on that plane,' Zoe said, sounding like the mum not the daughter. 'I'm fine, I promise. Beau and I will be fine. Don't you dare use me as an excuse to back out.'

'Okay.' Flick pulled Zoe in for one final hug and then let her go. Maybe she had been looking for an excuse to stay in her miserable comfort zone.

The moment she got onto the plane her phone beeped with a message. Guessing it was one of her farewell committee, she smiled as she dug it out of her pocket, but her heart squeezed when the name 'Sofia' flashed up instead.

Hope you have the time of your life. Love S.

Flick pressed the phone against her chest, her heart aching. The message reinforced the fact she was doing the right thing. Now that Sofia was living her best life, Flick needed to focus on herself and try to do the same.

With that thought, she found her seat, put her phone on aeroplane mode and sat back to try and enjoy the flight.

5

Felicity

'Welcome to New Orleans, where the time is now 6.52 pm and the temperature is a balmy eighty-two ...'

Eighty-two? Flick tried to convert that to Celsius in her head and put it at around twenty-six to twenty-eight degrees. Warm for an evening but not too bad.

'If you can reach your mobile phones, you may now turn them off aeroplane mode. We want to thank you for travelling with us and wish you a fantastic time in the Big Easy.'

The seatbelt sign flashed off and people shot out of their seats, madly rushing to grab their things from the overhead compartments. Flick reached for her mobile. She'd never seen the point of making a crazy dash to exit the plane, so instead of growing impatient like her fellow passengers crowding the aisle, she opened WhatsApp. Before she left, she'd set up a group for her friends and family titled 'Flick's New Orleans Adventure' in

36

which she promised/threatened to bombard them with photos and messages.

Felicity: Landed at Louis Armstrong. Am starving—plane food awful—and exhausted but proud of myself for getting this far. Dallas airport much better set up than LAX. Like one big circle with trains interconnecting all the terminals. Even managed to buy myself a coffee and do the tipping thing. Waiting to get off plane and go through customs, then I'll catch a taxi to the French Quarter and go scavenging for food.

Emma: Whee! How exciting! You made it! Patrick says he agrees with you about Dallas airport, and if you want a good meal go to Brennan's, Arnaud's or SoBou.

Zoe: Oh my God. Feels like you've been travelling for days. What time is it there?

Neve: Never mind about food, get yourself a Hurricane. I've heard they're potent.

Emma: Hurricanes are seriously overrated—expensive and more a young person's drink. More dinner suggestions: The Court of Two Sisters, or if you just want something fast but good, Patrick says the po-boys at Royal House are the best he's ever tasted and it's not far from where you're staying.

Flick: LOL—are you saying we're not young?

Neve: Em, turn off your inner travel agent and let Flick discover the place (and the cocktails) for herself.

Sofia: Thanks for the update—looking forward to many more. x

Toby: Glad you got there safely, Mum. What kind of aircraft was it?

Emma: I'm just trying to help.

Flick smiled down as the messages came fast and furious. She couldn't actually believe she was now on the other side of the world but the immediate connection to her friends and family eased her anxiety a little. Thank God for modern technology. She wished Sofia wouldn't add kisses to the end of her messages but didn't have the heart to tell her.

Finally, the people in the aisle started to move, so she said goodbye to the elderly couple who'd been sitting next to her from Dallas and tapped out one more message.

Felicity: Getting off the plane now—no idea what type, Tobes. Very comfy for economy anyway. I promise once I recover from jet lag, I'll eat at all those restaurants and try a Hurricane. Any other requests?

She slipped her phone into her handbag and reached up to get her overnighter. Even inside the terminal, the humidity in the air hit her the moment she stepped off the plane, and she cringed as she felt sweat erupt in her armpits and along her bra line. A few people called her crazy for coming to New Orleans so close to summer, but hey, Perth got hot—she could handle it. She might just have to change her bra more than she usually did.

Flick made her way quickly through the terminal, enjoying the lively jazz music from surround-sound stereo and taking everything in. The cafés advertised things like gumbo and po-boys, and where in Australian airports the shops sold fluffy koala and kangaroo toys, here they had alligators, turtles and little voodoo dolls on display.

'You're not in Kansas anymore,' she said to herself as she headed out into the baggage collection area. Miraculously, her first suitcase appeared almost immediately, and she couldn't believe it when her second followed close behind. If she was still looking for signs, surely that was a good one?

And getting a taxi was easy too. A young man with long jet-black dreadlocks that had a life of their own, introduced himself as Xavier in a southern drawl she could listen to for hours. He easily lifted her luggage into the boot—no, make that trunk, *get with the local lingo, Felicity*—of his big black beast of a car.

'Heading to the French Quarter, d'you say?' said Xavier, glancing at her in the rear-view mirror as he swung into the traffic exiting the airport. 'What hotel?'

'I'm here to work at Bourbon Street Taxidermy Art and staying in the apartment above.'

He raised an eyebrow. 'The place with all the dead animals?'

'That's the one.'

'I went in there with my mom when I was a kid. Never gone in again, place freaked me out. How'd you get that gig?'

Flick told him she was a taxidermist here to help a colleague. They filled the rest of the journey with Xavier pointing out landmarks and giving her tips about all the places she should visit. He got very excited about the Superdome—'It's home to the Saints!'—but she was more intrigued by an old cemetery they passed. It looked like something out of a gothic novel.

'Why all the above-ground tombs? I've never seen anything like them before.'

Xavier let out an amused snort. 'It's so the bodies don't wash away.'

39

Flick discovered he was only half joking as he explained about the early European settlers not taking into account the fact that the city was below sea level when they started to bury their dead.

'The coffins filled with water and rose back up to the surface. They tried drilling holes in them to let air escape and also filling them with rocks and sand, but it didn't really work. And the bodies didn't decompose properly. I think it was a Spanish dude who came up with the solution, but the cemetery tour guides will be able to give you the full story. Good thing about the above-ground tombs is that they deal with the corpses much more efficiently.'

'What do you mean?'

'Well, cos of the heat here, the tombs become like ovens and the bodies decompose much faster. After about a year there are only bones left, which means families can reuse them.'

'They reuse the tombs?'

'Yes. Here all members of a family are buried together.'

'Fascinating,' Flick said, definitely putting a cemetery tour on her mental agenda. 'How long have you lived in New Orleans?'

Xavier chuckled again—he seemed to find everything amusing.

'What's so funny?'

'Just the way you say New Or-lins—New Or-leens,' he mimicked her, dragging out the last syllable. 'Where you from anyway? Australia?'

When Flick nodded, Xavier said, 'Nice. I'm born and bred Louisiana. My family has been here for generations. I keep making threats to leave, but …' He shook his head and grinned. 'I reckon I'll be buried in the family vault.'

Flick asked him about his family and he happily shared his history. The conversation took them to the outskirts of the French Quarter, but the moment Xavier slowed the car on Canal Street, her eyes were glued on what she saw out the window.

Neon was the first word that came to mind, and there were people everywhere.

'Sorry, ma'am,' Xavier said, 'but I'm not gonna be able to drive you right to y'door because there's no cars that part of Bourbon. I'll try to drop ya as close to the shop as possible though, so we're gonna have to take a bit of a detour.'

'No worries.'

As Xavier drove he named the roads, pointing out more places and generally giving her an idea of the lie of the land.

'The Quarter is easy to navigate once you learn the roads on the grid. The streetcar is simple too and will take you further afield— Uptown, Downtown, to the Warehouse District, or if big fancy-schmancy houses are your thing, to the Garden District. Are you going to be driving while you're here?'

'I don't think so.' Harvey had offered his car, but said there was also a bike she could use, and she liked the sound of that better than trying to remember to drive on the right-hand side of the road in a strange city.

Xavier pointed out Louis Armstrong Park. 'Beautiful during the day but steer clear at night.'

He made a right into the French Quarter proper, and *oh my goodness*! This was what she'd lusted after on the internet that night she'd made the spur-of-the-moment decision to come. It was starting to get dark now, but the cutest lamps lit up the houses, shops and restaurants. The European influences were visible in the bright-coloured buildings with their intricate iron-lace balustrades and greenery hanging from large baskets on the balconies. Their quaint windows and shutters filled her with joy. Even the fire hydrants were charming.

'I'm going to drop you here on the corner.' Xavier pointed down the road. 'Your creepy dead things place is just down that way. If you hit Dumaine, you've gone too far.'

'Thank you,' Flick said, digging her purse out of her bag to pay him. Xavier already had her luggage on the sidewalk by the time she climbed out of the car and didn't waste time in jumping back into it and disappearing. She took a moment to get her bearings, looking in the direction he'd pointed for Harvey's place and the Blue Cat Jazz Bar where she had to pick up the keys for the shop.

'Hey, move it along, lady,' shouted some guy as he detoured around her suitcases.

'Sorry,' she said, realising the busy sidewalk was not the place to take a moment. Her handbag and overnighter secure on her shoulders, Flick took one suitcase in each hand and started wheeling them behind her, not an easy task on the uneven pavement.

Music wafted out into the street from the pubs and clubs on either side of the busy road, creating a weird cocktail of jazz, hip hop, rock and heavy metal. And then there were buskers in the middle of it all, adding their unique sounds to the mix. She passed an eclectic array of people, laughing and shouting to be heard over the noise, many sipping neon-coloured cocktails in plastic tumblers. There were women wearing twin-sets and pearls strolling near people wearing barely anything at all, men in suits and others dressed in tatty shorts and T-shirts as if they'd just fallen out of bed. Flick had assumed the French Quarter attracted mostly young people, but age didn't seem to matter here any more than the clothing or the music.

It wasn't long before she came upon the Blue Cat and saw Harvey's place right next door. The club wasn't as big as some of the venues she'd seen so far and didn't look much from the outside. There was a regular entrance, and also a window where you could get drinks to go—both bordered by bright blue shutters propped open by stone cat doorstops. A neon sign on the wall between them flashed 'Live Jazz'.

Flick lingered in the doorway. There were two women serving drinks—a younger one with bright blue hair in a short spiky cut, and a Black woman Flick guessed was in her sixties. She wore large hoop earrings, a bandana wrapped around her head and a massive smile. The venue was dimly lit with mismatched vintage lamps scattered throughout on tables that looked like they belonged in an old school. The chairs were all different too, as if they'd been collected from various garage sales—there were even a couple of old church pews. But despite the no-frills appearance, the place was packed with people, and Flick guessed that had something to do with the soulful piano music and the voice that accompanied it coming from deep inside.

Part of her wanted to plonk herself down on one of the pews and enjoy the show, but since there wasn't room for her to drag in her luggage and she couldn't leave it unattended outside, she went to the window instead.

'Hey, cher, what can I get you?' asked the woman with the hoops. 'We got four-dollar Hurricanes tonight or six-dollar Bloody Marys. And I challenge you to find better elsewhere in the Quarter.'

'Actually, I'm not here for a drink. My name's Felicity Bell and—'

Her face lit up. 'Oh, you're here to collect the keys. Harvey said you'd be dropping by. Welcome. I absolutely adore your accent.'

'Thanks.' Flick kept forgetting that she was the one who sounded different.

The woman dug into a big bowl at the back of the bar and plucked out a bunch of old keys. 'I'm Lauri-Ann,' she said as she handed them over. 'Theo will be sorry he missed you—he's currently on stage. But don't be a stranger. You just pop right in anytime you like some good music or a chat.' She winked. 'And drinks are on the house for neighbours. Welcome to the Crescent City.'

'Thank you.' Flick smiled as she took the keys. Harvey had told her Theodore was the owner, but he hadn't mentioned he was also a musician. 'Do you and Theo own the bar?'

Lauri-Ann threw her head back and laughed. 'Me and Theo? Hell no. I barely own the shoes on me feet.'

They were interrupted by three young guys wanting to buy drinks, so Flick excused herself, manoeuvred her luggage around the boys and made her way next door to the shop.

Two large bay windows sat on either side of a glass door, which was in desperate need of a good clean. A stream of fairy lights bordering both windows gently provided light for the displays and artistically stuffed animals. The main feature in the first window was an alligator, crouched as if ready to strike, but instead of the usual dull green, each of its armour plates was painted a different vibrant colour. The other window had a display of a black bear on its hind legs, its paws wrapped around a replica Bourbon Street sign.

Above the door hung a faded sign—'Bourbon Street Taxidermy Art—Established 1902'—and on it a paper notice reading 'Closed for family reasons. Back soon' had been stuck with sticky tape.

Flick found the key helpfully labelled 'front door' and slipped it into the lock.

6

Felicity

After a bit of jiggling, Flick eventually managed to turn the ancient key and push open the door. She dragged her suitcases inside and locked up behind her before she found the light switch and flicked it on.

In their email exchange about the handover, Harvey had sent a few photos of the shop and she'd seen some of the sale pieces on his Facebook page as well—for an old guy he seemed pretty social media savvy—but it was even more impressive in real life. Much more a gallery than a store, it housed animals of all sizes and although there was clearly a lot of local wildlife, he also had many species from around the world, including a tiger standing guard by the door, a highland cow with horns that looked like they could take out an eye, and even a giraffe.

Flick sucked in a breath. She'd always wanted to taxi a giraffe, but an alligator might be more realistic in these parts.

Some of the walls were painted a mossy green and others tomato red, although there was little colour visible, what with all the mounted animal heads. She smiled at a moose with rainbow horns, loving the mix of traditional taxidermy and quirky art. Old wooden cabinets with glass fronts contained some smaller animals and there were also chests with exhibits on top, some drawers artistically wedged open with displays inside.

The floor was polished concrete with a few animal-hide rugs strategically placed throughout. A deep-green leather sofa sat off to one side with a coffee table in front of it. On said table were a number of books on taxidermy, splayed open or on stands. Although most of the displays had a hefty price tag attached, there were a few pieces of jewellery in a glass cabinet by the counter that could suit a regular tourist budget. Harvey had certainly managed to fit a lot in a relatively small place and she knew that collectors from all around the world bought from him.

Towards the back was the studio area where he worked in view for anyone who wanted to watch and where he occasionally ran workshops. Flick wasn't expected to teach, but he'd suggested it would be good for her to choose some smaller animals from his large chest freezer and work on them while she attended the shop. She could hardly wait to see what was on offer.

Although she could have stayed there all night, marvelling over the various pieces, she'd be spending the majority of time over the next couple of months down here, so getting settled into the apartment above should be her first priority. That and finding something to eat, if her rumbling stomach had any say.

Weaving her way through the animals, Flick headed for the door at the back, which Harvey had left open. This led to a staircase and also to another door, which she guessed opened into the courtyard he'd also mentioned. She unlocked it and pushed it open to reveal a quaint little garden with cobbled stone paving, lots of plants in big pots, a little iron-lace table with an overflowing ashtray on it and two matching chairs.

Heading back inside, she heaved her first suitcase up the stairs and emerged, puffing, into an open-plan living area, the kitchen/dining room off to one side and a small hallway, which she guessed led to the two bedrooms. The colour scheme upstairs was much the same as in the shop and there were more stuffed animals as well. Sadly, the smell indicated Harvey smoked up here as well as in the courtyard. *Ugh.* The lingering smell, combined with something else—was it mould?—turned her stomach.

She marched across the space to a glass door that led onto a balcony overlooking Bourbon Street. As she yanked it open, warm air gushed inside, bringing with it the loud din from the street. Stepping out, she gazed down at the revellers. A group of loud and rowdy young men filled the balcony opposite, shouting lewd comments to the people below. One of the boys tossed a necklace of plastic beads to a woman. Wearing a bright pink veil and a satin sash across her body, she was clearly on a hen's night, and she proudly caught the offering and hung it like a medal around her neck.

Leaving the door open despite the noise, Flick stepped back inside, making a mental note to buy some scented candles tomorrow because fresh air was going to bring other issues. However, if not for the stench (and perhaps the neighbours across the way), she thought she could be very happy here in this old-fashioned apartment. Many people would be uncomfortable living, eating and sleeping surrounded by stuffed animals, but they made Flick feel immediately at home in this alien place.

In addition to the jackalopes and mounted alligator heads, there were also a few paintings adorning the walls. She thought of Zoe and wondered if these were local artists. Admiring the different styles and mediums, she gasped as she came across one particular painting of a skeleton wearing an elaborate wedding gown and veil. The haunting image sent a scuttle down Flick's spine. Dead animals she could deal with, but she couldn't watch horror movies, and couldn't understand why anyone would want something like this hanging in pride of place above the mantlepiece.

Turning away, she set to acquaint herself with the rest of the apartment. Once she'd put her first suitcase in the guest room, she went back into the kitchen and found a note from Harvey on the wooden table.

Dear Felicity

Welcome. I'm sorry I couldn't be here to meet you and show you around, but I hope you manage to make yourself comfortable. I think we've covered most of the business stuff via email, but here's a few quick words of wisdom from an old man who has called the French Quarter home all my life.

- *Don't fall for street scammers. They're aplenty.*
- *Don't bare your breasts for beads—it's tacky.*

Who did he think she was? Flick shook her head, thinking about what she'd witnessed outside and wondering what she'd come to.

- *Don't engage the uber Christians (sorry if you're a believer, but the ones on Bourbon are pains in the ass, always trying to pray for my salvation. Maybe I don't want to be saved!)*

She chuckled. Harvey sounded like quite the character and she was disappointed she hadn't had the chance to meet him.

- *Next door isn't bad for jazz music, but the real place to be is down on Frenchmen's. Tourists are less rowdy down there too.*
- *Watch your back when walking the streets, pickpockets love a naive tourist, and don't go out alone after midnight— especially on Dauphine Street.*

Finally, enjoy my city—it's the greatest one on earth. If you have any problems just see Theodore, or if all else fails, give me a call.

PS. I've left milk in the fridge and the cupboards stocked so you don't have to rush out and shop.

'Aw, what a sweetie.' Flick crossed over to the pantry, but her heart sank as she looked inside. Rows and rows of canned food—beans, stew, soup and sardines—but none of it appealed in the slightest. As her stomach made another disgruntled noise, her phone beeped a WhatsApp notification.

Zoe: *Mum, are you okay? What's going on? Have you fallen off the face of the earth?*

Emma: *Yes. Please give us an update. Am starting to stress a little. xx*

Felicity: *Sorry. I'm fine. Caught a cab to the shop and am now upstairs in the apartment. Bit smelly, bit hot, bit loud, but aside from that quite comfortable. Am starting to fade but am just going out to get a bite to eat. Photos incoming.*

Flick snapped a couple of quick shots of the apartment and sent them to the group, noticing the time on her phone. Geez, it was almost ten o'clock—if she wanted to get something to eat while heeding Harvey's warning, she'd better not dillydally. Feeling like Cinderella on a curfew, she sniffed under her armpits and made a face. No debating the fact she needed a shower, but food felt more pressing at this moment.

Back downstairs and out on the street, people were yelling, laughing and staggering on the sidewalk, and others carrying large signs were pestering everyone as they tried to lure them into various venues. Flick kept one hand on her cross-body bag as she followed her nose in the direction of sweet and spicy smells.

As soon as she could she turned off noisy, crowded Bourbon Street into St Ann and walked until she found herself on Royal, where the vibe felt a little more chill. But there were so many restaurants, the choice overwhelmed her as she peered through the windows. Some looked rather swish—their clientele dressed to the nines—others much funkier and laid-back, and there were also a number of pubs and sports bars. In the end, however, the thought of eating in any of those places alone had her buying a massive slice (more like a slab) of pizza for a ridiculously cheap price instead. It would be good to be able to take in the sights and soak up the atmosphere while she ate.

As she walked, she snapped more photos for the WhatsApp group.

Neve: Oh my, those buildings are to die for.

Felicity: They are beautiful, but up close, many of them are in dire need of TLC. Their decrepit state is part of their charm but if you wanted to buy one, you'd have to sink a lot of money into the upkeep.

Sofia: Looks amazing. Wish I was there.

Flick shoved her phone back into her bag and continued on, passing buskers every few minutes and, sadly, homeless people either begging for money or already curled up uncomfortably on cardboard. She dug into her bag every time, wishing she had more to give. Even though the evening was warm, the thought of sleeping outdoors left her feeling heavy. Most people just stepped around them, barely registering their presence, unless they had a dog or a cat with them—those with pets appeared to be doing much better business. She couldn't help noticing the number of cats and dogs both on the streets and in the shops—some lounging in windows, others on counters or on the floor. Nobody batted an eyelid. She even spotted a dog lying under a table in one of the restaurants.

Her stroll led her into an area signposted as Jackson Square. As well as more buskers, there were fortune tellers set up at card tables, artists at work trying to sell their wares, and at least three tour groups gazing around. The guides appeared to be trying to be the loudest, most enigmatic, as if in contest with each other as they waxed lyrical with creepy ghost stories. Flick heard a snippet from one guide about Saint Louis Cathedral being the most haunted building in the French Quarter.

Funny, she'd swear the tour guide from one of the other groups had mentioned something about an old convent owning that glory. At the end of the square, she glanced across the road to see a brightly lit café that looked to be doing a roaring trade. The sweet smells wafting towards her tantalised her tastebuds and she realised it was Café du Monde, a place she'd read about during her research. She snapped a photo as two white horses trotted by pulling a gorgeous Cinderella-esque carriage, which held a young couple too enamoured with each other to be noticing their surrounds.

Although alone, with so many people around, Flick didn't feel the danger that Harvey and others had warned her about. Everyone seemed to be having a good time and there was a real anything goes, non-judgemental vibe. Seb would have loved it here.

Sofia. She silently corrected herself, her good mood taking a hit. It was the first time in many years she'd thought of her as Seb and guilt immediately followed.

Trying to force thoughts of her ex aside, she continued on, focusing on the magnificent buildings and trying to soak up the relaxed holiday atmosphere as she people-watched. After a while, she came upon a guy with his long hair tied messily back in a bun, packing up paintings that were leaning against an ornate steel fence. Sofia wasn't the only person who would love this place—Zoe would be in heaven with the art. Flick must have passed at least a dozen galleries so far.

'Are you the artist?' she asked.

The man paused in the task of loading a canvas into the back of a cart attached to a bike and shook his head. 'Nah, I just sell his stuff. He's a buddy.'

'A very talented one,' she replied as she gazed down at a painting of a rabbit holding a red balloon. 'Is that a rabbit with a human body or a human with a rabbit head?'

He laughed. 'That's what I always want to know, but so far my friend has never cleared that up for me. You here on vacation?'

'I'm working here for a few months.'

'You alone then?'

Although his question didn't feel sinister, she suddenly remembered Harvey's words of warning and checked the time on her phone. Where had the last couple of hours gone?

'No, my … friend is just up ahead.'

'Have a good night then.'

'Thanks.' She gave the man a parting smile as she turned away. 'You too.'

Flick started back towards Bourbon Street, hurrying in what she thought was the right direction, but soon found herself on a dark street. Limited light flickered from the odd gas lamp but didn't so much light up her way as highlight the shadows, crevices and alleyways between some of the buildings.

A chill lifted the hair on the back of her neck. Getting a weird sense of being watched, she glanced behind as she picked up her pace even more. She was almost running, her sneakers slapping on the cobbled ground, when one of the shadows stepped out from an alleyway.

She screamed and slammed her hand against her heart.

'Didn't mean to frighten you, darlin',' slurred a tall man with a scruffy dark beard and scruffy dark clothes to match. 'How you doin?'

'Fine,' she said, her heart thumping loud and fast as she uttered, 'Have a good night,' and tried to continue on her way.

'Oh, I plan to.' The man blocked her path, so close she could see his dirty, possibly rotten teeth. 'You looking for a bit of company?'

Flick swallowed, trying not to recoil as his liquored breath feathered her skin. 'No, I'm just … I'm meeting my … husband around the corner.'

She pointed up the street and noticed she was on Dauphine. Wasn't that the one Harvey had warned her about? Her bladder threatened to let loose and judging by the smell of this dank place she wouldn't be the first.

Scruffy man looked at her with a smirk. 'You're not scared, are ya?'

She inwardly screamed. It felt like a trick question—if she said 'No' would that make him angry? But if she said 'Yes', would that give him the courage to do whatever his sinister eyes said he was planning?

Isn't New Orleans the murder capital of America? Neve's teasing landed in her head. Was the photo she'd just sent the last her friends and family were ever going to hear from her? *Calm down.* Surely psycho murderers were like dogs—they could smell your fear. And maybe she really had nothing to fear … just because this man looked and smelled dodgy and had stepped out of a dark alcove, didn't mean he *was* dodgy.

'I just don't want to keep my husband waiting,' Flick said, hoping he didn't notice the quiver in her voice. She surreptitiously looked around for someone who might be able to help, but the road was totally deserted. Where the hell had all the people gone?

'Fair enough, but this isn't a safe place for a woman alone,' he said, putting his dirty hand on the small of her back. 'How about I walk you to your husband. Wouldn't want you to meet any trouble on the way now, would we?'

Definitely dodgy, said a warning voice inside her head as her skin crawled. *Get out now!*

Before she realised what she was doing, she'd turned and kneed him in the balls.

He doubled over. 'Bitch!'

Bingo, she thought, barely able to believe what she'd just done. Emma and Neve would be so impressed.

Not if you don't run, said the voice.

Jogging had never been her forte, but she ran now like she'd never run before, not daring to look back until she turned on to Bourbon Street, still crowded with people. A stitch in her stomach, she sucked in air. The vibe had changed—the restaurants were now mostly closed, leaving only the strip and nightclubs open and there were no signs of any nice elderly couples. *Every* man felt like a danger.

Not making eye contact with anyone, Flick made a beeline for Harvey's shop. She cursed as she fumbled for the key in her bag, fear enveloping her, before her fingers closed around the bunch of old keys. Her hand shaking, it took a few goes for her to find the right one and get it in the lock. She glanced quickly back as she opened the door and, thanking her lucky stars there was no sign of the scruffy guy, slammed the door behind her and slumped against it. Were these old locks really any good? Flick tried to catch her breath, the oxygen burning as it heaved through her lungs.

Finally, when her breathing had begun to return to normal, she walked through the shop on shaky limbs and climbed the stairs to the apartment. The smell of tobacco and mustiness hit her immediately, but she no longer felt comfortable opening a window. She glanced around at her strange surroundings—the stuffed animals didn't offer the comfort they had earlier—and burst into tears.

What the hell am I doing here?

She could have been raped. Or killed. All the wonder she'd experienced earlier that night, all her excitement, evaporated in the wake of her shock.

Intuitively, she found her mobile in her bag and had brought Sofia's number up on the screen before she realised what she was doing. She desperately wanted to talk to her husband, to discuss what had happened and for him to tell her she'd be fine, he was proud of her for stepping out of her comfort zone, but the cold, hard reality hit her once again.

Her husband no longer existed. In his place was Sofia and Sofia had a boyfriend. Whereas Flick had no one. When would she finally be able to accept this?

No longer in the mood for a luxurious bath but feeling even more in need of a detox after having that man's hand on her back, she jumped in the shower, scrubbed herself clean, took two sleeping tablets and then fell into bed.

7

Zoe

'Another champagne?' Zoe asked a middle-aged couple—both immaculately dressed in designer labels, his hair too thick to be his own and her forehead suspiciously wrinkle-free—as they admired one of the paintings in the gallery's latest exhibition.

'Ooh, yes please.' The woman smiled and took a flute. 'What technique is the artist using here?'

'Impasto,' Zoe supplied, trying not to wince as her feet burned in her high heels. It felt like she'd been on them for hours. Who had the opening of a new show on a Monday night after they'd already put in a full day's work and would still have to get up and do it all again tomorrow? Gretchen, that's who, and because of who she was, people flocked.

'I like it,' the woman told her husband. 'I think it would make a wonderful statement piece in the entrance hall.'

The husband turned his head to one side and frowned. 'Really? I think it's a bit crude. Do you really want that to be the first thing people see when they step into our house?'

'If it was depicting a man in that position you'd likely think differently.'

Zoe quietly retreated, leaving the couple to argue as she continued doing the rounds with the drinks, answering questions about the exhibiting artists and their work as she went.

'Can I grab one of those?'

Zoe whirled around at the sound of a familiar voice and smiled genuinely for the first time that evening. 'Dad! What are you doing here?'

'Hello, honey.' Sofia pulled her into a quick hug, kissing her cheek. 'I was leaving the office and remembered you said you had a big opening tonight, so thought I'd stop by on my way to the station and say hi. Anything here I can afford?'

Zoe laughed as Sofia gestured to a massive painting depicting a woman giving birth on a beach. 'Not even close. How are you anyway?'

'Excuse me.' A tall gentleman cleared his throat and stepped between them. 'Can you give me some information about number twenty-two?'

Smiling apologetically at Sofia, Zoe stepped away to help the potential customer, silently praying this might be her first sale of the evening. She'd felt Gretchen's eyes on her every time she'd spoken to anyone and it seemed she couldn't do anything right. If she talked too long, she was wasting time; if she didn't talk long enough, she wasn't making their guests feel welcome. A sale would go a long way towards softening her boss. After a good ten minutes talking to the man, answering his every question in detail as best she could, he shook his head, grabbed another flute of bubbly, downed it and then walked right out of the gallery. Zoe almost burst into tears. Some days she couldn't wait to get pregnant, specifically so she could tell Gretchen where to go ... well, not exactly in those words. She'd definitely take maternity leave but whether she came back was undecided, so it wouldn't be wise to burn bridges.

Speak of the devil. Zoe gulped and wished she could claim a glass of champagne for herself as she saw her boss stalking towards her; she'd clearly witnessed the man's speedy exit.

Zoe forced a smile, preparing herself for the worst as Gretchen stopped in front of her and pointed over to where Sofia was sipping bubbly and admiring another painting.

'Do you know that woman? Did I hear you call her "dad"?'

'Um ...' Zoe wasn't quite sure how to answer.

Gretchen had no idea that as of four years ago, Zoe had two mothers, but very rarely slipped up and called one of them 'Dad'. It wasn't that she was ashamed of her situation—she was so proud of Sofia and how she'd handled coming out—and normally Zoe was an open book, but she and Gretchen simply didn't talk about anything not related to work. Not books they'd read, not TV shows they were bingeing, not music they liked and certainly not their personal lives.

Zoe had learnt the boundaries on her very first day when she'd mentioned something about Beau, and Gretchen had held up her hand and said, 'Stop right there!' She'd made it clear that Zoe was her employee not her friend and therefore they didn't need to waste time on small talk or pretending they cared about each other. Zoe didn't even know if Gretchen was single, partnered, straight or gay, although she sometimes speculated to amuse herself.

'Did I?' Zoe blinked, but Gretchen didn't seem to be listening.

She licked her lips as if Sofia was something delicious on a menu. 'She has fabulous style. You'll have to introduce us.'

'Oh ... I ...' Before Zoe could finish her response, Gretchen saw someone important across the room and swept away to go work her charms on them.

Her heart racing, Zoe hurried over to Sofia, almost spilling the last two glasses of champagne on the tray. 'You have to go,' she hissed.

'What?'

'I think Gretchen might have a crush on you.'

'Really?' Sofia's eyes widened, highlighting her pretty pink eyeshadow. 'I don't know whether to be terrified or flattered.'

'I'm not sure either, but please go and hopefully she'll forget she ever saw you. Whatever her interest, it won't be good for me. If you guys became friendly, she'd probably sack me—you know how much she detests mixing business with pleasure. Oh God, I'm getting a headache just thinking about it.'

When will this evening end?

Sofia squeezed her hand. 'Relax, honey, you're good at your job and she knows it. I'm not interested in Gretchen anyway.'

'That's right,' Zoe said. 'How's Mike?'

'He's great.' Sofia beamed. 'We've been working on the design for a new eco-friendly block of apartments in Subiaco. We're pitching to investors who are looking to choose a company to design this one and a number of similar ones across Perth.'

Zoe winked. 'I guess *you* don't mind mixing business with pleasure. When do I get to meet this Mike? I need to give him the Zoe tick of approval.'

It wasn't that she was particularly keen to do so. She suspected Mike had been the reason for her mother's sudden flight to the other side of the world, and it was still hard accepting her parents weren't together, never mind the fact her dad was a woman and now seeing a man. But she *wanted* to be supportive.

'What about Thursday night? You and Beau could come for dinner and I'll ask Mike as well?'

Thursday nights had always been family dinner night—even after Sofia and Flick had started living separately, the dinners had continued. But then Toby had gone off to Queensland and Zoe and Beau got busy with their new jobs and the dinners had gradually become fewer and further between. Now her mum, who usually cooked, was also gone.

'That sounds great. But,' Zoe squeaked as she saw Gretchen making her way back towards them, 'you've got to go! See you Thursday.'

After another two and a half hours of schmoozing and not one sale between them, the gallery finally emptied of people and Gretchen dismissed Zoe.

'Don't be late tomorrow morning,' she ordered. 'I've got a big day planned.'

'I can't wait,' Zoe said, fleeing before Gretchen changed her mind and found another job for her to do tonight.

She drove home on autopilot, dreaming of a nice long soak in the tub and maybe a foot rub from Beau. However, all her dreams were dashed the moment she stepped into the house and into her very worst nightmare.

8

Felicity

Is that rain? Flick wondered as she emerged from slumber the following morning and rolled over to check the time on her phone. She'd had a shocking night's sleep, taking hours to drop off after not being able to find her earplugs. The charming jazz music from next door had stopped not long after she'd climbed into bed, leaving only the headbanging noise of the surrounding clubs, which had gone on well into the early hours of the morning. If that wasn't bad enough the humidity had made her even more uncomfortable and she'd finally thrown off all her bedding and her pyjamas.

So much for arriving late in the day being good for conquering jet lag—she felt like she could play a zombie in one of Toby's favourite horror movies.

It wasn't the time or the notification telling her she had thirteen WhatsApp messages that caused her to gasp at her screen, but something she'd never seen before—time stamped 5.52 am.

61

EMERGENCY ALERT
Flash Flood Warnings in this area till 8.45 am CDT.
Avoid flood areas. NWS.

What on earth? She sat up straight and blinked, hoping her eyes were playing tricks, but when she opened them again the emergency warning was still there.

What did 'this area' mean? Flick sprang from the bed and rushed to the window. It looked like a totally different street to the one she'd walked last night. Water spanned from one side to the other, litter floating along like little boats. With the rain still falling, she guessed the water was also still rising. There were no people in sight, but an emergency vehicle drove slowly by, lights flashing and its tyres making waves, indicating just how high the water was.

Would it keep rising? Flick's head spun as she reached out to steady herself on the window frame. Would have been nice if Harvey's warnings had said something about possible flooding! She might be up high, but that didn't mean she wanted to be stranded here. At least she had his tinned goods if she got desperate. And she would *have* to be desperate.

Harvey! Suddenly she thought of the shop—could the water have got inside? Springing into action, she tossed her phone on the bed and scrambled for clothes. She shoved on a pair of shorts, threw an old T-shirt over her head and headed downstairs. No time for shoes.

She could hear the water lapping at the front of the shop even before she saw it. Her heart sank as she rushed to survey the damage. The animals guarding the entrance were already standing in a few inches of water and the rugs squelched beneath her feet. Glancing out into the street and marvelling at how fast this had happened, she began trying to move the exhibits out of harm's way, starting with the tiger and an alligator.

Sweat covered Flick's skin by the time she'd finished and she was searching for something she could use to try and block any more water from coming under the door when the ring of an old-fashioned telephone startled her.

She quickly identified the sound as coming from a red telephone plugged into the wall on the counter. She hadn't seen anything like it in years. Could it be Harvey? Maybe he'd received the alert on his phone as well—she didn't really get how these things worked because she'd certainly never signed up for such warnings. Hoping he'd be able to give her an idea of how to further protect the shop, she pounced on the receiver and lifted it to her ear.

'Hello?' she asked, slightly out of breath.

'Hey, it's Theo.' The deep voice paused a moment. 'From next door.'

'Oh, right, hi.' She felt ridiculously pleased to hear the stranger's voice.

'Look, I'm sorry I didn't get the chance to meet you last night ...'

Never mind niceties, she wanted to know when this was all going to be over. If she should be doing anything else. The emergency warning had been almost comically unhelpful: *Avoid Flood Areas.* Well, what if you were already smack bang in the middle of one?

'It's fine,' she interrupted. 'Does this happen a lot round here? How long will it last? What should I do?'

He chuckled. 'You do know we're prone to Mother Nature's wrath in these parts, don't you?'

'Well, yes, but ...' Of course she'd heard of Hurricane Katrina, she just hadn't expected anything like that would happen while she was here. 'Is this going to get really bad?'

'I'd say it'll all be over in a few hours.'

The panic that had been eating her insides subsided a little. *Thank God.*

'How's the shop looking?'

'Wet.'

He laughed again.

'I've moved what I can out of the way but I'm not sure if there's anything else I should be doing. The water's still coming in.'

'Harvey probably has some sandless sandbags lying around, but we haven't needed them for a while.'

'*Sandless* sandbags?' That was an oxymoron if ever she'd heard one, and why had Harvey failed to mention any of this? Maybe he hadn't wanted to scare her off? Right now, that was a real possibility.

'Yeah,' Theo said, seemingly oblivious to the irony in what he'd said. 'I'd bring some of mine over, but opening and closing the door will only allow more water in. We're stranded for now. You could give Harvey a call and ask though.'

'Thanks. I'll do that.' Hearing how unconcerned Theo sounded helped ease her anxiety a little.

'But I think the rain's letting up, so maybe don't stress too much.'

Flick glanced outside, relieved to see he was right. 'That's good to know. Thanks for the call,' she said, winding the phone line around her finger as she spoke. It gave comfort in a way modern phones couldn't.

'You're welcome. I'll see ya later.' Theo hung up before Flick could ask any further questions.

Feeling as if she'd done all she could, she took a few photos of the damage and also of outside through the windows, then tried to call Harvey, but he didn't answer, so she went back upstairs. May as well shower and have a much-needed dose of caffeine while she waited for this to pass.

She took longer in the shower than usual, washing her hair and all the grime of travel from it, before getting dressed in a fresh pair of shorts and T-shirt. She fingered her long dark hair into a ponytail and wrapped it in a messy bun on the top of her head, then swiped tinted moisturiser over her face. Neve would be appalled that she didn't apply any of the numerous anti-aging creams she'd forced her to buy and at least one layer of make-up, but with the task of cleaning up downstairs ahead of her, Flick didn't see the point of prettying herself up.

She texted Harvey an update, telling him about the flood.

Bit of a shock to wake up to, but all under control. Rain has stopped now, and I managed to get everything out of harm's way before it was too late. Is this a regular occurrence?

He replied after about five minutes.

Well, what an exciting start to your visit. Didn't I mention it? Thanks for doing such a splendid job.

Exciting? Flick snorted. That wasn't the word she'd use. She'd barely been here twelve hours, and after the altercation last night and the floods this morning, she felt like she'd been put through the wringer. Drinking the poor excuse for black coffee she made from what she could find in Harvey's kitchen, Flick was posting photos she'd taken to the WhatsApp group when she heard a noise downstairs. Someone banging on the shop's door. Taking one final gulp of coffee, she went to investigate.

A man of average height but *not* average appearance stood on the other side of the glass door. He was wearing faded denim shorts and a black T-shirt that hugged his body, and he was holding some sort of machinery with a tube attached, which made Flick think he must be someone from the council on clean-up duty.

'Can I help you?' she said, opening the door and noticing that the water had all but vanished from the road.

The man gave her a friendly smile. 'Actually, I've come to help *you*. I'm Theo from next door. Nice to meet you, Felicity.'

She took the hand he offered—it was warm and the grip firm but gentle.

'You're much younger than I imagined,' she blurted, before realising what she'd said. When Harvey had spoken about Theodore next door she'd envisioned someone more his vintage, but despite Theo's salt and pepper hair he had to be around her age instead.

He gave a deep, throaty chuckle. 'And I have to say you don't much look like a taxidermist.'

'Oh?' She withdrew her hand, blushing slightly. If she'd known she was going to have visitors she might have made a *little* more effort with her appearance. 'What exactly is a taxidermist supposed to look like?'

His lips quirked. 'Well, the only ones I know are Harvey and a couple of his friends that visit. Interesting lot, but mostly balding old men.'

Flick chuckled—she'd met plenty of them too—then pointed at what he was carrying. 'What's that?'

'It's a pump to help get your water out onto the street. Once we do that you can use Harvey's fans—' he gestured towards two big industrial-type pedestal fans in the corners of the shop '—to start drying everything out. Shouldn't take long.'

'What about your place?'

'I've got slate floors on a slant, and besides, everything of value is well above water level. There's a lot more to protect here.'

'Thanks.' Despite her qualms a few moments earlier, Flick had an almost irrepressible urge to hug him. Must be the jet lag wreaking havoc with her emotions, but it was nice to know *someone* here. 'That's kind of you.'

'Can I come inside then?'

'Of course. Sorry.' She stepped aside to let him in. 'I'm not exactly myself this morning. Didn't get much sleep, and then to wake up to this … I must admit, I'm starting to wonder if I made a terrible mistake coming here.'

Lord, why was she telling him this? He'd come to help her clean up, not offer therapy.

'This kind of weather is stressful if you're not used to it. But I promise we'll get this sorted in no time and then I'll make you a drink.'

Did he mean alcohol? At this time of the morning?

As if he was one of the psychics in Jackson Square, he added, 'I was thinking of coffee, but no judgement if you want something stronger. You've had a shock, and this is Bourbon Street, after all.'

'Oh, right, coffee would be great, thanks,' Flick said, feeling like a fool. She really needed to get some rest. She nodded towards the pump. 'How do I work this thing anyway?'

'I'll take care of it. You just try and relax a little.'

Flick was too tired to object, besides Theo had clearly done this before and would be far more competent than she could hope to be. They couldn't talk while he worked as the pump was pretty loud, which she was grateful for as, unlike Sofia, she'd always been shocking at small talk. As she watched she couldn't help noticing the way his arm muscles bunched while he worked and wondered how a piano player got arms like that? Perhaps it was from lifting heavy crates of alcohol in the bar. Not that it was any of her business, she was just happy for his assistance.

Bourbon Street was still deserted by the time they'd finished, save for a few people snapping photos while wearing disposable plastic raincoats that screamed tourist.

'I can't believe how fast the water went down,' Flick marvelled.

'We have a good drainage system in our city, that's for sure. And the odd flash flood is a blessing—especially in the Quarter. Cleans up the place a bit.'

'What happens to the homeless?' she suddenly wondered.

Theo looked pensive for a moment. 'It's toughest on them. Hopefully they find refuge. We have a number of shelters, but I always let anyone lingering outside come in during bad storms. There was no one this morning though.' He cocked his head slightly. 'Come on, what's it going to be? Coffee or something stronger?'

Flick smiled at the teasing sparkle in Theo's eyes. 'I feel like it should be me offering you coffee after all you've done to help, but sadly, I wouldn't push Harvey's stuff on my worst enemy and I haven't had time to buy anything else.'

'In that case ... I'd better cook you breakfast as well,' he said.

Flick's stomach groaned loudly and embarrassingly in response, making it very hard for her to turn him down. Besides, he was a neighbour and she didn't want to be rude, especially after he'd gone out of his way to help. 'If you're sure it's not too much trouble?'

'Not at all. Follow me.'

Empty of people, the bar looked vastly different from the previous night and Flick shivered as Theo closed the door behind them. She couldn't remember the last time she'd been alone with a man she wasn't related to, never mind one she hadn't even known twenty-four hours.

However, she didn't have too much time to feel awkward because a massive dog appeared from somewhere out the back and bounded towards them.

'Oh my goodness,' Flick exclaimed as the dog leapt up, its paws landing on her shoulders. Although she struggled to keep her balance, she laughed as it attempted to lick her face.

'Down, Roberta,' Theo ordered, grabbing the mutt by her collar and barely restraining her. 'Sorry. She's not used to visitors one on one. She's much more restrained when the bar's busy.'

Flick rubbed the dog around her neck. 'You let her hang here when you're open?'

'Yep. She's a gentle giant but if anyone tries anything, she helps get rid of them.'

'I can't imagine anyone trying anything with Roberta around. Is she a Doberman?'

'Yep,' Theo said as he continued on towards the back of the building. When Flick didn't follow, he turned back. 'You coming?'

'Where to?'

His lips twisted in obvious amusement. 'Well, since the kitchen's upstairs, I thought it would be easier to eat up there. But I can bring breakfast down here if that would make you feel more comfortable.'

'No. It's fine. I just didn't think ... So, you don't serve food down here?'

'Not food that requires a kitchen—Blue Cat's focus is quality music and drink, but we do bar food like chips, nuts, that kind of thing.' He smiled warmly again and jerked his head towards a doorway at the back of the bar. 'Come on, Felicity, I don't bite, but I can't make any promises for my cat.'

She opened her mouth to tell Theo he could call her Flick like everyone else but stopped herself at the last moment. In New Orleans no one knew about her past, they didn't know about Sofia, so they wouldn't feel sorry for her or pry. Here she could be whoever she wanted to be.

Here she could be *Felicity*—strong, independent and paving her own path. Maybe she'd even give herself a bit of a makeover!

'You have a cat as well?' she asked as they started towards the door, Roberta following closely at her heels.

'Yep, Tessa came with the bar,' he said as they went through the doorway and arrived at a staircase. 'In fact, usually you'll find her sitting on it, but she must be hiding because of the rain.'

'I love how animals have free roam in many of the shops here. That's not something you see often in Australia.'

'Our pets are important to us. Are you a dog or a cat person, or both?'

'More of a dog person. I've got a border collie cross lab back home, but I like cats too.'

Theo nodded as if he approved as they reached the top of the stairs and emerged into his apartment. 'Welcome to my humble abode.'

'Thank you,' she said as she gazed around. The place appeared to have almost exactly the same layout as Harvey's but a totally different decor and vibe. Theo's furniture was modern, and the walls were a soft off-white, littered with framed photos of musicians, instruments, records or actual lyrics, except for one that didn't fit in with the rest at all.

'Oh,' she exclaimed, her hand rushing to her chest. 'You have a weird skeleton bride painting as well.' And here she'd been starting to warm to him.

'*You've* got one of Miss H's paintings?'

'No. Definitely not. Harvey has one hanging above his mantelpiece.'

'Ah, right. The artist is well known in these parts.'

Flick tried not to let her distaste show too much on her face. 'Does this Miss H only paint these kind of … images?'

'I think so.' He smirked. 'I can see they're not to your liking. My ex-wife agreed, hence why I got this beauty in our divorce. Miss H lived next door to us actually. She gave us the painting as a housewarming gift. My ex reckons it cursed us.'

So, he was also divorced. *Interesting.* Not that it made an iota of difference to Flick.

'Anyway,' Theo cleared his throat, 'let's get you that coffee.'

Flick sat on a stool as he made her drink and then pushed it across the counter. She couldn't help noticing he had nice fingers, so slender and clean. You could often hazard a guess at a person's profession by looking at their hands. Hers in comparison weren't pretty at all—nails cut short so as not to get in the way of her work.

'Thanks.' She took a sip and had to concede it was much better than Harvey's coffee. 'How long have you had this place?'

'Just over two years. My family call it my midlife crisis.'

Flick found herself curious to know if this 'midlife crisis' was also the reason for his marriage break-up but did not want to risk a conversation where she might have to reciprocate and share the reason for hers. It wasn't that she was embarrassed about Sofia but people always wanted to know all the details.

Did she have any idea her husband identified as a woman? What was their sex life like? Surely there had been some sort of clue there?

Such conversations always made her feel stupid, because there had been clues, but she'd ignored them.

'What did you do before?' she asked instead.

'I was a probate lawyer. It's actually more interesting than it sounds, but I was ready for a second act.'

He certainly didn't look like any lawyer Flick had ever known. 'But you must have always sung and played the piano? I heard you briefly last night. You're very good.'

'Why, thank you.' He smiled as he cracked eggs into a bowl. 'Scrambled okay?'

She nodded and took another sip.

'I can't remember a time when I didn't play,' Theo went on. 'My mom was a classical pianist and wanted me to follow in her footsteps. When I clearly preferred jazz they steered me into a law career, like my dad. I did as I was told and toed the line until a couple of years ago. What about you? Have you always been a taxidermist?'

'Yup. Well, I did a Fine Arts degree and odd jobs before I actually was able to make a decent living out of taxidermy, but I wanted to do it since I was a little girl.'

'Seems a weird choice for a child. What piqued your interest?'

'My mum died in a housefire and most of our memories and photos were lost.'

'Shit. I'm so sorry.'

She smiled briefly at him. 'Thank you. Some of her jewellery was salvaged though and given to me. Among it was a grouse claw—I'd never seen anything like it before and I was fascinated with it.'

He frowned as he threw bacon into the frying pan. 'Excuse my ignorance, but what exactly is a grouse claw?'

'A taxidermied bird's foot made into a brooch, usually adorned with gemstones or coloured glass. They originated in Scotland during the Victorian era. Men would pin them on their kilts for good luck and later they were given as a sign of love and remembrance if people were going to be separated for a long period of time.'

'How romantic,' he scoffed.

Flick laughed. 'My mum was Scottish and this one had been passed down from her grandmother to her. Harvey has a few in his shop—I can show you if you like.'

Theo's horror shone on his face.

'Hey, I don't think someone with a skeleton bride painting can throw stones.'

'Touché.' He grinned, and she felt a flicker of something she hadn't felt in years. 'So how exactly does one get into taxidermy?'

While he finished fixing breakfast, she told him about the courses she'd done and the mentors she'd worked with. It felt odd, but also strangely normal sitting here at ten thirty in the morning drinking coffee with a stranger as he cooked for her.

'And this is your full-time job? Do you work for someone?'

She shook her head. 'Nope. I'm my own boss. I do a mixture of commissions for museums and galleries, but I also create my own art pieces to sell.'

'What about pets?'

'I only do them very rarely. There are other taxidermists that specialise in that, but people get very emotional where their fur babies are concerned. They often don't like the result; they don't think their pets look like they think they did.'

He chuckled. 'I guess that makes sense.'

'And I like to be able to be a little more creative.'

'Have you got any photos of your work?'

While they devoured his delicious scrambled eggs and bacon, and things that looked like scones but he called biscuits, Flick showed him some images from her Instagram account.

'They're really beautiful; you're very talented,' he said, his tone genuine. 'Is there a name for the type of taxidermy you do? The way you give the animals almost humanlike characteristics?'

She smiled, pleased that he seemed to get it. 'Mostly I'm an anthropomorphic taxidermist, which is exactly what you say. It began in Victorian England and I like it because I can really let my imagination run wild. I often wonder what animals are actually thinking when they're alive and so it's fun to play with that when I preserve them.'

'What's your most favourite piece you've ever done?'

'That's a bit like choosing my favourite child,' she admitted. 'Usually whatever I've just finished is my favourite, but I really love doing birds.'

Finally, Theo asked the dreaded question. 'So, what made you decide to come here?'

Flick hesitated a moment, not sure how much she wanted to tell him. 'It ... I ... It was a spur-of-the-moment decision really. My kids are grown, and I felt like a change. You know what they say, a change is as good as a holiday? Well, I thought I'd kill two birds with one stone.'

'You chose a great place for a holiday.'

'Hmm ... I'm still not convinced about that.'

'You're not going to let a bit of water discourage you, are you?'

'It's not just the floods.' Flick told him about her encounter the night before.

'Geez, I'm so sorry that happened.'

'It's my fault. I lost track of time and stayed out later than I meant to.'

'That tends to happen here,' he said, reaching to refill her now empty coffee mug. 'There's some sort of time warp—in the Quarter especially. Things that shouldn't take long do, while things that seem like they'd last a while don't.'

'I'm getting that impression.' She glanced at the time on his microwave. 'Thank you so much for breakfast—it was delicious— and the much-needed caffeine, but I should go check how the shop's drying out and I need to go buy some groceries. Where's the closest supermarket?'

'There are a couple of small grocers nearby—one on Dauphine and one on Royal—but they take advantage of the tourists. Your best bet is Walmart or one of the bigger places in Tulane, but they're not in walking distance.'

Flick thought of Harvey's left-hand drive car and decided she'd already had enough drama—she didn't need to add getting a ticket for driving on the wrong side of the road to her adventure. 'I don't need much just for me, so I'm sure one of the local ones will be fine. Thanks again.'

She stood and picked up both their plates.

'You're welcome.' Theo grabbed the mugs and joined her at the sink. 'Leave those, I'll throw them in the dishwasher later.'

As he escorted her downstairs, she asked, 'What time do you open the bar?'

'Usually about now.' As he spoke, they heard a key turn in the door. 'That'll be Roxy.'

Sure enough, seconds later the door opened to reveal a woman. Flick felt certain it was the younger bartender from last night, but today her hair was pink rather than blue.

'Hi there.'

'Felicity meet Roxy—she makes the best cocktails in town.'

Roxy rolled her eyes. 'He says that about all the girls.' But she beamed nonetheless.

'Roxy,' Theo continued, 'this is Felicity—she's taking care of Harvey's shop while he's away.'

Roxy held out her hand—her fingers were dripping with so many rings that Flick didn't know how she managed to lift them. 'Nice to meet you.'

'You too,' Flick said with a smile. 'I might pop by to try one of your cocktails later.'

'You do that,' Roxy said, stepping past and dumping her canvas bag on the bar. 'You won't find better.'

Theo escorted Flick out onto the street.

'Thanks so much for breakfast,' she said.

'You're welcome. I enjoyed the company.'

'Me too.' He'd made conversation easy.

'I was wondering ...' He paused, clearing his throat. 'Would you like to have dinner with me one evening?'

Oh Lord. Her stomach somersaulted. 'Do you mean ... like a date?'

So out of practice, Flick wasn't a hundred per cent sure, and although part of her would be flattered, a much bigger part of her squirmed at the notion. She hadn't come all this way to hook up with the first guy she met. Hell, she hadn't come all this way to hook up at all. Paving her own path didn't mean getting entangled with anyone else.

He nodded. 'It's not every day an interesting woman moves in next door.'

'What about the bar? And don't you have to play the piano?' she asked, biding time.

'Not always. I have a roster of musicians who come to do their stuff. I've also got great bar staff, which means I can get away for a few hours when I want a break. I make sure I have at least two nights off.'

When she deliberated, he looked down at his shoes. 'I'm sensing I might have just made things awkward between us?'

'I'm sorry.' Flick certainly didn't want to offend her new neighbour after he'd been so damn nice, but neither did she want to lead him on. 'It's not you, it's me. I'm divorced too, and I'm ... a little nervous about moving on.'

Then there was the fact she'd only be here temporarily. Neve would tell her to just enjoy the ride while she could, but Flick wasn't the kind of person to indulge in flings or one-night stands. Especially with neighbours.

'Ah, I see.' Theo gave her a sympathetic smile. 'I understand. Well, absolutely no pressure, but if you ever feel like a bit of company, drop by. No strings attached, I promise.'

Relief flooded her. 'Thank you. That sounds good.'

'Excellent.' His smile returned. 'Enjoy the rest of your day.'

'You too,' Flick said, before letting herself into the shop.

She barely noticed the wet musty smell because of the buzz inside her that she hadn't felt in years. Someone rather good-looking, friendly, talented and gentlemanly had asked her on a date. It was good to know she wasn't totally past her prime.

Reaching into her pocket for her phone, she was about to text her friends the news when she thought better of it. Emma and Neve would berate her for turning Theo down and she'd never hear the end of it, so Flick decided to keep this little gem to herself.

Instead, she sent a message to the WhatsApp group:

Felicity: Flood excitement all over now and I'm off to do my first grocery shop on US turf. Sorry, Neve, haven't tried a Hurricane yet, but the day is young, and I've had it on excellent authority that the bar next door makes really good ones.

9

Felicity

Just after 8 pm on her fourth day in the Quarter, Flick went to the door of the shop and looked out onto the street. She'd been busy until an hour or so ago with people wandering in to admire the pieces and ask her questions. Never before had she spoken about taxidermy so much. She mostly worked in solitude at home, and although her friends and family supported her art, they'd long since stopped asking questions about the ins and outs of the craft.

But the people who came into Bourbon Street Taxidermy Art were fascinated. As they watched her work on a baby alligator and a muskrat she'd chosen from Harvey's small stash, they asked her everything from intricate questions about her process to the history and ethics of taxidermy. Most were only window shoppers, unable to afford what Harvey had to offer, but she did field a couple of calls from collectors in other parts of America, sold a jackalope to a newly married couple from Oregon and a few pairs of Victorian rodent-paw earrings. There were also a couple of inquiries from people whose pets had recently died, but she'd given them the contact details for another taxidermist who lived out in the Bayou, as per Harvey's instructions.

After assessing that most of the people outside now looked to be in the mood to party rather than shop, Flick turned the sign on the door to closed. She checked her phone as she headed upstairs, finding a number of messages in the WhatsApp group, but none from Zoe. Her daughter hadn't replied to anything for the last twenty-four hours and hadn't sent any private messages either. Flick checked the time in Perth—it was just after 11 am. Zoe should be at work; no way Gretchen would let her have her phone on her, but it wouldn't hurt to try. Flick looked in the fridge as the phone rang.

Zoe's voicemail clicked in and Flick left a message: 'Hey, sweet, just wanted to hear your voice. Can you give me a call when you get a moment?'

She shut the fridge again, deciding to spoil herself by going out for dinner. If Zoe hadn't made contact by morning, she'd call Beau.

After a quick shower, Flick put on a summer dress she'd bought on the spur of the moment in a quirky boutique yesterday morning. The bright yellow, bohemian-style floral print went almost to her ankles and was more whimsical than anything she owned. But as she scrutinised herself in the mirror, doubts crept in. Could she really pull off this look?

She was about to take it off when that little voice reminded her that being here was about trying new things, stepping out of her comfort zone. She might not suit this dress, but her normal wardrobe of jeans and comfy shirts didn't suit the vibe or the climate of the French Quarter. Normally she wore her hair tied back in a sensible ponytail, but tonight she yanked out the tie and let it all hang loose. If she was going to let go, she might as well go the whole hog.

Before she could chicken out, she grabbed her bag and headed downstairs. The moment she stepped out onto the street she heard the mellow tones coming from next door. Although she'd explored the neighbourhood a little over the past couple of mornings before opening the shop, this was the first time she'd ventured out again at night—not just because of the scare that first evening, but also because she'd been damn exhausted. Tonight she'd be more careful and be sure to keep an eye on the time.

She hadn't seen Theo since the morning of the flood and she still hadn't had that Hurricane. It wouldn't hurt to pop in for a quick drink. The bar was busy again, but the crowd was mostly around her age or older, all sipping their drinks as they moved to the music in their chairs. Tonight, a trio of men played on the stage and Theo looked to be doing the rounds talking to some of the patrons. Lauri-Ann and a young guy Flick hadn't seen before were working the bar and a large ginger cat was perched atop it.

She tentatively reached out to rub its chin. 'Hello, gorgeous, you must be Tessa.'

'Wow,' said Lauri-Ann. 'She usually hisses if women stroke her. She's a total hussy and prefers the men.'

As if Tessa understood, she shifted slightly and swished her tail in Lauri-Ann's face. Flick tried to stifle a laugh.

'Good to see you again,' Lauri-Ann said. 'How are you settling in?'

'Really well, thank you. I'm meeting lots of fascinating people.'

She nodded, smile lines visible around her eyes. 'What can I get you?'

'I'd like to try a Hurricane, please.'

'A Hurricane?' Theo chuckled as he came up beside her. 'Way to stand out as a tourist. But if you're going to have one, better here than one of those cheap and nasty slushies they give you on the ghost tours.'

'I promised a friend back home I'd try one,' Flick explained, feeling her cheeks heating a little.

As Lauri-Ann made her cocktail, Theo lowered his voice. 'I'm glad to see you. I was beginning to worry I'd scared you off.'

She gave him a reassuring smile as her stomach tightened. 'No. Course not. I've just been finding my feet and trying to recover from jet lag.'

'And how's that going?'

'Well, this is the first night I haven't fallen straight into bed the moment I finished in the shop.'

'Here you are, cher.' Lauri-Ann placed the drink down in front of Flick.

She snapped a photo to post to WhatsApp and then took a sip. 'Gee, that's quite potent.'

Theo grinned. 'Enjoy. Excuse me.' He went over to the window to serve a couple takeaway drinks.

Taking another few sips, Flick leaned back against the bar as she watched the musicians on stage. She didn't know much about jazz music—hell, she didn't know much about any music—but she appreciated they were very good and couldn't help swaying a little in time to the beat. Theo chatted to her in between making drinks, explaining the trio had been playing at Blue Cat for longer than he'd been alive.

'How long is that?' Flick asked.

'Forty-nine years.'

'Snap,' she said. 'I'm forty-nine too. Big birthday coming up soon.'

He nodded. 'Next month as it happens. When's yours?'

'Not till December. You planning anything special?'

'Doubt it, I'm not really one to make a fuss.'

They sat in comfortable silence another minute or so and then Flick decided she couldn't finish her cocktail if she had a hope of walking any distance to dinner.

'As delicious as this is,' she said, placing the glass down on the bar, 'I need to go find some food.'

Theo frowned. 'You haven't eaten yet?'

She shook her head. 'It's not easy to do anything much but snack while the shop's open—I don't know how Harvey's managed to run it single-handedly all these years—so I've been eating later than normal.'

'I get that. My mealtimes are pretty all over the place here too.'

'Have *you* eaten?'

'I had a po-boy around the corner, let's see ...' He glanced at his watch. 'About seven or eight hours ago.'

'Don't suppose you want to come have something to eat with me?' The question was out of her mouth before she even realised she was going to ask it.

'Really?' He blinked a moment. 'I'd love to. Let me just clear things with Lauri-Ann and I'll be with you.'

Before Flick could say anything else, he went back behind the bar and whispered something to Lauri-Ann. Her eyes immediately sought Flick's, then she raised her eyebrows, nodded, and all but shooed him away.

Theo smiled as he gestured to the door. 'Let's go.'

Flick hitched her bag over her shoulder and ignored the loud thumping of her heart as she headed out with him. What game was she playing? She'd told him she wasn't ready to date and yet here she was inviting him out to dinner.

'Will Lauri-Ann be okay?' she asked.

He chuckled. 'She'll be fine, she's got Cooper and Roberta there as well.' Flick had seen the Doberman dozing on the floor behind the bar and she guessed the other bartender was Cooper. 'Now, where would you like to eat?'

'I have no idea. My friend recommended a few places, but I can't remember what they were. I'd like to try something unique to New Orleans. Maybe some gumbo?'

'I know just the place.'

They walked a couple of blocks to a restaurant on Royal Street. Theo opened the door and Flick stepped into a dimly lit venue with soft music playing overhead and individual gas lamps at each of the tables. Very charming.

'Evening, Theo, haven't seen you for a while,' said the young waitress.

'Hi, Nikki.' He gave her a quick peck on the cheek. 'Do you have a table for two?'

'Anything for you,' she said with a wink before leading them to a small table by the window.

They ordered drinks and then Nikki gave them time to look over the menu.

'You know her?' Flick asked.

Theo nodded over the top of his menu. 'The Quarter can be a little like a small town. We might have a large population of tourists, but those of us that have lived here a while know everyone.'

'I thought you'd only had the bar a couple of years. In Australia, I have some friends who live in country towns and they say you have to be there about thirty-seven years before you're a local.'

'Although I haven't lived here long, I've been playing at various venues since I was a teenager. I grew up not too far away and when I was a kid on weekends I used to sneak in here and busk.'

'What instrument did you play?' It wasn't like he could carry a piano with him on the streetcar.

'Saxophone. I still play it as well, but I like singing, and it's hard to do that with a mouthpiece, hence the piano.'

'Your parents didn't mind you busking?'

'Oh, they would have been horrified, but what they didn't know didn't hurt them. I wasn't always this old, boring and respectable you know.'

She laughed, already suspecting he wasn't boring at all. 'Bet you had quite an education growing up in these parts.'

Theo nodded, then winked. 'And, if you're lucky, maybe someday I'll tell you about it. Anyway, what are you going to have?'

She glanced down at the menu, slightly bamboozled by all the unique options. 'Do you have any suggestions?'

'I recommend the crawfish gumbo or the turtle soup. Although,' he leaned in close and lowered his voice, 'nothing beats the t-soup at the Commander's Palace.'

After a few moments' deliberation, Flick decided on the Chicken Andouille Gumbo with a side of salad, and Theo ordered something called 'jambalaya'.

'What part of Australia are you from?' he asked.

'Western Australia. Perth,' she clarified as she smoothed her napkin on her lap.

'Ah, the place with the quokkas?'

She was impressed. 'That's Rottnest Island. I actually did a commission for them a few years back—taxidermied a display of quokkas for their museum.'

'My younger sister would love to see that. She went backpacking Down Under in her early twenties and fell in love with those quokkas. She kept joking she was going to smuggle one home.'

'How many siblings do you have?'

'Four too many, all sisters.' Theo sighed, but there was a smile in his eyes. 'Three of them are also lawyers, all super successful, and one is a music teacher.'

'Do they live nearby?'

'Only Adelle—she teaches in the Garden District. What about you? Do you come from a big family?'

'No. I was an only child.'

'Lucky.'

'I don't know. I always felt lonely. I love watching my two interact with each other, even if sometimes they want to kill each other.'

Theo chuckled. 'Me and my sisters definitely had a love-hate relationship growing up. How many kids do you have?'

'Two. A boy and a girl. Well, a man and a woman now really. Zoe's twenty-four and Toby's twenty-one.'

'But they're always your babies, right?'

'Yes. How about you? Any kids?'

Theo nodded. 'I have two daughters, but I don't see them as much as I'd like. They're also in their twenties and too busy to spend much time with poor old dad.'

'I can relate to that,' Flick said, noticing the sadness in his eyes. 'I sometimes joke to Zoe I have to make an appointment for her to find time for me in her packed schedule. What do your girls do?'

'Anna is a video game designer and Olivia is at law school. What about yours?'

Flick couldn't help smiling proudly as she spoke about her kids. 'Toby joined the air force straight out of school. I don't see him nearly as much as I'd like. Zoe is the personal assistant to a curator of a pretty flash art gallery. She paints herself, so loves the work and it's a good learning experience, but her boss is rather demanding and a little eccentric.'

'Eccentric how?'

'Well, for one, she grumbles about Zoe needing to take a lunchbreak. She once told Zoe she doesn't know why she has to eat so frequently when she could make do with coffee and nicotine. Zoe said she's never seen Gretchen put anything in her mouth but coffee, champagne or cigarettes. Apparently she drenches herself in perfume to hide the smell.'

They were still laughing at Gretchen anecdotes when the food arrived. Theo watched as Flick took her first spoonful of gumbo.

'Well?'

She smiled at his intense gaze and wiped her mouth with her napkin. 'Give me a few seconds to let the flavours sink in.'

'Sorry.' He grinned back sheepishly and started on his jambalaya.

The gumbo was a bit like soup but much thicker—almost a cross between soup and stew. Its strong spicy flavour and the combination of both chicken and sausage meat was unlike anything she'd ever tasted.

'It's good,' she told him after a few mouthfuls. 'What exactly is jambalaya?'

'Here—try some.' He scooped up a forkful and held it out to her.

Flick took his offering and savoured the sharp, spicy, kind of African flavour. 'Is that some kind of sausage as well?'

'Yes. This one's made with Cajun sausage, vegetables and rice, but you can also use chicken, pork or seafood.'

'Everyone told me the food was amazing, but until tonight the only dinner I've had out is pizza.'

'Pizza?!' He gave her another look of horror. 'Thank God you came to me when you did.'

She laughed. 'Yes, thank God.'

Over dinner, they talked about the French, Spanish, and yes, also African influences in the local cuisine and also about New Orleans in general. It was clear Theo was besotted with the city and was as knowledgeable as the many guides that passed by the window with groups of eager tourists.

'So, what *is* the most haunted building in the French Quarter? I've heard a number of different possibilities.'

'Now that is a tough question,' Theo said, resting his cutlery on his dish. 'The history of this place means there's been many tragic and gruesome deaths. The belief is that people who come to such horrific ends can't find peace so they linger long after they've gone. Quite aside from the terrible mistreatment of slaves, there's been numerous fires and hurricanes, the Battle of New Orleans and other conflicts over land ownership, and of course the Yellow Fever epidemic. Over a period of about eighty years, over forty thousand people were lost to the disease. There were times when the death rate was so high, the city couldn't cope and had to resort to corpse wagons.'

'Corpse *what*?'

'So many people were dying of Yellow Fever that the authorities sent around wagons to collect the bodies. They'd be piled out on the street waiting to be removed.'

Nikki returned before Flick could express her horror.

'Sorry to interrupt, but would you like to see the dessert menu?'

'I don't think I could eat another mouthful,' Flick said.

'How about we walk a while and I give you a little ghost tour,' said Theo. 'We can get something later if we want?'

'Sounds good.' Flick was enjoying his company too much to want the evening to end just yet, and she was fascinated to hear a local's perspective of the places she'd seen so far.

Their first stop was Napoleon House, a tall, grey stone building.

'It was originally owned by Nicolas Girod, a mayor of New Orleans. The story goes he offered his residence to Napoleon as a refugee, but he never actually made it. These days it's a pretty good restaurant,' Theo told her as they stopped across the road from it.

'So,' Flick gestured to the building, 'are there any reports of ghosts here?'

'Quite a few, but apparently one of them claims a particular ghost isn't very nice and can become quite aggressive towards sceptical guests.'

Theo relayed a few stories of ghostly encounters people had reported there as they walked on towards Jackson Square.

'A lot of the restaurants were originally residences,' he said, pointing at a burgundy coloured building with a sign announcing it as 'Muriel's' hanging above a green door. 'They say this one used to house enslaved people before they went to auction. You can only imagine the kind of conditions they lived under, so it's not surprising that local clairvoyants say many troubled souls are still here.'

That was the second time that evening he'd mentioned slavery. It reminded Flick that although the Quarter was a popular tourist spot now and slavery had been abolished last century, its effects lingered even today.

As if sensing her solemn thoughts, Theo said, 'But Muriel's most famous ghost is a guy who bought the place in the late 1700s, Pierre Antoine Lepardi Jourdon.'

He said the name with a lovely French accent, which couldn't help but make Flick smile. 'What's his claim to fame?'

'You ever played poker?'

'I'm not sure played is the right word. My ex tried to teach me once, but I'm better at Scrabble.'

Theo laughed. 'I reckon I could teach you. But anyway, Lepardi was so bad at it he gambled his house and lost. He was so upset he topped himself.' He leaned close and pointed up to a window on the second floor. She felt his breath on her neck. 'That's where he spends his time. My barmaid, Roxy, used to do shifts up there and she reckons she's seen him. He has his own table and everything.'

'Do you believe in ghosts?' Flick asked, trying to distract herself from the way his proximity made her feel.

'I haven't had any encounters myself,' he said as they walked on a little further, 'but I've heard too many stories from people I trust to *not* believe.' He pointed across the road to the brightly lit Café Du Monde. 'Have you had a beignet yet?'

'No, but I read about them. Some kind of pastry right?'

'Kinda. They're a little like donuts but you have to try them to understand. Why don't we sit a while and I can tell you some more ghost stories. Unless you're ready to call it a night?'

Flick shook her head. 'Beignets and more stories sound delightful.'

They crossed the road, found a table, and a waiter greeted them almost immediately. 'Evening. Are you ready to order?'

'A serve of beignets and ...' Theo looked at Flick. 'Would you like café au lait or hot chocolate?'

'Think I'd better go the hot chocolate, or I'll never get any sleep tonight.' It was going to be hard enough as it was with her mind buzzing with all the haunted history Theo had told her.

The beignets were balls of fried dough, sweet and fluffy and tasting better than Flick could ever have imagined, although the chef had gone a little overboard with the icing sugar.

'You've got some on your ...' She pointed to her own upper lip, indicating the sugar on Theo's face.

'Whoops. Beignets are messy but worth it,' he said, wiping it off with a serviette. Flick couldn't help noticing the five o'clock shadow on his strong jawline. Neve and Emma would definitely deem him sexy, but Flick was just as captivated by his personality.

While they ate, Theo came good on his promise, sharing more stories of the Quarter's chequered past and haunted buildings. He was a wealth of local history and knowledge and she found herself hanging on his every word as she learnt about Old Absinthe House,

Arnaud's, the Morgue, Pirates Alley, Saint Louis Cathedral and more.

'There's something almost magical about this place,' Flick said. 'The colourful quirky people and little nooks and alleyways make me feel like I've stepped into the world of Harry Potter or something.'

He nodded. 'When I was a kid, I swore that the shops on Royal Street moved around and switched places.'

She laughed, but it wasn't hard to imagine thinking such a thing. 'Thank you for showing me round.'

'You're very welcome.'

When they'd finished their drinks, Theo led them down Decatur Street to show her a few more iconic buildings on their way back. Flick's phone was deep in her bag and she couldn't be bothered taking it out to check the time, but she could tell it was late—maybe even after midnight. Although it had still been busy at Café du Monde, the buskers and psychics around Jackson Square were gone, and there were no more tour groups in sight. But even as they walked down dark, nearly deserted alleys and streets, she never once felt unsafe with Theo.

'You asked about the most haunted building in the Quarter.' He nodded towards a mansion on the street corner. 'This one's a definite contender.'

Flick frowned—it didn't look any different to any of the other houses they'd passed. 'Why?'

'Because of Delphine LaLaurie.'

The way he said this name sent shivers scuttling down her spine.

'Undoubtedly one of the most evil humans to ever grace the Quarter. Hell, probably one of the most evil women ever to live anywhere. There are accounts that say she chained her cook to the oven, kept enslaved people in cages, gouging out their eyes, ripping off ears, tearing out fingernails. She'd stuff their mouths with animal faeces and sew them shut. When they were discovered, many had broken bones and wounds festering on their skin.'

Flick's own skin crawled as he described the horrors this woman had inflicted within the walls of this impressive-looking building. It was hard to reconcile such beauty with such brutality.

'One of her slaves eventually set fire to the house to try and alert the authorities. Many were already dead, but the rest were taken from her and sold at auction.'

'I hope they had a better life wherever they went next.'

'You'd like to think so, but apparently her friend bought them back and returned them to her.'

'That's awful,' Flick said, dessert now sitting heavy in her gut. 'Does anyone live there now?'

'It's owned by out-of-towners and has been converted into apartments. Nicolas Cage actually owned it previously, but rumour is he never dared to sleep there.' Theo paused. 'Though he does own a tomb in Saint Louis Cemetery No. 1—it's this massive pyramid— so I guess he might come back to town eventually.'

Back on Bourbon Street, they passed Lafitte's Blacksmith Shop Bar. It still heaved with loud music and was so crowded that people had spilled out onto the street.

'Oldest structure used as a bar in the whole of America. Also haunted,' Theo added with a wink.

Flick laughed. 'I think I'd be more surprised if you told me it wasn't. Is there an *un*-haunted tour, showcasing all the places that don't harbour lost souls?'

'Don't think anything like that's caught on yet. It might be a very short tour.'

Flick nodded. 'People would probably complain they hadn't got their money's worth.'

They were almost home and although more than ready for bed now, she couldn't help being a little disappointed the evening had come to an end.

'Thank you for tonight.' Flick smiled up at him. 'I had such a lovely time and feel like I've learnt a lot as well.'

'You're welcome. I enjoyed myself too—only hope I didn't bore you to tears. I've been told I get carried away talking about the Quarter sometimes.'

'Not at all.'

In fact, she couldn't recall having such a pleasant evening in a long time. If all dates were as easy as this one—not that this was technically a date, just a casual dinner between new friends—then perhaps Emma and Neve were right. Maybe it was time to step out of her comfort zone and open herself up to the possibility of something more with a man.

Flick was trying to work up the courage to ask Theo if he'd like to do this again, when his brow creased in obvious concern as he stared towards the shop.

'What is it?' she asked, her heart skipping a beat as she followed his gaze.

A woman sat on the steps in front of the door, her knees drawn up and her head resting on her arms. Golden blonde hair fell over her shoulders and a large duffel bag rested beside her. Flick gasped as they came closer, unable to believe her eyes. It had to be an apparition, or someone that looked the spitting image of her daughter.

The woman lifted her head.

'Mum!' Zoe screeched, jumping to her feet and throwing herself at Flick. 'Where've you been? I've been trying to call you for hours!'

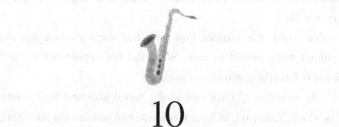

10

Zoe

Zoe flung herself into her mother's arms. She'd never been so happy to see her. As if the last few days hadn't been horrendous enough, the last couple of hours she'd been propositioned by drunks, preached at by some loony with a megaphone and had loose change tossed at her when someone clearly mistook her for a homeless person.

Right now she couldn't see the appeal of New Orleans at all, but she was happy to be as far away from Perth—from Beau—as she could get.

'Darling, I'm sorry, I was having dinner,' Flick said as she hugged her back. 'What are you doing here? Why didn't you tell me you were coming?'

Zoe burst into tears again, surprised she actually had any left. She'd done nothing but cry since Beau had walked out of their house and out of her life. She'd howled as she booked a plane ticket early the following morning and sobbed almost the entire journey here.

At one stage a concerned flight attendant had brought her an entire box of tissues and asked if there was anything he could do to help.

She'd told him to bugger off—his gender had done enough—and he'd retreated like a little mouse, looking as if he might be about to cry as well.

Zoe could only imagine how wretched she must look but she couldn't bring herself to care. What did her appearance matter? What did anything matter anymore?

'Oh, sweetheart,' Flick said as she pulled back and looked into Zoe's face. 'Come on, let's get you inside and you can tell me what's going on.'

'I'll get the bag,' said the strange man.

Zoe was too emotionally wrung-out to argue, but she was glad when he deposited it inside and then left them be.

'Who was that?' she asked as her mother locked the door behind him.

'Theo owns the bar next door. Let's get you upstairs.'

Flick led her through all the stuffed animals to the back of the shop and up a dimly lit staircase to the apartment above. It felt weirdly calming to be surrounded by taxidermy again—since moving out of home, Zoe had kinda missed her mother's dead animals.

'Sit,' Flick said, ushering her over to the sofa and easing her down. Only when her mum wrapped a crocheted throw blanket around her shoulders and placed another on her knees did Zoe realise she was shaking.

'I'm cold,' she whispered. So cold she felt as if she'd never be warm again.

'I know, sweetheart. Let me get you a hot drink.'

Zoe sat almost in a trance as her mother went across to the kitchen. She only vaguely registered the music playing outside and the musty smell wafting around her.

Flick returned a few moments later with a steaming mug. 'Drink this.'

Having barely consumed anything in twenty-four hours (except the free wine on the plane) Zoe obediently took a sip and immediately screwed up her nose. 'What's that?' She thrust the mug back at her mum.

'Malted milk. I don't have any Milo and I didn't think you should be drinking coffee at this time of night.'

Her body clock was so out of whack she didn't even know what day it was, never mind the time. 'Do you have anything stronger?'

Flick took the mug and stood. 'Let's see what I can find.'

Zoe leaned back and closed her eyes. Although she was exhausted, she wasn't sure she'd ever be able to sleep again. Every time she tried, she saw Beau and his hands on somebody else, and her heart broke all over again. She couldn't help wondering if somehow this was her fault, if somehow, *she'd* pushed him away. Things hadn't been great between them lately, but she'd never imagined it was down to something like this. She felt as if she had a zillion papercuts all over her body and she might die from the pain.

The tears were streaming when Flick returned with a glass of something amber-coloured. 'I found this in Harvey's stash.'

She didn't ask what it was as she reached out and took a large gulp, then winced as the liquid burned the back of her throat. She immediately felt a warm kind of relief.

Flick lowered herself onto the sofa beside Zoe. 'Do you want to tell me what's going on?'

She didn't. Not really. But her mum deserved to know why she'd come all this way. She took another gulp. 'Beau cheated on me.'

Flick's mouth fell open, but nothing came out.

'Oh, honey, no!' she said once she recovered. 'Are you sure?'

The shock was clear in her mother's eyes and voice as she vehemently shook her head, but it was nothing compared to the surprise and confusion Zoe felt.

'Unless he's a liar as well as a cheat, then yes. Effing sure.'

When she'd arrived home from work to find Beau standing at the end of their bed, piling his clothes into a suitcase, another one on the floor, her first thought was that she'd forgotten about a school camp.

'Hey, Zoe.' The tone of his voice and the fact he'd used her full name—he always called her Zo-Zo, babe or some other term of endearment—had chilled her to her bones.

'What's going on?' Her voice shook as she told herself she was probably panicking for no reason. Maybe he was whisking her off on a surprise Mediterranean holiday and the other suitcase was stuffed with bikinis?

The next words that spilled from his lips killed that possibility. 'There's no easy way to say this ... I'm sorry ... but I can't do this anymore.'

'This? What ... I-I don't understand.'

Beau looked close to tears, but Zoe had been too shocked for waterworks.

'What exactly do you mean you can't do this? Is this about the baby?'

'No. It's not about having kids. Well, not exactly.' He paused a moment, then, BAM! 'I've been sleeping with someone else.'

He may as well have punched her in the stomach. The air left her body and she doubled over, unable to believe her ears. But as she crumpled to the floor, the most awful thing about it was that he didn't rush over to her. He didn't tell her that this was some kind of sick prank. He didn't pull her into his arms and try to soothe her pain.

He simply stood there, awkwardly, as if he'd rather be anywhere else, which, judging by what followed, was obviously the case.

'Please … tell me you're joking.'

'I'm sorry. I … I didn't mean for any of this to happen.'

'Then how *did* it? Who the hell is she?'

'She's … I met her through school.'

'Another teacher?' Zoe mentally went through a catalogue of his colleagues, unable to imagine Beau attracted to any one of them. Then again, she'd never have imagined *this* at all.

'No. Natasha's … she's the mum of one of my students. A kid I coach swimming. We got chatting one day after a meet and …'

Zoe held up her hand, her stomach revolting. 'Stop. *Please.*' Part of her didn't want to know the details, but there was another part of her that wanted to punish herself with every single one. 'How many times?'

He blinked. 'How many times have we had sex?'

'No! How many times have you seen *The Sound of Music*?' She tended to get sarcastic when she was upset.

Beau's shrug felt like another blow to her gut. 'I don't know. A few.'

'A few?' She glared at him. Her best friend since she was fifteen, the love of her life, the man who'd promised in front of a priest and all their friends and family that he'd be true to her until death do they part, looked like a stranger. Suddenly the reason for him not wanting to sleep with her made oh-so-much sense.

Yet, even days later it was still impossible to process. That he'd slept with someone else—kissed another woman, touched her intimately. Unbelievable *and* unforgiveable. Not that he'd asked her forgiveness.

'She's the mum of a student?' Flick clarified now.

'Yes. She's, like, probably old enough to be his mother.'

Anger replaced the shock in Flick's eyes. 'I'll kill her. I'll kill *him*!'

Zoe knew exactly how she felt. In the hours that followed Beau's announcement, she'd gone through a myriad of emotions. Disbelief, denial, shock, then anger mixed with sadness and homicidal thoughts. If she hadn't fled the country, she might now be in jail.

'Did you have a chance to talk to him properly?' Flick asked. 'Or did you …'

'Just leave?' Zoe swiped at her eyes again, annoyed that she was still blubbering over such a wanker. 'I tried to talk to him, Mum. I told him everyone makes mistakes and that I was prepared to try and work through this, to try and forgive him, but he didn't want a bar of it. He doesn't want to be with me anymore.'

'Is he in love with her?'

'Eff knows,' she yelled, grabbing onto anger, which was easier than sadness. 'He says he's not, that it's just sex, but I can't believe anything he says anymore. He said he was flattered by a sexy, older woman paying him attention, but the fact that he followed through with it—and enjoyed it—made him realise he's not ready for marriage, kids, the whole package. He wants to have *fun* instead apparently.'

Zoe cringed as she recalled her reaction—how she'd thrown herself at his feet, desperately begging him not to throw away what they had. 'We can have fun. I know we've been busy lately. I know we've been stressed, but if you're not ready for parenthood, then okay.'

She'd promised they could wait a year or two, that she loved him and they could move past this, but he'd barely been able to look at her—glancing at the door instead, as if he couldn't wait to get out of there. 'I'm sorry, Zoe, but I'm not gonna change my mind. I don't want to be married anymore.'

And with those words he'd grabbed both suitcases. 'I'll message you in a couple of days to organise a time to come and get the rest of my stuff.'

'Are you going to stay with her?' she'd spat.

He sighed, as if he really didn't have time for this. 'No. I'm gonna stay with Zane for a bit.'

Zane was Beau's best mate from high school—he'd been best man at their wedding and had recently started dating a friend of Zoe's from uni. 'Does he … does he know?' She couldn't bring herself to say the words. 'Does Mikayla?'

She wondered if she was the last person to find out her marriage was a farce.

Beau groaned. 'Dunno. She might. I had to tell Zane something. Anyway, it's getting late. Goodnight, Zoe.'

Then, after ten years together—four of them married—he walked out of her life without even a backward glance.

She didn't know if he'd messaged her. She'd removed him from her social media, blocked his number on her phone. Even though it was impossible to imagine her life without Beau in it, she'd wipe him from her whole damn history if she could.

'I'm such a pathetic fool, Mum. I'm going to be the laughing-stock of everyone I know.'

'I don't think anyone will be laughing, Zo-Zo.'

'Maybe not to my face, but I know what they'll be thinking.' There'd already been plenty of sympathetic messages from their mutual friends and although they meant well, they only made her feel worse. 'And you may as well get it out of the way,' she added, taking another sip of the potent drink and bracing herself.

Flick's forehead creased. 'Get what out of the way?'

'Saying "I told you so". You and Sofia thought I was stupid to get married so young. Well, turns out you were right.'

99

'We *never* thought you were stupid. And I'm as blindsided by this as you—Beau is like a son to me.'

'*Was* like a son, Mum. He's dead to me now and he should be dead to you too.'

'Okay.' Flick squeezed Zoe's hand. 'Beau who?'

'Thank you,' Zoe whispered. 'There's just one problem. I have that bastard's name on my butt.'

'What?'

'We got matching tattoos on our honeymoon. A little heart with each other's name in it. It was supposed to be our secret and now some other woman has had her hands all over it!'

'You got a *tattoo* without telling me?'

Zoe glared at her. 'That's your biggest concern after hearing all this? I wouldn't have got married, never mind got a tattoo, if I knew this is how it was all going to end.'

'I'm sorry.' Her mum immediately looked chastised, put her arm around Zoe and drew her into her side. 'I'm struggling to make any sense of this.'

'You and me both … I keep telling myself it's a nightmare and I'm going to wake up any moment and everything will be normal again.'

'I know that feeling,' Flick said under her breath. 'Don't worry about the tattoo. We can get it removed. I'm sure there's someone round here who can help. But right now, how about something to eat? And then maybe a shower before bed.'

Zoe shook her head. 'I can't stomach anything at the moment.' The thought of trying to eat only made her constant nausea worse. 'And I'm not up for a shower. I just want to sit here. With you. Do you mind?'

'Of course not, sweetheart, whatever you need. I'm here for you. Now. Always.'

Flick pulled Zoe into her arms once again, holding her and stroking her hair as she'd done when she was little and upset over something. Her mum's touch had always worked magic, and right now, although it couldn't fix anything and she would *never* feel good again, it was exactly what Zoe needed.

11

Felicity

Sometime in the early hours of the morning, Zoe finally fell asleep. After making sure she was truly zonked, Flick extracted herself from the couch, covered her with a light blanket and retreated to her own bedroom. But, thanks to the shock of Zoe's arrival and the reason behind it, she couldn't shut off her brain.

It was hard to believe Zoe was actually here, in the flesh. Finding her waiting on the doorstep had been such a shock—part of her had been overjoyed to see Zoe's familiar face, but, as much as she hated to admit it, there'd also been a smidgeon of annoyance.

Flick hadn't even had a week to herself and she'd finally begun to relax and enjoy herself in New Orleans—perhaps even open herself to the possibility of romance. Who would have thought? But one proper look at her daughter and all her maternal instincts had kicked in with a vengeance. She'd wanted to hug her, feed her, do *something* to make everything better. Fix this. That was what mothers were supposed to do, but she had no idea where to even begin.

The thought of Beau cheating simply didn't compute. At least when her husband had finally told Flick he—yikes, *she*—identified as a woman and wanted to transition to Sofia, she hadn't been completely caught unawares. Confused, yes. Sad, yes. Questioning whether she'd really ever had the marriage she'd thought she had, yes.

But Zoe and Beau? She'd never have predicted this.

Glancing across at her baby girl now, sleeping a few feet away, her heart squeezed. She didn't look peaceful at all and Flick longed to reach out and try to smooth the creases from her brow.

Thank God she wasn't pregnant. Thank God they don't have kids.

That was the only good thing in all of this she could think of right now. Although she knew how much Zoe longed to be a mum, their separation—if it truly came to that—would be much more straightforward without the added complications of a family.

Flick took another sip of her tea, but it held none of its usual soothing qualities. Her thoughts were too loud. Her head ached. She wanted to talk about this with someone but didn't want to betray Zoe by telling Emma and Neve just yet. Her instinct was to call Sofia—the only other person who cared about her daughter as much as she did.

But hang on! Did Sofia even know what was going on? Surely, she'd have called to forewarn Flick of Zoe's arrival if she did. And *she* was Zoe's parent too. If the situation was switched Flick would want Sofia to call her.

Putting her own feelings aside for now, she grabbed her phone and checked the time in Perth—she still hadn't wrapped her head around the difference. Almost 5 pm. Sofia would be leaving work soon and catching the train home. Perhaps a message would be best.

Not sure if you know, but Zoe is in New Orleans with me. Things not good with Beau. Really bad actually. I can't talk right now as she's sleeping beside me, but I'll call you tomorrow.

Flick's phone started ringing and she stabbed her finger at it to reject the call, then switched it to silent.

A reply came almost instantly: *She's supposed to be having dinner with me and Mike tonight. How can she be in New Orleans?*

Flick stared at her phone, dithering, so stressed about Zoe she barely even registered the mention of Mike. She could sneak downstairs and call Sofia from there. Zoe looked dead to the world, and she'd never kept anything this big from Sofia before. But even downstairs felt too far away, so she went out onto the balcony and called from there instead. Bourbon Street was almost deserted now and there was only the distant sound of music coming from a few of the strip clubs.

Sofia answered before the phone barely had the chance to ring. 'Flick? What on earth's going on?'

The hormones may have altered Sofia's voice, but Flick still felt a comfort she didn't want to feel at the sound of her ex's voice. She leaned back against the balcony railing, her throat growing suddenly tight and tears sprouting in her eyes.

'Oh God, it's awful,' she sobbed as she began to tell Sofia exactly what Zoe had told her.

'Sweetheart, slow down, take a breath. I can't understand what you're saying.'

Flick started again, and this time from the expletives coming down the phone line, she knew she'd got the message through.

'I'll fucking kill the little bastard.'

'Calm down, please,' Flick pleaded. 'That was my first thought too, but anger isn't going to help Zoe. We have to focus on supporting her the best way we possibly can.'

'You're right. I'm sorry,' Sofia said. 'I just can't believe this. Beau's the last person I ever thought would hurt our baby girl. I thought they were the real deal.'

'You and me both.'

'Do you think it's really over? I mean, I'm not condoning his actions but everyone makes mistakes—maybe he'll see the error of his ways?'

'I don't know. But I do know Zoe doesn't deserve to be messed around. As much as I love—*loved*—Beau, she deserves a marriage where she feels secure and loved, a husband she can trust. I'm not sure I'd want her to forgive him.'

'I understand. But in the end, I guess that would be her decision.' They were both silent a few moments, then Sofia added, 'Look, I've got that conference in LA soon; maybe I should fly over there beforehand?'

'No!' However comforting it was to share this problem with Sofia, she'd be better placed to take care of Zoe if she wasn't dealing with her own complex emotions as well. 'I mean, I don't think that's necessary at this stage.'

Sofia sighed. 'Okay, well, if you're sure. I just feel so bloody helpless.'

'I know. I feel helpless too, but I promise I'll take care of her and keep you posted.'

Although Sofia deliberated a little longer, Flick managed to convince her that she had it under control.

'I've got to go,' she said eventually, noticing the sun peeking over the horizon. 'It's almost morning and I haven't even been to bed.'

'Okay. Take care. Tell Zoe I love her and that I'm here if she wants to talk. Phone. Facetime. Whatever.'

'I will,' Flick promised.

She went back inside and fell into bed, managing a couple of hours restless slumber before she woke properly again to the sun blaring in through the gap between the ancient lace curtains. She sat bolt upright, the events of the previous evening barrelling back into her head.

Zoe!

Flinging back the light sheet that covered her, Flick dashed into the living area and expelled a long breath when she found her daughter still asleep. Her mind immediately went into mum-mode. When Zoe woke, she'd need something comforting to eat, a shower and a good dose of caffeine, none of which would mend her heart but would hopefully be a good start towards making her feel human again.

Flick crossed to the kitchen and assessed her still meagre supplies. She could make scrambled eggs, but she needed fresh bread and she wanted to get Zoe a proper coffee—but that would mean leaving her, which she didn't want to risk doing just yet. A voice in her head said that was ridiculous, but Flick had never seen her so heartsore, and broken people did drastic things.

While she contemplated her next move, Zoe shifted slightly on the couch, slowly opening her eyes and taking in her surroundings. 'Mum?'

'I'm here. Morning, sweetheart.'

Zoe stretched and rubbed her eyes. 'What time is it?'

'It's just after eight. Do you want to have a shower and then we can go out and get some breakfast?'

'I'm not really hungry.'

'You have to eat something.'

'I don't want to go anywhere, Mum, but I'll be fine if you go. I promise I won't do anything crazy like jump off the balcony.'

They both glanced across at said balcony. Flick wasn't sure whether to laugh or panic. The possibility hadn't crossed her mind until Zoe planted it there.

'I could kill for a coffee though.'

Although Flick had bought more coffee, it still wasn't much better than Harvey's. 'Trust me, you won't kill to drink the stuff I've got here. If you're sure you'll be okay, I'll go buy us a proper one.'

'Thanks, Mummy-dear.' Zoe smiled but there was no joy in her eyes.

And why should there be? Her relationship with Beau may have started as a high school crush but it had evolved into something so much more. Flick had been happy when Zoe had missed the painful and dramatic break-ups her friends had experienced in their teens, but now she couldn't help wishing that Zoe and Beau had never become so serious.

'On one condition. You have a shower while I'm gone.' She didn't add that it would make Zoe feel better, because having had her own marriage fall apart, she wasn't that naive, but keeping up basic personal hygiene was a must. And if Flick had to bribe her to do so for now, she would.

'Okay.'

Leaving Zoe to acquaint herself with the bathroom, Flick grabbed her phone, keys and handbag and went downstairs, almost bumping into Theo as she left the shop. 'Sorry!'

He reached out to steady her and his smile morphed into a frown. 'Geez. You look awful.'

'Oh … *thanks*.'

'I just meant you look tired, stressed. Is it something to do with your daughter?'

'Yes. She's ... split up with her husband. She's completely broken. I didn't get much sleep.'

'I'm sorry to hear that,' Theo said.

Flick nodded. 'And now Zoe wants coffee, so I'm off to get her some and hopefully something she can't resist eating. I'm thinking beignets?'

'Good choice. Do you mind if I walk with you? I was off to get breakfast myself.'

'Not at all. Where do you recommend?'

'Café Beignet isn't too far away.'

As they walked the short distance up Bourbon Street, they chatted about inane stuff like the weather and various clubs and shops they passed, and it was exactly the reprieve Flick needed for a few moments.

The tables in the courtyard venue were almost all taken when they arrived, and a trio of jazz musicians were playing on the small stage. Flick ordered chicory coffees—hoping they'd be okay—and beignets to go. Theo went for the same and everything was ready almost immediately. Holding the coffees in a cardboard carrier and the beignets in a paper bag, they made their way back down Bourbon, Theo tossing coins at a few of the homeless folk they passed on the road.

'This street almost feels like a different place in the morning than it does at night,' Flick mused. 'And weirdly I think I prefer it when it's loud and buzzing.'

'The poverty is more obvious during the day. By night, it's all fun and frivolity, but tourists can forget that real people live here. Many of them homeless. There were issues before Katrina—problems going back generations. But so many people lost their houses and jobs in the hurricane and only the wealthy had the means to rebuild.

Not that I'm not grateful for the tourists,' he clarified. 'They keep me in business.'

They walked a little further, passing a voodoo shop where a woman with black frizzy hair, wearing a long black shirt and flowy black top was turning the sign on the door from closed to open. Theo waved at her as well and she popped her head out the door.

'Morning. And who have we here?' she asked, flashing Flick a wide smile.

'Hey, Luna.'

Flick smiled back as Theo introduced them. 'Felicity is taking care of Harvey's shop.'

'Ah, welcome. I heard he was off to Florida for a while. You must come see me some time for a reading.'

'Maybe,' Flick said, unsure whether she dared. Not that she really believed in such stuff, but would it have been better to have been forewarned about her own break-up as well as Zoe's?

'You seem to know everyone,' Flick said as they continued on.

'Can't help it, I'm a friendly kind of guy.'

She had to concede that was true but wondered if, in the case of the ladies, like the waitress they'd met and Luna, it was also to do with how he looked.

'Good luck with your daughter,' Theo said, his brow slightly furrowed as they slowed in front of the Blue Cat. 'Hope she enjoys the beignets.'

'Thank you.' Flick smiled and hurried into the shop.

Upstairs she found Zoe once again on the couch, but her hair was wet, and she had on fresh clothes at least.

'How are you feeling?' Flick asked and then immediately regretted the stupid question.

'Like I want to curl up into a ball, go to sleep and never wake up.'

Choosing not to encourage that line of thinking, Flick approached with the food and handed Zoe one of the takeaway cups. She put the other one on the coffee table and then unveiled the beignets.

'Welcome to New Orleans. These are a local delicacy.'

Zoe shook her head. 'I said I'm not hungry.' But thankfully she took a sip of her coffee.

Baby steps. Flick sat and racked her brain for some safe topic of conversation. Of course, the only thing that came to mind was Beau and this whole damn mess. She had lots of questions about how Zoe planned to move forward from this but didn't think they'd be welcome yet, so instead she scoffed three whole pastries, barely tasting them. If she kept stress-eating at this rate she'd be the size of a house by the end of next week.

'When do you have to open the shop?' Zoe asked, finally breaking the silence.

'I've been opening about ten, but I can do it later, or not at all. We can do whatever you'd like.'

'I don't want to get you in trouble with Harvey, and no offence, but I'd rather be by myself for a bit.'

'Okay.' Flick fought the desire to pick up *another* beignet. Maybe if she left them on the table, Zoe would be tempted eventually.

She reluctantly went to have a shower and ready herself for the day. When she emerged twenty minutes later, she sighed at the sight of Zoe asleep again. Flying halfway across the world was exhausting enough, but combine jet lag with heartbreak and Zoe would probably be in a zombie-like state for days.

Flick scribbled a note, telling Zoe she could find her downstairs if she needed anything at all, and then went to open up.

She'd discovered that Bourbon Street had good foot traffic most days, but Friday proved to be her busiest day so far. On the one hand this was a good thing, because the people coming in and out forced her to talk and think about something other than Zoe, but it also meant she didn't manage to check on her as much as she'd like. Each time she did, she made herself a cup of horrid coffee, because without it there was no way she was going to make it through the day. All but twice, she'd found Zoe fast asleep—the other two times she was staring at the TV, watching mindless shows. She appeared to be in a trance, unable to participate in any kind of conversation no matter how hard Flick tried.

Give her time. She's had the biggest shock of her life and it's only been a matter of days.

But a mother couldn't help wishing she could just kiss it better, stick a bandaid on and work the kind of miracle she did when her children were little and upset.

She barely made any progress on her projects and by five o'clock her eyes were no longer capable of staying open. Heeding Harvey's assurance that she could choose her own working hours, she went to lock up.

A figure appeared in the glass as she was turning the sign to closed. *Theo!* Tired as she might be, something fluttered inside her at the sight of him. She immediately forced it back in its box. Now was not the time.

'Hey,' he said as she opened the door. 'Closing up early?'

She nodded. 'I'm so tired that if I waited any longer, I wouldn't be able to climb the stairs.'

He smiled sympathetically and held up a couple of plastic bags.

'I brought some stuff for you—well, mostly for your daughter. But I also bought dinner from Brennan's as I thought you guys might be too tired to cook or go out.'

Flick peered into the first bag to find a couple of DVDs, some chocolate bars and a tub of ice-cream. She almost burst into tears.

'I know Harvey doesn't have any streaming services, but still has a DVD player. Thought his movies might not be to Zoe's taste, so I managed to dig up some she might like.'

'Oh my goodness, that's so sweet. How much do I owe you?'

'Don't be silly. It's a gift.'

'Thank you,' she managed, reaching out to take the bags.

'Do you want me to carry them upstairs?'

'I don't mean to be rude, but I don't think Zoe is in the right frame of mind for visitors right now.'

'Not rude at all; you need to look after your girl.' He took a step back and lifted a hand to wave. 'I'll lock the door on my way out. Yell out if you need anything else.'

'Thank you,' Flick said, and then went upstairs.

12

Zoe

Zoe looked up from the couch as she heard her mother climbing the stairs for the umpteenth time that day and contemplated whether to feign sleep again. It wasn't that she didn't want to talk to Flick, she just didn't want to talk about *Beau*, and yet she didn't want to talk about anything else either. Nothing mattered anymore.

Her life as she knew it was officially over.

Problem was she needed to pee, so she was going to have to get up sooner or later anyway. *Stupid bladder.* She hadn't eaten and had barely drunk anything since coffee that morning and yet still it insisted on going through the motions.

Flick grinned as she entered the room and saw Zoe up and about.

'What's that?' she asked, eyeing the bags her mother was carrying.

Flick put one of them down on the coffee table. The other looked to contain some kind of takeaway. 'It's a care package.'

'A what?'

'A few things to get you through the next few days—to try and help you feel a bit better.'

'Next few *days*?' Zoe couldn't believe the naivety of her mother. 'You think it's only going to take me *days* to get over Beau? Mum! He was the love of my life. I've never been with anyone else and I never wanted to be.'

'I know, honey, I didn't mean ...' Flick sighed. 'Anyway, this isn't from me. It's from Theo next door.'

'The guy from last night?' Zoe raised an eyebrow. She didn't appreciate her mother flapping her gums about her personal life to complete strangers. 'You told *him* about me and Beau?'

'Well, not the details. I just mentioned you guys had ... separated.'

Zoe flinched at that last word. 'Are you dating him?'

'What? No.' Flick's cheeks turned from peach to beetroot in less than a second. 'I've not even known him a week. He's just a friend. A nice guy.'

'You're delusional if you think there's such a thing. Turns out men are bastards.'

'Honey, while I understand you're upset, you can't write off all men. What about your brother?'

'Toby doesn't count.'

Flick looked as if she was contemplating arguing but decided against it. 'Do you want something to eat?'

'What have you got?'

'I don't know but it smells delicious. Why don't you take a look while I put the ice-cream in the freezer?'

Flick leaned forward to pluck a tub of ice-cream from the bag, but Zoe intercepted it. She still didn't feel like eating but could make an exception for ice-cream. Wasn't that the recommended cure for broken hearts?

'I'll have this, but I'm just popping to the loo.'

When she returned, her mum had optimistically set two places and the takeaway containers on the dining table. She'd also opened the balcony doors. Warm air, loud music and the occasional drunken shout wafted in from outside.

'What is *that*?' Zoe asked, screwing up her nose as she peered down at the three dishes. Two of them looked like something you'd serve up to folks in an old people's home who'd lost their teeth.

'There's some red beans and rice, pork gumbo, and also some vegetarian gnocchi.'

'That man is clearly trying to get into your pants,' she said, going to grab a spoon for the ice-cream.

'Zoe! There's no need to be so crass. He's just generous and probably wanted to make sure there was something for all tastes.'

'Don't be so naive.' She peeled back the lid, dipped her spoon into the container and shoved a large helping of peanut butter and jelly ice-cream into her mouth. 'But I'll give him this,' she said after letting the flavours melt on her tongue, 'he's got good taste in ice-cream.'

'I'll let him know.' Flick yawned as she began to scoop some of the red bean stuff onto her plate.

'How was the shop today?' Zoe asked as she sat.

'Quite busy. You know you're welcome to come downstairs and chat whenever you want.'

'I know.' Although hanging out with a bunch of stuffed animals was not Zoe's idea of a good time. 'I'm not really feeling up to much more than TV at the moment.'

She couldn't imagine ever feeling up to anything more ever again. She'd packed in such a rush she hadn't even brought any pencils, never mind a sketchpad or paints, but whereas normally she didn't go a day without at least doodling something, she hadn't missed them at all.

'Fair enough. But when you are, you should definitely take a walk around the Quarter. There are some really cute boutiques with gorgeous clothes, not to mention lots of funky art galleries too. You'd love them. I can always close the shop for a little while and come with you.'

Zoe made a non-committal noise—the thought of going anywhere didn't appeal in the slightest. And when she'd peeked over the balcony earlier in the day, all she could see were clubs and pubs, none of this so-called art culture. It would have been fine if she was here with a bunch of girlfriends, but it didn't look much like the kind of place you went with your mother, even if she were in the mood.

'Window-shopping is no fun and I can't afford to buy anything anyway.'

'Speaking of money … what have you done about your job?'

'I quit. No way Gretchen would have given me time off.'

As her mother's eyes widened, Zoe held up a hand. 'I don't need a lecture. I know I'll have to get another job eventually, but that's honestly the least of my problems right now.'

How could she think about hunting for work when her head was so full of thoughts about where she and Beau had gone wrong? Was it just the last couple of months since they'd decided to have a baby, or had there always been cracks in their relationship? Was it the sex? Until *Natasha*, they'd been each other's only sexual partners. Was he bored with the physical side of their relationship? She'd thought they were pretty adventurous, but maybe she was wrong.

She shuddered, imagining his older woman having all sorts of weird and innovative skills, taking him to places Zoe didn't even know existed.

'Can we please talk about something else?'

'I'm sorry, of course we can.' Flick yawned again.

'Or maybe you should go to bed. You look shattered.'

She opened her mouth to object, but Zoe held up her hand. 'I'll be fine,' she promised. 'I'll watch some more TV'—maybe sneak a little more of Harvey's liquor—'and see you in the morning.'

Flick hesitated only a moment. 'If you're sure. I am knackered.' Then she stood and started to clear up.

'I'll fix all that,' Zoe said. It was the least she could do after being the reason her mum had been up half the previous night.

'Thank you, darling.' Flick dropped a kiss upon her head. 'Also, when you're ready to sleep, why don't you come in with me. There's plenty of room and you shouldn't spend another night on the couch. Tomorrow we'll clean the bedding in Harvey's room and you can move in there.'

13

Zoe

Zoe frowned at her reflection in the tarnished old mirror as she ran her fingers through her oily hair. She'd always been a light golden blonde but now her hair had the brownish tint of the unwashed. She shrugged, unable to care about this any more than she could about her bloodshot eyes, the puffiness beneath them and her blotchy cheeks, which were a side effect of endless crying and spending all day since she arrived staring at the television.

She glanced towards the shower but decided she couldn't be bothered right now. She couldn't be bothered to change her clothes either, but if she didn't do that her mum would notice and nag her about hygiene again.

Zoe, have you had a shower? Have you brushed your teeth? You need to eat something, sweetheart. Why don't you get out for a bit of fresh air?

She'd forgotten how annoying living with a parent could be, but she'd rather be here than anywhere else right now. So, she reluctantly brushed her teeth, splashed water over her face and headed into Harvey's bedroom, which was now supposed to be hers but wasn't much more than a place to keep her clothes. Her mum had aired out the room, changed the bedding and lit a number of scented candles, but a horrible musty smell still permeated everything, and the couch was closer to the TV anyway. Over the past few days—Zoe had lost count as the minutes, hours and days all blurred—she'd become addicted to documentaries and reality TV. She even found home renovation shows more comforting than the rom-coms her mum's 'friend' Theo had given her.

Why would anyone want to watch that bullshit fantasy when they were suffering heartache? She guessed they were supposed to cheer people up with the prospect of a happy ever after, but there wasn't going to be a happy ending to her story. Beau had put paid to that.

The only thing she could really relate to right now was this weird painting that hung above Harvey's mantlepiece of a skeleton dressed as a bride. When she wasn't watching TV, she spent a fair bit of time staring at it. Something about the skeleton's expression spoke to her heart. It was like it understood how she felt, more than her mother or anyone else could.

Dead. Like an empty shell. With no future to look forward to.

Wondering about the man who had clearly abandoned the poor skeleton—did he leave her because he'd found someone else like Beau?—Zoe dug in her suitcase for a clean pair of undies and a change of T-shirt but decided the old pair of denim shorts she'd been wearing could go a little longer. She dressed and went back out into the living room.

Thankfully, Flick had finally retreated downstairs—her constant fussing was getting on Zoe's nerves—so she could continue to wallow in peace. She crossed over to the kitchen and made herself a coffee, then added a dash of Harvey's poison to the mug. Or at least she tried to, but nothing came out.

Miserably discarding the empty bottle, she pushed aside tins of stew and fish as she rifled through the cupboards, searching for another to no avail.

'Dammit.' How the hell was she going to get through the long day ahead without alcohol?

She'd tried to forget with mindless TV but more often than not the show didn't hold her attention and instead she found herself reaching for her phone and stalking her husband on social media. Although she'd blocked him across all platforms, they had enough mutual friends that she could still access his accounts. He hadn't posted at all since he'd left, but she kept checking back, dreading the day he'd update his status to 'single' or worse, 'it's complicated'.

But it wasn't complicated. There was no way she'd ever be able to misinterpret what he said and it made her question everything she'd believed over the past ten years. Did he ever *truly* love her? Was she always more invested than him?

She wasn't sure she wanted to know the answers and the only time she ever truly switched off was when she passed out from drinking.

Flick's eyes lit up as Zoe entered the shop a couple of minutes later, shoes on her feet for the first time in days and her oversized handbag hanging over her shoulder. She hadn't ventured downstairs since she'd arrived.

'Good morning, darling. You're looking lovely this morning.'

That was clearly a lie—Zoe had seen herself in the mirror mere moments ago. But she didn't call her mother on it. 'Thanks. Thought I'd get a little exercise.'

'Excellent. Do you want me to come with you?'

'No! I mean ...' She gestured to two women at the front of the shop, chatting over a stuffed fox. 'You've got a job to do, but I can buy you a takeaway coffee if you want?'

'Thanks, that'd be lovely.' Flick took a credit card from her pocket. 'Here, take this. The coffees are on me.'

Zoe headed out onto Bourbon Street, pulling maps up on her phone in order to find the nearest bottle shop. Even though it wasn't quite midday there were already people strolling down the middle of the road sipping drinks from massive plastic cups. She'd planned on buying a bottle to replace Harvey's, but as she headed in the direction of some place called Walgreens, a near-deserted, rustic-looking pub and the lure of cheap cocktails on a sign out the front caught her eye. It wouldn't hurt to have an actual drink en route.

It took a second or two for Zoe's eyes to adjust as she stepped into the dimly lit building but by the time she got to the bar, she could clearly see the rows and rows of bottles on the back wall. Her mouth watered. A tall man with a bushy mop of red hair was polishing glasses and glanced up as she approached.

'Morning, ma'am. What can I get you?'

'A cocktail, please. Something large and potent.' Zoe dumped her bag on the bar as she climbed up onto a stool. She'd never been called 'ma'am' before.

'I know just the thing. Coming right up.'

As the man turned to gather the ingredients for her drink, she felt the presence of someone else not too far away and looked up to see a young guy refilling pamphlets in a stand at the other end of the bar. He wore tight jeans with a stripy button-up shirt and thick-rimmed black glasses. Besides the men there were only two other patrons in the whole venue, a couple sitting at a table by the window, their heads bent close together as they looked out onto the street.

'Here you go,' said the bartender, stealing her attention again as he pushed an icy purple concoction in a large tumbler across the countertop towards her.

'What is it?' she asked, already taking a sip as she gave him her credit card.

He tapped it against the EFT machine. 'A voodoo daiquiri.'

'What's in it?'

He winked. 'Sorry, kiddo, that's a trade secret.'

Oh well. Zoe took another sip. What did it matter what was in it as long as it tasted good? And *damn* it tasted good.

The sound of a crying baby pierced the air and her eyes followed the noise to the couple at the table. She saw a baby carrier on the floor that she hadn't noticed before. As the man bent to scoop up the distressed little bundle, Zoe felt a stab to her heart and her eyes prickled.

That was supposed to be her and Beau. It wasn't only her heart that ached but also her ovaries. Who knew if she'd ever be a mum now? And what kind of people brought a baby to a bar, never mind to the French Quarter, anyway? Fighting tears, she turned back and downed almost half her drink in one massive gulp.

'Are you okay?'

She turned to see the geeky-looking guy with the pamphlets looking at her. 'Excuse me?'

'Sorry, I just thought you looked upset and ...' He nodded towards her glass. 'You're drinking that pretty quickly.'

'What's it to you?' she said, her fingers tightening around the tumbler. 'Are you the alcohol police?'

'No, I just ... Never mind.' He shook his head and turned away.

Zoe closed her eyes, a sudden wave of remorse washing over her. Like the flight attendant on the plane she'd snapped at, this stranger was only trying to be nice. 'No, *I'm* sorry. That was rude,' she called back.

When he turned to face her again, she added, 'You're right. I'm not really okay, but that's no excuse to take it out on you.'

He shrugged. 'I've got thick skin. But if you want to talk about it, I'm a pretty good listener.'

'Not really. But I wouldn't mind some company.' He could keep her mind off the couple with the baby while she finished what was left of her cocktail. 'Let me buy you a drink. Oh, unless you're not allowed to drink on duty.'

He frowned a moment, then chuckled. 'Oh, I don't work here. I was just delivering these.' He flashed one of the pamphlets, which turned out to be promotional material for a ghost tour company.

Her eyes widened. 'Do you work for them?'

'Yep. I'm a tour guide and paranormal investigator. And well, also a waiter, but between you and me, it's the ghost stuff I like best.'

'Paranormal investigator?' Zoe couldn't keep the scepticism out of her voice. 'You mean like *Ghostbusters*? That was one of my favourite movies as a kid, but then ... I grew up.'

The guy took a seat on the bar stool beside her and gestured to the bartender. 'Can I get a Coke, please?' He looked back at Zoe. 'Do I detect a sceptic?'

'Are you asking me if I believe in ghosts?' Amused, she took another sip of her drink.

'Well, do you?'

She laughed and shook her head. 'I'm sorry, but no. I think they make great fodder for novels and scary movies, but once you're dead, you're dead, and you can't come back to revenge-haunt people.'

He leaned a little closer and whispered, 'I'd be careful what you say in one of the most haunted bars in the city.'

Zoe raised an eyebrow and glanced around. 'There are ghosts here?' She felt a little chill on the back of her neck.

'At least two. Maybe more.' He pushed his glasses up his nose, then picked up his Coke to take a sip.

She studied him—he had a spray of freckles across his nose and looked more like an absent-minded professor than a ghost hunter. 'And you know this for a fact?'

'I do. I'm part of a local ghost-hunting group. We only formed recently but we're already getting a lot of work from people who feel other-worldly presences in their homes and want answers. We used this building as one of our first case studies, to test our equipment and stuff. There's been reports of ghost sightings and stories flying around for years about the spirits here, so we investigated to try and determine which ones had any truth to them.'

'And?' Zoe found herself hanging on his every word.

'And we discovered evidence of an adult male and a little girl. The little girl lingers near the fireplace over there and we have no idea who she is, despite lots of research of deaths that happened on this spot. And we think the man is the ghost of a French pirate who was killed in a brawl on the street just outside.'

'A pirate?' Zoe couldn't help smiling at that. This place felt like another world. 'And when you say equipment ... what exactly do you mean?'

'We use infrared digital cameras, EMF meters—' When she gave him a blank look, he elaborated. 'Sorry, electromagnetic-field detectors that highlight radiation. But we also use normal digital recorders to capture electronic voice phenomena and a number of other simple techniques.'

'Wow.' Zoe blinked. 'So, you really do believe in ghosts?'

He nodded, his dark hair flopping over one eye. He pushed it back behind his ear. 'I believe the world isn't black and white and that sometimes souls linger after passing on, yes. I've believed since I was a kid, but now I've got the evidence to prove it.'

Although cynical, she was fascinated by the clear passion in his voice as he spoke about his profession. She realised she didn't even know his name. 'I'm Zoe, by the way,' she said, thrusting out her hand.

He looked at it a moment before sliding his hand into hers and holding for a second longer than necessary. 'Pleased to meet you, Zoe. I'm Jack.'

'*Jack?*' It was such a simple, straightforward name but this guy seemed anything but simple and straightforward.

'What's wrong with Jack?'

'Nothing. It's just ... you don't look or act like a Jack.'

Jack's lips twisted into a grin. 'Is that right? And what name do you think *would* suit me?'

Zoe shrugged. 'I don't know—Arden? Or Cole? Or Huxley? Something more ... unusual?'

'Well, you, Zoe, can call me whatever you like.' He chuckled and took another gulp of his Coke. 'Enough about me anyway. Tell me about you? That accent's Aussie right?'

'Yep. But trust me, I'm boring in comparison to you.'

'How about you let me be the judge of that.' He pushed his too-long hair back off his face again. He actually wasn't that bad-looking beneath those glasses. 'Let's start with what you're doing in town? Business or pleasure?'

'Neither.' Zoe sighed. Was she ready to share the truth with a stranger? After a pregnant pause, she decided no. 'I'm between jobs so visiting my mother who's working here.'

'I see. And what is it you usually do for a living?'

'I'm ... well, until recently I was assistant to an art curator. I worked in a gallery doing her social media and stuff.'

'Are you an artist yourself?'

She blushed. 'I paint. A little.'

'A creative,' he said, his tone impressed as his phone beeped from somewhere in his pocket. He took it out and glanced at the screen. 'Dammit. Sorry. It's a reminder alarm. I've got a meeting with a possible client.'

'No worries,' Zoe said, although she couldn't help being disappointed. It had been nice not being alone with her thoughts, and simply talking to Jack had made her feel lighter than she had since she'd arrived home to find Beau packing. 'Thanks for keeping me company and for taking my mind off my woes for a while.'

'Trust me. The pleasure was all mine.' He touched his head as if he were tipping an imaginary hat. 'Look, I know you're a big sceptic and everything, but if you wanted to go on a ghost tour, I'm doing one tonight here at eight o'clock. You're welcome to come along. On the house. Maybe we could even grab dinner afterwards? That's if you're not too busy with your mom?'

Oh my God, was the geeky ghost hunter asking her on a date? He really must be desperate if he found her appealing in her current state.

It was on the tip of her tongue to turn him down, tell him she was sorry if she'd given him the wrong impression but she wasn't in the market for a romance, a holiday fling or anything of the sort. And even if she was, he was so not her type. Jack couldn't be more opposite to Beau if he tried ... but right now that held particular attraction. Maybe he was exactly what she needed to help her forget?

'Why, Jack,' she said, smiling coyly as she cocked her head to one side. 'That sounds utterly delightful.'

14

Felicity

Seven thirty Tuesday night, Flick was trying not to lose patience with the elderly couple who'd been in the shop for over an hour. The woman was interested in the modern exhibits, pointing to various displays and asking about inspiration. She was particularly intrigued by the displays of a local artist who combined the body parts of different species to create whole new animals. Flick told her as much as she knew about the artist, thankful she'd had time to study Harvey's notes before Zoe arrived.

'These things are pretty expensive, aren't they?' said the man, rapping his knuckles on the head of a mountain lion adorned with beads and a mask for Mardi Gras.

Flick winced. 'Please don't touch the exhibits.'

'Why not?' he asked, barely removing his hand. 'They're already dead, aren't they? Not like I can hurt them.'

Flick spoke through a tight smile. 'Physical handling of the animals can cause damage and most of these exhibits are for sale.'

'If you break it, you pay for it, darling.' The woman laughed nervously. 'And how long have you been working here, dear?'

Flick thought a moment, counting back the days. 'Actually, only just over a week. I'm taking care of the place while the owner looks after his sister in Florida.'

Her arrival was a distant memory—if not for the minimal progress she'd made on the muskrat, she wouldn't believe she'd only been here nine days. She might not have seen much of the Quarter since Zoe arrived, but these last few days felt like a lifetime and had been some of the most distressing of her forty-nine years.

'It's a bit like being a doctor of the dead, isn't it?' The man chuckled, finally stepping away from the mountain lion. While his wife showed genuine interest, he clearly thought taxidermy a bit of a joke and anyone who practised it a little off their rocker.

Flick didn't bother replying. There was nothing he could say she hadn't heard a million times before.

'How long will it take you to finish that rat?' asked the woman, her necklace swishing from side to side as she leaned annoyingly close over the work bench. 'And what will it look like when you're done? Are you planning on adding an element of fantasy too?'

Usually Flick would be in her element talking about the ins and outs of her craft, but tonight she just wanted them to leave so she could shut up shop and go check on Zoe.

'I'm sorry, but I have a prior dinner engagement, so I'm going to have to close up,' she said, starting to pack away her tools. 'It was lovely talking to you though.'

She practically had to push the couple out the door—the woman still asking questions and the man still making unfunny jokes—and she let out a long sigh of relief when she finally locked it behind them.

Earlier that day Zoe had emerged for the first time since she'd arrived Thursday night and had returned a couple of hours later in a much better mood, the fresh air and bit of sun clearly having done her the world of good. Flick hoped that meant Zoe had turned a corner in her grief and that maybe she'd finally be able to drag her out to a restaurant for dinner.

But the sight she found when she entered the apartment was better than she'd dared to hope for. Zoe had showered and blow-dried her hair, and she was dressed in a short black skirt and a sparkly sequin top. Devoid of colour since her arrival, she now looked much more her usual self. Maybe she'd had the same idea about dinner.

'Oh, hi, Mum,' Zoe said, looking up from the couch as she zipped up hot pink ankle boots. 'You all closed up now?'

'Yes, and you look fabulous, honey. I was just coming up here to tell you to get your glad rags on because we're going out to dinner, but it looks like you beat me to it.'

'Oh, sorry, Mum. I can't. I've got a date.'

'You what?' Flick couldn't have been more surprised if Zoe had told her she'd joined the Church of Scientology.

'Well, not a date exactly,' she said with a bit of a giggle. 'But I met this ghost-hunter guy when I was out today, and he asked me to join his tour tonight. Can't say no to a free ticket.'

'*Oh.*' Flick couldn't help raising her eyebrows. 'Well, maybe I could come along. A ghost tour sounds fun.'

'It might be fully booked already.'

'Or it might not be,' Flick replied, her gut telling her she couldn't let Zoe go out alone with some strange guy at night, especially not in this neighbourhood. 'Give me five minutes to change my top and freshen up.'

Zoe sighed and glanced at her smartwatch. 'Hurry up.'

Five minutes later, they made their way downstairs and out onto the busy street. Feeling like she'd been cooped up for days, Flick welcomed the fresh evening air as Zoe led them a few blocks away to a dingy looking pub. A woman out on the street was holding a large placard and shouting about last-minute ghost tour tickets.

'I guess I'm in luck,' Flick said, noticing Zoe scowl as she approached the woman to buy one.

Once she had her ticket, they headed inside to grab a drink. Pop music blasting from a surround-sound stereo, the venue was crowded with people and had an unwelcome aroma of cheap booze and sweat, but Zoe brightened again as she waved in recognition and then made her way across to a guy standing near the bar.

Flick hurried after her, blinking in surprise as Zoe leaned in and kissed the man on the cheek.

'Wow—you look stunning.' Flick lip-read the guy's words, watching him look her daughter slowly up and down as she came up beside them.

She cleared her throat, but her aim to make herself known was futile against the loud music. 'Zoe, are you going to introduce me?' she shouted.

'This is my mum,' Zoe shouted back, not even hiding the roll of her eyes. 'She insisted on coming with me. She's worried you might be a serial killer.'

'I did *not* say that,' Flick exclaimed.

'You didn't have to—I *know* you.'

The man gave her a charming smile as he offered his hand. 'Hi, Zoe's mum!' he yelled. 'It's a pleasure to meet you. I'm Jack and I promise I'm not a serial killer.'

'Good to know,' Flick replied, although she doubted serial killers went around introducing themselves as such. Still, he didn't look like a criminal—he had friendly eyes. But it wasn't Jack she was worried about, it was Zoe, and the fact she clearly still wasn't in her right frame of mind.

'Anyway, can I get you guys a drink before we start the tour?' Jack shouted.

Zoe nodded. 'Yes, please.'

'Not for me.' Flick wanted to keep her wits about her.

Jack turned back to the bar and after a few moments produced one of the largest cocktails in a plastic tumbler that she'd ever seen. It looked to be the equivalent of about five drinks.

'Thanks.' Zoe beamed and took a sip.

Flick wondered if this guy was trying to get her daughter liquored up, but when she glanced around, everyone in the bar had one just the same. For a moment there, she'd forgotten where they were.

'Right, let's get this show on the road,' Jack said, gesturing for Flick and Zoe to follow him.

Too loud inside the pub, Jack and the woman who'd been selling tickets gathered the group on the sidewalk just outside and introduced themselves.

'I'm Jack and this is Buffy,' he said, loud enough for everyone to hear.

Buffy? Seriously? But Flick seemed to be the only one who found this amusing.

'Before we start,' Jack continued, 'we're going to break up into two groups—those with a yellow ticket will go with Buffy and those with blue tickets, you're stuck with me.'

Flick glanced down at her ticket, relieved to see it was blue.

Once they were sorted into their groups, Jack led them a little way down the road to a quieter corner, where he directed them all to stand back as close to the building as possible, leaving room for people to pass. He stepped back onto the road and gave them the safety spiel. 'Any questions before we start?'

'Will we be able to get another drink?' asked a tall bulky guy with a South African accent.

'Yes.' Although Jack smiled, Flick thought she detected a hint of annoyance in his voice. 'We'll take a refreshments and restroom break halfway.'

When there weren't any further questions, they set off, Zoe walking right up the front next to Jack as he led them to their first stop. As Jack and Zoe spoke in hushed voices, Flick stayed a step behind, feeling very much like an unwanted chaperone. The rest of the group were with friends and no one paid any attention to the lone middle-aged woman in their midst. After a few minutes, they turned into a dim alley on one side of the impressive Saint Louis Cathedral and Jack gathered the group on the cobbled path beneath a flickering oil lamp.

'Welcome to Pirates Alley,' he said in the dramatic tones of someone in a pantomime. 'While this lane may look quiet, I promise you there's a lot more happening here than meets the eye. Officially called Rue Orleans, Pirates Alley was never meant to be a main street, but rather a throughway between Chartres and Royal Streets.'

Jack pointed out the notable buildings surrounding them and then got on with the spooky stories everyone wanted to hear.

While Flick found everything he told them about the ghosts of Faulkner House Books, the legend of Jean Lafitte, a friendly priest and a number of disgruntled prisoners fascinating, it was Zoe's interactions with Jack as they continued on their tour that really kept her attention, or rather bothered her.

It was clear that Jack found Zoe attractive, and she was hanging on his every word and basking in his attention, flirting right back, flicking her hair and fluttering her eyelashes, laughing if he made even the smallest joke. What the hell was she playing at? If Flick was one of the other paying guests she'd be annoyed at the way he gave Zoe all his focus, but everyone was in far too good spirits—no doubt because they were filled with spirits—to care.

When they paused for intermission, Zoe once again commanded his attention.

'So, Jack, were you born around here?' Flick asked, trying to distract them from each other.

'No, I moved here a few years ago,' he replied, not breaking eye contact with Zoe. 'And it was exactly like John Goodman said when he moved here—it felt like an incomplete part of my chromosomes got repaired or something. Coming to New Orleans felt like coming home.'

'Who's John Goodman?'

'An actor,' Flick told Zoe. 'Most of his big movies were before your time.'

'Right,' Zoe said, then smiled back at Jack. 'So where are you from?'

'I grew up in Pennsylvania.'

Zoe frowned. 'Pennsylvania? Aren't there lots of Amish people there?'

'Yeah. My family are Amish.'

'Wow.'

Flick watched Zoe's eyes widen—he clearly intrigued her even more now. Before either of them could ask any further questions, he glanced at his watch and announced it was time to move on. He gathered the group together and whisked them back out onto the street where they headed to the second last stop on the tour—the Ursuline Convent on Chartres Street.

'This building behind us is most famous for its association with the Filles a la Cassette,' Jack said, adopting a not too terrible French accent—although not quite as good as the one Theo had put on the other night. 'Women with suitcases. Better known now as the Casket Girls, there are many legends surrounding these women. So, who exactly were they? And what have they got to do with the Ursuline Convent?'

He went on to explain they were young women handpicked by the Bishop of Quebec on the order of the French king, sent here to marry the men who'd come to establish the ports of New Orleans. They weren't the first shipload of brides sent to Louisiana. Originally the bishops and mayors sent women from their jails and brothels, but when they were deemed undesirable by the men, an alternative plan was hatched. This time they sought virtuous young women from orphanages and convents, expecting them to be good candidates for marriage to the French colonists.

'The Casket Girls arrived in 1798 and many were sent to live with the Ursuline nuns until they were married off. The journey was a long and arduous one and legend says that the women looked pale and sickly when they finally arrived. So pale that our tropical heat reddened and blistered their skin. The fate of many of these girls was not good—they were disrespected by the men of the Vieux Carre, abused by their husbands, and some may even have been forced into prostitution. Eventually, the king decided enough was enough and he demanded the remaining unwed girls be returned to France.'

'Excuse me? Why are they called the Casket Girls?' called a woman.

'I was just getting to that,' Jack said with a patient smile. 'The suitcases the women brought with them were called "cassettes" and this word eventually morphed into "casquette" and that became "casket". Although apparently small, some say these cassettes looked a bit like coffins. More likely they were nothing but small chests, about the size of an overnight bag, but let's not let the truth get in the way of a good story, hey?'

The group chuckled and then Jack finished by explaining that the nuns kept the caskets on the third floor of the convent and one night all their contents vanished. 'Due to this mystery, the fact the brides were pale after getting off the ship and the supposed shape of their suitcases, some people believe that the Casket Girls were not only some of the founding "mothers" of New Orleans, but also the ones who brought the vampires here. But this is a ghost tour, so if you want to hear more about vampires, you should take our Voodoo and Vampire tour tomorrow night.'

As Flick listened to Jack's remaining ghost stories, she almost forgot her concerns about Zoe and her obvious interest in their tour guide, but the moment the tour ended, they came right back to the forefront.

'Where are we going for dinner?' she asked them brightly.

They exchanged a look—it was clear Zoe didn't want Flick to accompany them and Jack didn't appear enthused either, but too bad. Wasn't it a mother's duty to stop her children making stupid mistakes?

'You like pasta?' Jack asked, clearly too polite to ask her to bugger off.

Flick nodded. 'It's my favourite.'

'Awesome. I know just the place. Come on, ladies.'

Jack offered an arm to each of them as he led them to a restaurant on Bienville Street. Although it was busy, they were greeted almost immediately and led upstairs to a table on the balcony, tantalising smells wafting at them as they passed the kitchen.

'I'm Karan, and I'll be your server for the evening,' said a woman. 'Can I get y'all some drinks to start?'

Jack ordered a beer, Zoe another cocktail, and Flick decided one glass of wine wouldn't hurt, then Karan left them to read the menu.

'I'm just popping to the ladies room,' Flick said after making her selection. 'Can you guys order me the shrimp linguine, please?'

'Sure, Mum,' Zoe said absentmindedly before turning back to Jack.

Flick sighed as she made her way to the bathroom—they clearly weren't going to miss her.

After washing her hands, she dug out her phone and glanced at the screen, considering a quick call to Emma or Neve. What would they make of Zoe's sudden change in behaviour? She'd filled them in on what had happened with Beau and they'd been checking in regularly to see how Zoe was going, but suddenly her support network felt so far away. Despite her daughter being here, Flick felt more alone and distant than ever.

Her phone beeped with a text and her stomach dropped as she read the message from Zoe.

Sorry to do a runner, Mum, but you just can't take a hint. We ordered for you though. Enjoy your meal and don't wait up. I grabbed the spare key from Harvey's cupboard.

What? Her heart jolting, Flick rushed back to the table, only to find it empty except for their barely touched drinks. She couldn't believe Zoe had actually abandoned her. So much for Jack not being a 'date'; she'd thought ahead enough to take a key. Flick tried to call her but of course it went to voicemail.

'Hey,' came the tentative voice of Karan as she arrived with a steaming plate of pasta. Talk about fast food. 'Your friends said to apologise but they had to leave.'

'I'll bet they did.' She could tell Karan didn't buy the story any more than she did. 'Is it possible to get that to go?'

Flick didn't normally mind eating alone, but she'd lost her appetite.

'Sure.' Karan smiled sympathetically and went away to box up the dinner.

Flick took a large gulp of wine while she waited, wanting to be angry but unable to quell her worry about Zoe and the fear that Jack might take advantage of her in her current state.

Karan returned with a plastic bag and the bill, which she placed down on the table, topping off Flick's disappointing night. Of course, they'd left her to pick up the tab. Trying to tell herself to cut Zoe some slack—she was clearly not acting rationally—Flick took her doggy bag and headed home, keeping both eyes wide open for a sighting of her daughter or Jack as she walked.

None eventuated.

Defeated, she was almost at the shop, when the flickering neon sign out the front of the Blue Cat caught her eye and she realised she'd been so busy taking care of Zoe that she hadn't yet thanked Theo for the care package.

Despite having only heard him play once that very first night, Flick could tell it was him sitting at the piano the moment she stepped inside. His sound was unlike anything she'd heard before. It had the soulful, melodic notes of jazz but there was an element of something else there too. She hadn't heard any of the songs before and wondered if he wrote his own, but his deep voice would make any lyrics sound good.

Even though he wasn't available to talk, she couldn't resist lingering a few moments. She waved to Lauri-Ann who was serving customers at the bar as she went closer to the stage and found a spot off to the side where she could watch as well as listen. Theo played piano with his whole body, almost as if nobody was watching, yet at the same time he was attuned to his audience, engaging them frequently with eye contact, smiles and even the occasional question.

He was such a good entertainer that it seemed almost a waste for him to be performing here to a bunch of semi-drunk tourists. She filmed a quick video and sent it to the WhatsApp group:

Felicity: Hanging out in the jazz bar next door.

Emma: Wow—he's good.

Neve: And not bad looking either.

Toby: Glad you're having a good time, Mum. And Aunty Neve, can you keep those kinds of comments off this chat? There are some things sons don't need to think about.

Flick smiled, a wave of love for Toby coming over her. She hadn't communicated with him much since Zoe had arrived as all her time and energy had been consumed by her daughter and the shop.

Felicity: It's all right, Tobes. I'm here for the music only.

Surprise, surprise, there was no response from Zoe.

After a while Theo looked up from the keys and glanced in her direction. Their eyes met and he flashed her a smile that went a little way towards easing some of the anxiety currently plaguing her.

When he finished his number, he stood and announced he was taking a short break. 'Anyone else who has a song in them, feel free to take the stage.'

To Flick's surprise, a young man shot out of his seat and, to cheers from the rest of the patrons, took up the offer.

'Good evening, Felicity,' Theo said, arriving beside her. 'How are you?'

'That is not a question you want to know the answer to.'

He grimaced. 'Sounds like you need a drink. What can I get you?'

'I'll have a Bloody Mary, thanks,' she said, suddenly in no rush to get home. Biding her time a while here would be better than eating alone while she waited for Zoe to return.

'Coming right up.'

She followed him to the bar and commandeered a stool just in front of where Tessa was lounging on it. While Theo whipped up her drink, Flick rubbed the cat's neck, the sound of her loud purr relaxing.

'How's Zoe doing?' Theo asked, leaning a little closer to be heard over the music as he handed her a glass.

'Not great. She hasn't been eating, barely drinking. She's become an empty shell of a person. She's spending all day watching TV and every time I've tried to talk to her about how she's feeling, she shuts me down. Until tonight when it's like she's suddenly a totally different person.'

'What happened tonight?'

She told him about Zoe finally leaving the house, meeting Jack and then doing a runner with him.

'Well, that sounds like progress. At least she's left the couch.'

'Hmm ...' Flick wasn't convinced. 'I'm not even sure she's told him she's married.'

'Do you think there's any chance of her and her husband getting back together?'

She rubbed her lips together, then sighed. 'No. He cheated on her and then *he* left her. I don't see a chance for reconciliation.'

A lump formed in her throat at the thought. The world just didn't seem right anymore—she and Sofia, now Zoe and Beau ... none of it made any sense. Before she could stop it, a tear snaked down her cheek.

'Hey, she'll be all right.' Theo grabbed a paper napkin off the bar and handed it to her. 'Everything you've said sounds like normal signs of heartbreak to me.'

'Thanks.' Flick took the offering, wiped her cheek and sniffed, not wanting to fall apart in front of him. 'I just ... It was hard enough watching my usually bubbly girl in a near-comatose state on the couch, but I'm not sure today's about-turn is any better. I'm worried she's going off the rails.'

He raised an eyebrow. 'A night out with someone who sounds like quite a nice young man is hardly going off the rails.'

'Maybe. But I'm not sure this pretending she's fine and going on dates is any better. It's too soon. She needs time to recover from her marriage break-up before she even thinks about the possibility of getting entangled with anyone else.'

'As you say,' Theo said, 'she needs time. Maybe it is too soon to be seeing other people, but when push comes to shove, she's an adult. Sometimes we gotta let our kids make their own mistakes.'

Flick cradled her glass in her hand, unsure whether she completely agreed. 'I know, and I'm trying to be patient, but I just want to make everything better.'

'It wouldn't be right if you didn't. You love her, but it's still raw. She isn't some broken washing machine you can just fix. The best thing you can probably do for Zoe is to not even try. Just be there for her when she wants you to be. She'll recover from this, but everyone deals with trauma in their own way. You can't rush her.'

Flick thought back to the time when she and Sofia had just separated and Emma and Neve were trying to chivvy her up, tell her how to feel and how to act. How irritating she'd found their well-meaning attempts. She *still* found their meddling in that regard a little annoying. Maybe Theo had a point and she needed to let Zoe handle this her way. She only prayed she'd stay safe.

'How'd you get so wise?' she asked.

He smiled down at her. 'I haven't been called that in a long time, but I do have my fair share of experience in disappointment.'

'Oh, me too.' Flick sighed and took another sip of her drink. 'Anyway, thanks again—for the care package, the advice, and just for listening to me whinge about my parenting woes.'

'Anytime.'

'I should let you get back to your music.'

He glanced over to see the young guy who'd taken over from him still playing and singing, clearly having the time of his life. 'What are you doing tomorrow?'

Flick blinked. 'Tomorrow?'

Theo nodded. 'Isn't the shop closed on Wednesdays? I was wondering if you and Zoe would like to come on a day trip. We could go to a couple of plantations or visit a friend of mine who lives in the Bayou for some alligator-watching.'

'Both options sound great,' Flick said. She loved what she'd seen of the French Quarter so far, but of course she wanted to go further afield and learn more about the local history and culture. Having their own personal guide would be a bonus. 'But I'll have to check with Zoe, see if she's up for it.'

'Of course. No pressure. I'll drop by about ten o'clock. If you can come, great; if not, I'll take a raincheck.'

'Great. Thank you. I'll see you then.'

Theo headed back to the piano and Flick finished her drink and then went home, hoping that while she'd been next door Zoe had seen sense and returned. *Alone.*

But the apartment was dark and empty.

15

Zoe

'Wasn't that a bit cruel?' Jack said, glancing back at the restaurant as he and Zoe hurried down the street. She didn't know where they were going—just away from her mother who was seriously trying to cramp her style. 'I already get the impression your mom didn't like me, now—'

'Who cares what she thinks of you? Isn't it what *I* think that matters?'

'I suppose so.' He shouted to be heard over the noise of buskers, drunks and excitable tourists. 'And what do *you* think of me, Zoe?'

She slowed her steps then leaned into him as they caught their breath. 'I think all your ghost knowledge is super sexy. And I think you're actually rather good-looking ... in a nerdy kind of way.'

'That might just be the best compliment anyone has ever paid me,' he replied, sliding his hand up into her hair and yanking her mouth to his.

And *boy*, he did not kiss like a nerd.

As his tongue pushed into her mouth, Zoe steadied her hands on his shoulders, which were harder and bulkier than she'd imagined. Heat and desire crashed over her and she trembled at the surprising intensity of it. Although on some level she'd planned this, she hadn't expected kissing anyone but Beau to actually feel this good.

Beau! For a second guilt shot through her, but then she remembered that Beau had done a lot more than kiss somebody else, and so she slid her hands up Jack's neck into his hair and kissed him like she'd never kissed anyone before. Kissing a near stranger felt thrilling, illicit, unpredictable, and a little bit dangerous. It made Zoe feel reckless and alive, exactly what she needed after days of feeling dead inside.

'You hungry?' Jack asked when they finally came up for air. He had hot pink lipstick smudged all over his mouth and his hair looked even more mussed up than usual. Very edible indeed.

Reaching out, she pushed a few stray locks off his forehead and nodded.

'Have you had a po-boy yet?'

Oh, the man meant food, right. Well, she guessed they needed sustenance for what she had in mind. 'All I've eaten since I've been here is tinned stew and soup.'

He made a face and grabbed her hand again. 'Come on then, I'm going to introduce you to some proper Louisiana cuisine.'

As they walked up Decatur Street hand in hand, Zoe said, 'What exactly is a po-boy?'

'It's a kinda sandwich with salad, your choice of meat—but it's also so much more than any sandwich you've ever had before. You've really gotta taste it to understand.'

They walked the short distance to Johnny's Po-Boys, which Jack declared did the best in town. It didn't look much inside—yellowed walls with a load of old framed photographs and run-of-the-mill tables and chairs with red-checked cloths—but the queue of people waiting and the smells coming from the kitchen indicated others shared Jack's view.

As they neared the front, Zoe glanced up at the menu, which consisted almost entirely of nothing she'd ever considered belonged in a sandwich—alligator sausage, catfish, blackened chicken, crawfish, shrimp, oysters.

'Would you think me incredibly boring if I went for something like chicken and salad?' she asked Jack.

'Yes.' He gave her a stern look. 'You didn't come all this way to have plain chicken. Live a little.'

'Okay.' She shrugged, high on the night and the buzz of Jack's lips on hers. He felt like a light that had illuminated the darkest point in her life and right now she would probably swim with alligators if he told her to. 'I'll go with the alligator.'

'Good choice.' Jack nodded then turned to the counter to place their order. 'One alligator po-boy, one Johnny's special and a bottle of water.'

'Are you serious?' Zoe laughed as she realised he'd ordered a sandwich with beef, grilled ham and cheese. She punched him playfully in the arm. 'If I don't like the alligator, we're swapping.'

'Deal.' He took her hand, leading her off to one side of the takeaway joint while they waited for their order. Somehow their lips found their way to each other again and they were locked in another titillating kiss when their dinner was called.

'It's good to see you smiling,' Jack said, as they walked back outside with the po-boys. 'Are you feeling better than you were earlier?'

It felt like he was probing with this question, but she didn't want to talk about Beau. 'Better is an understatement,' she said instead. 'I think your lips have some kind of magical powers.'

He chuckled. 'Never underestimate a nerd.'

'Oh, don't you worry—it's not a mistake I plan on making again.'

'Good. Now, shall we take these down to the river?'

Zoe stopped walking a moment. 'When you say river … do you mean the actual Mississippi?'

'Yeah …' He looked a little bemused. 'At least last time I checked.'

'Haha. But yes, let's do that. I can't believe I'm going to see the Mississippi. When you were a kid did you used to try and trick people by saying "The Mississippi is a long word, how do you spell it"?'

Jack frowned. 'Don't think so. Maybe the joke didn't get to Pennsylvania.'

That reminded Zoe that his life growing up Amish was probably vastly different to hers and she was desperate to hear all about it.

'I can't believe you're Amish,' she said as they walked back towards Jackson Square. 'I only just watched a documentary about growing up Amish.'

'*Was* Amish,' he corrected.

'Was. Sorry. How many brothers and sisters do you have?'

'Four brothers and two sisters. I'm the second oldest.'

Thanks to the doco, she knew that families of this size weren't unusual among the Amish—contraception being one of many things they did not approve of. 'I used to want to have a big family.'

'Used to?' They passed a busker playing the ukulele and Jack tossed them a few coins. 'What made you change your mind?'

'Nothing,' she said quickly.

'And what about you? Do you have siblings?'

'I have one brother, Toby—he's in the air force. We used to fight like crazy when we were kids, but I kinda like him now. Are you close to your siblings?'

'I got along with some more than others growing up, but we don't see each other anymore.'

Of course. Zoe bit her lip. If he'd chosen to leave, he'd likely have been excommunicated by the Amish community but possibly also shunned by his family. This was all fascinating to her, but it was Jack's real life and she couldn't imagine how painful it must have been.

'I'm sorry, that must be hard.'

Jack shrugged. 'It is what it is. I made my decision and I don't regret it. I'm living the life I want to be living now. And hey, if I'd stayed in Penn, I'd never have met you and you'd never have discovered what a great kisser I am.'

'That would have been a travesty,' she said with a smile.

He pointed across the road to some steps. 'We'll cross over here.'

They navigated cars, people and even a couple of horse carriages. Although it was after 10 pm, the area surrounding Jackson Square bustled with people and the sound of the horses' hoofs clip-clopping on the road made Zoe smile.

She glanced to her left to see a building with green and white awnings all lit up. 'What's that place?'

He looked at her like she'd grown horns. 'How long have you been here?'

'About three days.'

'And you haven't been to the famous Café du Monde yet? What kind of tourist are you?'

She was not about to tell Jack that she was the kind that lay on the couch, crying her heart out into a spiked cup of coffee. 'I've been jet-lagged. What's so great about Café du ...?'

'Monde.' He shrugged. 'It's famous for its beignets—deep-fried dough basically, but delicious. There are other cafés that do good ones too, but you can't come to New Orleans without at least trying some. Let's head back this way and get dessert later.'

But no matter how good the beignets, Zoe had something else in mind for dessert. She was sure she'd heard somewhere that the best way to get over one guy was to get on top of another and, if Jack's kissing skills were anything to go by, he seemed as good a prospect as any.

They walked up the steps to the Washington Artillery Park, then down the other side and over a railway track to the riverfront, leaving the bustling French Quarter behind. Although it was well and truly dark now, there were a number of streetlamps lighting the path. Jack and Zoe made their way over to a wooden bench and sat down, the mighty Mississippi River in front of them.

The *actual* Mississippi. She remembered reading about it in *The Adventures of Huckleberry Finn* when she was in Year Eight.

'That's one massive river,' she said as she began to unwrap her sandwich.

'Not only wide, it's the third longest river in North America—it's so long that one droplet of water takes ninety days to get from one end to the other.'

'And what's that bridge over there?' she asked, pointing off to their right to a bridge that at this distance looked like it was lit with a string of fairy lights.

'The Crescent City Connection—it's actually two cantilever bridges and used to be called the Greater New Orleans Bridge. It's the farthest downstream bridge on the Mississippi River.'

Zoe smiled at his little speech. 'Aren't you a fount of general knowledge?'

'I have plenty more facts where they come from. But never mind the river or the bridges, what do you think of your po-boy?'

She took a bite and immediately gagged.

'That bad, huh?' Jack laughed and unscrewed the lid of the bottle of water.

She guzzled a few mouthfuls. 'I just … I don't know what I was expecting, but this is not it.'

He smirked. 'Here. Have mine. A deal's a deal.'

'Do you mind?'

'Not at all, I actually quite like alligator.'

'Oh my God.' She elbowed him. 'That's why you got this other one, isn't it? In case I didn't like the exotic.'

'It's an acquired taste.' He gave her a sheepish smile.

So, he was sweet as well as smart and sexy.

The roast beef was much better, and they watched the world go by as they ate. While it wasn't as busy down here, there were still plenty of people around, but the highlight was when a paddle-steamer called the *Natchez* cruised by, people singing and dancing on its balconies and its lights causing the water to shimmer.

'I can see why you like this place so much,' Zoe said.

'Not everyone gets New Orleans or the French Quarter, but those that do … well, it becomes a part of who you are. What brought your mom here?'

'She's a taxidermist and she's taking care of the shop on Bourbon Street while the owner is away.'

It perhaps wasn't a surprise that Jack, fascinated by dead people, also found Flick's profession intriguing, and for a while they spoke about taxidermy and what it was like growing up in a house full of dead animals. 'And what about your dad? Is he still around?'

'He's not dead, if that's what you mean. But he's also no longer a he.'

When Jack gave her a blank expression, Zoe went on to tell him the story of how her dad had announced that she'd never felt right in her body, that she'd always felt like a woman and she wanted to transition. It was much easier talking about Sofia's coming out and the demise of her parents' marriage than talking or even *thinking* about her own.

'That's why your parents split up?'

Zoe nodded. 'Mum considered staying married but, in the end, she just couldn't do it. They're still friends though.'

'That's pretty heavy stuff. How do you feel about your dad now?'

'I love her. She's still the same person underneath, but it's like she's also so much more than she ever was before. I'm really happy for her, and she's much more enthusiastic about fashion and shopping than Mum.'

'Do you still call her Dad?'

'I try not to.' It was a question many had asked. 'Calling her Dad seems disrespectful because of the masculine connotations, but sometimes I slip up. I guess it's hard to break the habit of a lifetime. We had a conversation when she first told us she was transitioning— she wanted to make it as easy for us as possible, but in the end my brother and I agreed that calling her Sofia felt the most reasonable. We've already got a mother, so calling her Mum would have felt weird.'

Jack nodded. 'That makes sense. She's lucky you were all so supportive.'

'I won't say it wasn't a shock, but in hindsight it actually makes so much sense. And it's not my life that's changed dramatically, so not supporting Sofia would be pretty selfish. We should all have the freedom to be who we truly are.'

'I agree. You want to go for a wander?' Jack suggested, now that they'd both finished their po-boys.

'Sure.' Zoe stood, enjoying the buzz of electricity as he took her hand. It was surreal being out in this alien city, across the other side of the world, with a man that wasn't Beau. If someone had told her a week ago this was how things would be she'd have thought they were on drugs, yet it didn't feel wrong.

'How long are you in town?' Jack asked as they wandered further along the river path.

'Not sure. Right now, I'm taking it one day at a time. As you say, I've been a terrible tourist up to now, so I need to make up for lost time. What would you say are the absolute must-sees?'

'Well, there's lots to explore in the French Quarter. If you're into jazz, you need to check out Frenchmen Street, and the markets down there are fun too. Of course, there's the old houses in the Garden District, and you gotta do a swamp tour and check out the cemeteries. You'd probably like the Museum of Art. Honestly, I've been here almost three years and I still haven't seen everything I want to.'

'You can tell me to mind my own business if you want, but what made you decide to turn your back on your old life?'

Jack took a moment. 'I felt stifled. I didn't like being told what I could and couldn't believe. I finished school at eighth grade and then had to work on the family farm, but I hated that. It didn't feel like me. I didn't want to stop school and I was curious about the outside world. So many things didn't sit right with me about our lifestyle— it wasn't the religion so much as the rigid rules that didn't make any sense. Why weren't we allowed to use electricity, have running water, drive cars? My family and our community did stuff simply because that's the way it had always been, but I felt no connection to that way of living.'

'Did you do Rumspringa?' Zoe asked. 'I've heard it's wild. Did you get drunk, do drugs, go to nightclubs and have sex with lots of girls?'

He laughed. 'You shouldn't believe everything you see on TV. That's the exception, rather than the rule. Not everyone goes crazy—it's more a chance to explore yourself, work out who you are and who you want to be. I'd already made my decision that I was leaving long before Rumspringa. What about you? Did you have a wild youth?' Jack slowed and turned to face her. 'Did you kiss lots of boys?'

Her breath caught in her throat as his mouth came close to hers. She licked her lips. 'Not nearly enough, but I've decided I want to make up for lost time. Wanna help?'

'How can I resist an offer like that?' he said, before dipping his head and kissing her again.

Her body melted against his and her heart raced. She'd thought his kisses back in the French Quarter pretty damn hot, but now she was in danger of combusting. The temperature inside her body at that moment would give a New Orleans summer a run for its money. Walking and talking with Jack had been more than enjoyable—he was an interesting guy—but *nothing* made her forget her troubles as much as when his mouth claimed hers.

Desperate to feel even more, she crept her hands under his shirt and palmed them against his bare chest. He groaned into her mouth, his grip tightening on the back of her head, and she felt something hard and delicious pressing against her stomach. She wanted to touch it. She wanted *him* to touch her. Who was she kidding? She wanted to do way more than touch. Her knees trembled as need rocked her to her core.

Would it be absolutely wrong to have him right here, right now?

That'd show Beau—he'd always wanted to have sex in a public place, but she'd been too shy, too self-conscious. Suddenly she didn't feel self-conscious at all, and this part of town was a lot quieter than the crowded streets of the French Quarter.

Emboldened, she moved her hand lower and slid it inside the waistband of his jeans. He sucked in a breath and she tore her lips from his long enough to whisper, 'Do you have a condom?'

His eyes widened. 'You want to have sex? Here?'

'What's wrong with here?' She felt her nerve wavering. She didn't want to discuss it, she just wanted to do it.

'I really like you, Zoe,' Jack said, staring intensely into her eyes, 'but I don't sleep with women on first dates. And even if I did, I wouldn't want our first time to be some quick fumble on a dirty sidewalk. You deserve better. What's the rush?'

'What's the *rush*?!' she yelled, yanking her hands out of his pants and stepping back. 'I'm not staying in New Orleans. It's not like this is going anywhere. I don't want a bloody relationship with you! I just want you to fuck me so hard and fast that I forget about my husband sleeping with someone else.'

'What?' He recoiled as if she'd hit him, glancing at her recently bare ring finger as he asked, 'You're married?'

'Well, technically, but only because you can't just download a divorce on the internet.' Zoe thought this pretty funny, but Jack didn't laugh.

'That's why you were so down today?'

She nodded, emotion burning the back of her throat and her eyes. 'And I said I didn't want to talk about it, remember?'

'How long were you married?'

'Almost four years, but we were together most of high school.'

'And how long ago did you break up?'

It was now Tuesday morning in Australia. 'Just over a week.'

'Shit, Zoe. I'm sorry. The end of a relationship is always hard, but a marriage—'

'Stop!' She held up her hands. 'Enough. I don't need your sympathy. I told you I didn't want to talk about it and I meant it.'

'Okay.' He nodded. 'I get it, but I won't be your rebound hookup. I'm not going to have sex that you'll probably regret when you wake up tomorrow morning. How about I walk you home instead?'

'Walk me home?' she scoffed. 'No thanks. I'm a big girl, I can walk myself.'

And with that, she turned and ran back along the river, angry tears spilling down her face. How could Jack kiss her like that and then let her walk away? Why did he have to be so damn principled? And what kind of man turned down an offer of no-strings-attached sex?

If only her husband had displayed half of Jack's ability to keep it in his pants she wouldn't even be in this predicament!

16

Felicity

Zoe wasn't asleep on the couch when Flick woke the following morning and for a moment she panicked. Had she even come in last night?

Anxiously, she made her way to Harvey's bedroom when a thought struck. What if Zoe was in there but she wasn't alone? Biting her lip, she dithered a moment and then knocked on the door, calling out tentatively. When there was no answer—not even a murmur—she barged right in. Checking Zoe's whereabouts and her safety was more important than the possible mutual mortification of catching her in a state of undress with the ghost tour guy.

At the sight of only one body in the bed, Flick exhaled. Even as an adult, Zoe looked so peaceful when she was asleep, but the warm fuzzy feelings of relief Flick felt on finding her there were short-lived.

She crossed the room and pulled back the doors, humming as blinding light streamed into the room. 'Rise and shine, sleeping beauty!'

'Mum, what the hell are you doing?'

'I'm welcoming the day—it looks like it's going to be a beautiful one. Perfect for a day trip with our neighbour.'

Zoe rubbed her eyes and then glared at Flick. 'What are you talking about?'

'Last night, while you were off doing who knows what, I stopped by the bar to thank Theo for the gift he gave us, and he offered to take us for a drive to see some plantations or visit the Bayou. He said he has a friend who runs swamp tours and he can get us cheap tickets.'

'What about the shop?'

'It's closed on Wednesdays. Why don't I make you a coffee and some breakfast, while you shower? Theo's collecting us in an hour.'

'Uh, no thanks. Why would I want to be the third wheel on your date?' Zoe groaned and rolled back over, pulling the covers over her head.

Flick had been quite prepared to forgive her daughter for last night, but her attitude got her back up all over again. 'It's not a date,' she said, 'but speaking of, how was *yours* last night? Or was it just a hook-up?'

She might be old, in Zoe's eyes at least, but she knew the lingo. And while she'd been standing here, she'd been scrutinising the room, looking for signs of sex or Jack. While she couldn't see any of either, she hadn't heard Zoe come in, so she could just have easily not heard him sneak off in the early hours of the morning.

'It was good,' came her mumbled reply, neither confirming nor denying the hook-up part, 'but it was late and I'm stuffed. Do you mind closing the door on your way out?'

Flick let out a half-laugh and crossed her arms over her chest. If Zoe thought she was just going to leave this discussion at that, she had another think coming. 'Aren't you at least going to apologise for leaving me stranded in the restaurant? That was a pretty ordinary move—you're not usually a nasty person.'

'And you're usually more perceptive, Mum. Jack and I wanted to be *alone*.'

When Flick didn't say anything but didn't make a move to go either, Zoe slowly lifted the covers off her head. 'I'm *sorry*, okay?'

It sounded like one of those apologies that weren't really an apology at all, but she decided not to push it. 'Did you sleep with him?'

'Oh my God, Mum! That's none of your business. What is this anyway? The Spanish bloody Inquisition?'

'I'm just worried about you, Zo-Zo. I don't want you to get hurt.'

She snorted. 'It's a bit too late for that.'

Flick made a move towards her and sat down on the bed, reaching out to stroke her hair as she'd always done when Zoe was little and upset. 'Darling, I get what Beau did has hurt you badly, but getting involved with someone else so soon, when you're still—'

Zoe swatted her hand away and sat up. 'You don't have any idea what you're talking about.' She scrambled on the bedside table for a packet of painkillers and popped two with a bottle of water that had been there for who knows how long. 'I'm not getting involved with him. It was just a bit of fun. It's not like I'm gonna marry the guy, okay?'

Flick wasn't sure whether this was okay or not. Then again, Jack seemed nice enough; if Zoe was going to have a rebound fling with anyone, she could probably do worse.

'Just because I deal with things differently to you, doesn't mean you're right and I'm wrong.'

'What's that supposed to mean?' Flick asked, taken aback.

'Ever since you broke up with Sofia, you've kinda checked out of life. Neve and Emma keep trying to get you to see other people, but even after all these years you're intent on staying in your own little bubble, feeling all depressed and sorry for yourself. Well, I don't want to do that. I don't want to waste my life pining for what was clearly never meant to be.'

'That's not what I'm doing.'

Zoe rolled her eyes. 'Could have fooled me.'

'What do you think coming here was all about? If moving across the other side of the world where I don't know anyone else wasn't getting out of my comfort zone—or my bubble, as you put it—then I don't know what would be.'

'Moving here was running away,' Zoe said as if she was talking to a two-year-old and rapidly losing patience. 'Here you can stay in your shell and you don't have to keep making excuses to your friends when they try to set you up with perfectly nice men.'

'I thought you didn't think any of those existed anymore?'

'You're right, I don't. But that doesn't mean we can't enjoy them. Men are massive jerks and incapable of being monogamous, so we may as well make the most of the one thing they're good at.'

Flick raised an eyebrow. 'Sex?'

'Got it in one, Mother. If you can't beat 'em, join 'em, I say.'

Flick hated hearing Zoe talk like that. 'Not everything is about sex, you know.'

'Then why are you making such a big deal about it?' Zoe threw her hands up in the air. 'Why are you so worried about me having it? And why are you so scared of it?'

'I'm ... I'm not scared of it.' Heat flared in Flick's cheeks—she couldn't believe the audacity of her daughter. 'Maybe if you weren't here, I'd be having plenty of it,' she snapped. 'Who knows what would have happened with Theo if you hadn't showed up on my doorstep out of the blue.'

Zoe's mouth gaped but she quickly recovered. '*Geez*, I'm so sorry I'm cramping your style, but don't let me hold you back any longer. Go enjoy your day out—without me hanging around like a bad smell, you won't have any excuse not to go for it.'

And with that, Zoe flung back the covers and stormed out of the room.

A few seconds later Flick heard the thump of the bathroom door and the pipes in the wall creaking as the shower started up. Shame, sadness and regret washed over her. The last thing she wanted was to make Zoe feel unwelcome. Fighting was so unusual for them. Even when Zoe was a teenager, they'd never had the screaming matches that some of Flick's friends had with their daughters, so this was a totally new experience. And one that didn't sit right in her heart.

Flick glanced out the window as Theo neared the arresting frontage of Oak Alley Plantation. It was easy to see where the place got its name. Gigantic oak trees grew on either side of a long drive, stretching over to form a picturesque canopy. Peeking through the trees, Flick glimpsed an impressive building with grand columns that had to be the plantation owner's house.

'It's like something from *Gone with the Wind*,' she said.

'Wait till you see inside. It's one of the more stately plantations, but it doesn't shy away from acknowledging the massive divide between the wealthy landowners and their slaves,' Theo said as he turned into a much more functional entrance that led them around the back to a parking area, filled with cars and tour buses.

Even today, when the temperatures were high, these destinations were clearly popular. Flick hoped that exploring the vast grounds and learning about the plantation's history would distract her from thinking about the argument she'd had with Zoe that morning and whether she had a point. *Had* she been wasting her life? *Was* she afraid of intimacy? Of sex?

'Felicity. Are you okay?'

At the sound of his voice, Flick shook herself from her recollection and looked up to see he was already out and holding her door open for her. 'What? Oh. Sorry, I was just …'

'Lost in a world of your own?' he said with a bemused smile. 'You've been a little preoccupied since we left the Quarter. Do I dare ask what you're thinking about?'

'Nothing really,' she said as she climbed out of the car. 'Just words I had with Zoe this morning.'

'Want to talk about it?'

Although Flick knew Theo was a good listener, no *way* was she going to tell him the crux of their conversation. 'Thanks, but it's nothing important—Zoe and I just don't necessarily see eye to eye on how to mend a broken heart.'

He nodded. 'Ah, I see. Kids, hey? You never stop worrying about them.'

'Ain't that the truth.' Flick hitched her bag on her shoulder. For the next few hours she was going to try and forget her Zoe woes and simply enjoy her day. 'Anyway, I don't want to think about children anymore. Come on.'

Absentmindedly, she offered her hand to Theo. The gesture clearly surprised them both; however, he hesitated only a moment before taking it.

For a second Flick froze. Holding hands might only be a small thing, but it was the most intimate connection she'd had with anyone in a long while. But then Theo squeezed gently and she relaxed.

Flick's first instinct when Zoe had refused to come had been to tell Theo she couldn't make it either, but now as they headed into the plantation, she was not only glad she'd come, but maybe also glad that Zoe hadn't.

They joined a group of people gathered in front of a gift shop waiting for the next tour and got talking to an elderly couple from Ohio who were so excited to be travelling after the gentleman had recovered from cancer. They were wearing matching Steamboat Natchez souvenir T-shirts. Couple goals.

'I thought I was going to lose Stanley,' said the woman, gazing into her husband's eyes. 'New Orleans has always been on our bucket list so the moment the doctors declared him in remission, we booked the trip. It also coincides with our fifty-fifth wedding anniversary.'

'Happy anniversary,' Flick and Theo said at the same time.

'Thank you,' replied the man. 'How long have you two been together?'

They exchanged a look and Flick realised that they were still holding hands and she didn't want to let go. It felt like the most natural thing in the world.

'We only recently met,' Theo said after a few long beats.

'Oh, how splendid.' The woman pressed a hand against her heart and beamed at her husband.

Just then a bubbly young woman wearing a uniform of khaki trousers and a blue shirt called for everyone's attention.

'Hi, y'all,' she shouted. 'I'm Nadine and I'll be your guide as we explore Oak Alley Plantation.'

She gestured for the crowd to follow her. In the distance Flick spotted the massive house they'd seen from the road.

Nadine stopped as they came upon two rows of white-washed wooden huts on either side of a wide gravel path. She gestured to the first one. 'This structure behind me is one of the six reconstructed slave quarters that we built in order to give our guests a small insight into what life was really like on Oak Alley. Each of the six huts have different displays, which tell the stories of some of the two hundred enslaved workers who lived ...' She paused a moment. 'And often died here. Sadly, we don't have the same kind of documentation—letters or personal journals—we have from the plantation owners; instead we have records of slave sales and other such documentation that show us just how dehumanised these workers were.'

'How many slaves were here at Oak Alley at any one time?' asked the gentleman Flick and Theo had met earlier.

'Well over one hundred—men, women and children. They were enslaved in the house and in the fields. As you can imagine life was gruelling for both, but the people in the fields often spent up to eighteen hours a day toiling in the hot sun. You might be surprised to know that often the particularly hard labour fell to the women. And you'll see from the displays in the huts the squalid housing and shocking conditions these people lived under. After the tour of the Big House, which you may only go through with a guide, I encourage you to look at the displays in the various huts at your own leisure. And also check out our blacksmith shop, sugarcane and Civil War displays.' As they moved on and approached the Big House, Flick could almost see the prestige and power oozing from it, but suddenly she saw it in a totally different light.

At the main entrance, Nadine spoke about the history of the building. Flick tried to focus as she pointed out the Antebellum architecture and explained that the twenty-eight Doric columns on the four sides of the square building were designed to correspond to the twenty-eight oak trees that formed the alley, but her mind was still back on those huts and also, Theo's hand in hers was damn distracting.

After a tour of the lower level—lots of beautiful polished floors, shiny chandeliers, antique furniture, gold-framed portraits lining the walls and a massive dining table set with fancy crockery—they had to break apart to go single-file up the slightly precarious staircase. She couldn't help mourning the loss of Theo's warmth.

'What do you think?' he asked, leaning close as they waited in the upstairs hall for the rest of the group to join them.

'Huh?' The feel of his breath against her ear distracted her and for a moment she didn't know what exactly he meant.

He smiled as if bemused. 'I know there's a lot to take in up here. Are you enjoying it?'

'I'm not sure enjoying it is exactly the right word. Some of it's a bit confronting, but this is a very beautiful house. It's hard not to be a bit affected by it.'

Well, it wasn't exactly a lie. How could you not be in awe of this home, the history that hung both on its walls and between them, and the contrast with what they'd seen outside? But she was having trouble focusing on anything but Theo. He was standing so close that whenever she breathed, all she could smell was the woody scent of his colongne. Her fingers twitched as she contemplated reaching out and grabbing his hand again. If holding hands had felt that good, she couldn't help wondering what it might be like to take things to an even more physical level.

Somehow, she managed to finish the tour of the second storey, taking in at least some of the facts Nadine imparted about the people who'd lived here.

When the official part of the tour came to an end, Nadine led them out onto the balcony. Although photos hadn't been allowed inside, they were encouraged here and everyone wanted to take a selfie with the impressive alley of three-hundred-year-old oak trees in the background. Flick could only imagine the joys and horrors that these natural beauties had witnessed in their lifetime.

When it was their turn, Theo leaned against the railing and wrapped his arm around her, pulling her close as he held his phone in his outstretched arm and snapped. Flick shivered. She hadn't been this close to a man in years and it felt far better than she remembered. Their clothes did nothing to protect her against the heat of his body, and once again she got a delicious whiff of him. The scent was intoxicating.

'There—what do you think?' Theo asked, bringing up the photo on the screen of his phone.

It took a moment for her to find her voice. 'I think it's perfect.'

When she sent this image to Neve and Emma later, they'd be impressed but it wouldn't be the scenery and majestic trees they'd want details about.

'Great,' he replied. 'If you give me your mobile number, I'll send it to you.'

Flick racked her brain for some witty response about only giving him her number if he planned on using it to ask her out. She needed to find some way to tell him that she'd changed her mind and wanted something to happen between them. But this was all so new. What if she'd misread the signs? She hadn't made a move or had anyone put any moves on her in well over twenty-five years. And, there'd been very few boyfriends before she got married, so she could hardly say she'd been experienced in the art of seduction back then either.

Dammit, she was thinking too much, and Neve always said that nothing good ever came from overthinking. Didn't actions speak louder than words?

Before she lost her nerve, Flick turned her head and brushed her lips against Theo's.

The kiss couldn't have lasted more than two seconds, but time stood still and the chatter of the rest of their group fell away as she felt the effect in little tremors all over her body.

Hallelujah. This confirmed it—she had definitely *not* checked out.

'That was ...' Theo began, his voice a low, sexy rumble. 'Unexpected.'

Flick's heart sank and she licked her lips nervously. 'That doesn't sound very ... good.'

'Are you joking? I've been wanting to do that for ages, but I've been trying hard to be on my very best behaviour, because I thought that's what you wanted.'

Flick's sigh of relief merged with a choked laugh. 'You've been nothing but a perfect gentleman, but ... maybe I don't want you to be a gentleman anymore?'

That seemed to be all the encouragement Theo needed. Shoving his phone back into his pocket, he yanked her closer and brought his mouth back to hers, kissing her in a way that would be very hard to misconstrue. His intentions were clearly as X-rated as she wanted them to be and she'd forgotten how good a simple kiss could be. Then again, there didn't feel anything simple about the way his mouth moved against hers.

'Ah, young love,' said the old woman from Ohio when they finally broke apart, but Flick and Theo barely acknowledged her.

'Shall we get out of here?' Theo asked, his voice thick.

Flick nodded, desperate to feel his lips on hers again.

'Don't forget to check out the other exhibits,' Nadine called after them as they hurried down the stairs. 'And I can strongly recommend lunch in our restaurant.'

But neither of them had any intention of doing anything of the sort. Food was the last thing on Flick's mind—she'd had gumbo, jambalaya and beignets, now it was time to sample one of the other delights New Orleans had to offer.

'You sure you don't want to get lunch?' Theo asked as they hurried past the restaurant emitting the mouth-watering smells of Creole—or was it Cajun?—cooking as they headed for the car. 'Or check out the displays.'

'We can get something later,' she said. The historic exhibitions here deserved her full, undivided attention and, thanks to Theo, that wasn't going to happen today.

17

Zoe

Zoe woke up feeling much better—physically at least—than she had when Flick had burst into her bedroom a few hours earlier and yanked open the curtains.

She couldn't believe her mum had actually gone off on a day trip with the guy next door without her. After a long shower, she'd been starting to feel halfway normal again and was thinking that maybe she could handle a bit of shopping and a long lunch somewhere at one of the local restaurants, but it was too late. Flick had already gone.

The one day she didn't have to open the shop, she'd chosen to spend with some stranger. Not that Zoe could really blame her— she'd pretty much told her to go. Still she couldn't help feeling annoyed and angry at the situation. After downing a cup of coffee and scoffing some toast, she'd returned to bed, hoping to sleep off a few more hours of her new, unbelievably shitty life.

It worked until just after one o'clock when she woke up to a still empty apartment, but she had to admit there were advantages to this. Without her mother breathing down her neck, she'd be able to lounge around on the couch watching TV without judgement. However, the moment she picked up the remote and turned it on, another Amish documentary flashed onto the screen. What were the chances? Talk about the universe conspiring against her.

As if she needed any reminder of last night's mortifying events. Part of her hoped propositioning Jack had been a bad dream, but when she touched her hand to her cheek, she felt the stubble burn she'd got from when they were kissing like a couple of savages. She shivered at the memory—pleasurable even though she didn't want it to be.

How could she possibly be attracted to anyone else so soon after her marriage had ended? What did that even say about her feelings for Beau? Was she just confused or had they never really been as strong as she'd believed?

Damn men.

Because of Beau she was here in a place she'd never planned to visit, with no job, not much money, and no idea what she was going to do with the rest of her life. Because of Beau she'd met Jack, and because of Jack, she was feeling even worse. And she *still* had no alcohol. After meeting him yesterday, she'd totally forgotten that her reason for going out was to restock Harvey's stash and had returned without it or the coffee she'd promised her mum.

Switching off the TV, she hurled the remote across the room, stormed over to the balcony and flung the doors wide open. The heat of the midday sun hit her the moment she stepped outside. It didn't seem right that the sun could shine so bloody brightly when her life was in such a shambles. And it wasn't just the stupid weather. Below on Bourbon Street, people were laughing and taking happy snaps, and an actual brass band played as they waltzed down the middle of the road. Tourists were following behind, singing, clapping and dancing along with the music.

Why did everyone look so damn happy? It made her want to march right down there and punch someone in the nose!

She couldn't understand the fuss about this place. Her mum raved about the charm of the buildings, and she supposed if you liked ghost stories or jazz music there might be something appealing, but couldn't everyone see the poverty? Late last night on her way back to the shop, she'd lost count of the number of homeless people she'd seen sleeping in doorways. Not to mention the stench. The aroma of spicy southern food had been overwhelmed by the smell of stale urine, fresh vomit and cheap booze.

Cheap booze. Her lips twitched a little; she could almost taste the relief as she went back inside. This was New *Bloody* Orleans. She didn't have to mope about inside wishing she had more alcohol, she could simply go and get some. Slipping on a pair of thongs—'flip flops' in this strange land—Zoe grabbed her purse and phone then headed downstairs. Her attempts to banish Beau from her mind by hooking up with someone else had backfired and her mother had deserted her, but Zoe had faith that this new plan—or rather her original plan—had merit.

Although the bar next door was open, jazz music had never been her thing and she didn't want to risk Flick and whatever-his-name coming back and interrupting her. She walked briskly along the street, passing a number of strip clubs with women in skimpy outfits hugging poles outside as they lured men inside. Nothing against the women—if they could make money off shallow pathetic men like her husband, go them—but also not the kind of joint she wanted to escape into. After last night, she didn't want to be anywhere near a man, never mind the type that frequented those places.

Turning off Bourbon Street, she kept walking until a chalkboard out the front of a trendy looking bar called to her:

Why should happy hour only be an hour?
Come in and enjoy our bottomless mimosas all day every day!

A bartender covered in tattoos and dripping with body piercings asked if she'd like any food with her drink. As she hadn't eaten anything since the po-boy last night with He-Of-All-The-Principles, she ordered a cheeseburger and fries from the woman, who wore a name badge that read 'Cherish'. Zoe had never seen anyone who looked less like a Cherish in her life.

'Why the long face?' she asked as she slapped Zoe's lunch down in front of her ten minutes later and topped up the drink she'd already half-guzzled. 'Boy trouble?'

'Got it in one.'

Cherish grinned. 'That's why I bat for the other team. So, what happened? Boyfriend bring you on holiday and then end up doing the dirty with someone else?'

'Close, but he was my husband.' Zoe popped a fry into her mouth.

'Ah, sugar, forget him. Plenty more fish in the sea.' She shrugged. 'Or on Tinder. Especially round here. You're too young to be married anyway.'

'Too young for my husband as well, apparently.'

'Let me know when you need another top-up,' Cherish said, before moving along to serve a family who'd just walked in.

The man and woman with their teenage son and daughter reminded Zoe of how her family had been when she was growing up. The woman even looked a little like Flick, with her long, straight dark hair parted down the middle and clearly dyed to cover up the greys. Of course, the guy—tall and buff, with a New York Yankees jersey and a matching cap—looked about as unlike her 'father' as one could get.

She turned back to her food, cursing as her eyes started welling up with tears again. Why did everything have to change? She longed for her life like it was back in high school. When Dad was still Dad, they all lived together at home, she and Beau were in the throes of new love—the cutest couple at school, the couple most likely to get married—and she and Toby drove their parents mad fighting about stupid shit.

She not only missed that life, she missed the friends she had back then. Friends she hardly saw now she was married, and everyone had jobs or itinerant lifestyles. Most of her schoolfriends had all but given up messaging her to catch up and it hadn't even really bothered her because she'd had Beau. He was her best friend and the person she liked hanging out with most in the world anyway. If she was honest, she'd felt superior to most of her friends, smug in the knowledge that she had the happy, loving relationship most of them craved, even if they wouldn't admit it.

Well, hadn't that backfired. Zoe didn't feel so smug anymore, she felt utterly alone and miserable. At least she still had her parents and Toby.

At this thought, she downed the rest of the mimosa, managed a 'Thanks' for Cherish when she refilled it almost immediately, then fumbled in her bag for her phone.

Just when she was about to give up, her brother answered. 'Zoe? What's wrong? Is it Mum?'

'Huh? No. She's fine. Why would anything be wrong?'

'It's three in the morning.'

She hadn't even thought about the time difference. 'Shit. I'm sorry.'

'It's okay.' He paused a moment. 'I'm really sorry to hear about you and Beau.'

One of their parents had obviously told him, which was fine, but she didn't want to talk about Beau now. 'I was just thinking about *you*,' she said, hoping Toby would get the message, 'and I wanted to hear your voice.'

'Are you drunk?'

She glanced at the mimosa. 'No.'

'Where's Mum?'

'She's out with some guy.'

'What? Who?'

Zoe sighed, starting to regret her decision to call him. 'He lives in the bar next door, he's a musician or something. They've gone sightseeing and I didn't want to go with them.'

'Is she dating him?'

'She reckons they're just friends. Anyway, how are you?'

'Fine. Tired.'

'Sorry.'

'It's okay. What were you thinking about me?'

She racked her mind for something, not wanting to admit how desperate she'd been feeling. 'Oh, not much, just reminiscing about growing up.'

He chuckled. 'So, you were thinking of all the ways you used to torture me?'

'I did not,' she objected, knowing she did exactly that. But what else were little brothers for?

'You're right. Making me get down on all fours and pretend I was a dog, bark and beg you to feed me biscuits, which you made me eat off the floor … that's perfectly acceptable behaviour.'

'Hah. I'd almost forgotten about that, but hey, it meant Mum and Dad finally bought us a dog, so worth it, really,' Zoe said, thinking of their very first labrador, Milly.

'Yes, because then you could cut my hair and try to blame a poor innocent puppy for it.'

Zoe grinned remembering the lopsided crew cut she gave him, which had taken months to grow out. 'I still can't believe you actually sat long enough to let me do that. See, we had some good times, didn't we?'

'For you, maybe.'

They both laughed, then Toby said, 'Look, Zo, as nice as it is to chat, I've got a busy day tomorrow. Are you sure you don't wanna talk about ... you know?'

'No. But thanks. You've given me exactly what I needed. Goodnight, little brother. Love you.'

'Uh ... love you too. It was good to hear from you. Call me whenever you need, okay?'

She hung up and took another sip of her most delicious mimosa as her eye caught a poster behind the bar. It said something about the person with the best dressed costume winning five thousand dollars.

'What's that all about?' she asked as Cherish returned to top up her glass yet again. Zoe was beginning to lose count.

'Ah, a few bars are having a Casket Girls pub crawl. Have you heard of them?'

'The Casket Girls?' said Zoe, once again thinking of Jack and trying not to scowl. 'They're the vampires who supposedly live on the third floor of the convent down the road, right?'

Cherish nodded. 'Once a year we have a bit of fun with the legend. People dress up as brides to honour those poor girls, and anyone in costume gets discounted drinks in participating bars. Each bar chooses a winner from the costumes they see on the night and then we get together and pick the overall best. That person is crowned Casket Bride for the year and wins the cash.'

'Wow.' So much about this idea appealed to Zoe—even cheaper drinks, the possibility of earning some much-needed money, and best of all, a chance to celebrate women triumphing despite the bastard men who disrespected and betrayed them. And, with her artistic talents, perhaps she could even have a chance of winning? 'Sounds fun.'

'Oh, it's a hoot,' Cherish said.

Zoe stared at the poster as she popped the last fry into her mouth. Today was Wednesday, the pub crawl was a week on Friday—that didn't give her much time to design and make a wedding dress, but she'd been worrying about cash and what she was going to do when she ran out of her meagre savings. She couldn't bludge off her mum forever, so this could be the answer to all her problems, or at least give her some time to sort herself out.

Leaving enough money to cover her bill and a tip for Cherish, she left the bar, headed back to the shop and scrambled around looking for some pencils and scrap paper. Then she began to sketch.

Not wanting to create a boring, romancey-type wedding dress, Zoe took inspiration from the skeleton bride painting that hung above the mantle. She wanted her dress to look a little bit gothic like the one in the painting but also modern. Hopefully there'd be some place nearby where she could buy cheapish material.

It felt unbelievably good to be scribbling again. Lost in her designs and surrounded by tossed-aside pieces of paper, she didn't even hear Flick open the door downstairs when she returned a few hours later.

'Hey, sweetheart.'

'Oh my God,' Zoe shrieked and slammed her hand against her chest as her mother appeared in the living room. 'When did you get back?'

'Just now,' Flick said, throwing her bag down on the table. 'Look, I wanted to say sorry for earlier. I didn't mean—'

'Mum, it's fine. *I'm* sorry. I didn't mean all those things I said, but you know how I am when I first wake up. Let's just agree to forget it.'

Flick hesitated a moment, then, 'Okay, but don't forget I'm here if you want to talk about ... about Beau.'

Zoe shook her head. 'No thanks.'

It wasn't like talking would change anything. It wouldn't change what he'd done and it wouldn't change the fact that everything she believed about love and even herself had been shattered.

'How was your day, anyway?' she added, returning her attention to her sketching.

'Amazing. Really, really, really good. Excellent.'

At her mother's weird-sounding voice, she looked up again and this time registered the massive grin on Flick's face. There was only one reason why a woman would be smiling so much it looked like her mouth might leap off her face at any moment and start dancing. It was the face her friends got whenever they were talking about a new crush.

Flick definitely had a thing for the guy next door.

Either that or she'd caught the New Orleans happy bug.

'Guess you didn't miss me after all?' she teased.

'Of course we missed you, darling,' Flick said, clearly full of BS. 'I think you'd have found the plantation eye-opening. We'll definitely have to go visit some ourselves.'

'*Plantation*? I thought you were seeing more than one.' They'd been gone so long they could probably have seen *all* of them and her mum's face was flushed as if she'd caught a bit of sun.

Flick blinked. 'That's what I meant—*plantations*. Anyway, enough about my day. How was yours? It's so good to see you drawing again. Is that a wedding dress?'

'Yes.' Zoe explained about the Casket Girls pub crawl and the possibility of winning five thousand dollars.

'Wow. That's a lot of money.'

'I know, and as you said, now I'm not working I need some way to earn money, and I think I'm in with a chance. Remember how good I was at sewing in high school? And I might not have designed clothes before, but I'm enjoying giving it a go.'

'And it looks like you're doing an excellent job of it. I think this is a wonderful idea,' Flick said, still beaming.

The mood her mum was in, Zoe got the impression she could say she'd decided to take up fortune-telling or drug-dealing and she'd be excited. 'Don't suppose Harvey has a sewing machine lying around?'

Flick thought a moment. 'Actually, I think I saw one in the workshop area downstairs. I'll just have a quick shower—it was hot out there—and then I'll go take a look for you. What are you going to do about material?'

'I googled places that sell fabric and second-hand clothes nearby. I thought if new fabric is too expensive I can buy some really cheap op shop type dresses and re-use the material.'

'Great idea.'

'I'm going to go shopping and see what I can find tomorrow. Do you reckon you could loan me some money for supplies? I'll pay you back.'

'Of course. In fact, how about I come with you? We can go in the morning before I open the shop.'

'That would be great. Thanks.'

After her shower, Flick made good on her promise to find the sewing machine. The ancient Singer looked like something out of a museum, but with a little TLC Zoe managed to bring it to life and tested it on an old tea towel while her mum hummed in the kitchen as she made dinner. It felt such a buzz to be doing something productive again and she couldn't wait to buy some material tomorrow.

'Shall we watch a movie?' Flick suggested when they'd almost finished their creamy pasta.

Considering all they had were the DVDs Theo had given them, Zoe couldn't think of anything worse. Besides, Flick's over-the-top chirpiness was starting to get on her nerves. It wasn't that she wanted her mum to be miserable forever like her, but there was happy and then there was taking the piss.

'Actually, I'm going out.' She stood, carried her bowl to the kitchen and started scraping her leftovers into the bin.

'With Jack?' Flick asked.

Zoe was glad she had her back turned—she'd never been good at lying, least of all to her mother. 'Yes,' she said. If Flick thought she was going out on her own, she'd insist on coming and that would defeat the purpose. She'd be monitoring how much Zoe drank, judging her, worrying and fussing.

'Okay then, honey. Have a good night. And be safe.'

'I will.' Zoe kissed Flick on the cheek and then went off to Harvey's bedroom to throw on some fancier clothes.

Half an hour later, she'd downed her first cocktail and was doing her damn best to lose herself on the dance floor of a nearby nightclub.

18

Felicity

'Are you sure you have to go?' Theo ran his hand over Flick's naked back as she attempted to put on her bra.

There wasn't one inch of her body he hadn't touched or tasted, more often both, since last Wednesday, and she'd loved exploring every little dip and curve of his as well. His body was much harder, more ripped than you'd expect of a middle-aged piano player—in fact, it was a pure treat, a thing of beauty, a work of art, and she liked looking at it and touching it almost as much as she liked the mind-blowing sensation of having him inside her.

'Yes, I do have to go,' she groaned. As much as she'd like to spend a few more hours curled up beside him, she wanted to get back before Zoe woke up.

Yet, when he snuck both his hands around her body and cupped her breasts as he pressed his lips against her neck, she knew she was a lost cause. Her bra slipping from her grasp, she leaned back against him, sighing as his fingers teased her nipples, making them immediately hard.

What difference would a few more minutes, or a few more orgasms, make?

'What's that you say? You've got to go?' Theo whispered into her ear, his hot breath skating across her skin. 'Don't let me keep you.'

In reply, she turned her head and met his mouth with her own. Within seconds she was utterly and completely lost in his kisses. Their tongues dancing, their hands roaming, every ounce of self-control she possessed evaporated as Theo drew her back into the bed, yanking the sheet over the top of them.

Smiling down at her, he brought his hands back to her breasts and every part of her caught fire.

Even after a few nights of exploring every intimate inch of each other's bodies, the intensity of the pleasure she experienced whenever he touched her was still surprising. Sex in her marriage had always been nice, comfortable—they knew what they liked and disliked and how to bring each other to an enjoyable climax—but it had never been like *this*. Maybe it was only good because it was new, because Theo was practically a stranger and that in itself was thrilling, or because they both knew it wouldn't last forever, but whatever the reason Flick couldn't get enough of it.

'What are you thinking about?' he asked now, frowning slightly.

'Nothing important,' she whispered as she pushed the thoughts of her ex out of her head and pulled Theo's mouth down to meet hers once again, smoothing her hands over the hard muscle of his shoulders. Already both naked, it wasn't long before their skin was slick with desire. Flick felt his erection pressing against her belly and she was more than ready to accommodate it, but if there was one thing she'd learnt about Theo it was that he did not like to rush. Whether eating a meal, walking Roberta, making a cocktail, telling a story, playing the piano or playing her, he liked to savour the experience.

And who was she to argue as he moved his mouth down her body, licking and nibbling, first her nipples, then caressing the curve of her breasts and swirling his tongue around her belly button, before moving lower. Much lower. She sucked in a breath and gripped the edges of the mattress as he wedged her legs apart with his broad shoulders and pleasured her with his mouth until she could take no more.

'Theo, please,' she urged.

She didn't have to ask twice. Crawling back up her body, he grinned as he positioned himself.

'You blow my mind, Felicity,' he said as he thrust into her, going even deeper than she'd thought physically possible.

Flick screamed out at the pure bliss that rocketed from her core and spread all through her body. Theo held her tightly yet tenderly as he thrust harder and faster, taking them both exactly where they wanted to be for the third time since she'd climbed into his bed ten hours ago.

'Oh my gosh,' she moaned, her bones feeling as if they'd melted.

The man was a machine, a sexual beast, and when she was with him it almost felt as if she turned into someone else as well. And wasn't that exactly what she'd wanted to achieve coming here?

'Now I really have to go,' she said, still panting a few minutes later as they lay in each other's arms. If she didn't leave his bed this second, she might never be able to bring herself to do so.

With a reluctant sigh, he let her go. 'I'll miss you.'

'Hold that thought until tonight,' she said, before quickly tidying herself up and pulling on yesterday's clothes.

'Don't you worry, I won't be thinking of anything else,' he promised.

With those words on replay in her head, Flick made her way next door, unable to stop smiling. Her facial muscles were actually starting to ache from overuse, and they weren't the only ones. She'd had more sex over the past week than she sometimes had in a year in her old life—it was surprising she could still walk. Suddenly she understood all the fuss Neve and Emma made about it.

But she and Theo didn't just sleep together in the hours they stole. She hung in the bar listening to him play piano, they ate delicious local takeaway in bed, he'd tried—and failed—to help her improve her poker game and they'd laughed lots, but there'd been plenty of time for talking as well. She'd learnt that Theo and his ex-wife had met at law school, started dating almost immediately, married just after they graduated and bought a house in the Garden District as soon as they were able to get a mortgage.

'She was very materialistic and also very ambitious,' he said. 'She didn't tell me until she was pregnant with Anna that she actually never wanted kids. I'd assumed we were on the same page, so it was a shock when I found out we had different ideas for the future. After a lot of consideration, she decided she'd keep the baby and she didn't like the idea of an only child, so we had another one eighteen months later. Although Rachel was a good mother—she excels at everything she puts her mind to—she never let anything get in the way of climbing further up the career ladder. She wanted me to be the same and had ambitions about us starting our own law firm, but the idea never really appealed to me.'

Theo explained that Rachel had thrived on the long gruelling hours of corporate life, whereas he'd resented the overtime at the office, which took him away from their daughters, his music and spending any quality time together.

'In the end, I went part-time at a much smaller firm so I could be at home more and also started taking on some pro bono cases, and every second Sunday I played the piano here. I guess that might have been the straw that broke the camel's back.'

'What do you mean?'

'Well, even though my income, combined with the tips I made and Rachel's salary was more than we needed, she wasn't happy. She hated the friends I made through music, and my lack of drive, as she called it, bothered her. She was constantly at me to apply for a promotion or move to a bigger firm. Money and status was all she seemed to care about,' Theo concluded. 'It's funny how you think you know someone and it turns out you didn't really know them at all.'

'I know exactly what you mean,' Flick said, thinking back to her early years with Sofia.

Of course, she didn't tell Theo about any of that—merely stating that she and her husband had also grown apart, also wanted different things for the future. She felt a tad guilty about the fact she hadn't told him the whole truth about her marriage, but she simply couldn't bring herself to. And what did it matter? Her past and Sofia had nothing to do with what she was currently very much enjoying with Theo. As Zoe would say, it wasn't like she was planning on marrying the guy! Flick didn't plan on staying in New Orleans and Theo couldn't imagine ever living anywhere else.

She was at the door of the shop, fumbling for the key in her bag, when her phone started ringing. Digging it out, she glanced down at the screen. *Speaking of exes*. She was in two minds about whether to answer it; she didn't want to risk a conversation with Sofia ruining her mood. But, if she didn't answer, her ex would only keep calling until she did. Sofia was nothing if not persistent.

'Hi,' Flick said, wedging the phone between her ear and shoulder as she found the key and let herself inside.

'Hey, sweetheart. Hope I didn't wake you.'

'Um ... no. I've been up for a while. What time is it there?'

'Eight o'clock. I've just had dinner. It still feels weird eating alone, especially on a Thursday,' Sofia said, sounding less cheerful than usual.

'Mike isn't around?' Flick surprised herself by asking. That had to show *some* kind of progress in her quest to move on.

'He had to go to his mum's place for her birthday.'

Clearly Sofia hadn't been invited. Flick couldn't help wondering whether that was because things between them weren't that serious yet or because Mike's family might have reservations if they found out his new girlfriend used to be a man. She really hoped it wasn't the latter. As hard as it was accepting her ex-husband's new life, Flick still loved her—always would—and felt protective. She didn't want her to be at the receiving end of any nastiness.

'Anyway,' Sofia went on, 'you and Zoe have been quiet for a few days, so I thought I'd check in and see how she's holding up.'

'We've been busy.' Flick closed the door behind her as quietly as she could. She didn't continue upstairs because she didn't want Zoe to overhear them talking about her or alert her to her arrival. She wasn't sure if their daughter suspected anything about her late-night expeditions—Zoe was always still out with Jack when Flick went next door and fast asleep by the time she snuck home.

It wasn't that Flick was ashamed or embarrassed, more that she was enjoying sneaking around like a teenager. It added an element of illicitness to their fling. The only people she'd told about Theo were Neve and Emma and, unsurprisingly, they'd been over the moon, texting her multiple times a day asking for updates.

'So what have you been up to? Are you doing a lot of sightseeing?'

'A bit, although I only have the one real day off a week,' Flick said. 'But Zoe's actually doing pretty well. We've been getting out for breakfast, even doing a bit of shopping together. You'd be impressed, I've even bought a couple of skirts and dresses.'

Sofia laughed. 'Wonders never cease.'

'And Zoe's sewing is keeping her busy while I'm working, which is a good thing.'

'That's right. She told me about the wedding dress competition. It sounds fantastic.'

'Yes,' Flick replied, detecting a hint of jealousy in Sofia's voice.

It reminded her of the time the three of them had gone hunting for Zoe's wedding dress—Sofia had been in heaven, whereas Flick had only been there because it was important to Zoe. Fashion had never been her thing—until recently she could never be bothered with the time and effort it took to put an impressive outfit together.

Flick did *not* mention Jack, the fact Zoe went out with him almost every night, or her suspicions that they were doing more than drinking, dancing and talking about all things supernatural. If their daughter wanted to mention him, she would. And, just as she'd had her reservations at first, Sofia would likely think it was too soon, but Zoe sewing by day and spending her evenings with the ghost hunter was far better than Zoe drowning her sorrows by binge-watching TV on the couch.

'Are you sure everything's okay there? You sound a little weird. Are *you* okay?'

'I'm absolutely fine,' Flick said, biting down on a smile. 'Better than fine,' she added, suddenly realising this was the first conversation she'd had with her ex where the light lilt that Sofia had added to her voice since she transitioned didn't make her want to cry. Distance was a wonderful thing. 'It's nice having Zoe here; we've been getting to spend some real quality time together. And this place is amazing—the history, the music, the food, the atmosphere, the architecture ...'

She was about to add that Sofia would adore it, but not wanting to put ideas into her head, she swallowed the words just in time. 'Anyway, I think Zoe's waking up,' she lied, 'so I better go.'

'Okay. Call me if you need anything and tell Zoe I love her.'

'I will,' Flick promised.

19

Felicity

Early that evening Flick looked up from where she'd been working at the desk as Zoe appeared from upstairs.

'What do you think?' she asked, a smile on her face as she twirled around in exactly the same way she had when she was a little girl excited about a new dress.

'I think ... *Wow*.'

Flick was a little speechless. She might not be an expert in fashion, but the dress was unlike any wedding gown she'd ever seen before. Zoe had cut all the various dresses they'd bought from op shops into tiny pieces and then sewn them together, like patchwork. There was lace, tulle, satin and silk in different shades of white, scattered with sequins and beads and buttons and ribbons, and somehow it worked. Fitted at the bodice and a tad more revealing than anything Flick would ever wear—but hey, she was twice Zoe's age—it flowed out from the waist and cascaded in layers to just above the ankle.

Of course, she'd seen the dress taking shape while Zoe had been making it, but she'd never imagined it would look as good as this on.

'Is that a good wow?' Zoe asked, adjusting the veil she'd also made.

Flick rolled off her plastic gloves. 'It's an "I can't believe you whipped that up in just a week" kinda wow. Seriously, Zoe, maybe you missed your calling.'

'Thanks, Mum,' Zoe beamed and smoothed her hands over her skirt. 'It was fun. Let's hope the judges think like you do. I know it's a little bit different, but I figured I needed to stand out to win the prize.'

'You certainly do that.' Flick went to hug her, but Zoe held up a hand.

'Love you, Mum, but can't risk the dress.'

'Okay, of course, sorry,' Flick said with a chuckle. 'Here, let me take a photo to send to Sofia.'

Their daughter obliged by posing for a number of photos, humouring Flick as she made her move about the shop to try and get the right light—the various pieces of taxidermy made the perfect backdrop for this slightly gothic gown.

'You know what this reminds me of?' Flick said, still clicking away.

'What?'

'That horrible painting upstairs. Not that your dress is horrible at all,' she rushed to explain. 'I quite like the dress in the picture, I just don't like the skeleton wearing it. I've thought about covering it up because it gives me the heebie-jeebies.'

'You're so weird, Mum. You're surrounded by dead stuff all day every day but you can't handle bones? Anyway, enough photos. If I'm going to hit all the participating bars and make sure the judges get a proper look at my dress, then I'd better be off. Wish me luck.'

'Luck,' Flick said. She almost asked if Zoe would mind if she tagged along—they'd only spent a couple of evenings together over the last week and Theo wouldn't be available until late, but Zoe was already halfway out the door. And she probably wouldn't want her mother hanging around anyway. The memory of being rejected and left in the restaurant held fresh in her mind. She let out a sigh, but as long as Zoe was safe and not dwelling too much on Beau's betrayal, that was all that mattered.

'Say hi to Jack for me,' Flick called as Zoe opened the shop door.

'Will do,' she called back, as she waved her hand and held the door open for a couple of women. They were both clutching cocktails in plastic skulls.

'Hey there. Welcome to Bourbon Street Taxidermy Art,' Flick said to the women as the door thumped shut behind them.

'Oh my God, you're Australian,' exclaimed the shorter of the two. 'Like us.'

Although Flick loved the southern drawl spoken by locals, she found herself delighted to hear a familiar accent. The women exchanged pleasantries, Flick explaining she was here short-term for work and the women, who she discovered were from Queensland, telling her they were on a girls' trip to celebrate their fortieth birthdays.

'What's going on out there?' asked the other one.

Flick looked out onto the street to see what seemed like hundreds of brides and a number of men and women dressed as grooms as well. Zoe clearly had plenty of competition. She explained about the themed pub crawl, which appeared to be a lot bigger than she'd imagined, and the women decided maybe they'd have an early night with room service in their hotel.

Flick laughed. She didn't blame them—not everyone came to the French Quarter for the wild partying and she had the feeling tonight was set to get even crazier than usual on Bourbon Street. The Aussies stayed a while longer checking out the exhibits and not long after they left, Flick shut up shop.

She went upstairs, showered, made herself a snack, replied to a few emails, exchanged some messages with Neve and Emma, sent the photos of Zoe to Sofia and then made her way next door as she did almost every night of late. She enjoyed nursing a drink in the Blue Cat and watching Theo work his magic on the piano almost as much as she enjoyed him working his magic on her. When she was younger, Flick would have been worrying about coming on too strong. Wondering if she should be playing hard to get. You know, a little treat 'em mean, keep 'em keen? But Theo had made it clear he couldn't get enough of her and, besides the fact they were too old to play games, she didn't want to waste any time. If this was only going to be a fling, she wanted to make the most of it.

She couldn't help smiling as she stepped outside—she'd never seen so many brides in her life. Even though the bar was only a few metres away, it took longer than usual to walk the short distance due to even more people littering the sidewalk. Most of the costumes were real wedding dresses and none of them as original as Zoe's. She crossed her fingers that Zoe would win—the money would help, but it would also give her a much-needed boost.

Leaving the craziness of the street behind her, Flick was relieved to find the Blue Cat mellow as normal. Not a bride in sight. The old church pews were filled with people chatting and laughing.

'Hello again,' Roxy said as Flick approached the bar.

Did she detect a hint of disapproval in the young bartender's voice? 'Hi,' she replied brightly, ignoring the niggle. 'Can I get a glass of white wine?'

'Of course.' Roxy turned to grab a bottle from the fridge.

Flick waved at Lauri-Ann, who was even busier than usual serving takeaways at the window, as Roxy filled a glass and put it down in front of her. 'So, you and Theo, hey?'

Flick didn't know how to respond to Roxy's wriggling eyebrows.

'Don't be embarrassed,' she said. 'I think it's great. It's actually good to see him pursuing a woman more his own vintage, if you know what I mean.'

Flick wasn't sure she did, and she wasn't sure she wanted to.

'And, you could definitely do worse for a holiday fling. For an old dude, Theo definitely has a pretty good body.'

Flick's cheeks heated. How was she supposed to respond? Roxy made it sound like she'd had personal experience with that body. Had Theo slept with *her*?

'Who says it's a fling?' she said, and then immediately berated herself. That's exactly what it was and she wasn't ashamed, but something in Roxy's tone had provoked her.

The bartender shook her head and gave a sympathetic laugh. 'Oh, sugar, Theo doesn't do anything else.'

As she turned to serve a couple who'd just arrived, Flick took a sip of her wine and glanced over to where Theo sat at the piano, bringing the instrument to life. The way Roxy spoke, piano-playing wasn't the only playing he excelled at. While she knew this thing between them wasn't serious, she couldn't help feeling a little disillusioned by the fact this probably wasn't as special to him as it was to her.

No wonder he was so good at sex. It sounded like he had plenty of it. And probably mostly with women half her age, if Roxy could be believed. She stared at the bartender's lithe young body. How could Flick ever compete?

Feeling a bit foolish, she was considering finishing her drink and heading back to Harvey's when Theo glanced up, caught her eye and winked. At this one simple gesture, heat flushed through her entire body and suddenly she felt stupid for almost letting Roxy bother her. What did it matter what Theo had done in the past? Or even what he might do in the future. Right now, his attentions were on her—they were having fun and that was the important thing.

She blew him a playful kiss as she made her way to a pew closer to the piano. For the next half hour she simply enjoyed the music, the wine and the atmosphere.

At about nine o'clock, Theo handed over to a female duo and made his way to her. 'Evening, Felicity,' he said, planting his lips on her cheek. It was the most chaste kiss they'd had in days, but they were in public, and it still held the promise of plenty more to come. 'You're looking stunning tonight.'

Flick had never been much good at accepting compliments, but the new Felicity had not only made a bit more effort after her shower this evening—straightening her hair, actually putting on make-up, earrings and one of the skirts she'd bought on her shopping expedition with Zoe—she also had the confidence to smile and thank him.

'Let me take you out to dinner,' Theo said.

'Like an actual date?' she teased.

He nodded. 'You deserve it and so does that outfit.'

His gaze skimmed down her body and lingered on her bare legs. She shivered.

'While that sounds lovely, have you seen out there tonight? It's an invasion of brides. I'm not sure we'll be able to get a table anywhere.'

'The brides will be in the clubs and pubs. I'll take you to a proper restaurant.'

'In that case, how can I resist?'

Five minutes later, after promising Lauri-Ann and Roxy he'd be back by closing, Theo took Flick's hand and led her through the hordes down Bourbon Street, on to St Ann and a little further to Muriel's on the corner of Jackson Square. She remembered the burgundy building and the stories about the resident ghost from their very first night out, but she was not prepared for the ornate elegance that greeted them when they stepped inside.

She'd thought that first restaurant he'd taken her to had been charming, but this place took charm to a whole other level. Their waitress greeted them in perfect French, which Theo actually understood, and then led them to 'The Bistro'—a beautiful dining room with polished wooden floors, chandeliers, high ceilings and deep garnet walls, one of which appeared to be decoupaged with old drawings and pictures. The skirting boards, door and window frames were in contrasting white and there were lovely old mirrors in gilded frames hanging on the other walls. It was easy to believe this place was haunted, because if she died here, she probably wouldn't want to leave either.

They were shown to a table dressed in a stark white cloth, bone china plates, and sparkling silver cutlery and glassware. It was right by the window, so they had the perfect view out onto Jackson Square. Theo held out the antique leather chair for Flick before taking his own seat. They ordered wine and then perused the menu, which all sounded so delicious she had no idea what to choose. She noticed that many of the dishes included Creole ingredients—creamy Creole dressing and Creole mustard—but no mention of Cajun.

'What exactly is the difference between Creole and Cajun food?' she asked. 'They seem pretty similar to me.'

'Take that back!' Theo pressed his hand against his chest, feigning horror.

She laughed. 'Well? Educate me.'

'So, Cajun food originated with the French who settled in Canada but were then exiled and came down to Louisiana and began combining some of their French culinary traditions with American ideas. Where the Cajuns were all French Canadians, the Creole culture refers to a mix of the colonial Spanish and French settlers but also the enslaved people that were brought across from Africa. Being a port city, so many ethnicities landed here and over time they mingled and began to influence each other's cooking.'

'I see. So, Cajun food is more French, whereas Creole is like—'

'A melting pot of nationalities and flavours.'

Flick frowned. 'But they both seem to have the same dishes? Like gumbo?'

'Yes, but there are subtle differences. Cajun food is generally hotter, Creole often creamy. Creole cooking uses tomatoes heavily, whereas Cajun does not. The Creoles generally had access to more ingredients, which is reflected in their dishes. If you're truly interested, you should take a cooking class at the School of Cooking on St Louis Street—maybe it's something you can do with Zoe? But if she's not interested, I'd love to go with you.'

'I'd like that,' Flick said, thinking about how much fun she could have in the kitchen with Theo.

In the end, under Theo's guidance, they decided on crawfish and goat cheese crepes to start, followed by panko-crusted salmon for her, blackened redfish for him, and some candied sweet potatoes with pecans and southern-style greens to share.

'We need to save room for dessert,' he advised, 'because Muriel's does some of the best you'll find in New Orleans.'

'So are you Creole or Cajun, or something else entirely?' Flick asked as their waitress retreated.

Theo smiled. 'My mom is French Creole—her family have been in NOLA since the late 1800s—but my dad's family is from LA.'

Before too long the food and the conversation flowed as naturally between them as it did when they were in bed. If Flick had known being with another man would be as easy as this, maybe she wouldn't have resisted Emma and Neve's attempts to get her to put herself out there again so ardently.

They chatted more about the ghost, who apparently resided mostly in the 'Séance Lounge', and also about the goings-on outside, watching the tour groups, the brides, the buskers, and the eclectic mix of everyone else who passed by.

'Did you busk in Jackson Square when you were young?'

He nodded. 'Yep, Jackson Square, down by the river, Royal Street … Occasionally we even dared to join the real talent down on Frenchmen Street. There probably isn't one corner in the Quarter I haven't played on at some stage.'

'Did either of your daughters inherit your musical talents?' Flick asked.

She'd spoken plenty about Zoe and Toby during their time together, to the point that she sometimes wondered if Theo would tell her to shut up, but he always listened patiently and seemed more comfortable talking about her kids than his.

'They both played various instruments when they were little, but it was always a chore to get them to practise. How about you? Have you ever played anything?'

'Not unless you count the recorder that they insisted we all learn at school. I was hopeless. Not a musical bone in my body.'

'I don't believe that. You're an artist and I've seen the way you drift into a world of your own when you listen to me play. Maybe you just never had the right teacher. I could give it a shot if you want.'

'What?' she scoffed. 'Teach me to play the piano?'

He nodded. 'Or the saxophone. I also know my way around a trumpet.'

'I'll bet you do,' she said glancing down at his beautiful long fingers. She leaned a little closer, very aware that her top gaped a little at the cleavage. 'You can teach me to play something, on one condition.'

His lips curled up at the edges. 'And what would that be?'

'I'll teach you how to taxidermy an animal. Your choice of the small ones in Harvey's deep freeze.'

'Hell no.' He grimaced. 'I love your end result, but I have a fear of blood and do not like getting these hands dirty.'

'Unless the animal died through trauma, there's not actually always a lot of blood.'

'I'll have to take your word for that.'

They both laughed and Flick took another sip of her very good wine as she once again glanced out the window. 'This has to be the greatest place on earth for people-watching.'

'I reckon it's the greatest place on earth for anything,' Theo replied.

Flick smiled at him. 'I'm beginning to think you might be right.'

When their waitress brought them the dessert menu, she shook her head. 'I don't think I can fit one more spoonful of anything else into my stomach.'

But Theo convinced her they couldn't leave before trying Muriel's famous pecan tart. 'I'll carry you home if need be.'

In the end, they ordered the tart and two liqueur-laced coffees.

'What do you think? Aren't you glad I insisted on dessert?' Theo asked as he held up the last forkful of their supposedly shared tart to Flick's mouth. She was slightly ashamed to admit she'd scoffed the lion's share of it, but who knew pecans could taste *that* good?

'I think if I spend much more time with you, I'm going to grow to the size of a house,' she said, before closing her lips around the fork and her eyes in bliss as the last of their dessert melted on her tongue.

'You'd be sexy whatever size, but luckily I know a way to help you work off the calories.'

'Do you now?' she teased as a waiter delivered a trio of young men to the table beside them. Feeling as if she were about to sink into a food coma at any moment, Flick didn't pay much attention to the new arrivals.

But when Theo had paid the bill and offered his hand to help her up, she got a proper look at one of the guys at the table.

'Jack?' she said, frowning.

The young man looked up and sure enough, her eyes weren't playing tricks on her. The tall, lanky, slightly geeky ghost tour guide hesitated a moment as if trying to place her, before pushing to his feet and smiling. 'Zoe's mum, right?'

Before Flick could answer, Jack turned to Theo and his smile widened. 'Hey, what's up, man?'

'Hey,' Theo replied as the men high-fived each other.

'You two know each other?' Flick asked.

'Jack lives in the apartments above the shop next door—on the *other* side.' He smiled at the younger man. 'How you doing? How's the ghost-hunting business going?'

Jack nodded. 'It's good. It's growing. Might even be able to quit waiting tables soon.'

'That's great,' Theo replied.

But Flick didn't give two hoots about whatever they were talking about. She nailed her gaze on Jack. 'Where's Zoe?'

He rubbed his chin as his eyebrows squished together. 'What do you mean? I haven't seen her since the night we met.'

'What?' Flick felt the floor shift beneath her feet, and she didn't think it was because she'd had too much to drink. 'But ... she's been out almost every night this last week. With you.'

Jack looked shocked, then shuffled awkwardly on his feet. 'Really sorry, but that's not true.'

'I don't understand. This doesn't make any sense. Why would she lie?'

He sighed. 'Look, I wish I could help you, but all I can say is that when Zoe left me that night, she was pretty upset. She'd just told me about her husband sleeping with someone else and ...' He glanced down at his feet as if he didn't want to say anymore.

'And *what*?' Flick asked loudly, turning the heads of a number of other patrons in the restaurant. Theo put his hand on her arm. She shook him off. She didn't care.

Jack's cheeks flushed crimson as he stepped a little away from the table and lowered his voice. 'She wanted me to ... ah ... help her forget her husband. When I tried to get her to talk about it instead, she got upset and ran off. I should have gone after her. I'm sorry.'

'Oh my goodness.' Flick pressed her hand against her suddenly burning chest as terrifying thoughts invaded her head. How could she have been so blind? She should have forced Zoe to talk about what was going on inside her head. Instead she'd only seen what she wanted to see—that Zoe was slowly but surely starting to heal.

She thought of the undesirable she'd met the night of her arrival, of Neve and Emma's teasing about New Orleans being the murder capital of the world, and prayed to a god she'd never believed in that Zoe would be safe. She'd never forgive herself if something happened to her daughter because she'd been too distracted by her hormones to realise that Zoe wasn't telling her the whole truth.

How stupid and naive Flick had been to think she was doing so well so soon after the only relationship she'd ever known had failed her. And now so had Flick. She'd promised Sofia she'd take care of their daughter and yet she didn't even know where she was.

Sleeping with Jack so soon after Beau had been worrying enough, but if Zoe *hadn't* been with Jack, where the hell had she been these last few nights? And who with?

'I have to find her,' Flick said, already starting for the door.

Theo caught up just as she stepped outside. 'Felicity, calm down. I'm sure Zoe's fine. She hasn't come to any harm the other nights—there's no reason to panic that she will tonight. Just because she hasn't been with Jack like you thought, doesn't mean she's been alone.'

'I know! That's what I'm worried about.'

'Maybe she's made some other friends,' Theo said with a shrug.

But no matter what he said, Flick couldn't ignore the bad feeling in her gut. Call it mother's intuition or something, but she needed to find Zoe and see for herself that she was okay. She glanced frantically from left to right, wondering where to start. There were brides in every direction. And Zoe's costume might look unique up close, but picking her out of this crowd would be like playing *Where's Wally?*

'Maybe you should try calling her?' Theo suggested as Jack emerged from the restaurant behind them.

Why hadn't she thought of that? Rummaging in her bag, she found her phone. Willing Zoe to pick up, she tapped her foot against the cobbled footpath as she listened to the ringing tone, but the call rang out and went to voicemail.

Shit. Her eyes burned and her hands were trembling almost as much as her heart, but now wasn't the time to fall apart.

'She's not answering,' Flick said after another three failed attempts.

'Hey.' Theo pulled her into his arms and held her close as she lost her battle with tears. 'Don't stress. She probably can't hear her phone over the noise of the crawl.'

But while logic told her he was probably right, fear sat alongside the heavy dinner in her stomach. She couldn't get the thought of that creepy man she'd run into on her first night in the Quarter out of her head.

She pulled out of his embrace and tapped out a message: *Call me the moment you read this!!!*

Then she looked back to the men. 'I need to find her. Do either of you know which pubs and clubs are participating in this Casket Girls thing? Zoe made a wedding dress because she wants to win the money.'

Jack and Theo shook their heads.

'Shouldn't be too hard to find out though,' Jack said, drawing his phone out of his pocket. 'I think there's a Facebook page for it.'

He started tapping and it felt like years before he finally angled his screen towards her. 'There.'

Flick stared at the list, which looked to include every second venue in the French Quarter. It would take all night to search even half of them. Her head spinning, she took a deep breath as Jack said, 'I'll help you look.'

'Thank you.' She should probably argue that Zoe wasn't his responsibility and insist he get back to dinner with his friends, but instead she let out a grateful sigh, then looked at Theo.

'Of course, I'll help too,' he said, sounding almost offended. 'We'll find her, I promise.'

'I hope you're right. We should probably split up and divide the list of venues between us?'

While Jack nodded, Theo shook his head. 'No way I'm letting you go wandering around alone either at this time of night. How about you and I take all the venues from Canal to St Louis and Jack can search the rest?'

'Good idea,' Jack agreed.

Flick almost said she could take care of herself, but these two knew the Quarter better than she did, so she swallowed her feminist retort. 'Okay.'

Jack and Theo exchanged phone numbers so they could alert each other if they found Zoe and then Jack went in one direction and Flick and Theo set off in the other.

A few minutes later, they slowed in front of the first club on their list. At the sight of the long line of people waiting outside to get in, Flick's heart sank.

'It's okay, I know the bouncer,' Theo said. Grabbing her hand, he went straight to the front of the queue, ignoring the loud complaints that they were pushing in. After a few quick words with the burly guy at the door, their hands were stamped with the club's logo by a skimpily clad woman and they were inside.

Bright-coloured strobe lighting pulsed above their heads in the otherwise dark building, making her feel as if she might have a seizure at any moment. The music was so loud that Flick could feel it thumping in her chest and the only lyrics she could make out were swear words. The scents of stale air, sweat, beer, vomit, hairspray, and what she suspected to be pot, would have been bad enough on their own, but they combined to create a stomach-turning aromatic cocktail. This kind of place had been Flick's idea of hell even when she was in her early twenties and nothing had changed. But she wasn't here to have a good time.

'Can you see her?' Although Theo shouted, she had to lip-read his words over the horrendous noise.

'No!' Flick yelled back, but that didn't mean anything. She could make out the people near the bar, but those on the dance floor were pressed so close together it was difficult to tell where one person ended and another began. She gestured towards it. 'Maybe we should try in there.'

Something almost akin to dread flashed across Theo's face but he nodded nonetheless and started towards the mass of pulsing bodies. Flick almost slipped when she stepped into a spilt drink on the floor, but Theo caught her.

When they emerged a few moments later, Flick felt as if she'd been violated—she'd been groped at least twice by men half her age—but they were no closer in their mission to find Zoe. She didn't *think* her daughter had been dancing but couldn't be a hundred per cent sure.

'Have you got a photo of her on your phone?' Theo shouted.

It sounded more like 'Do you have a piano accordion?' but thankfully her lip-reading skills were getting better by the second. She nodded and lifted her free hand where she'd been clutching her phone as if her life depended on it.

As they approached the bar, Theo released her hand so she could swipe open her phone to get the picture. Thank God she'd insisted on taking some photos this afternoon. Not that she didn't have plenty of Zoe, but the ones from today showed what she was wearing right now.

'What can I get you guys?' asked one of the bartenders.

Flick shook her head and flashed her phone at him. 'I'm just wondering if you've seen this girl?'

'Lady, you know how many brides I've seen tonight?' He shrugged. 'They all look the same to me.'

Almost certain Zoe wasn't here, they were making their way towards the exit, when Flick thought of the restrooms. 'She could be in there,' she said, gesturing to a line winding out of the female one.

Not waiting for Theo to respond, she started for the front of the queue.

'Hey, wait your turn,' yelled a number of disgruntled patrons.

'I don't need to go, I'm just looking for someone,' she explained, flashing her phone as she walked down the line. 'Anyone seen this girl?'

Of course, the answer was no and when she barged into the restroom and shouted Zoe's name, she reaped no rewards there either. The knot of anxiety in her stomach growing ever stronger, she returned to Theo and they made their way back out onto the street.

Sadly, he didn't have a contact at the next venue, so they waited impatiently in the queue for five minutes that felt more like five hours before being granted entry. This place—more pub than club— had an actual band playing something that sounded much more like real music and the lighting didn't mess as much with Flick's head in the way the previous venue's had. But, aside from these differences, the result was the same. No sign of Zoe at the bar, on the dance floor or in the restrooms, and no one who had any recollection of seeing her.

Two and a half hours, two bars, one Irish pub, three clubs, and almost a dozen stamps up her arm later, Flick wanted to scream. And cry. And maybe even hit someone. Her calves ached and sweat trickled down her back, making her clothes stick to her like a second skin. It felt like Groundhog Day—each place they checked making her feel less and less like they'd ever find Zoe. It was hopeless. There were brides everywhere and not one of them her daughter. It would be easier to find the needle in the proverbial haystack.

'Maybe she's gone back to the apartment,' Theo suggested as they left yet another headache-inducing venue and paused so Flick could rub her aching feet.

'You might be right,' she said, desperate for this to be true. What she wouldn't give to go back to the apartment and find Zoe sleeping peacefully, none the wiser about their efforts searching all over town for her. 'Maybe we should go check?'

As Theo offered his hand to steady her while she slipped her shoe back on, his phone rang.

Flick's heart jolted. 'It might be Jack?'

But Theo was already answering the call. 'Tell me you've found her!'

20

Zoe

Having managed to visit every venue along the Casket Girls pub crawl where she'd flashed her gown at all the right people, had her photo taken a zillion times and too many drinks to count, Zoe now wanted to do nothing but dance her sorrows away in much the same way she'd been doing most nights of late. The only difference being that tonight she didn't have a self-inflicted curfew because she didn't have to get up tomorrow and work on the dress.

What was she going to do now to fill in her days? It had been good having something to focus on. And it had kept her mum off her back as well.

Not wanting to think about that right now, she sculled a whole bottle of water, tossed the empty to the guy behind the bar and made her way right into the middle of the dance floor of the last club on the list. Joining the throng of jerking bodies, she threw herself around with pure abandon along to the head-banging music. Until recently she much preferred the kind of music you could bop to as you sang the familiar lyrics—stuff like Taylor Swift, Rhianna and Beyoncé. There was nothing familiar about the music tonight's DJ was playing, and Zoe could barely make out the words never mind sing them, but she didn't care. The best thing about venues like this was that they played the music so loudly she couldn't hear her own thoughts over the top of it. With so many people around she didn't feel as alone as she did during the day and the flashing lights that almost blinded her made her feel as if she were on another planet. Exactly what she wanted and needed right now.

For over an hour she kept on dancing, barely conscious of the other people surrounding her, not even caring when they bumped into her. Occasionally she found herself dragged into a group, then she'd happily dance alone again for a while before being caught up with some random. She never talked to the other person, rather used their body as much as her own in her attempts to lose her mind.

When one guy actually spoke to her, she found herself shocked and also a little annoyed. Her fellow dancers had almost become surreal to her, as if they didn't really exist.

'What?' she yelled to the man standing in front of her. He wore black jeans and a red checked shirt that along with his boots made him look like a cowboy. All he needed was the hat.

'Can I buy you a drink?' he shouted back.

Zoe contemplated his question—vaguely in the back of her mind she could hear a little voice warning her she should probably eat something before she drank anything else, but a free drink was a free drink. 'Sure, why not?'

'Excellent.' The cowboy grinned and offered his hand.

She took it, already too drunk to hide her flinch as his sweat squished into her palm, not that he appeared to notice as he led her over to the bar.

'What are you having?' he asked, gesturing to the row of bottles behind them.

She chose a cocktail and Cowboy ordered himself a bourbon on the rocks.

'You here on your own?' he asked, standing way too close for comfort as they waited. His hot boozy breath on her skin made it crawl.

She tried to move back a little, but the bar was crowded and there wasn't much space. 'Yes,' she answered, that little voice once again telling her to be careful, but unable to come up with anything but the truth in her current state.

'I really need to eat something,' she added, swaying a little.

'Whoa.' The cowboy caught her and smiled. 'You okay there?'

When she nodded, he didn't remove his sweaty hand from her side, and a feeling of unease slithered down her spine.

'What do you think of this song?' he asked, nodding towards the dance floor as the bartender put their drinks down in front of them.

She followed his gaze to the throng of people and was about to turn back and tell the cowboy she'd never heard it before, when a familiar face appeared in her vision. In her alcohol-addled state it took Zoe a few seconds to work out who it was, and she also totally forgot the way they'd parted the other night.

'Jack,' she exclaimed in glee as if he was a long-lost friend.

'Thank God,' he said as he stepped between her and the cowboy. 'I've been searching all over the Quarter for you! Looks like I found you just in time.'

'You've been searching for me, Jack? How sweet.' She palmed her hand against his chest, which felt just as hard and delicious as it had a few nights ago. That suddenly reminded her what had happened, or rather *not* happened between them. She pouted and picked up her drink, almost forgetting about the other guy. 'Does that mean you've changed your mind about us?'

But, as her lips closed around the paper straw, Jack snatched the whole thing out of her hand, spilling it onto her fingers.

'What the hell?!'

Jack didn't answer, glaring instead at the cowboy and then gesturing to the bulkiest of the bartenders. 'I'm pretty sure this drink is spiked,' he said, thrusting it at the man. 'I saw this asshole drop something in it. You should probably throw it out and I suggest you do the same with him—'

But the cowboy was already hightailing it out of the venue.

'Thanks, man,' said the bartender, shaking his head. 'We'll get this tested and check the security cameras for the fucker. There's been a bit of a problem with roofies around the Quarter lately.'

Jack nodded. 'So I've heard.'

'I know the police are on the scent but this'—the bartender held up the drink as if it were a dirty diaper—'and our security footage will hopefully give them a better lead.'

'Was that guy trying to drug me?' Zoe asked, finally catching up with the conversation. She didn't want to think about what could have happened if Jack hadn't come along when he did.

Would the cowboy have raped her? The hair on the back of her neck lifted at the thought. What was *with* men? Did they all have some jerk chromosome that made them think they were above the law? Above morality?

'Looked that way to me,' Jack said, letting out an exasperated sigh. 'It's not safe for you to be out alone at night around here anyway, especially when you're drinking.'

He spoke as if he was her father, not someone she barely knew. 'Are you saying this is *my* fault? That by daring to go out and dance on my own, I was practically begging to be taken advantage of? Talk about victim-blaming!'

She was done with this conversation, just as much as she was done with men. 'Goodnight, Jack,' she said, turning to go, but the room started spinning and her stomach lurched.

Jack caught her before she hit the ground and she found herself pressed against his body, his handsome face so close she could almost count the stubble on his chin. That's if she wasn't suddenly using all her brainpower trying not to be sick.

'I think I'm going to throw up.'

But her warning came too late for both of them. It was like an out of body experience. She watched in horror as the contents of her stomach shot up and exploded out of her mouth, raining down in a horrible colourful concoction all over his crisp white shirt.

'Oh my God, I'm so sorry,' she blurted, her hand rushing up to cover her mouth as Jack stepped back. 'Let me get you a tissue.'

She dug furiously in her bag, finding absolutely nothing of use. When she looked up, the bartender had come good with a box of tissues and a bottle of water. He glared at Zoe as he handed them to Jack, then returned immediately to the bar.

'Here, let me help,' she said, yanking a tissue from the box and reaching out to try to help Jack clean himself up.

But she couldn't do it. If looking at her vomit wasn't bad enough, the moment the horrendous smell hit her nostrils, she gagged and felt her stomach revolt once again.

No time to apologise, she turned and dashed past the queue of people waiting for the bathroom. Those at the front took one look at her probably green face and let her pass. She made it to a basin just in time.

As bile burned the back of her throat, her eyes stung with tears. This was quite possibly the worst day of her life. Second only to the one when Beau told her it was over. The only thing that could possibly salvage it would be winning the prize money for the dress, but after seeing just how much competition she had, she wasn't holding her breath for that either. She wouldn't be surprised if the judges simply put all the entrants' names into a hat and randomly picked a winner.

Ignoring the derogatory comments of the women around her, Zoe took a deep breath, rinsed out the basin as best she could and then splashed water onto her face. She looked a sight—panda eyes and streaky cheeks thanks to mascara that had clearly lied about being waterproof—but her appearance had nothing on how she felt inside.

'Woo-woo!' Somebody wolf-whistled and a couple of girls cheered, breaking Zoe from her thoughts. She glanced sideways to see Jack striding towards her, totally shirtless and looking much hotter than a nerd had any right to.

'Hey, sweetheart ...' The woman at the sink beside Zoe fluttered her eyelashes at him. 'I think you got the wrong bathroom, but I'm not complaining. Nice abs.'

Jack brushed off her hand as she reached out to touch him and addressed Zoe instead. 'You okay?' He held out a bottle of water. 'Here, drink some of this.'

'What happened to your shirt?' she asked as her fingers closed around the bottle.

'I ditched it. Easier than cleaning it.'

Oh Lord, he must be rueing the day he met her. If someone threw up on her like that she'd never forgive them. 'I'm so sorry,' she whispered, knowing her words didn't change anything.

'Don't worry about it,' he replied, his tone clipped. 'Drink this and then let's get out of here.'

She did as she was told, relishing the feel of the cool water as it slipped down her throat, and then Jack ushered her out of the restroom, his palm gently but firmly against the small of her back.

It might have felt good if she didn't feel so bad.

As they made their way through the swell of bodies to the exit, Zoe racked her mind for something to say. She thought another apology might only make him cranky and small talk seemed lame under the circumstances, but even though he probably wouldn't be able to hear her over the noise, she didn't like the silence between them.

'Why were you looking for me?' she finally thought to ask.

He didn't reply but the answer became clear the moment they exited onto still crowded Bourbon Street and came face to face with her mum and the guy from next door.

Flick yanked her into her arms. 'Thank God you're okay. We've been looking for you everywhere.'

Zoe glanced at Jack over her mum's shoulder. Did she mean they'd *all* been looking for her? This was even more mortifying than she'd imagined. And had Jack called them while she was in the bathroom or something? How did he even have Flick's number? Nothing made any sense and if she spent any longer trying to work it out, her head might explode.

'Why? Has something happened?'

Flick blinked. 'I was worried about you. Going out at night alone. Lying to me about what you've been up to. This can be a dangerous place, Zo-Zo. Anything could have happened to you.'

'I'm fine.' She tried to disentangle herself, but Flick refused to loosen her grip.

'That's not what Jack told us—he said some creep spiked your drink.' Flick looked at him. 'Thank you so much. How can I ever repay you?'

210

'Don't worry about it. I'm just glad she's okay,' he said, as if Zoe wasn't even there. He nodded once at her mum and then shook hands with Theo. 'I'll see you guys round.'

'What happened to his shirt?' Flick asked as Jack stalked off down the road.

'I threw up on it,' Zoe admitted.

'You what? Oh, Zoe, what are we going to do with you?'

'I just want to go home to bed,' she said, shaking free and hugging her arms to her chest. She glanced up and down the street, relieved to see they were actually only a stone's throw from the taxidermy shop. *Thank God.*

'Don't you have anything to say for yourself?' Flick demanded. 'You made me sick with worry and you ruined Theo's and Jack's evenings as well.'

'How did Jack get involved anyway?'

'We ran into him at dinner, which was when I realised you'd duped me. He could see I was worried, and he offered to help. And you didn't even have the decency to thank him. I know you're hurting but this self-destructive behaviour has to stop now. As do the lies. Who knows what would have happened to you tonight if Jack didn't find you when he did!'

'Okay, okay.' Zoe held up her hand as tears flooded her eyes— she couldn't stand here listening to her mother's lecture any longer. 'I'm sorry I lied, okay? I'm sorry I scared you, but right now all I want to do is go to sleep. Can we talk about this tomorrow?'

'I think that sounds like a good idea,' Theo said, offering her a sympathetic smile.

'Thank you,' she whispered.

This softened her mum. She took one more look at Zoe, shook her head, then folded her back into her arms before ushering her down the street and into the shop. Theo bid them farewell at the door and somehow, with Flick's help, Zoe managed to drag herself up the stairs and into bed, where she rolled onto her side and cried herself to sleep.

The truth was, tonight had scared Zoe just as much as it had scared Flick.

21

Zoe

Zoe woke to sun sneaking in through the gaps in Harvey's curtains, a pounding head, a furry mouth, and her mum sitting on the side of the bed watching over her. She could tell from the look on Flick's face that a lecture was imminent, and she suspected she might even deserve it, but couldn't actually remember why.

'Morning,' Flick said, offering her a glass of water and two painkillers.

'Thanks.' She took them gratefully, swallowed both in quick succession and then downed the rest of the glass. It barely put a dent in her thirst. 'Was I hit by a truck or something?'

'Do you have *any* recollection of last night?'

'Um ...' Zoe tried hard to think, but the last thing she clearly remembered was her mum taking photos of her downstairs in the wedding dress. She glanced down and realised she was still wearing it. *Ugh* ... Was it the gown or her that smelled like sour milk?

'You must have had even more to drink than I thought,' said Flick. 'Would you like me to refresh your memory?'

It was clearly a rhetorical question, so Zoe didn't bother nodding. Her head already hurt bad enough without unnecessary movement.

Flick launched angrily into an explanation. 'Let's go back a little. The last few nights, you've been lying to me about going out with Jack. You've been staying out all hours, doing who knows what. Who the hell have you been with if not him?'

At the mention of Jack, the memories of last night came gushing back into her head. Oh shit, *that's* why she smelled like vomit.

'I haven't been with anyone,' Zoe admitted. 'I've just been going to clubs and dancing. It helps.'

'And drinking? Let's not forget the drinking.' Flick held up an almost empty bottle, which Zoe thought she'd hidden better under the bed.

'Have you been snooping around my room?' Outrage felt easier than admitting she'd been adding a little dash of something to the litres of coffee that helped her through each day. Last Wednesday, she hadn't forgotten to stop at Walgreens on her way home and she'd bought enough to feed her habit for a while.

'It's Harvey's room, and you're here as my guest. I had to do *something* while I was watching guard, making sure you didn't choke on your own vomit. You were a mess last night. And you owe Jack a lot more than just a new shirt.'

'I know! I know!' Zoe yelled and then immediately winced as a knife-like sensation stabbed at her head. 'I remember now. Please, can we not go over it?'

Flick sighed, not one ounce of sympathy in her face. 'Fine. But why did you lie to me about seeing Jack?'

'Because ...' Zoe looked down at the bed. 'I never meant to lie. But you just assumed I was seeing him, and it was easier that way.

If you knew the truth you wouldn't have let me go out alone. You'd have insisted on coming with me and I didn't want to go out to dinner where conversation would eventually come around to Beau, or to boring bars to listen to jazz music and pretend this was just a lovely holiday from real life. I wanted to go to a club where I could drink and dance and forget without you judging my every move.'

'I'm not judging you, darling. I might be concerned, but it's only because I care and I want what's best for you. You were lucky last night, but that might not always be the case.'

Zoe shuddered at the memory of the cowboy, but Flick hadn't finished.

'Alcohol isn't the answer to fixing your heartache. Neither is shutting me out. You came all the way across the world to be with me, so let me be here for you. Let me support you through this.' She reached out and squeezed Zoe's hand. 'Believe it or not, I do understand what you're going through.'

'No.' Zoe shook her head—*ouch!* 'You might think you do but you don't. Your marriage may have ended but Sofia didn't betray you. She didn't cheat on you! She didn't choose someone else when she should have chosen you.' Stupid tears flooded her eyes again and she swiped at them. 'It was your decision not to stay with Sofia. You guys are even still friends. You have no idea what this feels like.'

Silence rang between them for a long moment, then Flick spoke gently.

'Heartbreak comes in many different forms, as does betrayal. I'm not blaming Sofia—in the end she had to be true to herself—but the marriage I thought I had was very different to the reality, and when the truth came out, it hurt. I loved my husband, I love Sofia in a different way, and in theory I want to stay friends and be supportive, but it's the hardest thing I've ever had to do. You're right, I did come here to escape. I needed a break. So, I know our situations are not exactly the same, but sweetheart, I do know what it feels like to think your life is going one way and suddenly have it switch directions without your consent.'

Her mother's words were so raw, so heartfelt, and her eyes were as watery as Zoe's. She looked at Flick properly for the first time since her parents had announced they were separating and saw a heartache that echoed her own. For once, she really took a moment to think about how her mum must have felt when Sofia came out. When it happened, Zoe had been more hung up on how it might affect her own life, and all her energies had been spent grappling with understanding and supporting Sofia, but now she saw the truth.

And she knew, *that's* why she came here. Not simply because when a girl is upset the first person she turns to is her mum, but because her mother would understand. Subconsciously, Zoe had known that all along.

'I'm sorry, Mum,' she sobbed, falling into Flick's open arms. 'I've really messed up, haven't I?'

'No, honey, Beau messed up. This is on him.' Flick held her close as she stroked her hair. 'But we're not going to let him ruin the rest of your life. Okay?'

Zoe managed a nod.

'Perhaps you need to see a counsellor or someone,' Flick suggested. 'If you can't talk to me, then maybe you can talk to someone else? It's got to be better than drowning your sorrows.'

'I'll think about it, but I promise I'm done with drinking. The way my head hurts right now, I don't think I'll ever feel like alcohol again.'

Flick laughed. 'Well, if you do, make sure you tell me, and we'll drink in moderation together.'

'Deal.' Zoe sniffed and Flick magically produced a box of tissues.

'Here.' While Zoe blew her nose, she added, 'And I may not be the world's greatest dancer, but if you need someone to go clubbing with, I'll give it a whirl.'

Now Zoe laughed too. 'Let's not get carried away.'

They hugged again and although Zoe knew she had a long way to go before she felt normal again, she no longer felt so alone.

A long shower and a couple of hours later, Zoe stood at the door to Jack's place and took a deep breath. She couldn't believe he lived so close, but maybe that was a good thing because it didn't give her time to chicken out.

You can do this. Apologies didn't have to be awkward, and Flick was right—she owed Jack more than just a shirt. Buying that had been the easy part. She clutched the parcel to her chest now as she summoned the courage to knock on the damn door.

It opened right in front of her before she'd succeeded, and there he was.

Maybe she was still a little intoxicated, but he seemed to get better looking every time she saw him. His dark shaggy hair was damp as if he'd just stepped out of the shower. He wore shiny black shoes, black dress trousers, another crisp white shirt, but also a black waistcoat and actual bow tie. He'd taken nerd to a whole other level, but on him it looked good.

'Well, hello there, Zoe,' he said, his gaze intense as usual and his smile more like a smirk. 'You're looking a little better than you did last night.'

It was hardly a compliment, but she took it anyway. 'Thank you.' She swallowed. 'Speaking of last night, I'm wondering if you have a moment?'

Jack glanced at his watch. 'About five. I'm working in the restaurant soon.'

Ah, so that accounted for the fancy dress. She almost asked him which restaurant, but that seemed like a delaying tactic. And what business was it of hers?

'Well.' She rubbed her lips together, her stomach twisting. 'I just wanted to thank you for helping Mum and Theo look for me last night. You didn't have to, and I certainly didn't make it pleasant, but I owe you one. If you hadn't seen that guy put something in my drink, I might be nursing more than a hangover today.'

'I'm just glad I turned up when I did.'

'Me too. And I'm sorry for using you as an alibi, roping you into my lies and ruining your shirt. Here—' She thrust the one she'd bought at him. 'It's not the same, but I hope you like it.'

Frowning slightly, Jack took the package and unwrapped it on the spot. He held the shirt up against him. It was black with little white ghosts that looked like Casper all over it.

'I know that's probably not what real ghosts look like, but ...'

He grinned. 'It's the thought that counts. Thanks. This is awesome. Where'd you find it?'

'Just at a boutique around the corner.'

'Well, you didn't have to do this, but I do appreciate it. To be honest, I'm kinda surprised you even remember what happened. You were pretty far gone.'

Zoe cringed. 'It came back in flashes. Mum's lecture helped. But I am truly sorry.'

'You don't have to keep saying that. We all have bad days and I get you're hurting, but I didn't realise how serious you were the other night.' He shoved his hands in his pockets and didn't quite meet her eye as he added, 'If you're still interested in hooking up, then—'

'What are you trying to say?'

'Only that ...' Jack cleared his throat. 'Only that if you're intent on sleeping with someone else because you think it might help ease your pain over your husband, then doing so with me has got to be safer than going out every night, getting drunk and picking up some random dude.'

Zoe didn't know whether to laugh or slap his face. 'Are you serious?'

'Don't get mad.' He shrugged and gave her a sheepish smile. 'It's just an offer. I'm trying to do you a favour here.'

'Oh my God. I won't sleep with you because you feel sorry for me. I'm not some charity case.' He couldn't actually find her attractive after witnessing her at her absolute worst last night. 'Besides, I've realised the error of my ways.'

Here she was thinking maybe they could be friends, but he clearly wasn't any better than Beau or the guy who'd tried to spike her drink last night.

'Zoe!' he called as she turned and started to storm away. 'I'm sorry. I didn't mean—'

'Go to hell, Jack!'

22

Felicity

Midafternoon, at the sound of the bell above the shop door, Flick looked up to see a woman enter. Her heart sank. She'd thought it might be Zoe and didn't have the energy to deal with anyone else. She shouldn't have bothered opening today. She'd barely spoken to anyone who'd walked in off the street, and although her work tools were spread out on the bench, she'd made next to no progress on her projects. It wasn't only that she was almost too tired to speak or think, but also that she'd been thinking too much. Alternating between worrying about Zoe, being thankful that Jack had found her when he did and wondering what would become of her and Theo now.

Of course, this led to the usual mother guilt—guilt that had begun the moment she'd found out she was pregnant with Zoe and she'd assumed would ease when her kids hit adulthood but showed no signs of doing any such thing. She shouldn't be worrying about her revived libido when Zoe's wellbeing and mental health clearly required her attention.

Flick sighed and rose to her feet, trying to summon some professional enthusiasm as the customer weaved through the exhibits towards her. Despite her advanced age and the frown lines nestled between her wiry white eyebrows, the woman could only be described as striking. Her pale hair fell in loose ringlets almost to her bottom, her wrists and fingers dripped with sparkly costume jewellery and she wore a long lacey cream dress. If she wasn't forty or fifty years older than the brides who'd invaded Bourbon Street last night, Flick would have assumed she was one of them, still out on the town.

'What are you gawking at?' snarled the woman, hugging a large patchwork bag to her chest.

Flick blinked. 'Um ... I ... nothing. Are you here to browse or can I help you with something specific?'

The woman narrowed her eyes. 'Where is Harvey?'

'Harvey's away for a few months visiting his sister,' Flick said, forcing a smile. 'I'm taking care of business for him. I'm Felicity Bell, and you are?'

'Aurelia Harranibar.'

What a mouthful. 'Are you a friend of Harvey's?'

'We are acquaintances. When you say taking care of business ... does that mean you too are a taxidermist?'

Flick nodded and Aurelia thrust the patchwork bag at her. 'Good. Then I guess you'll have to do. I need you to take care of Edward for me.'

Flick didn't need to ask who Edward was as her hands closed around the heavy bag. Having worked with dead animals for over twenty years, she could tell she was holding a cat, albeit a rather large, probably well-fed one. And it figured. If anyone looked like a crazy cat lady, it was this narky old woman with a fancy name to match her fancy dress.

Curiosity got the better of her and she took the bag over to the work bench and peered inside. A big Siamese cat looked up at her from glassy, bulging, pale blue eyes. Cold and stiff, rigor mortis had already set in.

Flick stroked her finger gently over its fur then looked back to Aurelia. 'I'm really sorry for your loss, but I'm not taking on any commissions while Harvey is away. However, he gave me the name of a couple of—'

'What do you mean you're not taking commissions? What's the point of you even being here if you're not working? And what's that?' she snapped, directing a long bony finger towards the baby alligator-in-progress.

Flick didn't owe her an explanation, but the poor woman was upset over the death of her pet. 'I'm here to keep the shop open and handle any sales, and I'm working on a couple of small projects of my own so that people who come in to browse can see taxidermy in progress.'

'Well, why don't you work on my beloved Edward instead?' Aurelia suggested.

Flick took a calming breath. 'I'm afraid that won't be possible—it would take at least two months to do a proper job on Edward and I might not have that long. However, Harvey did give me the name of a couple of other taxidermists who may be able to help you.'

'What do you mean you *might* not have that long?'

'Harvey's time away isn't set in stone and so I don't want to take on any jobs I might not be able to finish,' Flick replied as she went behind the desk. 'Besides, I don't actually do domestic animals.'

She brought the list up on the computer, printed it off and then handed the contacts to Aurelia.

Her scowl never wavering, the elderly woman held the list close to her face, scrutinised it and then thrust the paper back at Flick. 'No. These simply will not do. They're both miles away and I don't drive. It was effort enough to get here on the streetcar. This is where all my previous cats have been preserved and this is where Edward will be as well.'

Maybe if Aurelia had been a little more polite, Flick would have been more sympathetic and might have suggested keeping Edward here in the deep freeze while she checked with Harvey to see if he'd be willing to take on the commission when he returned. But after being up half the night dealing with Zoe vomiting, she was not in the mood for a customer who refused to listen. That the woman didn't travel wasn't *her* problem. Hadn't she heard of Uber?

'I'm sorry for your loss, but I can't help you,' she said, picking up the patchwork bag and handing it back. 'Do have a nice day, won't you?'

Aurelia harrumphed. 'I don't know where Harvey found you, but he will be horrified to hear how I've been treated with such disdain in his esteemed establishment.'

Without another word, the woman turned and stalked back towards the entrance, clutching the bag to her chest.

Just as she lifted her hand to open the door, it flung open.

What happened next happened so fast it was impossible to tell whether Aurelia had been hit by the door or Zoe had run into her. Either way the result was the same—an elderly woman sprawled on the floor, her patchwork bag flung off to one side, the tiger that usually stood guard on top of her, and Flick and Zoe gaping on in horror.

'Is she dead?' Zoe shrieked. 'Have I killed her?'

'Do I sound dead?' groaned Aurelia.

Zoe exhaled loudly and Flick sent a silent prayer of thanks to whoever might be listening. A death on her hands would be the icing on the cake of the last twenty-four hours' drama. Considering where they were, Aurelia would probably come back to haunt her!

'Well, don't just stand there,' came an irritated yet shaky voice from the floor. 'Would one of you imbeciles get this giant cat off me?'

Her words jolted Flick into action. 'Zoe, help me, quick.'

They carefully lifted the tiger off the older woman and put it to one side.

'I'm so sorry,' Flick said, crouching down on the floor beside her. 'How do you feel? Do you think you can get up? Can I help you?'

'Do you always ask such stupid questions? How do you think I feel? Like I was knocked over by a stupid girl and had a tiger land on me. But I'm tougher than I look.' She shooed Flick away and tried to push herself to her feet, but she yelped the moment she put pressure on her hand.

Zoe looked on helplessly. 'What's wrong?'

'Are you hurt?' Flick glanced at Aurelia's wrist and winced at the unnatural lump protruding.

'Another stupid question,' Aurelia spat, but Flick couldn't help noticing her eyes were glassy. Poor thing, she'd lost her cat and now this. Guilt swamped her.

'You're right, I'm sorry,' she said, much more tenderly than before. 'This is completely our fault.'

'Should we call an ambulance?' Zoe asked.

Flick nodded. 'Good idea.' Who knew what other kind of injuries Aurelia might have sustained in the fall? They probably shouldn't attempt to move her—she could have a concussion and her wrist clearly needed attention.

'I don't need an ambulance. The cost of them is outrageous,' she grumbled. 'I just need you to help me up and then I'll be on my way.'

'Call the ambulance,' Flick told Zoe, then spoke softly to Aurelia. 'I'll pay for it.' Fingers crossed it didn't completely break the bank. 'It's the least I can do. I'm fairly sure you've broken your wrist and I don't have a car to take you to the hospital, so try to relax and we'll get you whatever help you need.'

As Zoe made the call, Flick looked around for something soft to put under Aurelia's head. She went with a cushion from the sofa.

'Here.'

Miraculously, she let Flick lift her head and position the cushion under it. 'Is there anything else I can get you while we wait for the paramedics?'

Now cradling her bad wrist, Aurelia narrowed her eyes. 'Do you know that young woman?'

Flick nodded. 'She's my daughter.'

Aurelia snorted. 'That figures. You know I could sue you both for this.'

'I'm sure you could.' Flick thought of Theo; maybe she'd need him for more than friendship with benefits if Aurelia followed through on her threat. 'But in the meantime, can I get you a glass of water or anything?'

'They're on their way,' Zoe said, approaching again tentatively. 'Is she okay?'

'No thanks to you.' This from Aurelia.

'How long did they say they'd be?' Flick asked.

Zoe shrugged. 'The operator said they'd be here as soon as possible.'

'Can you go upstairs and get a glass of water and a blanket?' It had been a while since Flick had renewed her first-aid certificate, but she remembered you had to keep a person who was in shock warm. Although Aurelia didn't appear to be in shock, it couldn't hurt and

225

it would give Zoe something to do rather than stand there looking guilty.

'So,' Flick turned back to Aurelia as Zoe hurried upstairs, 'how long have you known Harvey?'

'Don't think distracting me with meaningless small talk will take my mind off suing you,' Aurelia barked.

'I wouldn't dare think anything of the sort.' Flick took a deep breath as she glanced out the window, willing an ambulance to appear.

Zoe returned a few moments later, panting from running up and down the stairs. She handed Flick the water and the blanket but kept at a distance.

'Would you like me to help you try and sit up a little so you can have a drink?' Flick said as she covered Aurelia with the blanket.

'I am a little thirsty.'

'Can you grab another cushion?' Flick asked Zoe.

Aurelia winced as they positioned another cushion under her head, but managed to drink a few sips of water before letting out a big sigh. The most awkward silence followed for what felt like hours until finally, *thank the Lord*, they heard the sound of a siren clearing the way outside.

'Zoe, go meet them,' Flick ordered.

Less than a minute later an ambulance pulled up in front of the shop and Flick was relieved to see a man and a woman dressed in navy-blue uniforms leap from the front. They exchanged a few brief words with Zoe before entering the shop.

'Well, what have we here?' said the younger of the two paramedics, kneeling on the floor next to Aurelia. He had short-cropped brown hair, big ears and a sunny smile that lit up his whole face. 'I'm Riley, and it looks like today's my lucky day—I don't usually get such gorgeous patients. What's your name?'

'Never you mind my name, just get me up off this floor.'

Riley chuckled. 'Yes, ma'am, I'm going to do exactly that, but first I just need to do a couple of quick checks, okay?'

Aurelia sighed loudly. 'Why are you still talking? Do what it is you need to do and then get me out of here.'

'Friendly, isn't she?' said the other paramedic to Flick and Zoe. She introduced herself as Mabel and asked them what had happened, before dropping down next to her colleague to assist.

They checked her blood pressure and other vital signs, and where Riley had failed to get Aurelia to answer any questions, Mabel mostly succeeded. When they were satisfied the only real damage was to her wrist, they strapped it up and secured it with a sling, explaining this was only a temporary measure until they got her to the ER.

They eased Aurelia up into a sitting position and while Riley supported her, Mabel went out to the van to get the gurney. Zoe held open the door, but it was Theo who appeared first.

'Is everything okay here? I saw the ambulance and—' He stopped as his gaze dropped to the floor. 'Miss H?' he exclaimed, rushing over. 'What on earth have you done to yourself?'

'Theodore,' she replied with very little emotion.

'Is there anyone you don't know in New Orleans?' Flick asked, as Mabel wheeled in the gurney and Theo stepped back to let her through.

He laughed. 'Almost everyone, but I've told you about Miss H before. She lived next door to me when I was married.'

'*She's* the one who does the skeleton brides?' Flick said.

'You mean the picture upstairs?' asked Zoe. 'Wow.' She looked over to where Riley and Mabel were lifting Aurelia on to the gurney, new-found awe in her tone. 'I love that painting.'

Flick humphed.

'I do too.' Theo sounded bemused. 'Anyway, what exactly happened here?'

Flick gave him a condensed version as the three of them followed the paramedics out onto the street. A crowd had already gathered near the ambulance, but once they saw it was merely an elderly lady with a bandaged wrist, they dispersed quickly.

'Does she have any family?' Flick asked Theo as Aurelia was loaded into the back of the van.

'Not that I know of. I don't think she had any visitors in the twenty or so years I lived next door.'

'Maybe I should go with her?' Flick said. No matter how rude the woman was, no one deserved to be alone in such circumstances.

Theo nodded. 'I can follow the van and meet you there.'

Flick peered into the ambulance where Riley and Mabel were settling Aurelia and securing the stretcher. 'Can I come with her?'

Before either of them could answer, the patient spoke. 'If anyone's coming with me, I want the younger one.'

Flick turned to look at Zoe.

She shrugged. 'If that's what she wants.'

'Are you sure?' Flick asked. Zoe wasn't in a good place and might not be able to handle the older woman. Then again, perhaps if they went along with her wishes, she'd be less likely to sue them. Flick wasn't sure whether Aurelia actually had grounds to do so, but it couldn't hurt to try and get her on side.

'Yes,' Zoe said, much more firmly this time. 'I'll do it.'

After a brief discussion, it was decided that Theo and Flick would follow the ambulance to the hospital. Zoe kissed Flick on the cheek then climbed into the back of the van.

Just as Mabel was closing the doors, Aurelia called out. 'What about Edward?'

Everyone looked confused except Flick, who thought of the dead cat lying on the floor in the patchwork bag. 'I'll take care of him,' she promised.

'Good,' came Aurelia's voice from inside the ambulance.

Flick released a breath as the lights on the ambulance flashed and it started off down the street. 'I hope she's okay.'

'Who? Aurelia or Zoe?' Theo said with a chuckle as he pulled her into his side and kissed her on the head.

Flick took a moment just to lean into him and take the comfort he offered. In the short time they'd known each other, there'd been a few occasions that she'd been happy he lived next door, but was she relying on him too much? She didn't think the definition of 'fling' included either this or last night's kind of drama.

'Thanks for offering to come to the hospital,' she said, pulling away a little, 'but I can get an Uber just as easily.'

He frowned down at her. 'And why would you do that when I have a perfectly good car?'

'This isn't your problem, and you have your own business to worry about.' She gestured towards the bar.

'It's fine. Cooper and Roxy are there and I'm not rostered on to play until tonight anyway. I'm happy to help. I've got a bit of a soft spot for Miss H myself. It'll be good to make sure she's okay.'

Flick couldn't help bristling at the mention of Roxy and the recollection of the younger woman's words last night.

'Is something else bothering you?' he asked, touching her arm gently.

'Have you slept with Roxy?' The words spilled out almost of their own accord and she regretted them the moment they did. What business was it of hers?

'What?' His head snapped back and his hand dropped to his side. 'Why would you think that?'

'I ... it's ... just something she said.'

Theo's thick eyebrows crept upwards and his lips twitched—she couldn't tell if he was amused or annoyed. 'I'm not gonna lie, I haven't been a monk since my divorce, but no way would I cross that line with one of my employees.'

'Okay.' Flick swallowed. 'It doesn't matter anyway. You can sleep with whoever you like. I better go close up the shop or they'll have discharged Aurelia and we'll be still here on the pavement.'

But Theo didn't seem in a rush to make a move. And he was definitely smiling now. 'You weren't jealous of Roxy, were you?'

'What? No.' Heat flooded her cheeks and she couldn't meet his gaze. 'I was just ... curious.'

Theo touched her chin and forced her eyes up to his. 'Good,' he whispered, 'because you, Felicity, have nothing to be jealous about, and right now, I'm not interested in sleeping with anyone but you.'

And then he kissed her right there on the pavement in front of the shop and pretty much all the tension of the last twenty-four hours evaporated.

'I've got to deal with a dead cat before we go,' she said, forcing herself to pull away.

Theo nodded. 'Okay. You do what you have to do. I'll just let Roxy and Cooper know what's happening. Come get me when you're ready.'

Flick went back inside, locked the door behind her, switched the sign to closed and then picked up the patchwork bag containing poor Edward and took him out the back to the deep freeze. Then, she scribbled a note on a scrap of paper—*Closed for emergency. Back soon*—and stuck it on the door.

23

Zoe

Zoe buckled herself into the seat across from where the skeleton bride artist lay flat on the gurney. The woman barked complaints at Riley, the paramedic, as he tried to make her comfortable.

'Careful. Where did you get your qualifications? On the world wide web?'

Zoe bit her lip—she hadn't heard anyone refer to the internet this way since she was a kid. To Riley's credit, he took everything she said on the chin, his smile never wavering. He probably had all sorts of difficult patients in this job.

Zoe tried not to stare as they started off down the street, but she couldn't take her eyes off this woman. Although about the same age as her grandmother on her dad's side—Flick's mum had died long before Zoe was born—she didn't look grandmotherly in the slightest. Her dress was actually a little like the one in her painting, her skin pale as if she didn't see daylight very often and her hair almost doll like. Thin and petite but not exactly frail, she was unlike anyone Zoe had ever met before and she couldn't help being intrigued. If not also a little daunted.

'Is that a South African accent?' asked Riley, interrupting her thoughts.

'Huh?' She stirred. 'No. Aussie.'

'Ah, right. I've always wanted to go to Australia. Are you here on holiday?'

'Kind of.' Zoe hoped her short answers would give him the hint she wasn't in the mood for talking, not to him anyway. She was done with men—whether they were cute and in uniform or not—and shouldn't his attentions be on his patient? Peering around him, she worked up the courage to address the woman. 'We didn't meet properly before. I'm Zoe Bell,' she said, deciding in that moment to go back to her maiden name. She liked it better than Thompson anyway.

'Aurelia Harranibar, but you can call me *Miss* Harranibar.' She spoke as if she were the queen, asking Zoe to address her as Her Majesty.

'Okay, Miss Harranibar. Look, I just wanted to say how incredibly sorry I am for what happened back there at the shop. I know this is no excuse, but I've had a crap couple of weeks, and I'd just had a run-in with someone I thought might be a friend and—'

'Good God, girl. Do you always talk this much?'

'No, Miss Harrin ...' *Oh shit*, she'd already forgotten that tongue-twister of a name. 'Only when I'm nervous or feeling guilty.'

The woman actually chuckled. 'I like your honesty. Apology accepted. Let's agree not to mention it again.'

'Deal.' Zoe nodded, relaxing back into her seat. 'How long is it to the hospital?' she asked Riley.

'Ten to fifteen minutes, depending on the traffic. So, have you seen many of the sights yet?'

Pretending she didn't hear his question, Zoe addressed Miss Whatever-her-name-was again. Perhaps she could distract her from the pain she must be in. 'You're an incredible artist,' she said. 'Can I ask what inspires you?'

'You've seen my paintings?' For the first time, the woman looked less than sure of herself.

'Yes. Well, one of them. It's upstairs above the taxidermy shop. I love it.'

'Oh, that's right, I gave that to Harvey a few years ago as payment for Louisa.'

'Louisa?'

'My dearly departed baby.'

Baby? Zoe and Riley exchanged a look of alarm as the woman let out a gut-wrenching sob and pressed her good hand against her heart. 'Harvey preserved her for me. First Louisa and now Edward. I've only got Charlotte left.'

'Oh, right.' *Of course*, Louisa must be a pet. But wow, taxidermy didn't come cheap, which confirmed what Zoe had suspected—her paintings must be worth a pretty penny. She gave a sympathetic smile. 'I'm sorry for your loss.'

Miss Whatever sniffed and Riley offered her a tissue.

'Are you interested in art, then?' she asked, wiping her eye.

'More than interested. It's my life. I did art at uni and used to work for an art curator. I paint and draw myself.' Zoe blushed. 'Nothing as amazing as yours, of course.'

'Don't put yourself down, child. What do you like to paint?'

'I love naive art or primitivism, mostly. A lot of my work is of places I love.' She thought of Beau's parents' painting sitting unfinished back in Perth and felt a lump form in her throat.

'What's naive art?' asked Riley.

Zoe had almost forgotten he was there. 'Um …' She shook her in-laws from her head. 'It's simple, unsophisticated—you know, like a kid could have done it, only it looks amazing.'

He quirked an eyebrow.

'It's hard to describe. You really have to see it. Google Henri Rousseau, he's one of the best-known artists in the naive syle.'

'Will do,' Riley said as Zoe turned back to Miss Whatever.

'I've also been experimenting a bit with mixed media lately.'

'I don't mind mixing media myself. If I recall, that painting I gave Harvey was done in oils, but I use whatever takes my fancy at the time. Pastels, water colour, pencil, acrylics.'

'Do you always paint such gothic images?'

'I paint what I feel.' She glanced down at her sling. 'Although I don't suppose I'll be able to paint much of anything for a while. Or do much of anything. I'm right-handed, you know.'

Zoe winced. 'I'm so sorry about that.'

'What did I tell you about apologising?'

'So—' Zoe swallowed the word and the two of them shared a smile.

'Why've your last few weeks been so awful?'

'That's a very long and boring story.' One that Zoe definitely wasn't quite ready to share with strangers.

'Let me guess, it involves a man?'

Zoe nodded, trying to ignore the sticky knot of emotion that squeezed in her stomach whenever she thought of Beau.

'Chin up, darling, it happens to the best of us. But you've got to keep on going or they win. Focus on your art is my advice. Art can't break your heart the way men can.'

Zoe wanted to ask who and how they'd broken Miss Whatever's heart, but before she could decide whether that was too forward,

Riley cleared his throat. 'Sorry to break up the conversation,' he said tentatively, 'but we're here.'

The ambulance came to a stop, the back doors opened and Mabel appeared again. Zoe stepped out of the way to allow the two paramedics to do their thing while she took in her surroundings. After her time in the French Quarter, surrounded by quaint and colourful architecture, the hospital's plainness surprised her, but then again, what it did was more important than what it looked like.

Riley and Mabel wheeled Miss Whatever out of the van and over to the entrance, where automatic doors whooshed open and they were immediately greeted by a tall woman in scrubs. The medical professionals briefly exchanged words and Zoe, feeling like a spare part, followed them into the building.

She hadn't been inside many hospitals in her life, but it felt like the set of every American medical TV drama she'd ever watched—during uni when she'd been working late, old shows like *ER*, *House*, *Scrubs* and *Grey's Anatomy* had been her comfort viewing. There were bright fluorescent lights overhead, people rushing in every direction, the beeping of machines and paging of announcements overhead. And all this was strangely comforting. Thank you, Netflix.

'Are you the next-of-kin?' asked a man with a clipboard who appeared from nowhere.

'Um ...' Zoe twisted the strap of her bag between her fingers.

'Yes, she is,' said Miss Whatever from the gurney, and Zoe was not about to argue.

'Great. I'll just take your details, then you'll have to stay in the waiting area while we assess Miss Harranibar.'

After taking down her name and number, he pointed to some double doors. 'Someone will come and give you an update as soon as possible. But grab a coffee, it could be a while.'

'Okay.' Zoe squeezed her new friend's good hand. Her skin felt papery soft and there was a vulnerability in her eyes she was clearly trying to hide. 'You'll be fine and I'm not going anywhere. I'll see you soon.'

'Thank you, dear.'

As they wheeled her away, Zoe wandered out through the double doors into a large waiting area. There were people scattered throughout—some staring vacantly at a TV, some chatting in hushed voices, and the rest scrolling on their phones.

Zoe got herself a cup of coffee—if you could call it that—and a chocolate bar from one of the machines, flopped down into a seat and got out her phone. She stared at the screen, deliberating whether to punish herself yet again. It had been a few days since she'd stalked her ex-husband online, but sitting here now, the temptation to check his socials again was strong. Her finger wavered over the search function on Facebook, but no good could come from such torture. She'd call her mum and see how far off she and Theo were instead.

But before she could, her phone started to ring. She didn't recognise the number flashing up at her. *Weird.* The only person she knew here was Jack and they hadn't exchanged numbers. Maybe it was Flick calling from Theo's phone for some reason.

'Hello?'

'Is that Zoe Bell?' asked a guy with a very strong southern drawl.

'Who wants to know?'

'My name's Tyler and I'm calling to let you know you've won the Casket Brides Fancy Dress contest. Congratulations.'

'Oh my God! Seriously?' Finally, something had gone her way.

Tyler laughed. 'Seriously.' He named the bar that organised the pub crawl, told her she could come collect her prize money whenever suited her, then hung up.

It was all Zoe could do not to leap from her seat and do a happy dance around the waiting room but, considering the solemn faces of almost everyone there, she contained herself.

'What are you looking so happy about?'

She glanced up to see her mum and Theo standing in front of her. They weren't holding hands, but they were standing so close they may as well have been, and Theo had the telltale sign of a lipstick smudge at the side of his mouth that exactly matched the only colour Flick ever wore. It was weird seeing her mum with someone else and Zoe couldn't help worrying. It wasn't that she didn't want her to be happy—she agreed with Emma and Neve that Flick needed to come out of hibernation—but either things would get serious between them and she might consider a permanent move across the world, or they'd end, perhaps badly, and her mum would be back to square one again. Zoe had little faith in men right now and if Theo hurt her mum, she'd personally make his life a living hell.

Of course, she tried not to let any of this show on her face— the man had driven Flick here so perhaps Zoe could be a tiny bit gracious.

'I won,' she said instead, still trying to keep her voice down despite her excitement.

'Won what?' Flick asked.

'The Casket Brides contest—I just found out they picked my dress as the winner.'

'Wow.' Flick dropped onto the seat next to Zoe and pulled her into a hug. 'That's awesome news. Congratulations, sweetheart. I'm so happy for you.'

'Congratulations,' echoed Theo.

'Thanks.'

'Any ideas what you're going to do with the prize money?' Flick said.

'No. Put it in the bank to start with. And I know I've been bludging off you, so I'll pay you some rent or something while I'm here as well.'

'Don't worry about that. As long as you promise you'll spend it wisely.' Flick didn't say exactly what that meant, but Zoe knew— her mum didn't want her to waste it on tools for self-destruction. 'And help out by cooking a few meals and cleaning up a bit, then that's payment enough. I think it's a good idea to take some time to work out where you want to go from here. Anyway, how's Aurelia?'

Zoe blinked; already accustomed to thinking of her as Miss Whatever, she'd totally forgotten the older woman's real name. 'Oh, she's being seen to now. She's quite a character.'

Theo chuckled and lowered himself into the seat next to Flick. 'That's for sure.'

'How exactly do you know her?'

'We used to be neighbours. She lives in an old decrepit house in the Garden District—she's a bit of a local legend around there.'

'Because of her art?'

He nodded. 'Partly, yes, but more so because of her eccentric nature. She keeps to herself mostly, going out only to shop, eat or do business with local art galleries. Story goes her fiancé left her at the altar fifty-odd years ago and she's never properly recovered. She always wears white and apparently hasn't cut her hair since.'

'Surely not.' Flick touched her own long hair. 'That's tragic. It's right out of Dickens's novel.'

'*Great Expectations*?' breathed Zoe. 'We had to read that in Year Twelve. I hated it.'

But there was Zoe's answer to how Aurelia's heart had been broken and it made her own heart ache all over again. She blinked rapidly as tears pooled in her eyes. To be jilted on your wedding day had to be one of life's cruellest blows. A day that was supposed to be joyous and magical transformed into an absolute nightmare. The sadness of rejection mixed with shame and public humiliation, everyone talking about you, everyone feeling sorry for you.

Her own heartbreak fresh, raw and mortifying, Zoe didn't blame Aurelia for becoming a little eccentric. At least Miss Whatever had channelled her affliction into something amazing. 'So that's why she paints skeleton brides?'

'I guess so,' said Theo. 'Tourists would love them no matter what because they're gothic and ghoulish, but when they hear the tragic story of the artist, they love them even more.'

'Do you know if she only sells the paintings around here? I've never heard of her or seen her work before. And that's crazy—if all her paintings are as good as the one at Harvey's place, she deserves wider recognition.'

'Sorry.' Theo shrugged. 'I've no idea.'

'Well, although I do feel sorry for her,' said Flick, 'I have to say fifty years is a long time to hold onto such unhappiness. She seemed a rather difficult person and I'm sorry you had to deal with her today, Zoe. But I'm proud of you for stepping up.'

'She's actually not that bad. I like her, and I think she likes me too.'

Flick raised her eyebrows. 'Well, as long as you're okay, that can only be a good thing. Maybe she won't sue us after all.'

'What?!' said Zoe and Theo in unison.

Flick explained what Miss Whatever had threatened and, after Theo assuring them that nothing would likely come of it and he would help if it did, conversation turned to what would happen next.

'She named me as her next-of-kin.' A role Zoe planned to take very seriously. 'But you guys don't have to wait around. I'm fine. I can make my way back later once I've made sure she's okay.'

'No.' Flick refused to leave Zoe alone and Theo didn't seem too eager to leave either. They agreed the three of them would wait to hear what was happening to Miss H (as Theo called her) before making any decisions.

'If she's okay to go home today,' he said, 'I can drive her.'

Decision made, more weak coffees were bought from the vending machine and the three of them sat there making surprisingly comfortable conversation. Zoe had to concede, Theo didn't seem too bad. He was clearly smitten with Flick, but they never once made Zoe feel like the third wheel. He asked her lots of questions about herself—mostly about her art, sensitively steering clear of her reason for joining her mum in New Orleans—and she reciprocated by showing interest in the bar and his music. She'd never had any interest in jazz, but he actually made it sound appealing.

After about an hour, the doors to emergency opened and a short stocky man in scrubs walked out, pushing Miss H in a wheelchair.

Zoe shot to her feet and rushed over, Flick and Theo at her heels.

'How are you?' she gushed, her eyes drawn to the fresh white cast on the elderly woman's forearm.

'I'll be better when I get out of here. I told this bozo I could get a cab, but he refuses to discharge me until he's satisfied I have someone to take care of me.'

'That's me,' Zoe said, smiling at the doctor or nurse or whatever he was. 'And Theo here is going to drive us home. Is there anything we need to know before we go?'

'Miss Harranibar has suffered a fracture to her wrist. Considering her age, she's lucky it wasn't a lot worse. We've prescribed some stronger painkillers.' He gestured to a paper bag in her lap. 'And we've made an appointment for a check-up in a month's time.'

240

After a few more instructions, Zoe signed the discharge papers—which, under the circumstances, Miss H couldn't do—and then they were dismissed.

'You can drop the wheelchair back at reception once you've taken her to the car,' said the man.

'Wheelchair?!' Miss H pushed to a stand, using her good arm to assist. 'I don't need a wheelchair. I've broken my wrist, not my feet.'

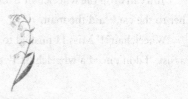

24

Felicity

'Here, let me carry your bag,' Zoe offered as Aurelia marched away.

She paused to hand her things over and then patted Zoe's hand. 'Thank you, dear. I just hate hospitals.'

'Don't we all,' Flick said, trying for a sympathetic smile. Despite Theo's assurances that she wouldn't sue them, you could never be too careful.

Aurelia didn't even acknowledge her as she slipped her arm through Zoe's.

'I'll go get the car and bring it round to the front entrance,' Theo said, surreptitiously squeezing Flick's hand as he told them where to meet him.

He was such a kind, sweet man, and she couldn't help being glad that he'd insisted on coming with her. When she and the others emerged from the hospital a few minutes later, he was already pulling up against the kerb.

After assisting Miss H into the front of his car, Theo tried to make conversation as they turned out of the hospital and into the traffic, but Aurelia closed her eyes, sighed dramatically and leaned her head back against the seat as if too exhausted to speak.

As they passed through the clearly trendy Warehouse District, Theo pointed out a number of art galleries and museums. Zoe leaned out the window, trying to take photos of murals on buildings with her phone.

'Careful,' Flick warned, worried her arm might get swiped by the streetcars that clattered up and down the middle of St Charles Avenue.

Before long the large brick buildings and converted warehouses gave way to massive houses and huge trees—'live oaks' according to Theo—on either side of the road.

'Welcome to the Garden District,' he said as he turned off the main road into the suburb proper, where trees formed a canopy almost right across the road. Light flickered between the branches, painting a pretty pattern on the bitumen, but it was the houses nestled in deep green immaculate gardens that took Flick's breath away.

They were simply magnificent. All at least two to three storeys with grand frontages, some were painted in bright colours but many of them were white with elegant Greek Revival columns. The streetlights were tall, iconic black gas lamps, the flame still flickering in some despite the time of the day. The whole street looked like a movie set.

'Oh my goodness, this place is gorgeous.' Zoe gaped out the window, snapping more photos on her phone. 'Sofia would be in heaven here.'

Flick stiffened at the mention of her ex—she'd been thinking the same thing but didn't want to talk about Sofia right now.

'What's that stuff growing from the branches,' she asked Theo, pointing at what looked like silver-grey threads hanging in the trees in the hope of changing the subject.

'Spanish moss. It grows like weeds round here but actually doesn't harm the trees.'

'It looks a little creepy.' Zoe sounded delighted.

Theo chuckled. 'The allure of New Orleans—beautiful *and* creepy at the same time.'

He turned into another street and immediately slowed in front of the corner house. 'Here we are, home sweet home, Miss H.'

As the older woman slowly opened her eyes, Flick tried not to grimace at the sight of the house. Her father always said you should buy the worst house in the best street, but this was taking it to extremes. Decrepit was the first word that came to mind as she stared at the dusty pink monstrosity, its exterior paint peeling. It had been a grand home once—a three-storey gingerbread house with a dark grey roof and fine white cast-iron lattice work, now rusted, around the verandahs. Faded curtains billowed like sad clouds in the tall windows, while two attic portals overlooked the street. Flick felt the sadness that seemed to have settled on the old mansion, as if it was caught in a memory it could never shake.

Where many of the other houses had been more beautiful than creepy, here the scales tipped the other way. The overgrown garden crawling up the porch posts to take over the house and a once-majestic three-tiered fountain in total disrepair only added to the foreboding.

Theo leapt out of the car and rushed around to help Aurelia who grumbled a little, but he smiled sweetly and did it anyway. Flick understood why she needed help—it looked as if an earthquake had torn up the pavement. Jagged slabs of concrete stuck out at all directions, thanks to the roots of the massive oaks pushing up from underneath.

How could a street with such grand houses have such a deadly footpath? This would never fly in Australia. It was an accident waiting to happen, and the last thing they needed was Aurelia falling again and breaking something else.

'What's with all the cracks?' Zoe asked as Theo guided the older woman towards the front gate, helping her navigate the hazards. 'Isn't there a council or something that fixes things like this? What if someone falls and sues them?'

'People round here are used to it, but folks on walking tours do occasionally hurt themselves,' Theo said. 'One fell badly a few years ago and tried to sue, but the city counter-sued for damage to the oaks, which are a protected species.'

Zoe laughed but Flick shook her head. Sure, the trees were magnificent but there must be something they could do to keep both the people and the grand old oaks safe.

Wanting to get Aurelia into the safety of her own house as soon as possible, Flick rushed ahead to the cast-iron gate. It creaked and groaned as she opened it, as if lamenting their arrival, but before any of them could go through, a high-pitched voice called from the garden next door.

'Theo? Is that you?'

Flick turned to see a woman in a knee-length black pencil skirt and colourful geometric blouse, her ridiculously high heels click-clacking on the pavement as she approached. Flick would be terrified one of the heels would catch in a crack, not that she ever wore shoes like that, but this woman strode towards them as if the path wouldn't dare mess with her.

'Rachel,' Theo exclaimed, kissing the woman on the cheek.

Although his tone was cool, Flick felt a stab of jealousy and immediately berated herself for it. Was this Theo's ex-wife?

'What are you doing here?' Rachel asked, her gaze jumping from him to rest briefly on Aurelia. 'Oh my goodness, what have you done to yourself?'

'I've gone and broken my wrist,' she sniffed.

'I see.' Rachel turned to look at Zoe and then her gaze finally landed on Flick. Salon-perfect champagne waves cascaded around her chin, but that was where her softness ended. She made no effort to hide her distaste as she looked Flick up and down, taking in her work pants, sensible dark T-shirt and long hair tied back off her face. 'And who are you two?'

'This is Felicity and her daughter Zoe,' Theo said. 'Felicity is working in the taxidermy shop next door to the bar. That's where Miss H fell and hurt herself.'

It wasn't like Flick expected him to announce he was sleeping with her, but it irked her that he introduced them as neighbours, rather than friends.

'Ah, so you're a taxidermist?' Rachel nodded as if this explained a lot.

'Yes. And you are?' Flick refused to be intimidated or made to feel less by this woman and her immaculately manicured nails.

'I'm sorry,' Theo interjected. 'This is Rachel, my ex-wife. She lives next door.'

Flick glanced over at the adjacent house, which was as tall, pale and sophisticated as the woman herself. She could only imagine how disgusted Theo's ex must feel to have her pristine white home and garden sitting alongside Aurelia's.

'Anyway, I don't have time to stay and chat,' Rachel announced. 'I just ran home to get some paperwork, but I have a meeting back at the office.'

Considering she lived next door, Flick thought she might offer to check in on Aurelia, or at least tell her to call if she needed anything, but Rachel did no such thing. She waved her hand in the air, then turned on her heel and hurried off without so much as a proper goodbye to any of them.

How could Theo, who was always so warm and charming, have spent so long married to this cold fish of a woman? Flick thanked the Lord her own ex was a genuinely nice person.

She turned back and held the gate open for the others. Aurelia shook off Theo's assistance as they entered her garden—which would be impressive if weeds were prized—and they followed her along the overgrown path and up three rickety steps onto the porch.

'My bag, please,' Aurelia barked at Zoe. 'I need the key.'

Zoe held it out as the older woman dug inside with her good hand. Flick was beginning to wonder if they'd be waiting all day when Aurelia finally held up a rusty, old-fashioned key, like a magician having conjured a rabbit.

'I *suppose* I should invite you all in for a drink,' she said, not sounding at all enamoured with the idea. Were all the women who lived on this street so unpleasant?

Although curious to stickybeak inside, Flick was about to tell Aurelia not to put herself out—she should be getting back to the shop anyway—but Theo answered first.

'Not necessary at all, but we'll just see you settled before we go,' he said, proving himself to be a much better person than Flick.

Taking the key from Aurelia, he slipped it into the lock and had the door open before she could complain or insist on trying to do it herself. With a slight huff, she tramped inside and they followed her into a vast entrance hall.

Goodness, Flick thought, glancing around—surely Aurelia couldn't live all alone in this massive place? It was like an overgrown doll's house that had been abandoned sometime in the last century. Paint flaked on the walls and the stair railing looked as if it would give you a splinter. Just as Rachel's house reflected her appearance, this one reflected Aurelia, but it was hard to tell whether the house had given up on the woman or the woman on the house. A tarnished chandelier hung above their heads, cobwebs clinging to it and the corners of the high, ornate plaster-moulded ceilings. Trying not to look obviously nosy, Flick peered into what must be a living room filled with antique furniture, a grand piano in the corner that if cleaned up a bit could fetch a nice price. On the far wall, a row of stuffed cats sat in pride of place on top of the impressive mantlepiece.

'Well, don't just stand there,' their host ordered, 'come through to the kitchen and I'll get you that drink.'

'Maybe you should sit down, and we can get you a drink and anything else you need to make you comfortable?' Flick suggested.

Ignoring her, Aurelia turned and led them further into the house, down a long hallway and into a kitchen, which although spacious, was as gloomy and oppressive as the rest of the place. A musty smell lingered and, fighting the urge to turn on a light and open a window, Flick shivered. These old houses were clearly built to withstand the extreme heat of the region, but this one could do with a blast of warm air from outside.

Aurelia pointed at a small wooden table on one side of the room. 'Sit. I've got whiskey or coffee, but no milk. And no cookies or anything either.' Her tone dared them to complain.

'I'd love a coffee, thanks,' Flick said, trying for friendly. Perhaps in her own home, Aurelia would feel safer, and would maybe even relax and thaw a little.

'Me too,' added Theo and Zoe.

'Can I give you a hand?' Flick offered again.

'I can manage,' Aurelia replied as a cat waltzed into the kitchen. It was almost identical to the one she'd brought into the shop that morning, except smaller.

Until this moment, Flick didn't think cats could actually scowl but there was no other word for the way this one looked at the intruders.

'Oh, Charlotte, my beautiful baby,' Aurelia cooed, stooping slightly and rubbing her good hand over its sleek fur. 'Did you wonder where Mummy was? It's okay, baby, I'm back.'

Aurelia spent a good few minutes bestowing affection on Charlotte while the others looked on. Flick almost felt as if they were intruding on an intimate moment. She took a step towards the window, chancing a look into the backyard, which was as overgrown as the front. Suddenly a breeze tickled her skin and she looked around. Maybe there was a window open somewhere after all?

'What are you frowning at?' Aurelia accused, choosing that moment to tear herself from the cat.

'Nothing.' Flick smiled. 'Just admiring your lovely home.'

Aurelia scowled in much the same way as the cat, then clumsily went through the motions of making coffee in a very ancient-looking plunger. Flick's grandmother had had something similar back in the eighties that she regularly used when entertaining—something Flick was pretty certain Aurelia rarely did.

While the coffee brewed, the older woman found four mugs in three different cupboards and lined them up on the counter next to the plunger. Flick tried not to grimace at the thought they could probably all do with a good wash. *A bit of dirt won't kill you.*

Slowly the nutty, mouth-watering aroma of fresh coffee began to dilute the staid air and when it was ready Aurelia lifted the jug with her left hand and attempted to pour. She missed the first mug entirely and as coffee splashed onto the bench, Flick swore she heard a curse word muttered under the older woman's breath. Still, she didn't dare offer assistance.

'Here, let me,' Zoe said softly, getting up from her seat. She gently pried the plunger from Aurelia's shaky hand.

Flick braced herself for an altercation, but miraculously Aurelia smiled. Until then she hadn't even been sure the woman's facial muscles were capable of such contortion.

'Thank you. I guess I'll get used to this one-handed business soon enough.'

Once Zoe had finished pouring the coffee and wiped up the spill, they all took a seat. Charlotte leapt up and sat on the table near Aurelia who didn't bat an eyelid. Almost in unison, they lifted their mugs to their lips—to Flick's surprise and relief it tasted a lot better than she'd expected. Or maybe she was simply in dire need of caffeine?

After a few long minutes, Flick could stand the awkward silence no longer. 'How long have you lived here, Miss Harranibar?'

'I was born upstairs in the master bedroom.'

'How wonderful. Has the house been in your family for a few generations?'

Aurelia nodded, giving no encouragement whatsoever.

It felt like trying to make small talk with a brick wall, but Flick liked a challenge, so she persevered, and Theo and Zoe chimed in as well. After a few more questions, either Aurelia began to let her guard down or decided conversing like a normal person wasn't that painful after all. Her answers became longer and more revealing and the four of them had what Flick would almost class a pleasant conversation.

They learnt that Aurelia had grown up in the Garden District and gone to the posh girls' school just down the road where Theo's sister now taught. Art had been her favourite subject and as an adult, she'd briefly worked there as a teacher herself. She didn't have any siblings and had inherited the house from her physician father, who had died of a heart attack just over fifty years ago.

When Zoe asked about her mother, she told them she'd never known her as she'd fallen ill not long after Aurelia was born and died in hospital. 'Cancer, I think. My father didn't like to talk about her.'

There was no mention of the fiancé Theo had told them about, or of any friends. Aurelia did speak of acquaintances—mostly gallery owners who sold her art—but gave the impression these were purely professional relationships.

Flick couldn't help feeling sorry for her lonely existence— although she'd craved a little solitude over the last few years, she couldn't imagine life without Zoe and Toby, Emma and Neve. She began to feel somewhat anxious about leaving Aurelia. Even though she'd fallen in the shop, she wasn't their responsibility, but how could they leave her to fend for herself in good conscience, when even pouring coffee had proven almost impossible?

Flick had visions of the woman wasting away because she couldn't buy groceries or cook for herself. And what about personal hygiene?

'Is there anyone who can come help you?' she asked. 'Did the hospital mention anything about a visiting nurse?'

'Someone's calling me in the morning to discuss possible assistance.' Aurelia's tone conveyed her displeasure at the thought, but the news eased the tension in Flick's chest.

'That's great,' she said enthusiastically. 'You should take whatever's on offer.'

'You know,' Zoe piped up, 'I'd be happy to help in any way I can as well. I could come over and do any jobs you need. Maybe shop for you, cook some meals, do some cleaning?'

'That's a very kind offer,' said Aurelia, 'but I'm sure a lovely young thing like you has much better things to do with your time than being cooped up here with an invalid.'

Zoe shrugged. 'As you said before, you're not an invalid, you've just hurt your wrist. And it isn't like I've got anything else to do at the moment anyway.'

'Well, if you insist,' said Aurelia, still stroking Charlotte, who was purring loudly. 'That sounds agreeable. I could even pay you for your time.'

'Oh no.' Zoe shook her head. 'That's not necessary, but I'd love to learn more about your art if you're willing to share.'

Aurelia offered her hand to Zoe. 'You, my dear, have yourself a deal.'

Grinning, Zoe accepted the handshake, which was more of a squeeze because Aurelia had to use her left hand. Zoe's offer surprised Flick, but maybe she too felt guilty about her part in Aurelia's accident? And maybe it wasn't such a bad arrangement? Hopefully becoming a companion of sorts would put paid to Aurelia's thoughts of suing them and it would also keep Zoe out of mischief for a bit.

'That's settled then,' Zoe said, smiling.

Soon Aurelia announced, 'I need a lie down,' which Flick guessed was her *almost* polite way of telling them she wanted to be left alone and, to be honest, she was more than happy to oblige.

Trying to get on the older woman's good side had been exhausting!

25

Zoe

Midmorning the following day, Zoe—bunch of flowers in one hand and a bag of basic groceries in the other—stood with a crowd on the corner of St Charles and Common Street waiting for the streetcar that would take her back to the Garden District.

She'd slept better than she had in weeks, maybe because it was the first night she hadn't had any alcohol since leaving Australia.

Rising early, she'd showered and dressed, and made her mum a coffee and breakfast in bed—she deserved it after all she'd put up with the last couple of weeks. They'd sat together on Flick's bed, eating, talking and laughing together like they hadn't done in a long while—not since Zoe was in her early teens and still used to climb into bed with her parents on Saturday morning, watch cartoons and talk about what the so-called popular girls were up to at school. It was nicer than nice. They hadn't talked about anything deep and meaningful—not the dramas of the last few days, not Beau or Sofia—but Flick made her laugh telling her about some of the people she'd met in the shop, and Zoe made her blush when she'd asked if she was serious about Theo.

At first Flick denied that anything more than friendship was blossoming between them, but Zoe hadn't let her off the hook that easily. Joking about role reversals, she'd nudged until her mum had eventually come clean, in exactly the same way Flick had once done when Zoe had crushes—pre-Beau—in early high school.

'Not serious, but lots and lots of fun,' she'd admitted.

'Is he good in bed?' Zoe had asked, turning her mum's cheeks an even deeper shade of red.

'That is not something I'm talking about with you, young lady.'

But the expression on Flick's face spoke volumes and confirmed what Zoe had suspected—that her mum had finally broken the drought.

Even when they'd eventually climbed out of bed to start their respective days, Flick couldn't wipe the smile from her face. It almost gave Zoe hope that perhaps one day—in the *very* distant future—she too might find someone to have fun with again. Almost. But until that day she was going to focus on herself and her art and, even more immediately, Miss H. Ever since she left Australia, she'd made one terrible decision after another, leading to one apology after another. This was her chance to do something right, something good.

After collecting her prize cheque from the pub—which still stank of last night's shenanigans—she'd shopped, then worked out where and when to catch the streetcar. By the time it pulled up, creaking and crunching as it juddered to a stop, and she joined the others scrambling to get inside, she was feeling more accomplished and better about herself than she had in weeks.

The few people who were clearly locals, tagged on using a card and machine system similar to the ones in Australia but Zoe waited in line behind a family of six trying to buy tickets. The driver sounded borderline exasperated as the family finally headed to find seats.

'Hi,' Zoe said, smiling at the woman. She held out a couple of notes, hoping it was enough. 'I'd like to buy a ticket to the Garden District.'

'And here I was thinking you wanted a rainbow unicorn!' With a roll of her eyes, she snatched both notes from Zoe's grasp and gestured to the seats. 'I don't have any change. Just sit. Next!'

'Okay. Sorry.' Zoe fled to the middle of the streetcar, feeling as if she'd been severely reprimanded (and possibly ripped off) when she'd simply been trying to pay her way. Her good mood plummeting fast, she found a seat next to a scruffy young guy wearing expensive-looking headphones and bopping away as if he were at a nightclub.

The moment they started moving, she decided maybe headphones would be a good idea. This had to be the noisiest mode of transport ever. As the streetcar headed down the middle of the road, it chugged loudly, almost like a giant dog panting. That on its own would have been bearable, but the constant clanking and screeching made her wonder if the whole thing would fall apart at any moment. It was suddenly very easy to tell the difference between the tourists and the locals—the tourists winced every time the sassy driver yelled something out the window at either another streetcar or a pedestrian or the whole car jolted, but the locals just went about their business, reading or playing with their phones.

After about ten minutes, they approached the stop where she needed to get off and she stood, along with half the other passengers— the Garden District was clearly a popular tourist destination.

As people filed off in front of her, Zoe chanced a glance at the driver. 'Thanks so much.'

'You're welcome, darlin,' she replied. Then, as Zoe turned to leave, she thrust out her hand. 'Don't ya want ya change?'

'Oh, thanks,' she said as a few coins dropped into her hand. Did this mean she needed to give the woman a tip? Perhaps she'd already accounted for that. *Argh.*

Flustered, she fled the streetcar, starting in what she hoped was the right direction.

On the way back to the French Quarter yesterday, she'd picked Theo's brain—trying to learn as much as he knew about Miss H and also fascinated to hear about the history of the area.

He'd explained that, like much of New Orleans, this part of town was once home to a number of plantations, which had been eventually sold off by one of its owners to a syndicate of American businessmen. The land had then been divided into parcels and bought by wealthy Americans who thought themselves too good to live in the French Quarter with the Creoles. The area became known as the 'Garden District' because each house had a large garden as opposed to the small courtyards in the Quarter. Apparently, the French had thought the Americans ostentatious for displaying their gardens out front, but these days it was the architecture that attracted the tourists as much as the gardens.

In addition to the brief history lesson, Theo had also driven around the neighbourhood, pointing out places of interest. He'd shown them the homes of John Goodman, Sandra Bullock and Anne Rice (celebrities that excited Flick more than Zoe), houses that had featured in movies, a couple of churches, a bright blue building that was apparently a renowned restaurant called the Commander's Palace, and Lafayette Cemetery No. 1, which gave Zoe the shivers even from the outside, with its dark foreboding brick walls and glimpses of the above-ground tombs. Cemeteries were creepy enough when the dead were buried beneath the earth, but despite Theo explaining the practical reasons for the tombs, to Zoe they looked like the setting of a horror movie. No wonder New Orleans was supposedly haunted—when graves had doors, it felt as if the dead could come and go as they pleased.

It was on the corner where this cemetery stood that Zoe turned into the gorgeous leafy street that would lead her to Miss H's place. Due to the fresh cream in her bag and the already warm temperature, she couldn't afford to dawdle but it took great willpower to walk briskly past such picturesque buildings. Although similar, each one of these grand houses told a different kind of story and Zoe found herself not only musing about the people that lived inside as she headed towards her destination, but also thinking about painting them.

Finally, she came to a stop in front of Miss H's faded pink home and felt a buzz of excitement that she could actually go inside this one. The gate squeaked as she opened it and the steps creaked as she marched up onto the porch. She raised her hand to lift the heavy cast-iron knocker and heard the sound echo through the old house as it thunked against the door.

And then she waited. And waited.

Zoe was starting to worry, wondering if Miss H might have fallen and hurt herself even more badly, when the door finally peeled back to reveal the woman. Still wearing yesterday's clothes, her hair was messy and she had bags under her eyes, making her look a decade older.

'Oh, it's you,' Miss H said, and Zoe couldn't quite tell whether she was relieved or irritated to see her.

'Good morning,' she said brightly. 'How's the wrist today?'

Miss H glanced down at her wrist then back at Zoe. 'That is the least of my worries. I've lost Charlotte.'

Who? It took a second for Zoe to twig. 'Oh, your cat. Where is she?'

'What part of I've lost her didn't you understand?' But although her words were harsh, Miss H's demeanour was anything but. The woman was a walking contradiction. It had been the same yesterday. One minute she seemed strong and independent, the next frail and vulnerable.

Zoe felt an urge to give her a hug but got the feeling Miss H wasn't the touchy-feely type.

'I'm sorry,' she said, stepping inside. 'Would you like me to help you look?'

As Miss H closed the door behind Zoe, she hesitated a moment. 'She doesn't like strangers, but I guess it couldn't do any harm. My search proved futile and your young bones mean you can probably look in places I couldn't.'

'How about I make you a cup of coffee and you can put your feet up while I take a look around?'

To Zoe's surprise, Miss H went along with the plan. In the kitchen, as Zoe worked out how to use the coffee plunger, Miss H explained that Charlotte hadn't even had her breakfast yet. 'Poor love stalked off in a huff when I couldn't manage to open her morning sardines and I haven't seen her since.'

Apparently, this tinned delicacy was the only food the cat would eat. That's why Zoe preferred dogs—they weren't so fussy.

Once the coffee was made, Zoe opened the sardines and put them in the bowl ready for Charlotte. Then, leaving Miss H at the kitchen table, she began her hunt, promising to turn the place upside down until she found the missing cat.

The ground level of the grand old house consisted of the massive kitchen, the vast entrance hall, a fancy dining room with a table that looked as if it could sit ten or more guests, a very formal living room, one bedroom with ensuite, a large laundry room, and the most divine sunroom out the back. It was by far the brightest room in the house with light streaming in through large picture windows that took up almost an entire wall. Judging by the easels, art equipment and a number of paintings leaned up against the back wall, this must be Miss H's studio and Zoe got the feeling she spent most of her time here.

'Found her?' Miss H called from the kitchen.

'Not yet,' she shouted back. *Where could the bloody thing be?*

'Perhaps you should try upstairs. Charlotte always used to retreat up there when her brother and sister had been picking on her. But go quietly. You don't want to scare her.'

Zoe took one last glance around, hoping she'd get the chance to take a closer look at the art later, and headed for the faded, blood-red carpeted stairs that would take her to the second storey. They groaned as she walked up as if they were surprised by the attention and the air grew staler the higher she went. At the top, she took a breath and surveyed the long hallway, which had about five or six doors—all closed—leading off it. While downstairs had by no means been a show home, up here everything was covered in a thick layer of dust—from the light fittings to the old-fashioned furniture and gilt-framed oil paintings on the walls.

'Charlotte? Puss, puss?' she called, peering under a side table as she repeated the words she'd said over and over like a mantra.

Her voice echoed back at her.

After walking the length of the corridor, Zoe could safely say the cat wasn't here, but she couldn't resist peeking into one of the rooms. Trying not to make a noise—she didn't want Miss H to think her a snoop—she turned the handle and pushed open the first door, finding it almost pitch-black inside. Feeling around on the wall, she flicked the light switch, but it did absolutely nothing. Giving her eyes a moment to acclimatise, she crossed the room and drew back the heavy drapes. Judging by the dust that rained down on her, the curtains hadn't been opened for years. Spluttering and coughing—so much for being quiet—Zoe glanced around to take in an ancient bed, side tables and a small, box-type TV that looked like it hadn't worked in her lifetime.

When the danger of having her first ever asthma attack finally passed, she ventured across to the wardrobe and despite the doors being closed—therefore unlikely to be hiding Charlotte—she pulled them open. Men's clothes hung from the rack, but the smell of mothballs almost overwhelmed her, and she snapped the doors shut quickly before she could take a proper look. Talk about an unsavoury sensory overload.

Zoe looked under the bed and around the rest of the furniture just in case cats could manipulate doors, but reaped no reward so went back out onto the landing.

That's funny. She frowned across at an open door—she would have sworn they were all closed a moment ago. Could Charlotte be in there?

This bedroom was much the same as the first—relics and dust, totally unliveable. She peered under the bed and squealed as a cockroach scuttled out to greet her. *Ugh.* As she was getting up, she heard a soft tread behind her and slowly turned, expecting to see the cat.

But there was nothing there. She shivered. Dimly lit old mansions were almost as creepy as graveyards. Either Miss H had no imagination, or she was very brave to live here all alone. As her paintings clearly showed her creativity, Zoe decided it must be the latter and it only made her admire the woman more.

Her heart racing stupidly, she hurried back into the hallway and almost yelped with joy at the sight of the small but fat Siamese cat, sitting just outside, her tail swishing from side to side. Zoe swore she looked like she was laughing at her.

'There you are, you ratbag.'

Feeling silly, she took a tentative step towards her, then bent down and scooped her up into her arms. Charlotte hissed her displeasure and struggled to get free, but Zoe kept a firm grip as she hurried down the stairs.

'Look what I found,' she announced on her return to the kitchen.

'My baby girl!' Miss H's face almost split in two at the sight of the cat. Her relief and delight were worth all the scratches on Zoe's arms.

Still holding the enraged beast—no way was she letting her escape again until she'd seen her precious sardines—she walked to the counter and dumped the cat next to the horrible fish. As Charlotte started tucking into her brunch, Zoe rubbed her stinging arms.

'Oh my goodness,' Miss H exclaimed. 'Look what she's done to you.'

'It's fine. I'm just glad she's okay.'

But Miss H was having none of it; she disappeared into the hallway and came back a few moments later with some bandaids and antiseptic cream. Who was supposed to be looking after who here?

When the cat was licking her paws post-meal and Zoe no longer bleeding, she turned her attention back to Miss H. 'Have you eaten anything today?'

'Oh, I don't have a huge appetite these days.'

Zoe guessed that was a no. She'd broken her arm swinging on the Hills Hoist washing line when she was eleven and could still remember how difficult it had made her life. Her parents had to feed, wash and dress her and she'd spent much of her six weeks in a plaster cast watching TV because she couldn't do anything else. Even going to the toilet on her own had been problematic. And judging by the fact Miss H still wore yesterday's outfit, had clearly not brushed her hair or removed her make-up and couldn't open the sardines for Charlotte, she might not have eaten because it was simply too hard.

Zoe desperately wanted to help but having your parents do all those things for you was quite different to a near stranger—she'd need to tread carefully so as not to offend or upset Miss H. 'Have you heard from the visiting nurse yet?'

'No, but the phone rang this morning and I didn't get to it in time. I guess they'll call back.'

'Is there anything I can help you with in the meantime? Anything at all?'

Miss H took a moment, then sighed loudly as if what she was about to say was almost too painful to verbalise. 'If it's not too much trouble, I'd love some assistance getting out of this dress and slipping into something more comfortable.'

'Not too much trouble at all.'

Leaving Charlotte still grooming herself, Zoe followed Miss H out of the kitchen and into the bedroom, which, unlike those upstairs, was clearly lived in. The light worked for a start.

With great care and trying to make sure she kept Miss H's dignity as much as possible, Zoe helped her out of her dress and into looser, easier to navigate clothes. When Miss H insisted on trying to attempt her face and hair left-handed, Zoe went back to the kitchen.

She put more coffee on to brew, washed the cat dish, commandeered a vase she'd seen earlier in the living room for the flowers, opened a few curtains and windows, then unpacked the ingredients she'd bought to make scones. It felt presumptuous just to start cooking in someone else's house, but Miss H would probably tell her not to bother and, as Flick would say, the woman needed some flesh on her bones.

By the time the lady of the house joined her, Zoe was cutting out circles in the dough, having managed to find a rolling pin and cutters right at the back of one of the drawers.

'I hope you don't mind, but I thought I'd make us some scones,' she said, her hands covered in flour. She'd never actually made them before, but Beau's mum always made great ones with the simple ingredients of flour, cream and lemonade, and had often said anyone could make them. So far it looked like she was right.

Miss H dropped into one of the kitchen chairs as if the process of tidying herself up had exhausted her. She'd done a pretty good job of it—the only clue that she'd struggled was red lipstick smudged across her cupid's bow. Zoe didn't say a word.

'You're a very sweet girl, you know that?'

'Hah, thanks.' Zoe laughed a little awkwardly as she slipped the baking tray into the oven. Being 'sweet' hadn't got her very far. 'These should take about ten to fifteen minutes. Is there somewhere you might be more comfortable?'

She hoped Miss H would suggest the sunroom and tried not to show too much excitement when she did. Charlotte followed them, settling on Miss H's lap when she sat down on the sofa.

'This is such a lovely room,' Zoe said, looking out at the desolate state of the backyard.

'I'm afraid I've let the rest of the house and garden go a little in the last few years. My knees started playing up and everything has just become a bit harder.'

'It's a massive place for only one person and it looks like you've been too busy painting masterpieces, but I meant it when I said I'd be happy to help. I could do some cleaning, some gardening.'

Miss H smiled thinly as she stroked Charlotte's back. 'So, cher, tell me about yourself.'

Zoe blinked. She'd been hoping to hear all about Miss H's artwork and the inspiration behind it, not talk about herself. 'What do you want to know?'

'Everything. It's not often I get a visitor. I plan to make the most of it. How old are you?'

'Twenty-four.'

'Do you have any siblings? Pets? Dark secrets?'

Zoe laughed. 'I've got one brother—he's three years younger than me—and I had a dog growing up, but he lives with Mum now. Well, he did, but he's staying with my … my dad at the moment.'

'Your parents not together then? Was it a particularly messy divorce?' Miss H almost sounded gleeful at the prospect.

'Not really.' At least not in the way she likely imagined, but Zoe wasn't sure how the older woman would react if she explained about Sofia, so she didn't elaborate.

A few more banal questions followed—where in Australia did she come from? What was her star sign? What did she normally do for a living? And then Miss H hit her with the biggie.

'Why are you here?'

Zoe blinked. She could lie and say she'd just come to visit her mum—take advantage of the free accommodation and all that—but she had the feeling Miss H would see right through her, and if anyone would understand it would be her.

'I recently found out my husband cheated on me.' Just saying the words brought a lump to her throat and she swallowed, refusing to show weakness by crying. She told Miss H everything—the words spilling out in an angry rush. How she'd loved Beau since they were fifteen and thrown together on a science project.

'Oh, honey.' Miss H lifted her hand from the cat and put it on top of Zoe's.

'It wasn't mine or Beau's favourite subject, but we had to spend hours together to get it done.' Possibly it had taken so long because while they'd been trying to produce a PowerPoint presentation about the elements of the periodic table, they'd discovered another kind of chemistry altogether. They'd married on their five-year anniversary and she'd thought their best years were still to come.

'Anyway, I felt so stupid, and the house felt so lonely without him that I couldn't bear the thought of staying there. And Mum was here …' Zoe shrugged. 'It just made sense to come. Less than five hours after Beau told me he was leaving, I'd emailed my boss to say I'd quit, packed my bag and booked a ticket. I flew out the following day. That's about as far as my planning went. But now that I'm here, I'm not exactly sure what to do with myself.'

'I knew it was something like that,' said Miss H, her tone ever so slightly smug. 'I felt an affinity with you from the moment I saw you but what you've been through is simply horrendous. You poor darling girl.'

'Thank you. What happened to you?' Zoe asked tentatively. She'd heard the rumours from Theo, but wanted to know if they were true.

Miss H moved her hand back to the cat, as if taking solace from her fur. 'Many, many years ago, I also foolishly gave my heart to a man and he tore it out, ripped it to shreds and then took it with him. Remy was a teacher—we met at work and fell head over heels. Ours was a whirlwind romance; he asked for my hand in marriage only three weeks after we met. Everyone thought we were crazy, but we were so in love we didn't want to wait.'

Zoe nodded—she understood that feeling. Everyone thought she and Beau were crazy getting married so young, and she hated that maybe they were right. Had the pressure of settling down while all his friends were sleeping around made him crack? Would they have lasted if they'd waited longer to get so serious?

'Our wedding was going to be such a magical day,' Miss H continued. 'It was springtime, all the magnolias were flowering, the weather was perfect, my dress was divine. I remember waking up in the morning and floating out of bed. I could just tell it was going to be the best day of my life. But it turned out to be the worst. That was the day Remy left me.'

'I'm so sorry,' Zoe whispered. 'That's such a cowardly thing to do. Did you ever hear from him again?'

Miss H hesitated a moment. 'No. Never. And I learnt never to trust a man with my heart again. Love makes you weak.'

'What's that smell?' Zoe sniffed, distracted by the scent of smoke. 'Oh, bugger. The scones.'

She leapt up, rushed back into the kitchen and opened the oven, expecting to see angry black lumps staring back at her. But they were fine—round and perfectly golden, exactly like Beau's mum made them.

See? She could have made a great mother too, if Beau hadn't turned out to be a cheating scumbag.

Telling thoughts of him to bugger off, she piled the warm scones onto a plate with a serving of butter and jam and took them into the sunroom to Miss H.

26

Felicity

Flick leaned back against Theo's pillows, her heart racing, her skin dripping with sweat and every part of her body thoroughly played. He wasn't only a gifted musician, his repertoire of sexual talents never ceased to amaze her.

At least half an hour had passed since she'd left a 'Back in 5' sign on the shop door. While Theo excelled at the quickie, he much preferred to take his time and she was easily led astray. But Harvey wasn't paying her to lounge around in bed all day.

'I've got to go,' she said, making no such move whatsoever.

Theo chuckled and smoothed his hand over her naked stomach. 'Your actions speak louder than your words.'

'And *your* actions are to blame for my actions!'

'What actions would they be?' he whispered, his warm breath caressing her skin.

'Oh, bugger it.' She threw her leg over his naked body. 'One more for the road.'

Almost an hour later, Theo and Flick made their way downstairs, hands linked tightly. Now that Zoe knew about them, as did Theo's staff, they didn't try to hide their liaison. Since Flick spent her nights with her daughter, she sometimes came over during the day for a sneaky lunchtime rendezvous. That way she got the best of both worlds—bonding time with Zoe, while also having a bit of fun. The young female jazz duo Flick had watched a number of times were on the stage entertaining a small but attentive crowd. She resisted the urge to linger, instead waving at them as she passed. She went to do the same to Lauri-Ann behind the bar but her hand froze midair.

Perched on a stool only a few feet away, wearing the most fabulous summer dress and looking far more glamorous than someone who'd just flown halfway across the world should, was Sofia, a sleek silver suitcase at her feet.

She turned slightly and their eyes met. Sofia cracked a big grin while Flick bit back a silent *What the fuck?!*

What the hell was she doing here?

'Flick! Oh my goodness, you look fantastic.' Sofia slid off the stool and sashayed towards her, her gaze sliding over Flick's new outfit before pulling her into a hug.

Ice flooded Flick's veins, replacing the warmth she'd felt moments earlier. 'What are you doing here?' she blurted, yanking out of Sofia's embrace.

'There was a sign on the shop door when I arrived, so I thought I'd get a drink while I waited.'

'No.' She shook her head, exasperated. 'I mean *here*, in New Orleans.'

'Ah right.' Sofia threw her a 'silly me' smile. 'Well, you know that conference I've got in California next week?'

Flick managed a brief nod—she vaguely remembered Sofia mentioning something about it on one of their phone calls.

'It seemed a waste to travel all the way to the US and not visit, so I decided to come over early and spend some time here first. I wanted to see Zoe, check that she was okay, you know. And you— you sounded a little weird last time we spoke.'

'I'm fine!' *At least I was until you showed up.* 'And so is Zoe. I told you that!' Over the couple of weeks she'd been visiting Miss H, she'd almost started to return to her old bubbly self and Flick figured the eccentric old lady was keeping her out of mischief.

'Excellent. Where is she?'

Before Flick could reply, Theo cleared his throat behind them. 'Are you going to introduce us, Felicity?'

Flick would rather a flash flood carry her off to sea, but she took a deep breath and gestured between the two of them. 'Theo, this is … Sofia, my …'

'Ex-husband,' Sofia said when Flick hesitated.

Actually, she was going to say 'friend', but the truth was out there now.

Theo's eyes widened but he covered his shock quickly and offered Sofia his hand. 'Welcome to New Orleans. It's a pleasure to meet you.'

'And you.'

Although Sofia smiled, she did a terrible job of hiding her assessment of Theo. Flick didn't know whether she was checking him out or trying to work out what was going on between them.

'I've got to be getting back to the shop. Come on,' she said to Sofia, unable to handle being in the same space with them both a moment longer. 'I'll see you later.'

Flick was already halfway out the door as she uttered the words. She heard a brief exchange between Theo and Sofia before the rumble of a suitcase and heels click-clacking behind her.

'He seems great,' Sofia said as she caught up to Flick outside the shop.

No comment. Her breaths came short and sharp as she fumbled to get the key in the lock, taking longer than usual.

'Here, do you want some help with that?'

'No. I said I was fine!'

'O-kay,' Sofia said as the door finally swung open. 'Wow, this place is magnificent. You must be in heaven here.'

Heaven? Flick sucked in another desperate breath. It felt like anything but heaven right now.

She left the 'Back in 5' sign on the door, locked it again behind them and eyed the sparkly silver suitcase. 'Where are you staying?'

'Um ... well ...' Sofia blinked. 'I haven't booked a hotel yet. Came straight here. Wanted to see my girls.'

Flick hesitated only a moment. 'I guess you can stay here.' It was probably exactly what Sofia assumed would happen anyway. Besides, Zoe wouldn't forgive her if she turned her other parent out onto the street.

Sofia's eyes lit up. 'Are you sure you have the room?'

Not really. But it wasn't the lack of space that unsettled her. 'As long as you don't mind sleeping on the couch. There's only two bedrooms.'

'Not a problem. You know I can sleep anywhere.'

Flick forced a smile. 'All right then, let's get you upstairs and settled and then I'd better come back down and open the shop.'

'You were longer than five minutes,' Sofia mused as they headed through the shop to the stairs at the rear. 'Is something going on between you and the guy next door?'

'No!' Glad she was ahead so Sofia couldn't see the expression on her face, Flick racked her mind for an excuse. 'He needed a hand moving some furniture.'

Sofia knew her too well to believe the lie—ridiculous as it was—but Flick didn't want to discuss her sex life with her ex any more than she wanted to hear about Sofia's. That was what had her fleeing Australia in the first place.

'By the way, who's looking after Dog?' Neve and Emma had taken turns over the years when the family went away, but if either of them had Dog now they'd have warned her about Sofia's arrival. It would have been nice to have had some kind of advance notification. 'Mike.'

'I see.' Flick didn't know what she thought about that. She had no idea what kind of person this Mike was. Would he take care of their beloved pet with the same care they would? If Dog didn't get her daily walk, her arthritis started playing up, but you couldn't push her too far either.

'You couldn't have checked if I was okay with that first?' she asked as they reached the top of the stairs.

Sofia panted a little as she dropped her suitcase to the floor. 'That would have ruined the surprise!'

And what a pity that would have been.

'You must be exhausted. Help yourself to whatever's in the fridge. The bathroom's up the hall if you want to freshen up or maybe you want to take a nap?'

Sofia marched across the room to the balcony and yanked open the doors. 'Nap?' She laughed as she gazed down onto Bourbon Street. 'How could you possibly sleep in a place like this?'

'Noise-cancelling earplugs are a blessing.'

Sofia turned back and frowned. 'Are you okay? You seem a bit … jittery?'

'I'm fine.' She took her smile up another notch. 'Just surprised to see you.'

A rare hint of uncertainty flashed across Sofia's face. 'Not a bad surprise, I hope?'

'Of course not.' She took a quick breath. 'You should take a coffee out on the balcony and people-watch.' It had always been one of Sofia's favourite pastimes.

'Are you going to come out and have one with me? I've missed you and I want to hear all about what you've been up to here.'

'I'd love to, but I *am* here to work,' Flick reminded her. Which sounded a bit rich considering what she'd been doing next door.

'Sorry. Of course you are. What time do you close? I'll take you and Zoe out to dinner. Where is our delightful daughter anyway?'

'She's in the Garden District, about ten minutes away by streetcar. She's become kind of a companion for an elderly woman.'

'How did that happen?'

Flick filled Sofia in as quickly as possible, leaving out the night on the town looking for Zoe and the fact she'd hit pretty much rock bottom, and instead beginning with the story of how Aurelia had fallen and broken her wrist in the shop downstairs.

'She's a bit of an enigma, and an hour or so in her company was more than enough for me, but I guess Zoe has connected with her over their art. She's been painting and also doing a bit of housework—although between you and me that place needs a lot more than a bit. At first, she only spent a couple of hours a day there, but that's been getting longer and longer. At least the friendship seems to be taking her mind off Beau.'

'How is she feeling about him?'

Flick sighed and leaned back against the balcony railing. 'She's still hurting, it's obvious in lots of ways, but she's doing her best to move on and has made it clear she doesn't want to talk about it.'

'Do you think we should try to make her? She can't just bury her head in the sand. She'll need to confront Beau eventually, if only to work out what they're going to do about their rental and their joint finances.'

'I know, but she needs a little more time. You're going to have to trust me on this one. I know she's our little girl, but she has to work out some things for herself.' It was bad enough Sofia's arrival was messing with Flick's equilibrium, she didn't want her to upset Zoe as well. 'It's barely been a month since everything she believed in crumbled, and anyway, she can't file for divorce until a year's up.'

'I suppose you're right. I just can't help worrying,' Sofia said as Flick's phone pinged with a message.

She glanced at the screen to see it was from Theo: *Are you okay?*

Her heart squeezed as she turned slightly away and tapped out a quick reply: *Yes. Sorry. I'll explain everything later.*

She turned back to Sofia. 'How long are you staying?'

'I've got five days before I have to head to California for the conference.'

Five days? She may as well have announced she'd emigrated. 'Great.' Flick's voice squeaked on the word as another message landed.

Don't worry about it. There's nothing to explain unless you want to. xx

'Might as well make the most of seeing all the sights, since I've come this far,' Sofia was saying. 'When do you think Zoe will be back?'

Flick shoved her phone into the pocket of her shorts. 'Um ... I'm not sure. She's usually back by the time I close up the shop.'

Sofia glanced at the smartwatch on her wrist. 'What time is that?'

'Normally about eight or nine o'clock.'

'That doesn't leave much time for dinner.'

'You can eat in a fancy restaurant at midnight in the Quarter, but I could always call her and let her know you're here? I'm sure she'd come home earlier if she knew.'

'No, don't do that. I want to surprise her. The look on your face when you saw me was priceless.'

Flick swallowed a sarcastic retort and forced a chuckle. 'Okay then. Well, I'd better go reopen the shop. Make yourself at home.'

'Thanks, babe.' Sofia smiled warmly. 'Maybe I'll have a nap after all—I want to be full of beans for tonight.'

'Good idea,' Flick said, then escaped downstairs to try and work out how the hell she was going to survive the next five days.

27

Zoe

When Zoe arrived just after 9 pm, her mum was shutting up the shop.

'How was Aurelia today?'

'Good. The home nurse visited, and she always feels better after she's had a proper shower.'

'That's great.' But Flick's tone did not match her words.

'Are you okay, Mum? Is something wrong?'

She smiled. 'No. Not at all. In fact, there's a surprise waiting for you upstairs.'

Zoe's heart froze. 'It's not Beau, is it?' She didn't mean to sound excited, but in the middle of the night, when Harvey's small bed felt enormous because she was in it all alone, she'd fantasised about him coming all this way to plead for her forgiveness and beg her to take him back.

Of course, she'd tell him to take a flying leap—in much more colourful language—but at least it would show she was worth fighting for.

'No.' Flick shook her head. 'I know the rules. If he dared to show his face here, I'd shove him in the deep freeze and then turn him into an exhibit.'

Zoe couldn't help laughing at the image of her husband stuffed like one of the many animals surrounding them. 'I always knew having a mum who was good with knives and scalpels would come in handy one day. What's this surprise then?'

'If you go upstairs, you'll find out.' Flick shooed her off.

'Okay, okay, I'm going.' Zoe climbed tentatively up the stairs and a familiar sweet perfume wafted out to greet her even before she saw Sofia sitting on the couch.

'Oh my God!' she shrieked as Sofia stood and the two of them launched into each other's arms. 'What are you doing here?'

'Came to see my two best girls,' she replied, squeezing Zoe hard.

'This is insane,' Zoe said when she pulled back. 'I can't believe you're actually here. When did you arrive?'

Sofia's smile stretched right across her face. 'Noon.'

Zoe turned to Flick. 'Why didn't you call and let me know?'

'Sofia didn't want me to ruin the surprise.'

'It doesn't matter.' She grabbed Zoe's hand, brought it up to her impressive bosom and squeezed. 'We're all together now and I'm so hungry I could eat a horse. Or maybe even an alligator? I hear it tastes like fishy chicken. Where should we go for dinner?'

Zoe was exhausted after a day of hard labour and had already eaten a light dinner with Miss H, but she couldn't bring herself to disappoint Sofia.

'There are so many good places ... Mum and I have been meaning to try SoBou; it looks super funky, but I have to get changed first,' she insisted, glancing down at her dusty, paint-splattered clothes.

'Me too,' Flick said and hurried to her bedroom.

Forty minutes later Zoe and her parents were shown to a table in an intimate corner of SoBou, which apparently stood for 'south of Bourbon'. She'd walked past the restaurant a few days ago but, like everything in the French Quarter, it looked even more magnificent at night.

Heavenly sweet and spicy aromas swirled around them as they entered and all three were enamoured by the chic interior, with its exquisite feature wall of hundreds of decorative glass bottles glittering like art as they provided light for the room. Although the bar off to one side of the venue still buzzed with people, due to the late hour, Zoe and her parents found they had the beautiful dining room and an attentive waitress, Angela, almost to themselves.

Sofia's eyes lit up when Angela suggested their signature martini and although Zoe felt the slightly disapproving gaze of her mother, she ordered one as well and in the end so did Flick. Zoe had stopped drinking almost entirely since the night Jack 'rescued' her, but what harm could one drink do?

Angela went over the evening's specials and her recommendations, but then gave them time to explore the menu while she went off to get the drinks.

'Everything sounds so delectable,' Sofia said. 'Shall we order a number of different plates to share?'

'As long as we can get the beef,' Zoe replied, her mouth watering at the description of cast-iron seared meat, flavoured with black garlic and smoked sea salt, alongside black truffle butter and charred sweet peppers.

'Ooh, yes, that sounds good.' Sofia nodded in approval. 'What about you, Flick?'

'I'm not actually very hungry.'

'That's a turn-up for the books. One of the things I always admired about you was your healthy appetite.' Sofia chuckled as she turned back to the menu.

'Well, things change,' Flick said, and Zoe detected a sharp edge to her voice.

Thinking back to the conversation they'd had the week before, she suddenly realised her mum might not be quite as excited by Sofia's arrival as she was.

Sofia, seemingly oblivious, added, 'Of course we've got to get the gumbo, and maybe some shrimp corndogs and alligator tacos for starters.'

'I'll pass on the tacos,' Zoe said, her pseudo date with Jack coming to mind. She'd been trying *not* to think of him, but every time she walked to the streetcar stop and passed by where he lived, she couldn't help herself.

Their waitress arrived with three colourful martinis and Flick drank almost half of hers in one gulp. Angela asked if they were ready to order.

Sofia did the honours and then, once Angela had retreated, lifted her glass. 'I think we should have a toast.'

'What are we celebrating?' Flick asked.

'Life! The three of us being together again in this magical place. Just like a family holiday.'

'Not *quite* like our family holidays,' Flick said.

'You're right.' A thoughtful expression crossed Sofia's face. 'Toby's not here. Maybe we should toast to him?'

Flick raised her glass—'To Toby'—and then downed the rest of it.

While they waited for their meals, Sofia dropped her chin into her hand and smiled at them enthusiastically. 'I want to hear all about what you've been up to. You said you were working on something, Flick?'

'A couple of things actually. A muskrat and also a baby alligator. Harvey has a racoon in the deep freeze I'm hoping to get to as well, but we'll see.'

'And is the shop busy? It seems a little out of place among the clubs and pubs on Bourbon Street.'

'You'd be surprised. Harvey has a wide-reaching reputation.' Flick caught the eye of Angela and gestured to her empty glass. 'Can I get another one of these?'

This confirmed Zoe's suspicions. Her mum didn't usually drink that much—at least not so quickly—and if asked about what she was working on, she'd normally go into far greater detail.

If Sofia noticed too, she didn't say anything. 'So, what else have you two been up to? Hope you saved some of the touristy spots for me so we can see some sights together.'

'We didn't know you were coming,' Flick said. 'But I only have Wednesdays off anyway.'

'And I'm kinda busy with Miss H at the moment,' Zoe apologised.

'Miss H?' Sofia asked.

'She's the woman I told you about,' Flick said. 'The one who hurt her wrist in the shop.'

'Ah right.'

At the crestfallen look on Sofia's face, Zoe felt compelled to say, 'Although maybe we can work in some sightseeing around that? And you should definitely come check out the mansions in the Garden District.'

'Well, I don't want to get in your way,' said Sofia, 'and I can see there's plenty to do in the evenings round here. I can explore on my own by day, but maybe we can all go on a ghost tour together one night?'

Zoe and Flick exchanged a glance.

'We've already done that.' And, as it would increase her chances of running into Jack, Zoe didn't fancy a repeat performance.

'But you should totally do one,' Flick encouraged as Angela arrived with her fresh drink. 'Thank you.'

Angela smiled. 'You're welcome. Your starters will be out in just a moment.'

'So, Zo-Zo, tell me about this old lady you're helping?' Sofia asked, taking a sip from her pink martini.

'She's actually only seventy-three. And she's super talented. Did you see the painting above the mantel in Harvey's apartment?' When Sofia looked blank, she added, 'The skeleton in the wedding dress.'

'Oh yes, I loved it. So striking. I've never seen anything quite like it.'

Zoe beamed proudly as if the compliment was for her own work. 'Isn't it clever how she manages to paint emotion into a skull?'

Sofia nodded. 'And the detail on the bride's dress—the lace looked almost 3D. She must spend hours getting it to look like that.'

'Yes, each dress is totally different too. Although the gothic element is cool, I'd love to see her paint some more modern dresses. Of course, she can't paint at all at the moment, but she's been giving me some pointers and is letting me use her supplies and her studio to do some stuff of my own. She says she likes watching me paint.'

Their meals arrived and although Flick made the right noises when Sofia and Zoe gushed about the various dishes, she only picked at her food and was very quiet throughout the whole evening. Sensing her mum wasn't in the mood for conversation, Zoe carried it as much as she could, starting with telling Sofia the tragic story of Miss H's fiancé leaving her at the altar on their wedding day.

'I get the feeling she hoped he'd change his mind and come back to her, that she's been waiting for him to turn up again after all these years.' Or maybe it was a bit like she felt about Beau—she wanted the chance to break *his* heart like he'd broken hers?

'How terribly sad,' Sofia said, digging in her handbag for tissues.

Flick spoke for the first time in a while. 'How she's managed to put fifty years in doing nothing but painting is a mystery.'

'She doesn't *just* paint. She's actually very well read. You can't see from the hall, but two entire walls of the living room are lined with bookshelves that are overflowing. There are books in her sunroom and upstairs as well. Every week she goes to the Garden District Book Shop and buys four or five. I went with her yesterday and I was in heaven. It smells like proper book shops should. I bought a couple of local history books and also a book-smelling candle. You should check it out, Mum.'

Zoe also explained that as well as doing some painting herself and taking Miss H out to the book shop and for coffee, she'd been helping with a bit of tidying up and bringing her into the twenty-first century.

'We got her an iPad so I could help set her up on Instagram and Facebook. Although you can find her paintings in many of the galleries around here, it wouldn't hurt to lift her profile online. She's actually a quick learner and is enjoying navigating the world wide web, as she calls it.'

Flick had already followed Miss H on social media the day Zoe had set up the accounts, but Sofia got out her phone now and did the same.

'She sounds like a fascinating character,' Sofia said as she scrolled through Miss H's new Instagram account and admired the paintings they'd already posted.

'I'm thinking of reaching out to Gretchen to see if she might be interested in doing a show in Australia. But I haven't told Miss H yet, because it would be a huge undertaking.' She also wasn't sure her old boss would be that pleased to hear from her, considering how she'd left her in the lurch.

'Aurelia is lucky to have you doing all this for her for free,' Flick commented.

'It's not a chore. I'm really enjoying her company, but I have to admit, her house is a little spooky.'

'What do you mean?' Sofia asked.

Between mouthfuls of beef that was as delicious and tender as the menu made it sound, Zoe told her parents about the things that had happened when she'd ventured upstairs looking for Charlotte. 'It's not quite as bad downstairs where Miss H spends all her time, but I do sometimes get the sense that someone is watching us.'

'So, you think it's haunted?' Sofia leaned forward, clearly excited by the prospect.

'I think it would be hard to spend time in that place and not start imagining ghosts,' Flick mused. 'All the buildings here are old and full of character, but Aurelia's house looks like something out of *The Munsters* or *The Addams Family*.'

Zoe had never heard of *The Munsters*, but she got the gist and her mum was right—all the scary movies she'd watched in her teens were playing havoc with her imagination. 'It's not that bad,' she said with a nervous laugh. 'It was amazing how much better the living room looked once I put the vacuum over it. I'm cleaning it up a bit each day.'

'You'd need years to fix that place up properly. Probably the best thing would be for it to burn down and allow something new and safe to be built on the land.'

'Mum!' Zoe exclaimed. 'That's awful. And where's your sense of history?'

'Now, now, ladies,' Sofia joked. 'Have you asked Miss H about it, Zo-Zo?'

'No, I don't want to sound stupid—I mean, I don't really believe in ghosts. But I also don't want to upset her or put ideas into her head. I don't know how she manages to live there all alone as it is.'

'Me either,' agreed Flick. 'But didn't she mention her father died there? If there is a ghost—and I think you know my thoughts on *that*—maybe it's just him watching over her.'

'Maybe. Anyway.' Zoe shook her head as her mum took *another* long sip of her drink. 'I shouldn't have mentioned it. Now I'll probably have nightmares tonight.'

'You can always come wake me up if you do, sweetheart. I'll probably be awake at all hours anyway due to the jet lag.' Sofia patted her stomach and picked up the dessert menu that Angela had delivered to the table. 'Now, who has room for something sweet? And maybe another round of cocktails?'

Zoe grinned. 'My arm could be twisted. The bread pudding lollipop sounds interesting.'

'Actually,' Flick pushed back from her chair, 'I'm tired. I think I'm going to call it a night.' She stood and scooped her bag up from the floor. 'I'll see you both tomorrow.'

'We'll come back with you,' Sofia offered. 'Isn't it dangerous to walk alone at this time of night round here?'

Flick shook her head. 'I'll be fine. It's only a couple of blocks away. You two stay, eat dessert, have fun.'

'Okay, Mum. Love you.' Zoe blew her a kiss.

'Love you, too,' Flick replied as she turned and hurried out of the restaurant. Zoe knew it could be dangerous, but she also suspected her mum had found the last couple of hours hard and needed a breather.

Sofia frowned after her. 'Is she okay? She's been acting kind of strange since I arrived. Maybe she's getting sick?'

'I don't think that's it.' When Sofia still looked perplexed, Zoe realised she was going to have to spell it out. 'I'm sorry, but I think it's you.'

'Me?' Sofia touched the base of her neck. 'What do you mean?'

'I know Mum acts all strong and like she's fine with everything that's happened over the last few years, but she's only human. She's still hurting from your divorce and you being here only reminds her of everything she's lost.'

'She hasn't lost me. We're still friends.'

'I know.' Zoe reached across the table and took Sofia's hand. 'I appreciate that, really I do, and I'm stoked to see you. But this was meant to be Mum's time to find her feet again, to make a new life for herself, just like you're doing. She came all this way because she needed to put some distance between you guys.'

'Really? That's why she came?'

Zoe nodded glumly.

'Are you sure it's not because of that man in the bar next door? She was there when I arrived, and I suspected there was something going on between them. I'd be happy for her if that's the case—I'm not here to make things difficult for her.'

Zoe wasn't about to betray Flick's confidence, although she suspected her feelings for Theo were deeper than she was prepared to admit. 'This isn't about another relationship, it's about Mum. I know she comes across as tough, but ... I think you need to give her space.'

28

Felicity

Flick gasped for fresh air as she left the restaurant, tired of pretending everything was normal and that she was okay with Sofia being here when she was absolutely not. While Zoe had been chatting about Aurelia and Sofia hanging on their daughter's every word, Flick had been trying not to scream.

When her ex had suggested dessert, she knew she had to get out of there before she said, or did, something they all regretted. But now what?

Although she'd told them she was heading to bed, the thought of going back to the apartment where Zoe and Sofia would soon return to didn't appeal in the slightest. There was only one place she wanted to be right now and that was in Theo's arms. But even the thought of seeing him filled her with trepidation because it meant she was finally going to have to explain some things she still didn't entirely understand herself.

Barely noticing the hordes of people high on spirits and French Quarter magic, she walked briskly back to Bourbon Street and right into the Blue Cat before she could chicken out. Theo was centre stage and she paused a moment to listen to him play, waiting for it to work its magic, but even his tender melodies couldn't calm the storm inside her. Roxy and Cooper were busy behind the bar, but Flick resisted the urge to order a glass of Dutch courage—she'd already had more than enough—and went and found a vacant seat mere metres from the piano.

She thought she'd have a while to work out what to say, but as soon as Theo saw her, he drew his number to an end. He stood, pressed a button on some kind of sound system behind the stage and pre-recorded jazz spilled out of the speakers as he made his way to her.

'Are you okay?' he asked, concern in his brow as he lowered himself into the seat beside her and took her hand.

'Okay enough that you don't need to annoy your patrons for me. I need to talk to you, but it can wait until you've finished the set or even till close.'

'Everyone's so drunk they probably won't even notice I've stopped playing.'

That wasn't true at all—the Blue Cat didn't have that kind of clientele—but Flick felt warm inside at the thought he was prepared to cut his set short for her. And maybe it would be good to get this conversation over and done with. 'Are you sure?'

He nodded and reached for her hand. 'Come on, let's go upstairs.'

His staff would assume they were going up to his apartment for a little hanky-panky, but Flick didn't care—this wasn't a conversation she wanted anyone listening in on.

'Can I get you something to drink?' Theo asked, flicking the light on as they stepped into his apartment. 'Wine? Whiskey?'

'Maybe just a coffee, please.' She didn't usually drink caffeine this late at night, but sleep would be unlikely anyway.

'Coming right up.' He gestured to the couch. 'Take a seat.'

Flick did so, wishing that Roberta or Tessa had followed them upstairs so she could run her hands through their soft, warm fur. Fidgeting with her handbag—which she settled on her lap like some kind of security blanket—did not have the same effect.

'Do you want anything to eat?' Theo called from the kitchen, the consoling scent of coffee already wafting towards her.

'No, thank you. I've just come from dinner, but you have something if you want.' Geez, she sounded so polite, so nervous.

'Where'd you go?' Theo asked.

'SoBou.'

'Great choice.' He went on to talk about knowing the chef there or something and although Flick tried to pay attention, she barely registered a word, until he came up beside her and offered her a mug of steaming coffee.

'Thank you,' she said quietly as she closed her hands around it. It had still been balmy outside, but there was something so soothing about holding a warm drink in your hands, no matter the weather.

'You're welcome.' Theo sat down beside her, cradling a drink of his own.

Flick turned to meet his gaze. 'I'm sorry about this afternoon. I owe you an explanation.'

'You don't owe me anything, and certainly not an apology. But if you want to talk about Sofia, your marriage or whatever, I'm all ears.' When she didn't say anything, he added, 'If you'd rather play a game of strip poker, that's fine too.'

Flick had just taken a mouthful of coffee and almost spat it out, but she managed a smile. 'I want to tell you. It's just hard to talk about my marriage. I don't even know where to start.'

'There's no rush.' Theo put his hand on her knee and squeezed. 'Why don't you start by telling me about Sofia?'

'Okay.' Flick swallowed. 'It was about eight months after we met. We were already engaged and living together by that time. One evening, I came home from a night class and when I was getting ready for bed, I found a bra and some knickers that didn't belong to me.'

She paused and took a deep breath. Aside from Neve and Emma, she'd never told this whole story to anyone.

Theo didn't say a word, just waited patiently for her to continue.

'Of course, I jumped to the obvious conclusion—an affair. My husband had to tell me the truth to stop me from walking out. That wearing women's clothes made her feel good and she confessed to trying on my stuff and using my make-up when I wasn't there.'

'And you accepted that?' Theo asked.

'Well, I figured it wasn't like having an affair. She said I was the first person she'd ever told what she thought of as her shameful secret. I felt sad that she carried so much guilt about something that really wasn't hurting anyone. I remember thinking I could leave this kind, good man because of his slightly unconventional habit, or I could accept him for who he was and marry the man of my dreams. I mean, everyone has their quirks, right?' Flick sniffed.

Theo gave her an encouraging smile as he dug in his pocket and passed her a hanky. 'It's clean, I promise. I keep them on hand for wiping the piano keys, but I haven't used that one.'

'Thanks.' She buried her face in his now familiar scent.

'So Sofia didn't tell you she wanted to transition then?'

'No. It was a few years later she told me she got into character and called herself Sofia when she wore her women's clothes, but still not that she'd ever considered transitioning.'

'I see.' Theo nodded. 'Did your kids know?'

'No. I was firm about that. Nowadays people are a lot more accepting, but even not that long ago when Zoe and Toby were in primary school that wasn't the case. So it was always our secret, and I felt honoured to be trusted with it. We had a good marriage—we were friends, even the sex was good.' She blushed a little—now that she'd experienced it with someone else, maybe it hadn't been as satisfying as she'd imagined.

'So what changed?'

Flick was unable to keep the bitterness from her voice. 'One day a plain envelope arrived addressed to my husband and I can't exactly explain why, but I had a funny feeling about it. I know I shouldn't have, but I opened it—after all we weren't supposed to have any secrets. It was from a ...'

It was still hard to think about that afternoon, never mind talk about it.

The afternoon her world had shattered. The afternoon she realised her husband wasn't who he'd professed to be, which meant her marriage wasn't as rock solid as she'd assumed. It had been like walking on solid ground only to suddenly look down and find yourself underwater.

'You don't have to talk about this if it's too hard,' Theo said when she'd been quiet a while.

But Flick wanted to. However casual things were supposed to be between her and Theo, if she didn't explain there would be a weirdness, an elephant in the room between them from now on. She wanted him to know the real her. And however much she'd tried to run from it, Sofia had shaped the person Flick was now.

She took a breath. 'The letter was from a gender reassignment clinic confirming an appointment.'

'Shit.'

'Oh, believe me, I said a lot worse than that. I felt so betrayed, not only because I hadn't known that she wanted to take things that far, but also that my husband was keeping secrets from me. Secrets about things that had the potential to change both our lives and the kids' as well. She said it was only to get information, to talk about options, but I lost it. We fought worse than we ever had before. I asked why the sudden decision to take this big step ...'

'And?' Theo prompted.

'It was because the world was changing so fast and what had once felt like an impossibility, now might actually not be. For years Sofia hadn't allowed herself to even dream about this option, hence why never confessing it to me.'

'How long ago was that?'

Flick rubbed her lips together—she knew the exact date of that conversation because it was imprinted in her mind, but she merely said, 'About four years.'

She took another deep breath and told him the rest. How she'd tried her damnedest to be supportive. How she'd accompanied Sofia to the initial appointments at the clinic, how they'd gone to counselling. How she'd come to understand how necessary and important it was for Sofia that this go ahead and how they'd tried to work out how a future could look for them. Together. Toby was finishing high school and Zoe planning her wedding, so they'd agreed Sofia wouldn't announce her intentions until those two events had passed.

'I planned to stay married to Sofia,' she told Theo, 'but I think I secretly hoped that maybe she'd realise this wasn't something she needed to do after all.'

'But she didn't.' It wasn't a question.

'No. The day of Zoe's wedding, she was so excited, because in the days following she was finally going to announce to the world who she truly was and officially start transitioning. I wanted to be happy and enjoy the day too, but I couldn't. And I was so angry at Sofia for ruining the wedding for me. I had an epiphany that day—I couldn't stay.' Flick took a quick breath. 'I actually contemplated killing her.'

Theo's eyes widened and she immediately regretted that last bit. She'd never actually told another soul, and now that she'd said it aloud, she understood why. What must he think of her?

'It was only for a couple of seconds,' she explained. 'I never really would have done it, but in that moment, I knew that by staying with Sofia I might be upholding my wedding vows, but I wouldn't be being true to myself. That night, I told her that I was proud of her, that I'd always love her and support her as best I could through her transition, but that I wanted to get a divorce.'

Tears leaked down Flick's cheeks as she spoke. It all still felt unreal. 'I didn't realise that even if we weren't married, supporting her would be the hardest thing I've ever done.'

Theo shifted closer, put his arm around her and drew her close.

'I know it sounds awful,' she sobbed, 'but sometimes I feel like it would have been better if my husband *had* died. In some ways that feels like the case—he is gone and in his place is this amazing, wonderful, kind, lovely woman who feels so familiar, yet at the same time feels like a complete stranger. I don't know what to do with that.'

'How did your kids react when the truth came out?'

'Better than me. I was so worried it would ruin their relationship with their father, but although Toby took a little longer than Zoe, they both came around fairly quickly. Now they're Sofia's biggest champions.'

Flick pulled back and looked Theo in the eye. 'I realise that not telling you all this before might make it seem like I'm ashamed of her, but that's not the case. I've been by her side through appointments, hormone therapy and surgery. She amazes me constantly. I'm proud of her for having the courage to tell the world who she truly is, to face physical hardships and other people's prejudice as she navigates this journey. I'm proud of her for taking risks and putting herself out there again. It's me I'm ashamed of. Because while I say one thing, I'm often feeling something else entirely.'

'You've got nothing to be ashamed of,' Theo said. 'I think you're amazing.'

But Flick shook her head. 'A better person would have stayed married—plenty do in our situation. Maybe if I was a better person, I'd have reacted differently way back in the beginning. Maybe if I hadn't reacted so badly, she'd have felt comfortable enough to tell me the truth back then. Maybe Sofia wouldn't have spent another two decades living in the wrong body?'

'Or maybe you'd have ended things then and there and never had Zoe and Toby?'

Flick shuddered. That didn't bear thinking about.

'Life is full of maybes,' Theo said softly as he stroked her hair off her face. 'But sometimes things work out just the way they're supposed to. Sometimes what you think is going to be the most painful time of your life, simply turns out to be the storm before the rainbow. Sofia seems happy enough now; maybe it's time you stop beating yourself up and give yourself permission to be happy too?'

That was a nice thought. Flick swiped at her cheeks, but she felt lighter for getting it all off her chest. 'I'm sorry. I feel like between my Zoe dramas and this, you're getting more than you bargained for with me.'

Theo was silent for a moment, then cupped her cheek with his warm hand. 'Felicity,' he murmured, 'don't apologise. I want to be here for you, in whatever way you need, whatever shape that takes.

293

I'm glad you finally felt comfortable enough to tell me, because …
I think I'm starting to fall in love with you.'

Flick's breath caught in her throat. The door to his balcony
slammed as a gust of wind blew it shut, taking all the oxygen in the
room with it.

Love? That wasn't what they'd agreed on, but weirdly it didn't
freak her out as much as she thought it would.

'You don't have to say anything,' he rushed to reassure her.
'I'm sorry. It was probably the worst timing of all to tell you, but I
couldn't help myself.'

Touched by the way the usually self-assured Theo suddenly
sounded a little uncertain, she leaned forward and kissed him hard
on the lips.

It was scary even to think about what it might mean if she loved
him back—a feeling she hadn't allowed herself to even contemplate
until that moment—but she couldn't deny the rush that came
hearing those words on his lips. The tension that had built up inside
her from the moment she'd seen Sofia sitting at the bar evaporated
as if a magician had come along, waved his wand and ordered it to
disappear.

One thing led to another and soon they were no longer upright
on the couch. Theo's hands moved from Flick's face, down her
body, yanking her T-shirt up and lifting it over her head. He skilfully
unhooked her bra with one hand, while the other moved to her thigh,
pushing her skirt up towards her waist. Instinctively, she arched
her hips towards him, silently praising the Lord she'd decided that
evening to wear one of her new skirts.

'Theo?' she hissed as he puffed hot breath onto her now bare
nipple and teased his finger back and forth over the scrap of cotton
that called itself her underwear.

He glanced up. 'Yes, Felicity?'

Their eyes met.

'I want you.'

'I want you too.' With a grin he rolled her knickers down her legs and tossed them over his shoulder.

She laughed, wondering as he stood to shuck his jeans if they could possibly make a proper relationship work. New Orleans pumped through Theo's blood and the bar wasn't only his livelihood but his passion. As a taxidermist working for herself, Flick could pursue her career almost anywhere. After selling the home her children had grown up in, she had felt displaced, but could she leave her family and friends for good to start all over again here with him?

Oblivious to her musing, Theo pressed the length of his body against hers and as he surged into her, she wrapped her legs around his waist and lost the ability to think about anything but the sensations rocketing right to the very centre of her. She'd worry about the love thing later.

'Well,' Theo said when business had concluded and he was snuggling her in his arms, 'that was a pretty good reply.'

'I don't *not* love you,' she whispered. 'I'm just ...' Confused, all over the place, surprised by the seismic-like intensity of her feelings for him but unsure whether she could trust them. Unsure whether she could risk her heart again. Unsure whether she could bring herself to be that close to another person.

Then again, she had just told him her deepest darkest secret and wanted to learn every single one of his as well.

Was *that* love?

'It's okay.' He pressed a finger against her lips. 'I'm hopeful one day you might feel the same way as me, but I don't want to pressure you.'

'Thank you,' she said, feeling deliciously warm and fuzzy inside.

'As much as I don't want to …' Theo said with a sigh a few minutes later. 'It's getting late, so I suppose I should go help the others close up downstairs. Are you going back next door, or can I convince you to stay?'

Of course she *wanted* to stay. She hadn't since that night they'd searched all over the French Quarter for Zoe because she didn't want to leave her alone, but her other parent was there tonight. Still, Sofia had no idea of the full extent of Zoe's self-destruction, and also, something about hiding away at Theo's felt cowardly. She couldn't let her ex make her feel uncomfortable in her own home (even if it was only a temporary one). After her conversation with Theo, she felt stronger, more able to handle her newest house guest.

'Not tonight,' she said simply.

Theo nodded, then dragged himself off the couch and offered her his hand. They cleaned up and dressed quickly then went back downstairs.

'Night, Cooper. Night, Roxy.' Flick waved at the bartenders, resisting the urge to tell the other woman she was wrong about Theo. Maybe he simply hadn't met his match yet?

That thought took her home and she was smiling as she quietly unlocked the shop door and climbed the stairs, not wanting to alert Zoe and Sofia to her arrival.

The apartment was dark when she reached it and she paused a moment, waiting for her eyes to adjust so she could see if Sofia lay asleep on the couch.

'Well, well, well, look what the cat dragged in?'

'Oh my God!' Flick startled at Sofia's teasing voice coming from the balcony.

She crossed over to the door and peered out to see Sofia wearing pretty purple PJs, sitting back in a cast-iron chair, her feet resting up on the railing. 'What are you doing out here?'

'Couldn't sleep. Knew I shouldn't have had that nap this arvo.'

Flick lowered herself into the seat beside Sofia.

'When you left the restaurant, you didn't come home to bed, did you?' Sofia asked.

She shook her head.

'Were you next door?' When Flick nodded, Sofia added, 'I knew there was something going on between you and that guy. What's his name? Leo?'

'Theodore, but everyone calls him Theo.'

'And he owns the bar?'

'Owns it and plays in it. He's a jazz pianist. He's brilliant.'

'Why didn't you just tell me when I asked about him earlier?'

'Because I was in shock! Because this is weird!' Flick threw her hands up in the air, both emotionally and physically exhausted and definitely still a bit drunk.

Sofia flinched and Flick hoped she hadn't woken Zoe.

She took a deep breath and spoke more calmly this time. 'Most exes can't stand to look at each other, never mind talk about new partners. Most exes don't just show up on each other's doorsteps and hang out together.'

'But I thought that's what you wanted? For us to stay friends?'

'I thought I did too, but not having that clean break that most people get when a marriage ends has made things even more confusing. The night of Emma's wedding, I was even wondering if I'd made the wrong decision. I was contemplating whether we should give our marriage another shot.'

Sofia's eyebrows crept upwards. 'Is that what you want?'

'No.' Flick shook her head, more certain than ever now. 'I was just lonely, I think, and struggling with how to move on when you're still such a big part of my life.'

'That's why you came here?'

'Yes.' Flick didn't want to hurt Sofia and being with her felt less difficult now she'd had a heart-to-heart with Theo, but it was time to tell the truth. 'I needed to get away from us. My head wants to be friends, and maybe in time that will be possible again, but not right now. We can't have the kind of friendship that I have with Neve or Emma—it's just too hard. I need time to work out who I am without you, and time to open myself up to the possibility of something more with someone else.'

'Like Theo? Are things serious between you and him then?'

She hesitated a moment. Her impulse was to say no, but that wasn't the truth. 'Yes, I think they could be.'

'Wow,' Sofia breathed. 'That happened fast.'

Flick smiled. 'When you know, you know, right?'

Sofia nodded. 'Does that mean you're going to move here permanently?'

'I don't know. It's early days.' *Very* early days, but her mind was becoming clearer with every second. 'Right now, I'm just enjoying feeling happy again.'

'I'm glad. I really am. All I ever wanted was for us both to be happy.'

'I know.' Flick felt her own eyes misting a little.

They sat in silence a short while, then Sofia said, 'I've changed my flight to California for tomorrow morning. Since it's winter in Perth, it'll be nice to spend a few extra days in the Golden State.'

'You're leaving already?'

Sofia nodded. 'Zoe told me that me being here is difficult for you and tonight you've confirmed it. I'm sorry I was so blind that I couldn't see for myself how hard it was.'

Wow. Flick couldn't believe Zoe had been so astute. She'd begun to grow up in these last few weeks in a way that even getting married hadn't achieved.

'I'm sorry too,' she said. 'I should have been more honest. But there's really no need for you to go that quickly. I can always stay next door with Theo and you can have my room.'

But Sofia shook her head. 'No, I'm not going to put you out of your own home. Go to Theo if you want, but don't feel you have to go there because of me.'

'Thank you.' Flick lost her battle with tears and this time it was she that reached out. She squeezed Sofia's perfectly manicured hand.

'I'll always love you, Flick,' Sofia said, choking up.

'Me too.' Just not in the way she'd imagined when they said their vows all those many, many years ago.

'I'm sorry I couldn't give you what you needed.'

'Me too,' Flick said again.

And then they hugged, holding each other tightly before finally pulling back. It almost felt like they were breaking up all over again, but this time there was no confusion about the future, no blurred relationship lines. As hard as it was, Flick knew she'd made the right decision.

She suggested Sofia take her bed so she would get a proper night's sleep and then she went next door to Theo.

'Well, this is a pleasant surprise,' he said ten minutes later when he unlocked the door to the bar and let her inside.

Roberta stood beside him and Flick reached out and rubbed the dog's fur. 'I hope you don't mind a late-night visitor but there's something I need to tell you.'

'Sounds ominous.' Theo stiffened slightly.

She took a quick breath. 'I'm falling in love with you as well.'

'Seriously?' His face split into a broad grin but his tone suggested he might be dreaming.

She nodded and laughed, feeling a lovely release having got it off her chest. 'How could I possibly not? You're charming and funny and kind and talented, not to mention sexy and incredibly good-looking. You make a mean scrambled eggs, and don't even get me started on your accent.'

'Is that it?' he asked when she'd finished.

She whacked him playfully but he caught her hand and yanked her into his arms. 'I kinda like your accent too,' he murmured, before lowering his mouth to hers.

It was a long, slow, tender kiss. Comfortingly familiar yet exciting all at once.

'So what do we do now?' she asked when they finally came up for air. Admitting they were in love was wonderful, but it brought with it a whole load of obstacles to overcome. The fact they lived on two different continents for starters.

'We go upstairs and get some rest,' Theo said, still holding her close, 'because it's late and you've had a very emotional day.'

'That sounds like a very wise idea.'

And, although they did go up into his room and climb into his bed, it was another few hours before they finally fell asleep. They couldn't help themselves. Like two excited teenagers, they lay there in the dark, spooned against each other, talking about what the future might look like for them and how they planned to bridge the gap of geography.

In the end, Flick had the best sleep she'd had in years. When she returned to Harvey's apartment early the following morning, Sofia was already gone.

29

Zoe

On the second Friday of their acquaintance, Miss H told Zoe they were going for lunch to the Commander's Palace—the bright sea-blue restaurant she passed every day on her walk from the streetcar to the house.

'You deserve a treat after all the work you've been doing around here, and I've got a hankering for some strawberry shortcake.'

Zoe wasn't about to put up an argument; she was excited to try the restaurant where Theo said many renowned American chefs had cut their teeth. So, after a couple of hours cleaning, Zoe helped Miss H into one of her many white dresses.

The last week or so, she'd mostly been getting around in what Zoe would call loungewear—loose white pants and muslin blouses that Miss H managed to take on and off herself, but apparently the esteemed establishment had a strict, smart casual dress policy. She wanted to look her best, and also insisted Zoe borrow a pair of closed shoes from her because the summer sandals she was wearing weren't allowed. Luckily, she and Miss H had similar sized feet. What did it matter if the style had gone out of fashion decades ago? Zoe thought, as the two of them walked the short distance to the restaurant.

They were greeted almost immediately upon arrival.

'Good afternoon, Miss Harranibar,' beamed a middle-aged man with a dark moustache, a shiny balding head and wearing a suit almost the same colour as his facial hair. His ample belly gave Zoe the impression that he didn't simply work here, but also regularly sampled the efforts of the chef. And if the aromas that hit her as they stepped inside were anything to go by, she couldn't blame him.

'Afternoon, Stanley,' returned Miss H, almost giving him a rare smile.

'And I see you've brought a visitor today?'

'Yes. Is my usual table available?'

The man dipped his head and smiled. 'It certainly is. Come with me, ladies.'

As he led them through the lower level of the restaurant, Zoe admired the numerous bronze chandeliers that hung from the ceiling. The walls were mostly painted cream with the occasional mint-green feature and beneath their feet was a spread of old-fashioned patterned carpet. The tables were dressed in crisp white cloths, matching crockery and polished silver cutlery. Whereas SoBou had a modern, funky vibe, this place clearly embraced the past.

One thing Zoe had to say for New Orleans—she hadn't had a bad meal anywhere and each restaurant had its own special character.

Although a huge space, most of the tables were taken already and Zoe was beginning to wonder where this special table of Miss H's was hiding when they came to a staircase and Stanley stood back to allow them to go up first. On the second level, he showed them to one of many smaller dining rooms leading off a main one. Its interior was just as elegant as the rest of the restaurant—all cream and gold—but cosier. Here there were only four small tables and none of the others were occupied.

Stanley held a seat out for Miss H and then did the same for Zoe, before unfolding white napkins and placing them theatrically upon their laps. 'Your server will be with you shortly. Enjoy your lunch, ladies.'

He'd barely disappeared before another guy arrived, this one younger and taller than Stanley and dressed in black pants, white shirt, black bow tie and waistcoat, and a long white apron almost to his ankles.

'Good afternoon, Miss Harranibar,' said the man, smiling widely. 'It's lovely to see you. What have you done to your arm?'

'Broken it. What does it look like, Felippe?'

His smile did not falter. 'I'm very sorry to hear that, ma'am. And who is your lovely guest?'

Miss H introduced them, and he offered his hand to Zoe. She took it, slightly bemused—waiters were not this solicitous in Australia.

'It's a pleasure to meet you, Zoe. I'm Felippe and I'll be taking care of you both this afternoon. Can I start by offering you a drink?'

'We'll have two martinis,' Miss H said sharply.

Felippe went on to explain there were four different flavours of their famous twenty-five cent martini. Apparently, you could have a total of three with lunch—at that price, Zoe understood why they needed a limit. She chose the blue-hued martini, created to match the exterior of the building, to start with and Miss H went with the same. Felippe then went through the specials of the day and left them in peace to consider the menu.

Zoe had barely begun when another waiter appeared with a pitcher of ice-cold water. This woman greeted Miss H by name as well and then poured them both a glass before retreating again.

It seemed everyone who worked here knew her. Zoe was heartened that although she didn't appear to have what you'd call real friends, Miss H clearly got social interaction from dealing with gallery owners and going about her everyday business. It was the same when they visited the local bookshop—the owner knew Miss H well. She was as much a part of the Garden District as the pretty houses, fancy blue restaurant and the cemetery. Zoe wouldn't be surprised if her house and her story were on the itineraries of the tour guides that brought walking groups around these streets.

'What are you grinning at, girl?'

'Nothing. Just admiring the beautiful decor.'

'Well, concentrate on the menu for now.'

As if telepathic, Felippe returned the moment Zoe had made her decision. She'd decided to be brave and try the turtle soup, follow it with griddle-seared gull fish, and then strawberry shortcake to finish because she'd never had it before and Miss H said it was the best she'd ever tasted.

'Your usual?' Felippe asked Miss H.

She nodded.

While they waited for their starters, Zoe and Miss H chatted about the Stephen King book she'd been reading that morning and also the Netflix show they were currently bingeing together. The older woman hadn't been much of a TV watcher until she'd broken her wrist, but she had more time in her day now and so Zoe had set up a few streaming services for her. Between television, books, giving Zoe painting tips, discovering social media and online shopping, she was managing to pass the time until she could paint again. As they spoke, other guests were led into their dining room and the three remaining tables were filled.

Zoe decided that this lovely setting would be the perfect place for her to broach the subject of sending some of Miss H's paintings to galleries further afield and was just about to do so when Felippe returned, accompanied by two new waiters with their first course. Felippe laid a basket of warm bread in the middle of the table and then motioned each waiter to step forward in turn and present their dish. It was like a theatre production with a cast of many seeing to their every need.

The first waiter presented Miss H with a plate of the most exquisite-looking strawberry salad Zoe had ever laid eyes on. Her mouth watered and she had buyer's remorse, but then the second waiter stepped forward to serve her bowl of turtle soup and she gasped as she looked up into his face. All thoughts of food forgotten.

'Jack?' He wasn't wearing glasses and his hair was neatly gelled back off his face, but still she couldn't believe she hadn't recognised him immediately. If she'd known this was the restaurant where he worked, she'd have made some excuse to Miss H about not coming.

Although her heart squeezed as their eyes met, he nodded once with the utmost professionalism—'Good afternoon, Zoe'—before stepping back to stand alongside the other waiters.

Felippe asked if they required anything else and then wished them a good meal, before giving a nod for the others to exit. Zoe immediately picked up her spoon, dipped it into her soup and shoved it into her mouth.

Miss H plucked up her fork and pointed it at Zoe. 'Do you know that boy?'

'Why do you think that?' Zoe fanned her face. It suddenly felt sweltering. Was the air conditioner not working properly?

'Quite aside from the fact you called him by name, he looked at you with an air of familiarity.'

'Um ... well, we ... we're sort of acquaintances. I met him not long after I arrived in the French Quarter and he invited me to go on a ghost tour he was running.'

'Ghost tour?' Miss H's lip curled.

'You don't believe in ghosts?' Zoe said, hoping to distract them both from the subject of Jack.

'Pfft.' She shook her head. 'I no more believe in ghosts than I do in fairies, dragons or unicorns, but there's no denying our local tourism trades on such nonsense.'

'Really? What about your house? You've never felt the presence of something there?'

Miss H frowned. 'Have *you* felt anything?'

'Well ...' Zoe didn't know what to say. The whole doors opening of their own accord, cold draughts and stairs creaking sounded so fantastical—they were the clichés of every horror movie she'd ever seen. 'Sometimes I get the feeling there's someone watching us, and I've also smelled smoke when nothing's been burning.'

'If you're talking about that time you made those scones, I'd say that was because I hadn't used the oven for a long time.'

That wasn't the only time Zoe had smelled smoke, but it was clear that Miss H didn't sense anything sinister and she'd lived there her whole life. Maybe it really was Zoe's imagination. If she hadn't had her head filled with spooky ideas by Jack, she wouldn't have felt anything out of the ordinary at all.

Miss H cackled. 'If I thought I had a ghost living with me, I'd paint the house haint blue.'

'*What* kind of blue?'

'Haint,' she clarified. 'It's a southern variation on the word "haunt" and you'll see half the houses round here painted in that specific shade of blue, because blue represents water, and apparently spirits can't traverse water. Therefore, folk believe if they paint their homes blue, it'll keep the ghosts away.'

Her expression told Zoe exactly what she thought of that idea.

'Anyway,' Miss H nodded towards Zoe's bowl, 'you'd better eat your soup before it gets cold.'

Zoe lifted another spoonful to her mouth and tried to focus on the unique flavour. She'd expected the soup to taste like seafood, but it was actually more like pork.

After a few mouthfuls, she said, 'I've been wondering if you'd allow me to send images of some of your paintings to a colleague of mine back in Australia. She knows art collectors all over the world and I think she'd be ...'

Zoe completely lost her train of thought as Jack, Felippe and the other waiter returned to the room, this time with plates for the table behind them.

'Um ...' She reached for her martini and took a much-needed sip. Why was his presence bothering her so much? Probably because she couldn't stop thinking about how they'd last left things—with Jack's *gentlemanly* offer to sleep with her. Of course she'd done the right thing when she'd told him where to go, but when he was this close, she couldn't help imagining what it might have been like to follow through. Her body flooded with warmth at the thought.

Jack retreated once again and Zoe did her best to uphold her side of the conversation, over-compensating by talking fast and spilling out all the ideas she had for Miss H's artwork—postcards to sell in local shops, prints that were cheaper than the originals and could be sold online, doing a few with more modern wedding dresses, the list went on.

'I feel like there's more to the Jack story than you're telling me,' Miss H said when the trio of waiters left the room for the fourth time.

'Oh?' Zoe swallowed, her soup now gone and also her martini. 'Why do you say that?'

'Every time he enters the room you go a deeper shade of tomato and start talking like a lunatic. He keeps sneaking glances at you too, you know?'

'He does?' Zoe didn't mean to sound so happy about that. Her body was at war with her head when it came to him.

'What happened? Did you two have a romantic liaison?'

'No. Not exactly. He asked me out to dinner after the ghost tour and then ...' Zoe's voice drifted off again.

'Then what?' The older woman leaned closer. 'Did he try something untoward?'

'No, nothing like that. He just wanted more than I did.' Zoe felt bad about this half-truth, but she didn't want Miss H to know how weak she'd been, how she'd thrown herself at Jack and he'd been the one to reject her. Sure, he'd later offered himself on a platter, but only because he felt sorry for her! 'He just ... well, we didn't part on the best of terms,' she concluded.

'Men don't like rejection,' Miss H snarled as she stabbed the final piece of strawberry. 'It's all right when they're dishing it out but quite another thing if a woman dares turn them down. You made the right decision though—you need to guard your heart.' She put down her fork and patted Zoe's hand in a rare show of affection. 'However, if he makes you feel uncomfortable, I can tell Felippe we don't want him serving in here anymore.'

'Oh no! Don't do that.' Whatever had gone on between them, he didn't deserve to get into trouble at work because of her. Especially when she wasn't telling the whole truth.

'Very well then.'

Almost the second Miss H placed her cutlery together on her plate, two new waiters swept into the room and cleared all evidence of their starters from the table. Felippe followed them with two more martinis—she couldn't recall whether they'd actually ordered them—and asked if they'd like a short break before their mains.

Miss H declined the offer and not much later the servers delivered their orders of gull fish, shrimp and grits to the table. The older woman glared daggers at Jack. Zoe almost felt sorry for him.

'Was your husband better looking than him?' Miss H asked as she tucked into her meal.

Zoe blinked—did she think Jack was ugly? If so, she needed her eyes tested. 'Um … Beau and Jack are very different—physically and personality-wise. Beau is a sports teacher and exercise fanatic, so he's more buff, and he's blonder and tanned from all the time he spends outdoors.'

Miss H nodded.

'What about Remy?' Zoe said. 'Was he handsome?'

'Oh yes.' A wistful expression came over her face. 'Incredibly so. He was very tall, big too, but not fat, just manly. He had dark hair, a bit like that boy's actually.' She shook her head. 'Doesn't matter anyway, men aren't judged on their looks like women and it makes them conceited. That Jack clearly thought he had a chance with you when you are way out of his league.'

Zoe wasn't sure whether to thank her for the compliment.

'Anyway,' Miss H continued, 'let's not waste our time talking about men.'

'Good idea.' Zoe smiled and picked up her own cutlery. She preferred to pretend Beau no longer existed and she wanted to enjoy this wicked meal—it wasn't every day you got to eat in a place as fancy-pants as this one.

They spoke a while about the Creole influences that inspired their dishes, before Miss H said, 'How long are you planning on staying in New Orleans?'

Zoe sighed. That was the million-dollar question. 'I don't know. I suppose I'll have to return to Australia when Mum does. I'll need to look for another job or try to get my old one back.'

The prospect did not fill her with joy. Here she could forget about the things she'd have to sort out with He Who Was Now Dead To Her, but when she went home, she'd have to face them. She'd have to initiate divorce proceedings, see people who knew what had happened, and find somewhere else to live. They'd paid their rent monthly and in advance, so she hadn't had to worry about this expense yet, but the next payment was imminent. Neither of them could afford it on their own—maybe his lover could move in with him? Whatever, Zoe certainly didn't feel it should be *her* duty to take care of this, but she didn't want it to affect her rental history on top of everything else. *Argh.*

'Did you hear me?' Miss H's sharp voice drew Zoe from her thoughts.

'I'm sorry. What did you say?'

'I have a proposition for you. I know you refused to accept any payment from me initially, but what you've done for me and around the house, and your ideas about how I can get more out of my paintings has gone above and beyond a favour. And, I've enjoyed your company immensely. I'd like to offer you a job. Would you consider coming to work for me more long term?'

Zoe's mouth fell open, but she quickly recovered. 'What would this entail exactly?'

'I would like you to continue to do a bit of cleaning and cooking for me. I can't deny I'm getting on a bit and you're right, I can't look after my big old place by myself, but I don't want to live anywhere else. Going into one of those residential care facilities would kill me. May as well take me straight to Lafayette No. 1.'

Zoe tried to smile but as much as she'd enjoyed the last couple of weeks, she had higher hopes for the future than cleaning for a living.

As if Miss H could read her mind, she went on, 'Of course you'd be much more than a housekeeper. What I really want is an assistant. I love your ideas for my business and you clearly know your way around the world wide web. I'm also getting tired of dealing with gallery owners and the like, so you'd handle that side of things for me as well. I'd pay you a generous wage and we could work out a commission-based bonus as well. But there is one condition.'

'Oh?' Zoe thought it sounded too good to be true.

Miss H nodded. 'That whatever time you spend daily helping me around the house, you also spend on your own art. You have far more talent than you imagine. I don't want this website you're talking about just to sell *my* prints, I want you to sell yours on there as well. So, what do you say?'

'Wow.' That was about the only word that she could manage for now.

'Maybe if the sales take off, we can hire someone else to do the cleaning to give you more time to paint and concentrate on the important things.'

'That sounds amazing. I'd need to look into getting a working Visa or something though. And also, I'll have to find some place to live once Mum leaves. Have you any idea what the rent is like around here?'

Miss H waved a hand in the air. 'Oh, you don't need to worry about any of that. My lawyer can help us with the Visa issues when she draws up your contract, and of course, board will be part of that. It would be stupid for you to pay rent elsewhere when I have a massive old house full of empty bedrooms.'

Zoe gulped. She should have known there'd be a catch. Spending even a couple of minutes upstairs had given her the creeps, never mind taking up residence alongside the dust, cockroaches and who knows what else. Did she have the guts?

Possibly misunderstanding her hesitation, Miss H added, 'We won't live on top of each other—you'd practically have the entire second storey of the house to yourself as my knees prevent me from going up there much these days. And you would only work business hours with two full days off a week. Anyway, there's no need to be hasty in your decision-making—take some time to think about it if you want.'

As Miss H turned her attention back to her shrimp, Zoe shook her head. 'No, I don't need any time. If you're serious, then my answer is yes.'

She'd be crazy to turn down this opportunity to pursue her art, make some valuable contacts and gain some business experience as well. It probably wasn't the kind of career move her parents would approve of, but she couldn't bludge off her mum forever. And besides possible poltergeists, the only other negative would be the potential of occasionally running into Jack—and that was much more bearable than the thought of running into people who knew what Beau had done.

'Glorious.' Miss H gave a rare smile. 'I'll get Felippe to bring us some champagne to celebrate.'

30

Felicity

At the sound of the bell above the door, Flick looked up from her work desk and smiled at the sight of Zoe entering the shop. She downed her tools as her daughter wove her way through the exhibits towards her.

'Well, hello hello. What brings you home so early? Did Aurelia finally get sick of you?'

Zoe grinned. 'Ha-ha! Quite the opposite in fact. Have you got time for a quick chat? I can make you a cup of tea and bring it down?'

'Actually, why don't I close up for half an hour and we'll go get some coffee and cake somewhere? I could use some fresh air and there's generally a lull this time of day anyway.'

After washing her hands and hanging up her apron, Flick put the 'Back soon' sign on the door, then she and Zoe walked a short while, soaking up the late afternoon French Quarter atmosphere, until they came to a café on Royal Street. After road-testing a number of local establishments, Flick had decided this one had the best coffee in town and she'd been coming here almost daily. So far she'd resisted the delicious-looking cakes in the glass cabinet, but not today. Her mind had been working in overdrive as she contemplated her future and she was in dire need of something sweet.

'What do you want?' she asked Zoe as she gestured to the display. 'My shout.'

Zoe shook her head. 'I don't think I could eat another bite after my lunch—I had the most amazing strawberry shortcake. But you have something.'

They ordered two iced coffees and a slice of Doberge cake, a multi-layered creation that alternated buttermilk cake with chocolate pudding and was topped with icing. Flick had never seen anything like it but was on a roll of trying new things. New country. New relationship. New cake.

'So, what do you want to talk about?' she asked as they sat at a table on the sidewalk. The café's concertina doors were pushed wide open, blurring the lines between inside and out.

'Well,' Zoe cleared her throat. 'Today, Miss H offered me a job.'

'Wow. What kind of job?'

'She wants me to be her assistant,' Zoe said, going on to explain that she'd still help with jobs around the house but mostly be in charge of selling her art to galleries and online. 'I know this might sound like a step down from what I was doing with Gretchen, but Miss H is *so* much more encouraging of me pursuing my own art. She wants me to dedicate time each day to painting and to sell my own prints as well as hers on the new website I'm planning. Plus, she's also going to speak to some local galleries about taking some of my work on commission.'

Excitement radiated from Zoe, but she was clearly nervous about what Flick would say. It was an unusual job offer, and if she wasn't in the process of trying to work out how she could move here permanently herself, she'd probably have major reservations. But Zoe had real talent and Flick knew how hard it could be when you were just starting out. Aurelia obviously saw her daughter's potential as well, and this softened her towards her.

And having Zoe in New Orleans would mean there was even less left for Flick in Australia. Maybe they could get a place together once Harvey returned and Flick had her own future sorted out.

'And before you ask, the job comes with a room, therefore my living expenses will be minimal.'

'Oh?' Flick's heart squeezed a little. So much for that idea. 'When do you think you might move there?'

Zoe opened her mouth but was interrupted by the arrival of their coffee and a massive slice of cake. They thanked the waitress who winked at them and disappeared back inside.

'It'll probably take me a couple of days to get everything sorted,' said Zoe. 'I'm not moving into a room upstairs until I've completely detoxed it.' She made a face and visibly shuddered. 'So, maybe a week? I'll come visit lots though and, while you're still here, you should come see us too. We went to this awesome restaurant for lunch today—I definitely want to take you back. The only problem is, Jack works there.'

'Jack, as in Amish ghost-hunter Jack?'

'How many Jacks do you think I know here?'

'What happened between you and him anyway?'

Zoe sighed. 'I made a bit of a fool of myself—seems to be a habit whenever he's near. But I don't really want to talk about it. Let's just say you were right—I'm not ready to start anything with anyone else. I'm not sure I'll ever be. The prospect of dating is terrifying. It was all so easy with Beau, but from what I've seen during my brief life as a single woman, good men are few and far between.'

Zoe was too young to sound so tired and cynical, but Flick understood it was all part of the process of moving on. She also suspected her daughter's feelings for Jack were more complicated than she cared to admit. It would be good for her to spend some time alone, working out who she was before getting involved with anyone else. It had taken Flick four years to feel ready to move on. You couldn't rush these things.

'So,' she said, picking up the fork and digging it into the cake. 'Are you one hundred per cent sure this job is what you want? You're not doing it because it's easier than heading back to Perth and … you know, facing things?'

'I'm sure.' She nodded. 'I won't deny that staying here is appealing, but I do know I need to talk to Beau, split our finances, sort the house, et cetera. And I will, I promise, but he's got nothing to do with this. I love spending time with Miss H and I really believe I can learn a lot from her. Besides, she's paying me to paint—no way will I find another job like that.'

Flick had to concede that point. She only hoped Aurelia wasn't also schooling her in the ways of becoming a bitter spinster. At least Flick would be nearby to keep an eye on the situation. 'Are you sure she has the money to pay you?'

'Apparently. She's getting her lawyer to draw up a contract asap, but I get the impression she's actually rather wealthy. Her paintings go for well over two thousand dollars apiece, and her father came from money.'

Flick couldn't believe anyone would pay that much, but she kept her mouth shut. What did she know about that kind of art? Plenty of people didn't understand the appeal of taxidermy. As long as Zoe was happy, so was she. 'It certainly does seem like a wonderful opportunity. Congratulations, darling.'

She lifted her mug and held it up to Zoe.

'Thanks, Mum.' Zoe beamed as they clinked their mugs and, as if the universe was joining in their celebrations, music exploded up the street.

There was always music playing somewhere in the French Quarter, but this was getting louder and sounded like some kind of jazz parade coming their way. Zoe and Flick peered down the road, craning their heads in the direction of the music.

First to appear were two police officers cruising down the street on shiny blue Harley Davidsons, white helmets on their heads and dark sunnies on their faces. People were slowing on the sidewalks, lifting their phones to take snapshots of whatever was approaching. As the bikes slowly passed by, Flick and Zoe got their first glimpse of what all the excitement was about.

A bride and groom were dancing down the middle of the road behind the cops, the deep sounds of brass instruments and drums rumbling behind them. The bride looked stunning in a frilly cream dress that flowed out in layers from the waist, a little like a tiered wedding cake. She waved a pretty lace parasol above her head as she moved in time to the beat of the band, and Flick laughed when she caught a glimpse of the sneakers under her skirt. You couldn't make moves like that in stilettos. Dressed in a cream suit to match and a bright red bow tie, her groom looked as all grooms should—besotted and completely oblivious to everyone watching them, his eyes only for his new wife.

A group of well-dressed revellers followed the newlyweds and the band came up behind them.

'What's going on?' Zoe asked when the waitress reappeared to clear the table beside them.

Like everyone in this place, she took her sweet time answering, pausing first to admire the band who looked to be having the time of their lives in their smart hats and black and white uniforms. Behind them there were even more people, carrying cocktails in plastic tumblers and/or paper fans as they danced and laughed their way down the street.

'It's a second line parade,' the waitress explained. 'Must have seen a zillion in my life and they never cease to make me happy.'

Flick knew what she meant—it was impossible not to smile watching it all unfold.

'What exactly is a second line parade?' Zoe asked.

'Oh sorry. Well, African-Americans have been having second line funerals forever but round here we celebrate nearly every occasion with one—business openings, festivals and especially weddings. Following the reception, you parade through the city with your bridal party and a brass band.'

Flick gestured to the crowds shadowing the bride and groom. 'So, all those people are wedding guests?'

'Nah. The lot before the band are the bridal party and some after them will be the guests, but the magic of a second line is that everyone celebrates with you.' She had to shout over the din of the music and chatter. 'Friends and strangers alike. By the time they've finished their walk round the Quarter, they'll have hundreds following them. It's about becoming one with the music and the city. It's almost a sin to get married in the French Quarter without a second line, and why would you want to? You can be sure if I ever tie the knot, it'll be me dancing down that street.'

The waitress did a little jig on the spot, rocking along with the passers-by. 'It's a once in a lifetime experience.'

'Unless you get married more than once,' Zoe said as she guzzled her drink like it was alcohol. She had to be the only person in the vicinity not smiling like an idiot.

The waitress gave her a funny look and then got on with her business.

As the wedding parade disappeared down the street, Flick turned back to Zoe. 'Actually, you're not the only one with news. Speaking of second weddings ... Theo asked me to marry him.'

'What?!'

Flick reached out to catch Zoe's drink as she almost dropped it. 'Well, you know how I said things weren't serious between us?'

Zoe nodded.

'Turns out I didn't know what I was talking about. I'm ...' She felt her chest expanding as she spoke. 'Theo and I are in love. I honestly didn't think I'd ever feel this way about anyone again but—'

'Did you say yes?' Zoe interrupted, her eyes wide.

'No.' Flick took a quick breath. 'And it's not exactly what you think. He was kind of joking. We're not at that stage quite yet, but we do want to pursue a long-term relationship. And I like it here. Actually, the longer I spend here, the more I can't imagine living anywhere else.'

'I know what you mean.'

'And it makes much more sense for me to relocate than Theo because he has the bar. I can get commissions anywhere and being here would feel like a proper fresh start. But I can only stay permanently if it's for work or I'm—'

'Married,' Zoe finished.

Flick nodded. 'Exactly.'

'Look, are you sure about this? I've got nothing against Theo, but ...' She shook her head. 'I just hope you know what you're doing.'

'I'm not going to marry him, Zoe, at least not straightaway—apparently it's not as simple as the movies make out to get hitched for a green card anyway. But what I'm trying to tell you is that it looks like you won't be the only one staying in New Orleans. I'll probably have to go back to Perth for a while to sort out the house, work out what to do with Dog—although I'm sure Sofia will take him. And most importantly, I have to find a way that I can stay here longer. I'm going to talk to Harvey about the possibility of him sponsoring me. Even if he doesn't actually pay me, I can take commissions, and that might mean I can live here on a working Visa, like you.'

'And if you can't get a working Visa through Harvey?' Zoe absentmindedly picked up Flick's fork and stole a bit of cake.

'Well, then Theo might employ me as a bar manager or something.'

'Because you've got *so* much experience in that area.'

'It would really only be on paper—I'd still practise taxidermy. There's plenty of work round here. I've already got my first commission.' When Zoe frowned, Flick added, 'Edward. You can tell Aurelia I'll take care of him now.'

'But you don't taxi pets?'

'I'm going to make an exception for this one.'

'Thanks, Mum.' Zoe gave her a warm smile. 'So, will you live with Theo?'

'That's definitely on the cards. There's plenty of room in his apartment—he even said he'd be happy for me to set up a studio in one of his spare rooms.'

'It seems pretty fast, Mum. I mean … how long have you known the man?'

'A little over a month, but it honestly feels a lot longer. He's a good man. He's made me feel alive again.' Flick bit her lip to stop her smile exploding.

'Am I gonna have to call him Dad now?'

'No.' Flick shook her head and grinned. 'Definitely not.'

'Well then, I'm happy for you.' Zoe's tone didn't quite match her words, but Flick decided not to call her on it. She might be all grown up, but no matter what your age, it would be difficult coming to terms with your parents having new partners.

'Who'd have thought that when you made the crazy decision to come to New Orleans, we'd both end up here? And perhaps more than temporarily.'

'Yes. I know.' Flick thought back to the night of Emma's wedding when she'd been feeling at her lowest—if she hadn't been so down, she'd never have looked twice at Harvey's message and she'd never have met Theo. 'Life certainly works in mysterious ways.'

They sat a little longer, discussing what they both needed to organise while they finished their drinks and cake. Flick was enjoying Zoe's company and was in no rush to get back to work, so they popped into a few cute boutiques as they walked back. Zoe bought a couple of lovely scented candles for her new room at Aurelia's and Flick bought some postcards to send to her dad, Toby, Neve and Emma.

'Have you told Tobes about Theo yet?' Zoe asked.

'No, I'm going to call him tonight. Have you spoken to him lately?'

'Yes. He's been such a great support. He's started checking in on me every couple of days.'

Flick smiled, proud of her children and the close relationship they had now they were adults. She slowed in front of the voodoo shop and gestured to a flashing neon sign in the front window: READINGS. 'Should we get our fortunes told?'

Zoe raised her eyebrows. 'Are you serious? I didn't think you were into stuff like that, and don't you have to reopen the shop?'

'Soon ... but no one really keeps time in this place, so a little longer won't matter. And it's just for a bit of fun. It's what you do when you visit the French Quarter—you take a ghost tour, you drink Hurricanes and you get your fortune told. Come on, let's see if Luna can fit us in.'

'Luna? Do you know the reader?' Zoe asked.

'Not really, but Theo does—he introduced us a while back.'

Flick led the way inside the building that from the outside looked like something out of Diagon Alley. They gazed around as their noses acclimatised to the powerful smells. Flick detected scents of lavender, rosemary, and possibly jasmine or something else. Every surface from the walls to the ceiling and even much of the floor was covered in the kinds of things you wouldn't find in most shops. There were wooden masks with terrifying expressions, skulls of all sizes, spells that proclaimed to do all sorts of wonderful things, candles, charms, rosaries and other types of beads, dreamcatchers, rows and rows of tarot cards, horned beasts, crystals, and voodoo dolls that weren't half as cute as the ones you found in the souvenir stores but looked like maybe they could actually do some damage.

'Maybe I should get some of this for Miss H's place?' Zoe said, holding up a bottle of something called 'Away All Evil Spirits' furniture cleaner.

Flick chuckled as she checked out the bottle beside it, which was some kind of house blessing spray.

Off to one side of the busy shop was a voodoo altar with a number of candles flickering in front of a morbid-looking doll. There were also bones, jars filled with dark liquid, some shells and crosses among other things. The whole place had a fascinating mix of African spiritual, Catholicism and French Creole culture.

There were so many people milling about that it was probably a long shot, but Flick decided to go to the counter and ask if Luna had any available reading appointments anyway.

As if she had sensed Flick's presence, the woman herself appeared from the back through a purple and gold curtain. 'Good afternoon, Felicity.'

Flick was impressed she remembered her at all—never mind her name—from that one brief meeting a few weeks ago. 'Hello. I was wondering if my daughter and I could book in for a reading with you?' She gestured to Zoe, still holding the bottle of 'Away All Evil Spirits'.

'When were you hoping?'

'Sometime this afternoon … as soon as you can?'

'As it happens, you're in luck.' Luna smiled as if even she was surprised by this. 'I'm free right now.'

'Great.' Flick smiled back. 'How much does it cost?'

'I don't charge for my services,' Luna said, which somehow made her seem more legitimate. 'But if you feel like leaving a tip, I will not object.'

'Of course. And can we come in together?'

Luna shook her head, her frizzy black hair swishing around her face. 'No. I don't do group readings.' She pointed at Flick. 'You first.'

Leaving Zoe to wander around the shop, Flick followed Luna through the curtain into a small, dimly lit room. The smell of incense was even stronger in here; the walls were painted a deep orange, there were fairy lights strung across the ceiling and the only furniture was a small table covered with a jewel-green velvet cloth, its golden tassels brushing the floor, and two chairs either side. Luna indicated for Flick to sit.

After taking a deep breath, she grabbed hold of Flick's left hand, smoothing her cold thumbs over it. 'I see things and I sense things through energy transfer,' she said, closing her eyes. 'Sometimes I'm visited by souls that have left this earth. You need to relax and let me do the work.'

Flick shivered as silence descended on the tiny room.

After a few long moments, Luna's voice broke it. 'I see two children … one is very close to you.'

Well, that wasn't hard, Flick thought dubiously—hadn't she just introduced her daughter? You couldn't get much closer than the very next room.

'And the other is a … boy? I feel as if he is scared of great heights.'

Flick couldn't help raising her eyebrows. How many people with acrophobia wanted to fly planes?

As if reading her thoughts, Luna added, 'It could be a metaphorical fear. This child has his eye on a dream, and he works hard to strive towards it, but sometimes he is scared of his own potential. He gets that from you—you sometimes feel great fear as well.'

Fear? The only thing she was scared of was something awful happening to her children and she reckoned that was a universal parental fear. Thankfully, Luna had her eyes closed so didn't see the scepticism on Flick's face.

Luna spoke a little more about her children, but Flick got the feeling she was simply saying things she thought a mum would want to hear. They were both going to be successful in love and careers, she would be a grandmother multiple times over—Zoe might be interested to hear that!

She went quiet for a little while and then squeezed Flick's hand. 'Oh, I'm feeling a presence … You lost someone close to you when you were very young …'

Although Flick's heart leapt, her inner sceptic reminded her that hardly anyone got to her age without losing a loved one.

'A woman?' Luna opened her eyes and looked directly at Flick. 'Your mother?'

Forgetting herself a moment, Flick nodded, ice flooding her body.

'Yes.' Luna's face softened into a smile. 'She wants you to know she misses you a great deal but she's proud of the woman you've become. She has a message for you.' Luna closed her eyes again and moved her thumbs in a circular motion across Flick's palm. 'She knows you have suffered heartache recently and she wants you to know you will find meaning again—a love deeper and more stronger than your first. But in order to embrace that love, you must stop re-reading the last chapter of your life. Does this make sense to you?'

Unable to speak, Flick nodded.

'However, she has one more word of warning.' Luna paused a moment. 'Remember, not everything is always as it seems.'

Hah. Flick didn't need a clairvoyant to tell her that; her marriage had taught her that lesson all too well.

Luna let go of Flick's hand abruptly and cleared her throat. 'I'll see Zoe now.'

As she stood, Flick tried to remember if she'd told Luna her daughter's name. She thanked her, gave her a generous tip and left the tiny room, gesturing for Zoe to go in.

'What a load of BS,' Zoe exclaimed when she came up beside Flick about five minutes later.

'Oh? What did she say?'

'She told me wedding bells were in my future, and when I told her that I think she means divorce, she changed her tune—said that although I'd suffered a great betrayal there was joy to come, that I just needed to open my heart to opportunities. Why does everyone think that's all anyone cares about? There's more to life than so-called love, which is what I told her. So then she changed her tune and started talking about all this travel she sees in my future.' Zoe sniggered. 'Considering my accent, that wasn't much of a leap. She ended by telling me I should be wary of taking things at face value.'

'That's interesting,' Flick mused. 'She said much the same to me.'

Zoe snorted. 'As if we both don't already know *that*. No wonder she didn't want us to go in together. I reckon she gets her material off fortune cookies.'

Flick told her what Luna had said about Toby and they both burst into laughter as they exited the shop.

'Oh well,' Zoe said, 'you were right—it *was* fun.'

31

Zoe

A week later Zoe officially moved out of Harvey's apartment in the French Quarter to Miss H's mansion in the Garden District. A couple of days earlier on Flick's day off, they'd taken an Uber to the Walmart, which was closer to Miss H's place than the Quarter but still too far to walk carrying all their purchases.

Although Zoe's chosen room upstairs already had a bed and furniture, she wanted to freshen it up and make it feel like hers. So, as well as working on some canvases she planned to hang on the walls, washing and rehanging the heavy curtains, vacuuming and scrubbing until her fingers ached, she'd bought herself some cheap bedding and a few other accessories to splash about. The fact the sheets and decorative cushions she chose were mostly blue had *nothing* to do with what Miss H had mentioned about haint paint. She'd *always* liked blue.

And the fact she'd bought 'Away All Evil Spirits' from the voodoo shop and rubbed it all over every available surface was simply because she liked the smell of it.

The wardrobe in her bedroom had been empty except for a few boxes, which she transferred into another one of the rooms, before airing it out and hanging up her clothes. As she'd packed in a rush, most of her stuff was still in Perth, but Sofia had promised that as soon as she got home from California, she'd go over to Zoe's old place and strip it of everything she owned. Her parents had also kindly offered to pay out their lease and, although she hadn't been able to bring herself to actually talk to Beau, she'd emailed him and asked him to notify the landlord and organise the vacate clean. It was the *least* he could do. Much of her belongings she'd asked Sofia to box up and store at her place, but she was going to send a few more clothes and Flick would probably bring some more when she went back to Australia.

By the time Zoe had worked her magic on the bedroom it was looking great and hardly recognisable as one of the rooms she'd peeked in on that first visit.

Between a bit of cleaning and cooking, the website she'd been creating and her own painting, her days were full and she was loving the job. Although Miss H had told her she could do whatever she wanted in her free time, they spent most evenings together as well. They never talked business at night, having decided that since they lived and worked together, they needed boundaries. Instead, after dinner they'd return to the sunroom where Zoe would paint while Miss H watched TV, because the light wasn't good enough for her to read at night and she still wasn't able to do much else. They were rapidly working their way through a number of shows on Netflix.

So far tonight they'd watched a couple of episodes of *How to Get Away with Murder*, which was turning out to be one of Miss H's favourite shows, and the last episode of *Virgin River*. Miss H spent most of her time making derogatory comments about the handsome male characters, and Zoe suspected she only watched it so she could make scathing remarks about romance.

'Do you recommend any good Australian television shows?' Miss H asked now as the credits rolled up the screen. 'I feel that as I have an Aussie living with me, I should educate myself on the ways of your people.'

Zoe managed not to smirk. 'Well, we're pretty similar to you Americans really, but we do have some good dramas. I'm not sure what will be available on Netflix here, but I can take a look,' she said, resting her brush on the edge of her paint palette. 'What kind of thing were you thinking of?'

'Something that shows the landscape,' Miss H said after a few moments. 'Remy and I planned to travel and the Australian outback was at the top of our list.'

'Really?' Zoe was always fascinated when she mentioned her runaway groom. 'Where did you guys plan to go?'

'Oh everywhere. Remy taught geography and he had grand dreams to travel to all the places he studied. I was going to accompany him and paint.'

'Did you ever think of going by yourself?' Zoe asked, wondering if the infamous Remy had disappeared because he'd decided he'd rather travel solo. Maybe he'd got cold feet and chosen to sow his wild oats across the world before settling down?

'Once or twice the thought crossed my mind, but I realised that everywhere I went I'd have been imagining what it would have been like if we were together. The idea lost its shine.'

At that moment the lights flickered above them and Zoe glanced up at the ceiling.

'Damn faulty wiring,' Miss H grumbled.

'Would you like me to call an electrician tomorrow to see if there's something they can do about that?'

Often when they were sitting here at night, the lights dimmed a little and then returned to normal. Like the noises the house made, Miss H always put it down to its age.

'Perhaps.' The older woman sighed. 'You know what, I think I'm actually ready for bed. Maybe we can start a new Aussie show tomorrow?'

'Okay.' Zoe nodded, despite being disappointed. She'd been hoping to hear more about Remy and Miss H's romance and besides, it was only just after nine o'clock. No way she was ready to venture upstairs just yet. Even being down here in this big house at night was a little eerie without company. 'Would you like some help?'

'Just a little if you don't mind.'

They went into the bedroom and Zoe helped Miss H out of her day clothes and into pyjamas and then left her to finish getting ready for bed alone. The visiting nurse still came a few times a week to help Miss H shower and Zoe mostly helped her dress, but she was getting pretty good at managing everything else with only one arm.

After bidding her goodnight, Zoe went into the kitchen and made a cup of tea, resisting the urge to help herself to the bottle of whiskey she'd seen in the back of one of the cupboards. She'd promised her mum she wouldn't drink alone, and she really did not want to regress to where she'd been a couple of weeks ago. So, taking her tea into the sunroom, she put some upbeat music on her phone, popped in her ear-pods, and tried to focus once again on the scene she was painting.

But being alone with her thoughts wasn't healthy. Every few minutes she'd realise her hand was hanging limply in the air, hovering over the canvas, and she was staring into space ... thinking of Beau.

Thinking of how she'd lost a husband, a lover, and also the best friend she'd ever had. Or so she'd *thought*.

Argh! She slammed her paintbrush down and flopped onto the sofa. What was the point of being halfway across the world if she couldn't banish him from her head?

Frustration coursing through her veins, she glanced at the time on her phone. It wasn't really that late. Maybe she should go out? If she ventured back to the French Quarter, Bourbon Street would be alive and pumping for hours more. But after her run-in with the cowboy, she didn't want to hit the pubs and clubs alone. And that presented a problem. The only other person around her age she knew here was Jack, and no *way* was she calling him!

She sighed and her eyes prickled. How were you supposed to meet new people in a new town at her age? While she liked working for Miss H, it wasn't exactly going to provide a lot of opportunity for meeting people her own age.

Tinder? Bumble? No, that wasn't what she was after. She didn't want to hook up or date anyone, she simply wanted someone— preferably female—to hang out with after work. She wanted friends she could start fresh with. Friends who didn't know her past. Was there an app for that kind of thing?

Damn you, Beau, for putting me in this predicament.

Instead of throwing herself on the mercy of the internet, she called Flick. Maybe she could go over there? It was never too late to visit your own mother, right?

Just when she thought the call was going to drop out, her mum answered.

'Hey, sweetheart.' There was music in the background, meaning Flick was either outside on the balcony or next door in the bar. 'How are you?'

'Oh, *great*. Just been doing a little painting and I was thinking—'

'Hang on a moment,' Flick shouted over the top of the music. Zoe heard the muffled sounds of conversation and then she came back on the line, the background quieter now. 'Sorry, I was in the bar and it was a little loud. I'm just waiting for Theo to finish his set and then we're going to go grab some dinner.'

Zoe's heart squeezed—even her mum had a better social life than she did. She could hardly ask to come over now. Flick would say it was fine, but she didn't want to gatecrash a romantic dinner.

'Anyway, I'm glad you called,' she said. 'I was going to ring you tomorrow and ask you something.'

'Oh?'

'It's Theo's fiftieth birthday on Friday. He doesn't want much fuss, but I wanted to do something special so I've decided to surprise him with a cake. I'm going to invite all his staff, even the ones who won't be working that night and Lauri-Ann is going to try and round up some of his friends. I'd love you to come too—you can bring Aurelia if you want?'

'What a wonderful idea. I'll definitely be there, but I'll probably come alone. Don't think it'll be Miss H's scene.'

Zoe felt more excited than she probably should by the prospect of spending an evening celebrating her mum's new boyfriend's big five-o, but some of his bar staff were young. Maybe one of them could become a friend? Or at least introduce her to more people?

'Fantastic.' Flick sounded equally as excited.

'So, is there anything I should bring? Besides a present of course?'

'You don't need to bring anything. I'm going to go shopping first thing tomorrow morning to buy the ingredients, that way I can make the cake before opening the shop and ice it Friday morning.'

'What kind of cake are you thinking?' Zoe asked, wanting to keep her mum talking as long as possible.

'I'm going to make a piano.'

'Like the one you made for me for my tenth birthday when you and Dad were trying to encourage me to keep practising?'

'Yes.' Flick laughed. 'Or is that too cheesy? Maybe I should just make one of those cakes with chocolate bars exploding out of the top?'

'No, go with the piano. He'll love it.'

They spoke a bit longer before Flick announced, 'Sorry, darling, but I'm going to have to go. Theo's finished playing.'

'No worries. You have a good night and I'll see you Friday. Love you.'

'Love you too, sweetheart.'

Feeling much lighter, Zoe went back to her painting for another hour or so before her eyelids began to feel heavy and she finally made the trek upstairs. The lights were already on because she'd put them on before it got dark, not wanting to spook herself with shadows.

Sometimes she didn't know what was worse—the thoughts of Beau or the thoughts that Miss H's house was haunted. The latter she could laugh off during the day but was harder at night when everything was pitch-black.

She headed into her bedroom, changed into her pyjamas and then went down the hallway into one of the two bathrooms on the second floor to do her nightly face routine and brush her hair and teeth. Spitting into the sink, she wiped her mouth with a flannel before straightening again and glancing into the mirror.

Her whole body froze.

There was someone standing in the doorway behind her.

Instinct kicked in and she spun around, raising her fists, ready to defend herself but ... there was nobody there.

She blinked and shook her head. Then, like one of those Too Stupid To Live characters in scary movies—how many times had she yelled at the TV, 'Stay the hell where you are!'—she rushed out into the hallway, glancing wildly up and down. She stilled, listening for sounds of footsteps … *anything*. But all she could hear was her own ragged breathing. All the doors except to her bedroom and the bathroom were closed, everything out on the landing exactly as it had been, except … was that the smell of smoke again?

Heart thudding, she followed the smell down to the end of the hallway to a door she knew led to the attic, yanked it open and peered up the narrow staircase. Although there were shards of moonlight coming in from the windows she'd seen from the street, there was no way she was venturing up there—she wasn't that TSTL. She hadn't even been able to bring herself to check it out during the day.

Closing the door, she sniffed again, but could no longer detect anything except the furniture polish she'd smothered over everything.

'You're clearly going crazy,' she whispered, half-laughing to herself, because right now it seemed not only the most likely explanation but also the least terrifying. No real person could have disappeared that fast. And why would they?

What had they looked like anyway? It was all a blur. She couldn't even be sure whether the vision was a man or a woman.

And, if she couldn't be sure what they looked like, how could she be certain they were even there? Clearly her imagination was playing tricks on her again.

Nevertheless, when Zoe went back into her bedroom, she checked under the bed, in the wardrobe, behind the curtains, then closed the door and almost broke her back dragging a heavy wooden dresser in front of it.

There. She smiled. That would stop any intruders in their tracks or at least alert her to their attempts. As she glanced around the room looking for something she could use as a weapon, another thought struck. The dresser might be able to protect her from a person but ... couldn't ghosts walk through walls?

Unease slithered down her spine as she climbed into bed. Was that true or was it just a myth? Along with things moving around of their own accord and strange electrical glitches.

Of course it was myth, she told herself as she snuggled under the covers.

After another hour or so of lying in bed, wide awake, listening for noises that went bump in the night, Zoe finally drifted off to sleep. In the morning, in the light of day, with the dresser still firmly across the door, her experience last night didn't seem quite so terrifying.

In fact, she was pretty certain she'd imagined the whole thing.

32

Felicity

Thursday morning, Flick snuck out of Theo's bed and quietly dressed so as not to disturb him—she couldn't afford to be waylaid today. She went back next door, showered, and ate a quick breakfast while she read messages that had come in overnight.

Since Zoe had arrived and Flick had started seeing Theo, she'd abandoned the group chat and had been texting privately with Neve and Emma instead. There'd been lots to discuss and a zillion messages over the last few weeks, but also a couple of Facetime calls, including one when Flick confessed how serious things had become between her and Theo.

It appeared her friends were still digesting her 'good' news.

Neve: *I can't believe you're leaving us.*

Emma: *I know ... book club just won't be the same via Zoom.*

Flick smiled at the screen. She was going to miss her two closest friends like crazy, but she knew they'd come around eventually. Neither of them would think twice about moving to *Mars* if that was the only way they could be with James and Patrick.

Felicity: You were the ones who encouraged me to start dating again.

Neve: We told you to go out and play the field, have sex, have fun, a holiday fling, NOT find the man of your dreams and never come back. If you were ready to find Mr Right, we'd have made you stay right here and do it!

Emma: But as heartbroken as I am that you are moving across the other side of the world, I'm happy for you. Just hope it's not too long before we can meet him.

Neve: Yes, we need to make sure he's good enough for our Flick.

Felicity: I can assure you he is.

Emma: We'll be the judge of that.

Neve: Well, you're the travel agent, Em—when's the best time of year to get a good deal? James and I are definitely up for a holiday. Why don't you and Patrick come with us?

Emma: That sounds like lots of fun.

Felicity: I agree—it does, but right now I need to organise a birthday cake. I'll chat with you guys later.

Flick slipped her phone into her handbag and then plucked Harvey's car keys off the hook in the kitchen where they'd remained untouched since she arrived. If she was going to be staying, there were a few things she needed to address. Getting better at tipping was one thing and conquering her fear of driving on the right-hand side of the road another. Today, when she needed to buy the ingredients for Theo's fiftieth birthday cake, seemed like the perfect opportunity to try the latter.

She only hoped the car started after being idle for over a month. And that she could actually find where Harvey kept it. Most of the residents of the French Quarter parked on the streets, but on Bourbon there wasn't such luxury, so both Harvey and Theo parked in a rented garage within walking distance of the shop and bar. Flick was relieved when the engine started after only a little encouragement. She repositioned the seat, checked the mirrors, played with the indicator and windscreen wipers and then held her breath as she reversed out.

'Woohoo!' She actually shrieked as she turned onto the street, following the directions spoken by her phone. *Step one, accomplished.*

Now she just had to remember to keep right and try not to mount the kerb, which felt a lot closer than it usually did.

There were a couple of near misses. The side of Harvey's car almost kissed a trash can (see, she was learning the lingo) and she was beeped at twice for stopping at an amber light (better to be safe than sorry). But she arrived at Walmart only a little later than her GPS had initially predicted with both the car and herself still intact. She felt as if she'd just won a gold medal and could not wipe the smile off her face as she headed inside.

Back home Flick dreaded grocery shopping—years of doing it for her family had taken any joy out of it—but here she was like a kid let loose in a candy store. After looking through the homewares section and finding a couple of tins that would be perfect for Theo's piano cake, she couldn't resist checking out the book section. She threw a couple of paperbacks into her trolley and then progressed into the grocery part of the superstore, which was just as fun as the rest. She took her time going up and down every aisle, taking it all in, grabbing everything she needed for the cake and more. Most of the brands were different from Australia, so there were lots of completely new things to discover and the sizes were ginormous.

She slowed in one aisle and marvelled over the mammoth bags of sugary cereal, unable to resist snapping a photo and sending it to Toby because she knew he'd get a kick out of them: *Maybe if we'd had cereal boxes this big in Oz, I wouldn't have had to go shopping so much when you were still living at home!*

Feeling nostalgic and resolving to make a detour via Queensland on her trip back to Australia, she absentmindedly pushed her trolley—also enormous—around a corner and almost crashed right into someone. 'Oh my gosh, I'm so sorry.'

'Careful where you're going,' exclaimed the woman, who was hugging a massive bag of kale. Looked like it wasn't only sugary cereal that came in crazy sizes around here. 'Wait a minute ... do I know you?'

Flick registered that she did indeed know her. *Theo's ex-wife.* Before she could reply, Rachel clicked her fingers.

'That's it. You were with Theodore that day he brought Miss H back to her house.' She glanced into Flick's trolley, eyed all the sweet stuff she'd got to decorate the cake and did not at all try to hide her distaste. 'You're his neighbour, right?'

Something in Rachel's haughty tone compelled Flick to smile and say, 'Actually, we're a little *more* than neighbours.'

Whoops. The second the words were out she regretted them. Theo hadn't had the chance to tell his daughters about their relationship yet—he'd wanted to do it in person, and now his ex-wife would likely do the honours for him.

'Really?' Rachel appeared to find this highly amusing. 'Well, congratulations then. I wish you the best of luck. Let's just hope he's a lot more faithful to you than he was to me.'

'What?' Flick breathed, her knees threatening to give way under her, but Rachel was already stalking towards the checkouts, the tapping of her heels echoing behind her.

Flick almost wanted to run after her and demand she explain herself, but she also didn't want to hear what she might say. Had Theo had an affair? Multiple, judging by the way his ex-wife spoke!

She felt sick, as if she'd scoffed one of those enormous bags of cereal, and she stood there at the end of the aisle, her hands tightly gripping the trolley as the other woman's words sunk in.

Let's just hope he's a lot more faithful to you than he was to me.

Was he really that type of man? Perhaps she'd been blinded by lust and pheromones?

But no—her grip loosened and her nausea eased—she couldn't believe it of Theo. He'd told her he and Rachel separated because they drifted apart, that it had happened over a period of years. Flick had no reason not to believe him. Why would he lie? His ex was clearly just trying to make things difficult for him for the sake of it. Even though she was married to someone else, she didn't want to see her first husband happy and moving on as well.

Flick would not let Rachel's malevolence get to her. She would put her remarks behind her and get on with her day—making a fabulous cake for a fabulous guy.

Yet, although fully on board with this plan in theory, she went through the checkout on autopilot, barely registering the chirpy woman who tried to make conversation as she scanned her items. All she could think about was Rachel's words—*Let's just hope he's a lot more faithful to you than he was to me.* They were on repeat in her head like a broken record.

Flick had a little reprieve on the way back to the French Quarter because remembering to drive on the right-hand side required every ounce of brain power. When she got back to the apartment, she threw herself into the task at hand. She liked baking and usually it calmed her—after she and Sofia had officially separated there'd been *so* much cake in her life. But today, it didn't deliver the boost it usually did. She poured too much sugar into the butter and got eggshell in the mixture.

Could Rachel possibly be telling the truth? Had Theo cheated on her?

Once the two square tins were in the oven, she took a cup of coffee out onto the balcony and tried to distract herself with the happenings below on Bourbon Street. Although only midmorning there was plenty going on, but even an elderly woman wearing a skimpy white outfit and dancing as she preached the gospel did not take Flick's mind off Rachel's words.

Let's just hope he's a lot more faithful to you than he was to me.

Of course she wanted someone she could trust—someone who wouldn't be tempted to look elsewhere—but it wasn't only the possible infidelity she had a problem with.

Time ticked by as she sat there stewing, and it was only when she smelled something burning that she remembered the cakes.

Dammit.

341

Rushing inside, she shoved her hands into mitts and yanked open the oven. Smoke poured out like a dementor and Flick jumped back as the heat licked her face. Immediately the smoke alarm started shrieking and flashing red.

'Shut *up*!' she screamed as she flapped her hands, trying to clear the air, but it was no use—the alarm was well out of her reach. Her eyes and ears stinging, she turned back to the oven and peered inside to see two black squares looking back at her.

'Dammit. Dammit. Dammit. Dammit,' she muttered as she removed the charred cakes and dumped them—tins and all—into the kitchen sink.

They sizzled as they hit the steel and Flick fought the urge to burst into tears. She couldn't recall the last time she'd burnt anything. Was this an omen? And if so ... what did *that* mean?

An urgent banging on the door downstairs joined the alarm, creating a cacophony that would have given her a headache if Rachel's words hadn't got there first.

'Felicity? Are you okay?' Theo's voice drifted up through the open balcony doors, only just audible above the alarm. 'Felicity!'

If she didn't reply, he'd probably call the fire brigade or climb up the building himself.

She dashed out and looked down at him—a small crowd had already gathered around and were glancing eagerly upwards as if hoping they were about to witness something exciting.

'I'm fine,' she shouted. 'Just accidentally set off the smoke alarm and now it won't shut up.'

Hopes of a drama thwarted, the crowd immediately dispersed.

'Let me in. I'll help you,' called Theo.

Flick almost tripped on the stairs as she hurried down to open the door. Thankfully he didn't try to hug or kiss her and she followed him back up to the apartment. He was faster than her and by the time she got there he was already standing on a chair, stretching up to wave a tea towel at the blasted noise. His shirt had crept up, treating Flick to a tempting glimpse of his six-pack. Was there a sexier man on the planet?

What does it matter what he looks like if you don't really know him?

'I think this must be faulty,' Theo said, dropping the tea towel to his side. 'I'm going to disconnect it for now.'

'Yes, please. Do whatever you need to.' She couldn't think straight with the noise, never mind the view.

'Do you have a screwdriver?'

She crossed to a drawer where she'd seen some basic tools, grabbed one and handed it to him.

'What caused it to go off?' he asked as he began to unscrew.

'Um ...' Flick glanced into the sink. 'I was trying to make you a birthday cake.'

Theo stopped and smiled down at her. 'Aw, that's so sweet. How'd you know?'

'I remembered you telling me it was this month when I first arrived, so I asked Lauri-Ann for the exact date.'

He succeeded in loosening the cap and the ear-piercing noise instantly ceased. Theo leapt off the chair, looking pretty damned pleased with himself, and Flick could have kissed him—if not for the knot in her stomach.

'Thank you,' she said instead.

'Not a problem. And don't worry about the cake; it's the thought that counts.'

He took a step towards her as if about to pull her into his arms, but she held up a hand. She wouldn't be able to get on with her day, never mind make more cakes or survive the birthday celebrations tomorrow, if she didn't know the truth. 'We need to talk.'

Theo frowned. 'Sounds serious.'

She nodded. 'Can I get you a cup of coffee?'

'You're scaring me. Whatever you have to say, just get on with it.'

Flick sucked in a deep breath—it didn't help. 'I ran into Rachel today ...'

'What? My ex-wife Rachel? Where?'

'At Walmart, when I was buying ingredients for your cake. She ... she said something that ... that doesn't quite match up with what you told me about the end of your marriage.'

'Oh?' His Adam's apple moved slowly up and down.

'I told her we were together and she said, "Let's just hope he's a lot more faithful to you than he was to me".' Flick rattled off Rachel's words like a memory verse, hoping Theo would scoff and adamantly deny it, but instead he lowered his gaze and tiny beads of perspiration appeared on his forehead. 'Is it true? Did you cheat on her?'

'Yes.' Theo ran a hand through his thick hair, his voice choked. 'Well, technically. But it's not what it sounds like.'

'What does that mean?'

'Things were already bad between Rachel and I. Sadie was just another musician that I met at a gig. We played together ... had a few drinks ... one thing led to another. It didn't really mean anything; we only hooked up a couple of times.' He paused for a quick breath. 'Rachel and I hadn't been intimate for over a year, but I felt so guilty about it, I confessed and begged her to come to counselling with me to see if we could make things good again, but she refused to even consider it. I guess my fuck-up was the excuse she'd been looking for to end things in a way that made me look like the bad guy.'

'You said you don't see your daughters much. Is this why? Are they angry at you for your affair?'

'It wasn't an affair,' he said vehemently. 'But yes, Rachel didn't only use it in court to get as much as she could out of me, but also to hit me where she knew it would hurt the most. It's ironic really, because I only stayed as long as I did because of Anna and Olivia. If I'd left when I first contemplated it, then I'd never have given Rachel something to use against me.'

Silence descended as Flick tried to digest what he'd said and how she felt about it.

'Look, I promise you.' Theo reached for her, holding her upper arms as if he wanted to shake sense into her. 'This has *nothing* to do with us. I promise I will never cheat on you.'

Did she believe him? Probably. Maybe. He spoke with such raw emotion, and even from only two brief interactions with Rachel, everything he said made sense. But her issue wasn't so much that she was scared Theo might cheat on her, it was that he hadn't *told* her about it. And, if she didn't know this about him, what else didn't she know? What else had he kept from her?

A chill swept through her body, despite the warm breeze blowing in from outside. Flashbacks landed in her head, bringing back awful memories of the day she'd opened the letter and discovered the person she was married to wasn't exactly as she thought them to be. It made her feel vulnerable in a way she'd never wanted to feel again.

'Why didn't you tell me?'

'I just … honestly, it's because I was scared. I didn't want to see you looking at me the way you are now, when it's not who I am. Our marriage was already over, but no matter the circumstances, I'm not proud of what I did. I didn't want one stupid indiscretion to change your opinion of me. And hey,' Theo shrugged, 'you didn't tell me about Sofia until you had to either.'

'We weren't supposed to be serious then. Up until the day Sofia arrived, you and I had agreed to a holiday fling—a bit of fun. But that night, when you told me you loved me, when I told you I felt the same and we started planning a future together, everything changed.' She stepped away, putting distance between them again. 'I opened my heart to you, I trusted you with my past, and in return I expected the same kind of honesty from you.'

'That wasn't the right moment,' Theo argued.

'I don't know, I think that would have been the perfect moment. But there've been plenty more opportunities for you to tell me since; instead I had to hear it from your ex-wife. I spent over two decades in a relationship where there were secrets, and I can't risk being in another one like that again.'

'No, Felicity, please—don't throw what we have away. I promise you there *aren't* any more secrets. That's it. You can ask me anything you want. I'm an open book.'

Maybe Theo meant it, maybe not, but how could she be sure? Flick suddenly saw the man standing in front of her as the stranger he really was. She'd barely known him a month. It had been crazy enough to jump into bed with someone she'd only just met, never mind let her heart get involved and decide to change her whole life, to move away from her family and friends for him. It had all happened way too fast. And the intensity of her emotions terrified her.

She'd known Sofia over half her life and look how that had ended.

She'd forgotten for a while, but Theo's confession had been a stark reminder that you could never truly know another person and Flick wasn't willing to open herself up to the vulnerability that came with that. One soul-crushing heartache had been enough for one lifetime.

'I'm sorry,' she sniffed, tears swimming in her eyes. 'I told you when we met that I wasn't ready for another relationship and I meant it. It was a mistake to let things get so serious.'

'Felicity, don't say that. You're breaking my heart,' Theo breathed.

She didn't want to hurt him, but she had to protect herself. Better to end this insanity now, because the deeper she got, the worse *her* heart could shatter.

'Thank you for coming to help with the alarm,' she said, 'but I think you'd better go now.'

HOW TO MEND A BROKEN HEART

33

Zoe

Early Thursday evening Zoe and Miss H were sitting down to a dinner of toasted cheese sandwiches when the heavy knocker sounded on the front door. Its boom echoed through the house, making Charlotte scurry under the table.

'Who on earth could that be at this time? Probably a religious caller or someone wanting to have a look inside, as if my home is some kind of museum.' Miss H snorted. 'The audacity of some people!'

'I'll tell them to piss off,' Zoe said, jumping to her feet. 'Back in a mo.'

She headed out of the kitchen and down the hallway, ready to put on a stern voice if need be, but when she peeled back the door all thoughts of confrontation were forgotten.

'Mum? What are you doing here?'

Flick smiled in the too-bright way people do when they don't feel like smiling at all. 'You said I could visit whenever I wanted. Well, I

348

thought it was high time. And, I bought you a housewarming gift.' She thrust a bottle of wine towards Zoe.

'Thanks.' Zoe took it as she scrutinised her mother. Quite aside from the fake smile and the fact she'd brought alcohol when she'd been trying to discourage Zoe from drinking it, she did not look good. Her eyes were bloodshot and her face had the puffiness of someone who'd been crying. 'What's the matter? Has something happened with Theo?'

Flick's attempt at a happy facade crumbled as she nodded. 'We broke up. It's your turn to say, "I told you so".'

'Oh, Mum, as if. Come in.' Zoe pulled her inside and into her arms. 'What happened?'

'I—' Flick's answer was cut short by a shout from Miss H.

'What's going on? Who's there?'

Releasing her mother, Zoe glanced into the depths of the house. 'We were just about to eat. It's just cheese toasties but I can make one for you if you want to join us? Otherwise I'll make sure Miss H is okay and then we can go upstairs and talk.'

'I'm not sure I could eat much, but let's go attempt dinner. I don't really want to discuss what happened, but I didn't want to be alone either.'

'I understand. Come on.' Zoe took her mum's hand and led her into the kitchen to where Miss H was sitting at the table. 'Wasn't a religious caller after all.'

Flick attempted a smile. 'How are you this evening, Aurelia? Hope you don't mind me dropping in like this, but I wanted to see my daughter.'

'Of course not.' Miss H patted the side of her mouth with a napkin. 'This is Zoe's house now too, so she can have as many guests as she wants.'

Zoe almost laughed at that—not only did Miss H's welcome not really sound very welcoming, but she made it sound like Zoe might throw a house party any moment. A little tricky when the only people she knew in New Orleans that she actually liked were sitting at this table. And if Flick and Theo had broken up that likely meant the birthday party was cancelled, so there went her opportunity to meet more people.

'Thank you,' Flick said, gesturing to the bottle that Zoe now carried. 'Would you like to share a glass of wine?'

'I don't know about sharing, but I won't say no to a drop myself. You can tell me how Edward is going.'

Flick nodded and Zoe went to fetch glasses. After she poured the white wine, she said, 'I'll make you a sandwich, Mum.'

'No.' Flick shook her head. 'I'm not hungry and you don't want yours to go cold.'

As her mum explained in gruesome detail what she'd done so far on Miss H's dearly departed feline, Zoe tried to guess what could possibly have happened with Theo. Yesterday, when they'd been talking about the cake, she'd sounded on top of the world. What could have gone wrong so quickly?

'Have you heard from Harvey at all while he's been away?' Miss H asked when she and Flick had exhausted all conversation about stuffed cats.

'Yes, we email often and speak about once a week—he likes to get the local gossip.'

'And how is his sister faring?'

'Harvey said she sleeps a lot of the time now and isn't eating much. He doesn't think she'll last much longer, but he's glad he can be there with her.'

'Zoe says you're staying in New Orleans even after he returns?'

Flick stared down into her wineglass. 'That was the plan, but I'll be going back to Australia now.'

'Oh?' Zoe said. Of course, this made sense if things between Flick and Theo had ended, but she hadn't thought it through that far yet and she couldn't help being disappointed.

'Don't you think about leaving until you've finished Edward,' Miss H commanded.

'I'll do my best.'

'Well, good. But why your sudden change of plans?'

Flick took a big gulp of wine. 'Theo and I broke up.'

Although her mum had said she didn't want to talk about it, Zoe couldn't help asking, 'What happened?'

'I ran into his ex-wife and found out he cheated—'

'He cheated on *you*?' Rage whirled inside her. 'With *her*?'

'No, no, not me. He cheated on his wife, that's why *they* broke up. Well, part of the reason.'

'Oh.' Zoe frowned, not sure exactly what that had to do with Flick.

'It's not the past that upsets me so much as the fact that he wasn't honest with me about it. I think I was blinded by lust for a while, but I realised today I don't really know him at all. It was all moving way too fast.'

'Still, once a cheater, always a cheater,' Miss H snarled. 'You're smart to get rid of him.'

Zoe sighed. 'I didn't used to think it was true that all men cheat, but I'm beginning to believe the statistics.'

'Anyway, enough about Theo. Who needs a man when we have each other?' There was an almost hysterical edge to Flick's voice as she reached out and squeezed Zoe's hand.

'I'll toast to that,' Miss H agreed, 'but I think this situation calls for something stronger. Besides we appear to be almost out of wine.'

Although not sure this was a good idea, Zoe got up and plucked the bottle of whiskey from the back of the cupboard.

'Are you sure I can't get you something to eat?' she asked Flick.

'I'm fine, sweetheart.'

But it was very clear she wasn't fine at all. She actually looked worse than she had the day she and Sofia had told Zoe and Toby that their father identified as a woman and their parents were getting a divorce. This trip was supposed to be about Flick finding herself and happiness again, but it looked like she was right back where she'd started emotionally.

And if Flick went back to Australia, where would that leave Zoe? While she liked Miss H and the job, the house and a craving for social interaction were already getting to her. She wasn't sure she wanted to stay here anymore without her mum, but she didn't exactly want to go back to Perth either.

And how would she tell Miss H she'd changed her mind?

The older woman was right—men had so much to answer for. Sometimes Zoe thought it would be easier to be a lesbian ... if only she was sexually attracted to women.

'Here.' Miss H handed Zoe the bottle. 'You do the honours.'

'Shall I get some fresh glasses?'

The others shook their heads, so Zoe poured whiskey straight into the same glasses.

Miss H lifted hers with her good hand high in the air. 'To us! And to hell with the men!'

Zoe and Flick joined in the toast and Charlotte jumped up onto the table as if even she agreed.

'I've got to say,' Flick said after taking her first sip, 'I'll miss the sex.'

'Mum!' Maybe it was time Zoe *forced* her mother to eat something—the alcohol had clearly gone to her head. Although she

352

understood the sentiment; she hadn't gone this long without doing the dirty since she'd lost her virginity. And *that* was a depressing thought.

Flick swished the whiskey around her glass. 'I should have listened to Luna.'

'Huh?' Zoe said.

'Remember she warned me that things weren't as they seem? She must have been talking about Theo.'

While Zoe raised an eyebrow, Miss H asked, 'Who's Luna?'

'She's a clairvoyant,' Flick explained, 'from the voodoo shop on Bourbon Street.'

'Ah, right.' Miss H nodded. 'I've heard she's very good.'

'You believe in stuff like that, but you don't believe in ghosts?' asked Zoe.

'Oh, not the ghost thing again.' Miss H glanced over at Flick and smirked. 'Do you know your daughter thinks my house is haunted?'

'Zoe always had a very good imagination. When she was little she used to make up the most outrageous stories. I actually thought she'd become an author at one stage.'

'Ooh I'd love to hear some of your stories, Zoe. Shall we take this conversation somewhere more comfortable?' suggested Miss H.

'Good idea. Do you want to come and see what I've been working on, Mum?' Zoe would rather discuss her painting than some tales she'd made up when she was a kid.

'Yes, let's go into the sunroom. I could do with putting my feet up a while.' Miss H hobbled to a stand and scooped Charlotte up with her free hand. The Siamese cat clung to her like a baby, but Zoe had to admit she was warming to the animal.

'Shall I make us some tea?' she asked.

'Tea.' Miss H grunted. 'Who needs tea when we have whiskey?'

The four of them migrated to the sunroom. Zoe switched on the lights and Flick crossed over to the easel set up in the middle of the room.

'Wow, that's gorgeous, sweetheart.' It was a painting of Miss H's house—or at least how Zoe imagined it looked in its glory years. 'What are you going to do with it when you're done?' Flick asked.

'Well, I think this one is going upstairs in my bedroom, but I'm also going to put it on our website and sell it as a print.'

'You can put me down for one. My unit is looking a little bare and … actually …' Flick moved on to look at some of Miss H's work, including the painting that sat unfinished, waiting for the artist to be able to return to it. 'I'll order one of these as well.'

Zoe knew her mum didn't love the skeleton brides, which meant one of three things—she was either drunk-buying, simply being polite, or her recent heartbreak had helped her see it in a new light.

Once Flick had selected a painting, they sat on the sofas and drank more whiskey. The conversation quickly returned to the uselessness of men. It was amazing how satisfying such a discussion could be and, after a couple of whiskeys herself, Zoe stopped trying to force-feed her mum and relaxed.

Just after nine o'clock, right on her usual schedule, Miss H yawned and announced she was calling it a night.

Flick went to stand up as well. 'I'd better be going, but thank you for such a great night. I feel much better after spending time with you two—don't think I've laughed so much in years.'

'Don't feel you have to rush off on my account,' said Miss H. 'You're welcome to stay as long as you like. Stay the night—we've got plenty of room.'

'Yes, good idea … You can share my bed.' Zoe didn't want her mum trying to make her way back to the French Quarter after so many drinks, but she'd also sleep a lot easier with Flick beside her.

'Are you sure it's not too much trouble?' Flick asked, already resting her head back against the sofa.

'Not at all,' Zoe and Miss H replied in unison.

'Okay then. Thanks. You've twisted my arm.'

Zoe went to help Miss H change, promising her mum she'd be back in a moment. But when she returned, she found Flick asleep on the sofa—one arm tucked under her, the other flung up over her head and her mouth wide open.

'Hey, Mum,' she whispered, gently shaking her shoulder. 'Come upstairs. You'll be more comfortable in bed.'

'I'm fine right here,' Flick moaned and rolled over.

Zoe covered her with a crocheted blanket and then went into the kitchen. She filled a glass with water from the tap, downed it almost in one go, then refilled it and took it back to the sunroom where she left it within easy reach of Flick.

'Night, Mummy.' Zoe felt an overwhelming rush of love as she kissed her on the forehead and then headed off to bed herself.

As she stumbled up the staircase in the dark, she realised she'd forgotten to turn on the lights, but weirdly she didn't panic. Maybe it was the fact she'd had a bit to drink, maybe the knowledge her mum was downstairs made her feel safer, or maybe she no longer felt threatened by whatever extra presence was, or was not, in the house. Even if ghosts did exist—which they probably didn't—they weren't all bad, right? Miss H had lived here her entire life and no one had harmed her.

There was no logical reason for Zoe to be afraid.

34

Zoe

'Mum?' Zoe whispered a few hours later when she woke to the sound of someone coming into the room. Everything was dark except for a slither of moonlight coming through the curtains but at the end of her bed she could only just make out the silhouette of a figure.

Her mouth went dry and her pulse leapt into overdrive. This was not her mother. The figure was taller and broader than Flick. Taller and broader even than Sofia.

She tried to regulate her breathing for fear she might start hyperventilating. Should she scream or pretend she was asleep? Maybe they hadn't heard her say 'Mum'?

And maybe the Pope's an atheist. Oh God!

Lying rigid, Zoe's eyes slowly began to adjust to the darkness and despite the terror racing through her veins, she couldn't look away as the shadow became clearer, but ... not quite solid. Large though, and definitely male. Zoe knew without a doubt that this was what she'd seen in the mirror last night.

And something told her they weren't real. At least not in the sense that she was real.

This actually made her feel less vulnerable and, as her breathing began to return to something close to normal, she got an undeniable whiff of smoke. Once again, she ignored it—if something was really burning, surely her mum or Miss H would smell it too and wake up.

Who the hell was this? Zoe racked her mind trying to remember what Jack had said, if anything, about communicating with ghosts. Had he said something about simply talking to them? Asking questions? It sounded too ridiculous to work but then again, this whole situation was ridiculous. If Zoe wasn't living it herself, she'd never have believed it possible.

After a quick breath, she whispered, 'Hello. I'm Zoe.'

She waited for a response but all she could hear was the sound of her own heart beating. Still the figure just stood there—it probably saw her as the interloper.

'I don't want to do you any harm,' she tried. 'Did you used to live here?'

The silhouette faded slightly and then came back again. Was that a sign? A message?

Zoe swallowed. 'Are you related to Miss H? I mean ... Aurelia? What's your name? How did you die?'

The figure disappeared—no puff of smoke or anything dramatic like you might see in the movies. One minute it was there and the next it simply wasn't.

Dammit. Maybe she'd pushed too hard? Or maybe you weren't supposed to ask about a ghost's death. She should have tried to take a photo or pressed record on her phone. Of course *now* she recalled

Jack saying something about electronic voice phenomena. Could a mobile do the trick?

Slowly, she reached for hers on the bedside table, turned it to silent, then opened the voice recording app and pressed 'Record'.

'I'm sorry,' she called softly. 'Are you still there?'

No reply.

She waited about thirty seconds before ending the recording, then held it to her ear to play. *Nothing.*

Disappointed, she stared at her phone: 2 am. She'd never get back to sleep now. Weirdly, she didn't feel spooked, but instead desperate for information. As she lay there in the dark googling and reading up on everything she could about ghosts, a thought landed in her head.

Why would Miss H's father be haunting the place? According to all the research she could find, ghosts generally only stayed in this world if they had unfinished business. So either he had some, or it was someone else who'd lived and died here. Perhaps tomorrow she'd try and find out more about the house's history. She could ask Miss H, and if she didn't know, there had to be records in the local library or something. Maybe she could go ask the fortune teller if she had any insight?

Zoe laughed to herself but then sat up straight in bed as a disturbing thought landed in her head. 'Oh my God!'

What if it was Remy?

A cold clamminess settled over her skin. Once the thought was in her head, she couldn't cast it out. And hadn't Miss H said Remy was a big man?

But if the ghost was Remy … did that mean …?

Her chest hurt as if her rib cage was trying to crush her—maybe it wasn't the ghost she should be scared of?

Flinging back her sheets, Zoe climbed out of bed and tiptoed downstairs, creeping past Miss H's room and into the sunroom where Flick still slept on the sofa.

'Mum!' Zoe hissed, shaking her not quite as gently as she had a few hours ago. 'Wake up!'

'What is it?' Flick blinked and shook her head. 'Where am I?'

'You're with me at Miss H's and I've just ... I saw something upstairs.'

'What are you talking about?' Flick sounded too tired to comprehend anything.

Zoe tried to be patient as she explained exactly what had happened. She could tell from the expression on her mum's face that she was sceptical.

'You mentioned tonight what Luna said to us about not taking things at face value, that not everything is as it seems. Well, what if that wasn't just some vague sentiment she tells everyone after all or a reference to our pasts with Sofia and Beau? What if your message was specific to Theo and mine was to Miss H?'

'What do you mean?'

'What if the person I saw tonight was Remy?'

'Huh.' Flick frowned. 'I'm not following. Who's Remy?'

'Her fiancé. Or he was. The guy who left her at the altar ... or so she says. But what if that was an elaborate lie to cover up the truth—that she killed him?'

Flick snorted. 'You really think that's possible?'

'Shh!' Zoe pressed her finger against her mouth and glanced towards the door—thank God she'd thought to shut it. 'And yes. It all makes sense now. Her favourite show is *How to Get Away with Murder* and she refuses to acknowledge there's anything weird going on in this house. That's probably why she's never left, despite the place being way too big and unmanageable for her—Remy must be hidden here somewhere and if she sells the house, there'd be the risk of someone else uncovering the bones.'

'Look, I think you should calm down.' Flick suddenly sounded much more awake. 'Just because Aurelia likes watching crime shows and is a little eccentric, doesn't make her a murderer. But if you feel that uncomfortable here, maybe you should come stay with me again.'

'I didn't imagine him, Mum, and I'm not scared. Well, not exactly.' Zoe didn't think the ghost would hurt her, and as long as Miss H didn't suspect she knew anything then she had no reason to harm her either. 'I just want to get to the bottom of this.'

'Okay.' Flick reached for the glass of water. 'Did you leave this for me?'

'Yes.'

'You're a sweetheart, you know that?' She took a sip. 'So, what happens next, Detective Zo-Zo? How exactly do you plan on uncovering the truth?'

Flick took an Uber back to the French Quarter early in the morning and a few hours later, after telling Miss H that she wanted to go and make sure her mum was okay, Zoe took the streetcar there too.

It had been an awkward morning—at least on her part. Now that she had her suspicions about Miss H it was impossible to act normal around her.

'What's wrong with you this morning?' the older woman asked over breakfast of tea and toast.

'I'm just tired and worried about Mum,' had been Zoe's reply.

She wasn't sure Miss H bought the excuse, but she could hardly confront her with her suspicions. Not yet. Not until she'd found some kind of evidence—a body? Bones? She shuddered.

Even then it would probably be best to take her discovery to the authorities. And she definitely needed more than a hunch to do that, which was why she was now swallowing her pride and standing on the doorstep of the only person she knew who might be able to help her.

Her finger twitched a little as she lifted it to press the buzzer on Jack's front door.

Seconds after the sound echoed inside, the door opened and there he was, looking ... all ... *Jack*! Dark jeans, a pale green polka-dotted, button-up shirt pushed up to his elbows, his hair tousled and in dire need of a haircut. He was wearing his glasses and an expression that said the world bemused him—or maybe it was just her?

'Zoe?'

'I need your help,' she said, ignoring the way her insides fizzed like champagne when he said her name.

Jack's lips curled upwards and his eyes twinkled. 'Well, you'd better come in then.'

'Not like *that*!'

'Pity.' He shrugged as if it was no skin off his nose either way. 'What else can I do for you then?'

Zoe glanced around—the door to his ground floor apartment was in a pretty open place. A homeless guy and his dog slept a few feet away and tourists were already littering the sidewalk. 'Maybe it would be better to have this conversation inside after all?'

And maybe she was a little curious to see where he lived.

'Suit yourself.' He stepped back to let her in. 'I was just making coffee. Want some?'

'That'd be great, thanks.'

His apartment was much smaller than Harvey's and smelled a lot better too. They stepped into an open-plan living room. Covered with papers, books and an open laptop, Jack's dining table looked more like a desk than any place you'd eat. The furniture was shabby chic, but probably not on purpose, and the table wasn't the only thing covered with books—they were everywhere, and coffee mugs too scattered on every available surface. It was messy, but not dirty. Eclectic, but warm. It had a real mad professor vibe going on and suited him perfectly.

'Sorry. If I'd known I was going to have guests, I'd have cleaned up a bit.'

He didn't sound sorry and that made Zoe smile.

As he began to make coffee in the kitchen, she surreptitiously glanced through an open door into the bedroom. Jack's navy-blue sheets were rumpled, the bed unmade. She could even see a dent in the pillow where his head would have been not all that long ago.

'So,' he said, making her jump. 'To what do I owe the honour of your visit?'

'You know that lady I was with at the Commander's Palace?'

'Yes.' He handed her a mug and gestured towards the small couch.

'Well,' Zoe began as she lowered herself onto it, 'I've started working with her, and now I'm living in her house in the Garden District. And something odd is going on there.'

'What kind of odd?'

She hesitated. How much should she tell him? Was this like seeing a fortune teller—better not to give them leading clues? 'I think I have a ghost problem.'

'Really?' There was undeniable interest in his voice. He put his mug down on the coffee table, miraculously finding a spot among the clutter.

Zoe nodded and told him everything—the flickering lights, the cold spots, the doors that sometimes opened on their own, the sound of light footsteps, the almost ever-present scent of smoke, the mirror and her nocturnal visitor. It all sounded so stupid when she said it out loud, but if *Jack* didn't believe her then no one would.

'You don't need to be scared,' he said when she'd finished. 'Dead people—especially ones that clearly have nothing to do with you—shouldn't be feared.'

'My mum is a taxidermist—I'm not scared of *dead* things! I just want some answers.'

Jack smirked. 'I thought you didn't believe in ghosts … are you sure this isn't some elaborate scheme to spend time with me? If you want to hang out, Zoe, you only need ask.'

'You've got tickets on yourself.' She shook her head but found herself fighting a smile. 'If I knew any other ghost hunters, I'd be asking them but as it happens, you're it. So, will you help me or not? I'll pay you whatever the going rate is.'

She hoped it wasn't too expensive, but she had her first week's pay and then money from the Casket Brides prize if need be.

'We can talk about payment if I uncover anything. And I can begin tonight, otherwise I'm booked solid for the next few days. We might need longer than one night, but you never know, we could get lucky.'

'Tonight's fine.'

The sooner the better as far as Zoe was concerned. Hopefully Jack would declare there was no paranormal activity in Miss H's house, and she could get on with life—without him or a ghost in it. If the worst was confirmed and she was living with a murderer, she'd move out pronto and work out what the hell to do with the knowledge.

'You'll have to wait until Miss H goes to bed—usually around nine o'clock—because she can't know what we're doing.'

'She doesn't feel this presence too?'

'It's complicated … She says she doesn't, but I'm not sure I believe her. Have you heard anything about her?'

'Not much. I don't do the Garden District tours, but I know she's some kind of artist and that lots of the guides show her house. The crew at the restaurant are also kind of fascinated by her. She's usually rude and demanding, especially to the male waiters, but they find her amusing so fight to serve her. That day I served you guys was my first time.'

'It was also almost your last.'

'What?'

'Never mind.'

Jack cocked his head to one side. 'Do you have suspicions about who this ghost could be?'

'It could be ridiculous, but I'm wondering if it could be her fiancé,' Zoe said and then told him everything she'd told her mum.

'Okay. We'll keep an open mind, but here's what you need to try and do for me before tonight. I need a name for this guy.'

'Remy.'

'Surname?'

'Don't know it.'

'Find out. That way we can try and track him down, see if there's any trace of where he went after he supposedly left. Also, find out if he had any family in the area. If he did leave, he might not have made contact again with Miss H, but his family likely heard from him. If we can find him, we rule out your theory.'

'She doesn't talk much about him. Occasionally she lets something slip but mostly it's just ranting about how he ruined her life when he left her.'

'And you're living with this delightful woman, why?' It was a rhetorical question. 'I've got a bit of time today, so give me the address and I'll see what I can find out about the history of the house and the land.'

Zoe felt relieved as she told him. Bringing Jack on board had been the right thing to do. He had contacts in the area and would likely find the information faster than she could.

'There could have been multiple deaths on the site,' he added. 'That whole area was a plantation first and Lord knows the horrors that were inflicted on the enslaved people there. You said you smell smoke?'

She nodded.

'There were often fires on plantations.'

'That's great,' Zoe exclaimed and then realised how bad that sounded. 'What I mean is, it'll be great if we find out the ghost is from long ago and nothing to do with Miss H.'

Jack grinned at her.

'What?' she asked, his intense gaze making her skin tingle.

'I just think it's cool ... that you've joined the dark side. Once you start opening your mind up to the possibility there's more to life than meets the eye, you really start living.'

Zoe took another sip of her coffee to stifle her smile. It felt like he was welcoming her into a secret club, but that's not why she was here. She hadn't come to *bond* with him.

'I wouldn't say I'm a full believer just yet. It's equally as likely I've lost the plot entirely.'

'I guess that's what we're going to try to find out.'

That felt like a good place to leave the conversation. 'Yes.' She put her mug down on top of a magazine—something called *Fate*— and stood. 'Thanks for the coffee.'

'You're welcome.' Jack stood too.

'So, should we exchange numbers or something? That way I can text you if I find anything and also let you know when the coast is clear?'

'Good idea.' He pulled his phone out of his pocket. 'I've got a tour tonight, so I won't be available till nearer ten thirty, but I'll text you when I'm on my way. What's your number and I'll send you a message now.'

As she rattled it off, Jack tapped his screen and seconds later her phone beeped with a message.

'Gotcha,' she said and then cringed because that sounded stupid. 'Anyway, is there anything I should do in preparation for tonight?'

'I'll bring everything we need, but this time you can provide the coffee.'

She nodded. 'It's a da–deal.'

OMG—she'd almost said 'date'!

35

Felicity

Of course this morning when Flick had a stinking headache, the shop was busier than it had ever been. She didn't know how she was ever going to find the time to dash up to the loo or make another much-needed coffee.

After returning from the Garden District and trying to make herself presentable following a night on the whiskey—which she was *never* drinking again, by the way—she'd contemplated not opening the shop at all. It had been so tempting to crawl under the bedcovers and try to sleep away her sorrows, but she decided it would be better to keep busy. Besides, she owed it to Harvey.

Although right now she didn't feel very favourably towards him. If he hadn't put that ad on the taxidermists' Facebook group, she'd never have given New Orleans a second thought, never mind come all this way. And, if she hadn't come here, she'd never have met Theo and right now her heart wouldn't feel as if it had been shattered into a zillion pieces.

How was it even possible to be feeling this miserable after a break-up when the relationship had lasted less time than it took to finish a piece of taxidermy?

'How much is that jackalope over there?'

Flick looked up from where she'd been trying to work on Edward and forced a smile for the young woman. 'Sorry, what was that?'

'That jackalope in the corner. The one wearing the red coat? My parents collect them and it's their fortieth wedding anniversary soon. It would make the perfect gift.'

'Just give me one moment.' Flick removed her gloves, washed her hands, then left the studio part of the shop and went over to the counter. Harvey's inventory and price list was already open on the computer screen.

The woman smiled when Flick told her the price. 'Okay, great. That sounds reasonable. I'm going to ask my brother and sisters if they want to go in with me. We're just about to go on a cemetery tour.' She pointed to the bored looking guy beside her. 'Can I get you to put it aside and I'll come back later in the day?'

'Sure.' As the couple left, Flick took a sold sign from under the desk and went over to attach it to the jackalope.

'Hey, Mum.'

'Oh my goodness.' She startled as Zoe spoke right behind her. 'What are you doing here?'

'And it's lovely to see you too.' Zoe offered her a cup of takeaway coffee. 'Thought you could do with one of these?'

'Thank you.' She accepted it and took a sip.

'You're welcome.' Zoe glanced around. 'It's busy in here today.'

'Yep.' Flick nodded, then raised an eyebrow. 'You didn't come all this way to bring me coffee and check up on me, did you?'

Zoe gave a sheepish smile. 'I've just been to see Jack.'

'Really?' That was an interesting development—hadn't they all sworn off men last night?

'Yes. He's agreed to help me. Tonight.'

The penny dropped. 'Oh, with the *ghost*?' Flick had thought she'd imagined that conversation, but it all came flooding back. 'You're really following through with ... with this investigation?'

'I know you think it's stupid, but there's no harm checking it out.'

'I guess not.' But Flick couldn't help wondering what might happen between Zoe and Jack if they were alone in the dark for hours.

Someone nearby cleared their throat and she and Zoe both turned to see a woman waiting patiently.

'Can I help you?' Flick asked.

'I'd like to buy a pair of bird claw earrings, please.'

'Of course.' Flick left Zoe a moment to assist the customer.

'Sorry about that,' she said, when the happy customer had gone.

Zoe grimaced. 'They are *so* creepy. Why would anyone want to wear dead bird feet on their ears?'

'Shh, that's not the kind of sentiment we want in this shop, thank you very much.'

'Sorry. Anyway, I'd better be getting back to Miss H before she starts getting suspicious.' Zoe leaned in to give her a hug. 'I'll let you know how tonight goes.'

'Yes, please do. But do you mind watching the shop just a moment while I rush up to the loo?'

'Sure.'

Flick went upstairs and when she returned a few minutes later, the place was empty except for Zoe. 'Did you scare off all the customers?'

Zoe grinned. 'You're welcome. You look like you could do with a little peace. Are you going to be okay?'

'Yes, but *you* be careful.'

'I will. Love you, Mum,' Zoe said and then flounced out of the shop.

Although she hadn't admitted it to her daughter, Flick had felt something in that house as well, and she'd barely spent any time there. But ghosts weren't real. She blamed New Orleans for the fact they were even contemplating such a thing. It was easy to get caught up in the spooky vibe. And she couldn't really believe the slightly frail, elderly woman capable of murder either but, as her grandmother used to say, *stranger things happened at sea*. And this was her little girl. She'd worried about much smaller things.

She downed the last of her coffee then returned to the work bench. As she slid her hands back into her gloves, the bell on the door dinged and Flick looked up to see Theo coming in.

Had he been watching, waiting for the shop to be empty? If not, he'd miraculously chosen the one time there were no other people she could focus her attention on. This was why having a fling with the guy next door had been a bad idea. He could just drop in whenever he pleased.

It was hard enough knowing how close he was, but *this* was too much. The shop suddenly felt claustrophobic.

'What are you doing?' she called, her pulse racing as he locked the door behind him and turned the sign to 'Closed'.

'We need to talk,' he replied unapologetically as he strode towards her.

'There's nothing to talk about,' she said, refusing to meet his gaze or take a proper look at him. She didn't want her resolve to be swayed by his sweet face and gorgeous body. If only they'd just left things at sex. If only he hadn't gone and told her he loved her. If only she hadn't gone and fallen in love right back.

'That's where you're wrong,' he said in that deep gravelly voice that serenaded locals and tourists alike every night. 'I've thought about nothing but you the last twenty-four hours and I'm not going to let you give up on us.'

'You don't have a choice.' Flick dug her hands into a bowl of pickling salt.

'Please, hear me out.' When she said nothing, he continued. 'It was wrong of me not to tell you the whole truth about me and Rachel, but history doesn't have to repeat itself. Until I met you, I didn't think I'd ever feel like settling down again, but you snuck into my heart and made me want more than just— What *is* that?'

'It's a cat. Or it was, and it will be again.'

Theo frowned. 'I thought you didn't do pets?'

'I don't usually, but this is Aurelia's cat. Remember the reason she came into the shop that day? Since she's been so kind to Zoe, I decided to make an exception.'

'Ah, right. What exactly are you doing?'

'I'm salting the skin—it's part of the tanning process. It sets the fur and keeps the hide from decaying.' It was much easier to talk about taxidermy than feelings.

He screwed up his face and went a little green. 'Do you think you could pause just a moment? I can't talk properly while you're doing that.'

She shook on some more salt. 'I'm sorry, Theo, but nothing you can say is going to make me change my mind and you're only prolonging the agony for both of us by trying to.'

He sighed. 'I thought because it was my birthday you might give me another chance, but maybe I should have given you more time.'

His birthday. In all the drama, she'd completely forgotten, but Flick wasn't going to be guilted into a about-face simply because he played the birthday card.

'I hope you have a good day, Theo, but it doesn't matter how long you give me, my mind is made up. I'm going back to Australia.'

'I could come with you?'

'What? No! That's not the issue.' There were bigger things than geography at play here. 'You lied to me. I don't know who you are. I can't trust you.'

'I didn't lie. I just omitted a bit of information.'

She rolled her eyes. Such a lawyer thing to say.

'But I'm sorry for that. I wish I could go back in time and tell you, but I promise you'll get nothing but honesty from me from now on.'

'I bet that's what Rachel thought when she married you as well!'

Theo flinched and Flick felt a stab of remorse. That wasn't fair. This wasn't about Rachel, not really, but he refused to take no for an answer.

'I guess you're right. You can never be sure of anything in life but that doesn't mean we should stop trying. Expecting the worst is a terrible way to live. Shouldn't we be able to learn from the past?'

'I have,' Flick said. 'That's why I'm ending this now. And you need to respect my decision. It's over, Theo.'

He pursed his lips. 'If that's really what you want, I'll go, but I'll never forget you. These last few weeks with you have been the best of my life. I think if you'd given us a chance, we could have had something really good together.'

Flick's resolve wobbled at what sounded like heartfelt words, but then she reminded herself he was a songwriter *and* an ex-lawyer—of course he'd have a way with words, but she needed to stay strong.

'Goodbye, Theo,' she said firmly. 'Thank you for a wonderful holiday fling.'

He shook his head sadly and headed back to the door.

As he disappeared, Flick's eyes filled with tears. She prayed this would be their last goodbye because she didn't know how many more she could take.

36

Zoe

Even though Zoe had been staring at her phone, she jumped when it finally vibrated with an incoming text message at ten thirty that night. *Jack.*

I'm waiting outside.

She got up from where she'd been pretending to paint in the sunroom, switched off the light, then crept into the kitchen and grabbed the two travel mugs of strong coffee she'd made just after Miss H went to bed. Travel mugs she'd bought after seeing Jack that morning, although she suspected she might not even need the caffeine. Despite trying to nap that afternoon to prepare for the night, sleep had been impossible with so much on her mind.

Trying not to make a sound, Zoe skulked through the near-dark house to the front door and opened it.

As expected, there stood Jack—a silhouette, with the light of the moon behind him and the tiny white Caspers on the shirt she'd given him almost glowing. Something hummed inside her at the sight of him wearing her gift. He carried two big black bags, which she guessed held his ghost-hunting paraphernalia.

What on earth had her life come to?

'Evening,' he mouthed.

'Hi,' she mouthed back. 'Nice shirt.'

He looked good, like he'd gone to a bit of an effort, and Zoe was relieved she'd showered, put on fresh clothes, blow-dried her hair and even splashed on some make-up. She'd ummed and aahed over whether to bother—she didn't want Jack to think she was trying to impress him. But in the end, she'd wanted to look better than she had the night he'd rescued her in the Quarter.

As she stepped back to let him inside, she got a whiff of something yummy on his skin. Not like he'd overdone it with the aftershave or anything, just like he'd had a shower with really good soap.

'Come on. Let's get this show on the road.'

Forcing all thoughts of Jack in the shower from her mind, Zoe gestured for him to follow as she headed for the staircase, holding her breath the entire way. The wood creaked under their feet and she winced, praying if Miss H heard that she'd just assume it was Zoe heading up to bed—*alone*.

It wasn't pitch-black upstairs, but tonight she'd left on only the bathroom light and her bedside lamp, some weird notion inside her that ghosts were more likely to appear in darkness. That's why you hunted them at night, right? She didn't know if that was even true, but here she was—at night, with a guy who professed to know how to go about such things.

'This place is something else,' Jack said, his voice just above a whisper as they emerged at the top of the landing. 'Are you sure someone actually lives here? It's like an abandoned museum.'

'You should have seen it before I moved in,' she replied, starting to relax now they were further away from Miss H.

Jack took a step further down the hallway, put his stuff on the floor, and then glanced around. 'Right, so this is the level where you've felt or seen the presence?'

She nodded. 'I occasionally walk through a cold spot or smell smoke downstairs, but the things I can't write off as draughts or electrical glitches have all happened up here.'

'Right. Can you show me where?'

'Yes. Of course,' Zoe said as she began the tour. She liked that they were getting straight down to business and her pulse leapt at the thought of what they might uncover. She wasn't quite sure whether she wanted to be proven right or wrong.

After showing him the bathroom, the area just outside the attic door where the smoke was often strongest, the bedroom she'd looked in that first day when she'd been searching for Charlotte, and the other rooms she'd barely been into, she finally took him into her bedroom. Unlike his bed, hers was made perfectly and piled with the cheap decorative pillows she'd bought herself at Walmart.

As Jack looked around, his gaze lingering a few moments on the bed, she remembered the mugs she was still holding.

'Oh, here, I promised you coffee,' she whispered, thrusting one towards him.

'Thanks.' Jack took it and their fingers brushed in the exchange. She felt an undeniable buzz of awareness. 'Relax, Zoe.'

'I am relaxed,' she snapped, silently cursing her traitorous body.

He took a sip. 'This is good coffee.'

'Thanks.' She forced a smile and they stood there a few minutes awkwardly. At least Zoe felt awkward, but Jack looked pensive so maybe he was simply thinking about what they were about to do.

'Do you feel anything?' she asked eventually.

He took his time replying, rubbing his lips together. 'Nothing specific, but ...'

'What?' she breathed, goosebumps sprouting all over her skin.

'I just feel like we're not alone.'

Zoe swallowed—perhaps she wasn't going crazy. 'So how exactly does this work? Do we just sit here hoping something will happen or do we try and summon the dead?'

He chuckled. 'We're not going to conduct a seance if that's what you mean.'

'I'm sorry, but I've never done anything like this before.'

'Okay.' He took another sip of coffee, then put the cup down on her bedside table and went back out into the hallway.

She followed him and found him squatting next to his bags as he produced what looked like some kind of camera from one of them.

'What exactly is all this stuff?' she whispered, curious despite being unsure whether they should be talking or not. She guessed Jack would tell her to be quiet if that were the case.

'This is a night-vision video camera,' he explained, pulling out a tripod. 'We've also got a laser grip infrared thermometer, a digital voice recorder, a shadow detector, a binary response device and a ghost box. These are the basics. We might not use all of them tonight, but I'll give you the lowdown in a moment.'

He may as well have been speaking Swahili. Zoe recognised a few words but had no idea what they meant put together.

Jack stood and began to set up the camera and tripod at one end of the hallway, just at the top of the stairs.

She watched him closely. 'Why weren't you wearing glasses at the restaurant?'

He gave a sheepish smile. 'I sat on my old pair and had to wear my contacts until I picked up a replacement.'

She laughed and then quickly covered her mouth—hopefully Miss H was a deep sleeper—but sitting on his specs seemed like such a nerd thing to do. 'I like you with glasses better.'

'You *like* me?'

Whoops. Her stomach twisted. 'Well … I … I just think you wear glasses well. They suit you. Some people look good with them and some people don't. You do. It doesn't mean anything. I'm just saying.'

And shut up now!

Jack's smile turned into that self-assured smirk. 'Good to know, Zoe, good to know.'

She sighed and glanced around as he finished fiddling with the camera. Where the hell was the ghost? She needed him to turn up and rescue her from herself.

'Did you find out the fiancé's surname?' Jack asked after a while.

'Nope,' she said, happy to be back on topic. 'I tried to start a conversation about Remy with Miss H a number of times but didn't get anything useful. No name, nothing about his family or even whether he came from around here. What about you? Did you—'

Jack held up his hand, silencing her.

'What?' she mouthed, the rest of her body stilling.

He nodded towards the other end of the hallway and Zoe slowly turned her head to see what he was gesturing to. Her heart lurched. Jack saw it too. She stood frozen, waiting for him to do something, say something.

Moving slowly, he reached back to press a button on the video camera, then stooped next to the bag and pulled out a few things, thrusting something about the size and shape of a TV remote at her.

He straightened and took a few tentative steps towards the apparition. In one hand he held a small digital camera, in the other something black and yellow that looked a little like a gun, except for its digital screen. Zoe hesitated only a moment before following, unable to breathe as Jack aimed the black and yellow device.

Immediately, the figure turned and disintegrated into the door behind it.

Dammit. Zoe wanted to yell at Jack—it probably saw the gun or whatever it was and thought he wanted to do it harm. Not that you could technically kill someone that was already dead but still, it looked threatening. And now they'd lost him.

But Jack's eyes were bright as he looked at her. 'You've definitely got yourself a ghost,' he whispered, his voice animated with excitement. Then he glanced down at the device in his hand. 'Darn it.'

'What?'

'I wasn't close enough to get a reading.'

Zoe gestured to the gun thing. 'What exactly is that?'

'A laser grip infrared thermometer—it takes the temp of a specific object with a laser, so you can compare it with the baseline temperature of an area.'

'And that's useful why?'

'You know those cold spots you mentioned?' When she nodded, he added, 'Well, in order to manifest, spirits draw energy or heat from the air around them, which causes a sudden drop in temperature.'

'Ah right. So, what do we do next?'

'We're going to go into the attic and see if—'

Zoe held up a hand. 'You want *me* to go up *there*?'

There was that smirk again. 'Do you want to get to the bottom of this?'

'Of course.'

'Well then, I could go up alone but whoever it is has appeared to you twice before now, which indicates they trust you. They may be more likely to communicate with you than me.'

'Okay.' She nodded, searching deep within herself for some courage. Jack knew what he was doing. And he was pretty muscly underneath that nerdy facade—she reckoned if anything happened, they'd be able to protect each other.

He gave her a quick rundown of the equipment they were going to use—explaining that if they registered any cold spots with the laser grip, or radiation with the EMF detector, or if the figure showed itself to them again, then Zoe could give the binary response device a shot.

She gulped, glancing down at the two devices she now held—the new one was black and shaped like a pyramid. 'You mean try to have a conversation?'

Jack nodded. 'Didn't you try that last night anyway?'

'Yes, but I didn't get any response.'

'You also didn't have one of these and were likely asking the wrong kind of questions. Ask direct questions that he can give a yes or no answer to, and if he does, he'll harness the energy in this device to respond. "Yes" will light up this side.' He pointed to one side of the gadget. 'And "no" this side. But who knows if we'll get to this point tonight? Ready?'

Zoe didn't think she'd ever be completely ready for this, but she whispered 'Yes' nonetheless.

Jack gave her a nod of approval, then, juggling the digital camera and the laser grip in one hand, he turned the handle and pushed open the door.

Zoe held her breath as she followed him up the narrow staircase, keeping closer to him than was perhaps strictly necessary. They were only halfway up when they both started coughing and spluttering due to the dust.

'You okay?' Jack whispered, glancing back over his shoulder.

'Yes,' she lied. 'You?'

He nodded and continued up. Zoe's eyes began to adjust to the darkness and when they emerged into the attic, the moon cast a fair bit of light through the windows. They took a moment to look around the cavernous space. It was like what you'd expect—equal parts dust, old boxes and furniture. She could make out a few distinct shapes—a birdcage, a world globe and a rocking horse, all things that must have been once well-loved and then forgotten.

Jack sat on a big old trunk in the middle of the room and tapped the spot beside him. 'Let's sit a little while, let the dust settle and see what happens.'

Zoe lowered herself down, barely breathing, and not just because of the dust. Her heart pounded and she wasn't sure whether it was the close proximity to Jack or because of what they were attempting to do. Nothing felt safe or normal anymore. She desperately wanted to fill the silence between them but couldn't think of anything mundane to say—and shouldn't they be quiet and listen?

After what seemed like eternity, Jack spoke softly. 'Hello? Is anyone here? I'm Jack and this is Zoe. We don't want to do any harm. We're here to help you. You can trust us.'

All Zoe could hear in response was the beating of her own heart and the leaves of the live oak outside swishing against the window.

'You try,' Jack suggested eventually.

Her heart hitched. 'What should I say?'

He slipped his hand into hers and squeezed. Warmth flooded her body. 'Introduce yourself.'

'Okay.' She sucked in a breath, her hand clinging tightly to his. 'H-h-hi. My name is Zoe, and this is my friend, Jack. We want to help you. Can you give us some sort of sign if you're here?'

Behind them a box clunked as it toppled onto the floor.

'Oh my God!' Zoe leapt onto Jack's lap before she realised what she was doing.

'Well, hello there,' he whispered, his face barely an inch away, his hands steadying her. 'You okay?'

'Did you hear that?'

He nodded but neither of them made a move to even look towards the sound. Their eyes locked. Why when she was scared beyond her wits could she think about nothing but the way his body felt against hers?

Whatever, this was hardly professional ghost-hunting behaviour. Disentangling herself from Jack, she picked up the laser-thingy that was now on the floor by his feet and started towards the errant box.

'Hello?' she called softly again. 'We don't want to harm you. Are you there?'

As she got closer to the spot, she aimed the gun in the air above where the contents of the box had spilled all over the floor. How had Jack said it worked?

'You have to press the button,' he murmured, coming up close—really close—behind her.

Never mind cold spots, all she could feel was the warmth of his body. Somehow, she did as he said and they both watched the little screen, waiting for a reading.

'Nothing,' he whispered, sounding as disappointed as she felt.

Zoe took a step towards the box. 'Are we allowed to use a torch?'

'A what?'

She frowned. 'You know … a flashlight?'

'Ah.' Jack pulled a small one from his pocket and shone it down where Zoe was now crouched.

'It looks like essays or school reports,' she said, lifting one to take another look. 'Oh my God.'

382

'What is it?'

'Remy's surname—*Walker*.' Zoe couldn't remember the last time she'd been so excited by anything. 'That will help you track him, right?'

Jack nodded as he picked up another bit of paper and aimed his torch on it. His eyebrows drew together.

'What is that?'

'I think it's a wedding certificate,' he replied.

She leaned in to take a closer look. 'It's *their* wedding certificate. But … but that doesn't make sense.'

'I thought he left her at the altar?'

'I know.' A chill lifted the hairs on the back of Zoe's neck, but she felt more curious than afraid. 'This doesn't make sense,' she said again. 'Maybe he left just after they got married?'

'I thought you suspected she killed him?'

'Well, that's possible too. She still could have told people he left.'

But this possibility didn't seem as plausible anymore. There were as many holes in her theory as there appeared to be in Miss H's version of the past.

'Yeah, I suppose so,' said Jack. 'Okay, let's give it another shot.' He switched off the torch. 'Hello? Remy Walker? Are you here?'

They waited for … nothing.

Jack went back to the trunk where they'd left the rest of the ghost-hunting gadgets. Of course she followed him—she might not be scared, but she wanted to stay close to the one thing she knew was real right now.

He picked up the TV remote lookalike and the pyramid thing. 'We're going to record on this while you ask questions. If we're lucky we'll get a response, but if not, we'll listen back and see if the recorder has picked up any EVP.'

'Electronic voice phenomena?'

He nodded. 'You're catching on.'

They returned to the spot near the fallen box and when Jack gave her the go ahead, Zoe said, 'Is anyone here?'

No response. No light appeared on either side of the binary response device.

She tried again. 'Are you Remy Walker?'

Again nothing.

They tried a few more questions with no response, making Zoe more and more frustrated.

'Why isn't he responding?' she whispered. 'Why keep appearing and then refusing to cooperate? Maybe the ghost is just playing tricks on us? Maybe it doesn't want our help after all?'

'Hey, don't be so disheartened. It might not feel like it, but we've had quite a successful night so far. It probably took the spirit a lot to appear to us downstairs and then lead us to the box. He gave us a name. Let's see if we can find anything else.'

They went through the rest of the box and the ones around it, searching for another clue, but all they contained were old geography assignments and textbooks, which had clearly belonged to Remy.

'Let's take a break,' Jack said. 'Go back to your room, finish our coffees and listen to see if the recorder caught anything.'

'Okay.' Zoe let out a long breath, feeling emotionally exhausted.

They retreated to the second storey. She felt a little weird about shutting the door—the only guy she'd ever been alone with in a bedroom before was Beau—but they didn't want to risk Miss H hearing voices.

'Shall I turn on the light?'

'Up to you,' he said, glancing around as if looking for some place to sit. There was only her bed. 'We might be more likely to get another visit if it's dim.'

She nodded and gestured to the bed, pretending her heart wasn't pounding. 'Wanna sit?'

'Sure.' He scooped up his discarded mug and climbed onto the bed.

Zoe sat down next to him and they both leaned back against the bedhead, their legs stretched out in front of them like an old married couple who no longer had anything to say to each other.

Jack pressed play on the recorder and held it up between them. Zoe leaned in to listen, but all they heard was her asking the questions.

'Do you think there was a window open up there or something that caused the box to fall?' she asked.

'No.' He took a sip of coffee. 'Boxes full of paperwork are heavy—they don't just blow over. Besides, that box was very specific.'

They both looked down at the wedding certificate still in Zoe's hand.

'Maybe I should confront Miss H with this tomorrow. Ask her outright why she lied about him leaving her at the altar?'

'Maybe,' Jack said, although he didn't sound convinced.

'Hey, so did you find out anything about this house?' she asked.

'No. I didn't get a chance, but I'll get onto that tomorrow. I'm meeting a colleague in the morning to do some research on a place in the French Quarter, so I'll kill two birds with one stone. I'll try and find some more information about Remy Walker as well.' Jack dug into his pocket and pulled out a tube of mints. 'Want one?'

'Thanks.' She took one and popped it into her mouth. 'Jack?'

'Yes.'

'I just ... I just wanted to say thanks for coming here and helping me with this, especially when I haven't been particularly nice to you since we met.'

'What are you apologising for? Throwing yourself at me? Using me as an alibi in your lies to your mom? Throwing up on me?'

She cringed. 'Yes. All of that.'

He chuckled. 'Apology accepted. And I'm sorry for being an asshole when you tried to apologise before. I guess I'm a little nervous around pretty girls and it makes me do and say stupid things.'

Pretty girls.

'Could have fooled me,' she whispered, her cheeks heating.

Their eyes met in the near darkness. Zoe suddenly found it almost as difficult to breathe as she had in the attic. Her gaze drifted to his lips as she remembered the way they'd felt on hers. *Sweet. Salacious. Magical.* You'd never guess from looking at him that he was such a great kisser. But he was. And right now, she wanted him to kiss her again.

She wanted to kiss *him* even more than she'd wanted to the night they met, but this time she wasn't aided and abetted by alcohol. And she didn't know what to do with such lust.

'Zoe?' Jack's voice sounded choked. 'How are you feeling … you know, about your … your husband?'

'*Ex*-husband.' Or as good as. She sighed, annoyed that Beau had broken the moment. 'I'm better than I was. It still hurts—perhaps it always will—but I can see light at the end of the tunnel now. Maybe.'

'What actually happened between you two?'

Although Zoe brushed them off whenever her family tried to get her to talk about Beau, she found herself telling Jack everything. She told him about how she'd thought they were soulmates, how she'd longed to have a baby and how Beau had crushed her with his betrayal.

'He not only broke my heart, but he made me wonder what was wrong with me that he had to look somewhere else.'

'There's absolutely nothing wrong with you,' Jack said, squeezing her hand. 'I promise. He's the one who needs his head read.'

She almost smiled. 'But I married him—I thought I knew him. I didn't think he'd ever have been capable of hurting me. How could I have been such a terrible judge of character?'

'You're not a terrible judge of character. You're simply a good, kind person who sees and expects the best from people. Your ex's actions have nothing to do with you.'

'Thank you,' she said, gazing into his soulful eyes, wanting to believe him.

He stared back at her and the air between them seemed to crackle and fizz. She swallowed as Jack reached out to cup her face.

'I'm not going to lie,' he said. 'I really, really, really want to kiss you right now. And call me presumptuous, but I'm getting a similar vibe from you.'

'You're not presumptuous, but ...' Her voice trailed off, uncertainty swimming like a plague of insects in her stomach. Why couldn't her head and her libido be in sync?

'*But* I get the feeling that what you could really do with right now is a friend?'

She nodded, frustration, disappointment and relief flooding her.

Jack smiled and dropped his hand. 'Then, if you'll have me, I'd love to fill that spot?'

'I might have to check your references,' Zoe said, trying to lighten the mood when she felt anything but light.

'Damn. I was hoping you wouldn't ask that.'

They both laughed then and, as disgruntled as her hormones were with this decision, Zoe knew it was the right one. Sex—while good in the moment—complicated things. Friends were far less likely to break each other's hearts and she knew hers couldn't handle another knock right now.

'So ... tell me about the first time you saw a ghost?' she asked, sitting straighter and putting some distance between them. 'Who was it?'

'My dad,' Jack said simply.

Her heart jackhammered. 'I'm so sorry. You don't have to tell me.'

'It's okay.' He twisted the tube of mints between his fingers. 'It was a long time ago. I was thirteen. He'd died only a couple of weeks earlier in a farm accident or so we were told, but it never kinda sat right. Anyway, me and my older brother had to take on most of his duties. I was milking the cow one morning when I first saw him. At first I thought I was going crazy, but by the third time I couldn't keep it to myself. I ran back home and told my mom and my brothers and sisters. I think Mom actually wanted to believe me, but as our people don't believe in the paranormal, she sought advice from the ministers in our district. I was told I was a liar and that I was not seeing anything. I was warned I must stop talking nonsense or I'd be shunned.'

'They threatened to shun a child?'

He nodded.

Zoe could only imagine how terrifying that must have been. It made her want to take him in her arms and comfort him, but he wasn't thirteen anymore and, considering the chemistry between them, she didn't think that would be a good idea.

'But I wasn't lying,' he added. 'I did see him. And that's when I started to question our way of life, when I started to resent being told what I could and couldn't believe. Remember you asked me about Rumspringa?'

She nodded.

'I ran away from home when I was sixteen. Never even got to Rumspringa.'

'Oh my God. Where did you go? How did you survive?'

'There are places, people who left the church who take in others that do the same. After a couple of nights hitchhiking and sleeping rough, I found refuge in Baltimore with friends of a friend. They helped me, got me a job in a diner, gave me a roof over my head until I'd saved enough money to stand on my own two feet.'

'Wow. And how did you end up in New Orleans?'

For the next hour or so, they swapped stories—Jack told her of all the places he'd been in his quest to learn more about the paranormal, making her realise just how sheltered her existence had been in Perth. He told her how he realised he might not have been able to help his dad, but maybe he could help other lost souls.

When Zoe finally began to grow tired, Jack said, 'Why don't you try and get some rest?'

She frowned. 'Are you leaving?'

He shook his head. 'I'll stay, unless you don't want me to? I can sleep on the floor, and that way if anything more happens, I'll be here, and we can try and collect some evidence. I'll pack up my things and sneak out early.'

'You don't have to sleep on the floor. I promise I can keep my hands off you,' she joked.

'It's not you I'm worried about,' he replied. 'But I'll do my best as well.'

37

Felicity

Flick's mobile rang as she was heading down to open the shop and she was happy to see Zoe's name flashing up at her. Maybe tonight they could go out for dinner or something. She couldn't stand the prospect of another night upstairs alone with her thoughts, music coming through the walls from the Blue Cat, taunting her.

'Morning, sweetheart.'

'Hey, Mum.' Zoe sounded out of breath.

'Are you okay?'

'We had a very late night—or rather early morning—and I overslept. I'm rushing to get dressed because Miss H is probably wondering what the hell's happened to me.'

'*We?*' Even as she asked the question, the answer clicked. 'Oh right, you and Jack.' After the conversation with Theo yesterday, Flick had almost forgotten about the ghost-hunting plans. 'Was it a success? Did you guys feel anything?'

'We more than felt something. I saw him again, Mum, and so did Jack. Unfortunately, he hadn't quite got the camera set up, so we didn't get any concrete evidence, but we're pretty sure it's Remy.'

'Really?' Flick's hand paused on the light switch as she entered the shop. 'Jack saw him too?'

'Yes. We'd barely started when he appeared, and he seemed to lead us upstairs—into the attic. So, we went up there and ... and we found their wedding certificate. He can't have left her at the altar because there's proof they got married.'

'What?' Flick turned the open/closed sign and unlocked the door. 'But—'

'I know. Why would she say that if it wasn't true? I still think there's something fishy going on. I'm sure Remy's dead. How or why he died I have no idea, but Miss H's behaviour screams guilt to me and I'm more determined than ever to get to the bottom of it.'

'What are you going to do next?'

'Well, I was thinking maybe I could just show her the wedding certificate and ask her to explain herself.'

Flick didn't know if that was a good idea. She'd heard Aurelia talking about being abandoned on her wedding day, so she was either a liar or a lunatic. Both options left a very uneasy feeling in her stomach.

'But Jack's also going to do some digging and see if he can find any more information now that we have Remy's full name. I checked online this morning but didn't find anyone who fits the bill. I'm not sure whether to wait and see what Jack uncovers or confront her?'

'Definitely wait,' Flick said. Young people thought they were invincible and although Zoe could probably overpower Aurelia if need be, who knew what the older woman was capable of? *If* she had murdered her husband—and that seemed highly unlikely—she'd gotten away with it for fifty years.

'And maybe you should make an excuse about moving out for a few days while we work out what to do.'

'You really think that's necessary?'

Before Flick could respond, her phone beeped, indicating another call coming through. She checked the screen. 'Sweetheart,' she said quickly, 'Harvey's trying to phone. I'll ring you back in a few minutes, okay?'

'Sure. Talk soon.'

Flick accepted the other call. 'Hi, Harvey. How are you?'

'Morning, Felicity.' His sombre tone delivered the news before he did.

'I'm so sorry,' she said.

'Thank you, dear. It was expected of course, but it's never easy to lose a loved one, especially when she's your last living relative. Well, aside from her children, but they barely know I exist. They're vultures, the lot of them.'

Flick listened patiently and made sympathetic sounds as Harvey grumbled about his nieces and nephews and how they'd started bickering about their mother's will mere moments after she'd taken her last breath, but her mind wasn't completely on the conversation.

'And if that's not bad enough, they're refusing to adhere to some of her wishes for her funeral. They think I'm just an old man they can walk all over, but I'm standing my ground. Mary will get the send-off that *she* wanted, even if it kills me.'

'Death and grief can cause people to act out of character sometimes,' Flick said.

He snorted. 'This has nothing to do with grief. As much as I love Mary, she and that fancy-man husband of hers raised those kids as spoiled brats.' When he'd exhausted the topic, he sounded quite deflated. 'Anyway, she's at peace now and I'm itching to get back to the shop. My fingers are seizing up because they're not working.'

'When will you be back?'

'Well, the funeral's next week—I'll stay for that and then I'm on the next plane out of Florida.'

Next week? Flick slumped back in the seat. While relieved on one hand that she could now book a ticket home, she couldn't quite summon the necessary enthusiasm when there was even the smallest possibility that her daughter was living with a murderer. Being a little unsociable and eccentric was one thing, but could there be any truth in what Zoe suspected?

'But don't feel you have to rush off,' Harvey continued. 'You and Zoe are welcome to stay on till the three months are up if you like. A deal's a deal, and it'll be nice to have some company for a change.'

'That's a very kind offer, but I'm ready to go home. And actually, Zoe is no longer living here. She's started working in the Garden District.'

'Has she indeed? How did that come about?'

'Um … you know the painting you have upstairs above the mantlepiece?'

'Aurelia's?'

'Yes.' It was the first time she'd heard anyone call the elderly woman by her first name. 'Well, she came into the shop a couple of weeks ago and wanted me to preserve her cat. When I told her I couldn't do it, she got a little agitated.'

She explained how Aurelia had fallen and broken her wrist, which had led to Zoe helping her, which in turn had led to a job offer and also Flick agreeing to take on Edward out of guilt. 'Do you think you'll be able to finish him off for me?'

'I've never collaborated with anyone before, but I can't see why not. Poor Aurelia, her cats have been dropping like flies these last few years.'

'Are you two good friends?'

'I wouldn't say we're friends exactly, but I have known her a long time. We knew each other as kids.'

'Really? Did you know her ... husband?'

'No, never met the man. It was a whirlwind courtship—he came to work at the school where she taught, and next thing everyone knows they were getting married. By all accounts, she was besotted. Such a tragedy what happened to him.'

Flick's heart skipped a beat. 'I thought he jilted her on their wedding day?'

'That old story?' Harvey chortled. 'No. He *died* the morning *after* their wedding.'

Flick almost dropped the phone. 'He what? *How?*'

'There was a very small fire in the house ... the kitchen I think, a saucepan catching alight or something, if I remember. He put it out and there wasn't any damage. But then later that night, he suffered a fatal asthma attack triggered by smoke inhalation.'

'Oh my God.' Flick's hand rushed to her chest. 'But ... I don't understand. I haven't just heard the story from other people.' Her mind briefly flickered to Theo. 'Aurelia herself has spoken about her fiancé leaving her—to both me and Zoe—more than once.'

'Ah, yes.' Harvey sighed. 'Well, that's the second part of the tragedy.'

38

Zoe

Across the other side of town, Zoe grew tired of waiting for her mother to return her call. She sent a quick message to Jack who had succeeded in sneaking away from the house before sunrise.

How's progress? Anything yet?

Patience, my friend, these things take time.

A selfie of him surrounded by a pile of paperwork at the library accompanied his text. She smiled at his goofy grin and the way he called her 'friend', recalling the deeply personal conversation they shared in this very room.

Sorry. I'll do my best.

The thing was, Zoe had never had a patient bone in her body. She swiped some gloss over her lips, her gaze falling on the wedding certificate sitting on her dresser. Uncertainty battled with curiosity inside her. She reached for the certificate, pulling her hand back again. She did this little dance four times before her fingers finally closed around the aged piece of paper and she headed downstairs.

Assuming Miss H would already be in the sunroom, she was halfway there when her mobile started ringing. Seeing it was her mum, she detoured into the barely used living room and quietly closed the door behind her.

'Hello?'

'Remy did die,' Flick said in lieu of a greeting. 'He's buried in the cemetery down the road.'

'What?' Zoe exclaimed, and then quickly lowered her voice. 'I *knew* it. But hang on, how did *you* find out?'

'Harvey. We got talking about her because of someone needing to finish Edward when I leave.'

'And what did he say?' Zoe discarded the wedding certificate on the piano and lowered herself onto the stool.

'They did get married, but there was a small fire in the kitchen the next day and although he put it out before it could do any real damage, he was an asthmatic and complications from the smoke inhalation killed him.'

'Holy shit! That's why I always smell smoke!' A chill swept over her skin and this time she didn't know whether it was Remy or simple shivers. 'But hang on … if he's dead, why does everyone think he left her? Why does *she* say he did?'

'Apparently Aurelia had some kind of mental breakdown after Remy died. She never returned to work after the funeral, she refused to visit his grave and became very angry with anyone who tried to talk to her about him. In the end, her friends stopped visiting because they didn't know what to do with her. You've heard about the stages of grief, right?'

'Yes.'

'Well, Harvey believes Aurelia got stuck somewhere between anger and denial and somehow her memories got warped. She felt abandoned when Remy died, and rewrote the past to one she could deal with better.'

'Is that even possible? And how is it any better?'

'Maybe not better, but I guess she needed a reason to stay angry. The mind is a strange thing. You believe what you tell yourself, therefore memories are never one hundred per cent reliable, but this is clearly some kind of disorder.'

Zoe's mind was spinning. 'But why didn't anyone ever help her? If Harvey knows her so well, why didn't he?'

'They're not really more than acquaintances. And Aurelia's father had died not long before Remy, so she didn't have any family support. Also, people of that generation aren't as likely to stick their noses in each other's business.'

'Helping someone isn't sticking your nose in!'

'Sweetheart, calm down. I didn't say I agreed with it, I'm just saying, it wasn't unusual fifty years ago. Other people's grief— even straightforward grief—can still be uncomfortable today. Sometimes it's easier to ignore something when you don't know how to fix it.'

Zoe shook her head, so confused it hurt. 'But that doesn't account for why everyone thinks Remy left her.'

'Zoe? What are you doing in there?'

She startled at the sound of Miss H's voice and looked up to see her standing in the doorway. Zoe hadn't heard the door open and didn't know how long she'd been standing there.

'Mum, I gotta go. Talk soon.' She gulped and summoned a carefree smile. 'Hello, that was Mum. She's just ... she's not really coping with the whole Theo thing.'

'I see.' Miss H frowned. 'And what about you? Are you okay? You slept very late today.'

'Yes ... sorry ... must be delayed jet lag or something.'

Miss H raised one of her thin, grey eyebrows. 'Is that possible?'

'Yep, I think so,' Zoe said, looking at the older woman in a totally different light. At first she'd felt in awe of her, a little inspired, then suspicious, and now? Now she didn't know what she was supposed to do with what Flick had told her. It was the saddest thing she'd ever heard—poor Miss H—but should she just go on as they were or try to help her? What would be the kindest thing?

Although she didn't have any clue, she did know that in times of crisis, tea was always a good idea. 'Shall I make us some tea?'

'Looks like you could do with some coffee yourself.'

'Coffee it is then. Come on.'

Miss H followed her into the kitchen and spoke about trivial things while Zoe made the coffee. Zoe wouldn't have been able to say what the conversation was about because all she could think about was Flick's discovery.

'What's on your agenda today?' Miss H asked as Zoe carried the tray into the sunroom.

'Huh? I'm sorry?'

'Are you going to paint first or is there internet stuff to do? I thought I might—'

'I'm sorry,' Zoe interrupted as she set the tray down on the coffee table. 'But do you mind if I go out for a while?'

'Out?'

'Yes ... um ... I think I should check on Mum again.' It was the first excuse that came to mind. 'I'm worried about her.'

Miss H sighed but nodded. 'You're not a prisoner here. You can come and go as you please. You're a little skittish today and I sense

I'm not going to get any good out of you until you've done what you need to do. Go on, be off with you then.'

'Thanks. I won't be long. Promise.'

Then, without even grabbing her bag, Zoe hurried down the hall and out the front door. A tour group stood on the sidewalk, the guide waxing lyrical about the crazy old artist who lived here. She paused mid-sentence and blinked as Zoe appeared and opened the gate.

Without a word, Zoe charged through the middle of the group and started down the street towards Lafayette Cemetery No. 1. Flick said Remy was buried there and Zoe felt compelled to see his grave for herself. By the time she reached the arched entrance of the iconic cemetery she was puffing. No longer scared of the unknown, no longer scared of the dead, she strode right on in.

She paused a moment and glanced around for some kind of sign or someone who might be able to direct her, but although there were plenty of people, none of them looked like they had any kind of authority. Most were clearly tourists, milling about taking selfies with the mammoth tombs in the background.

Zoe no longer felt like a tourist. She felt like a part of this dark and beautiful place. Strangely proud of what New Orleans had to offer but also protective. When some guy climbed on top of a grave so his partner could get a better picture, she almost yelled at him to show some respect. But that wasn't why she was here, so she went to the first far corner of the cemetery and systematically began to make her way through the aisles.

Like everywhere else in the Garden District, the paths here were fractured, grass and dirt poking up between the cracks. The graves, while imposing, were mostly dilapidated, blackened by mildew, and only a few looked as if they still received regular TLC. Zoe couldn't help pausing to read the inscriptions on some of the gravestones. Yellow fever had wiped out whole families, but it was the names of the babies that brought tears to her eyes.

Many of the monuments were well over a hundred years old and so weather-beaten they were hardly legible. As fascinated as she was, Zoe started to lose heart. Would someone who'd died as recently as fifty years ago even be buried here?

Hope came moments later when she found a grave with a date as recent as 1983. Remy would have died over a decade earlier, but it was encouragement enough for her to continue.

Another aisle, a few more tombs, and Zoe halted as her gaze caught on the surname Harranibar. The dates of the dead listed went back to the early 1800s and right alongside it was another, much newer, much smaller monument.

Remy Walker—1945–1971
Beloved husband of Aurelia.

'Oh my God!' Both hands rushed to cover her mouth and tears sprang to her eyes. He'd been just down the road all the time and, judging by the lacklustre appearance of the stone and the weeds climbing around it, his grave had long been forgotten.

She needed to take a photo. She needed to call Jack. She needed to call her mum.

Giddy with excitement, Zoe reached into her pocket only to discover she'd left her phone back at the house. *Dammit!* She must have left it in the living room after Miss H had sprung her.

Oh no! She'd left her mobile *and* the wedding certificate in full view.

It'll be fine, Zoe said to herself even as her breath quickened. Miss H hardly ever went into that room, and she didn't have any reason to today either. Still, she'd better get back there. She had to call Jack and tell him to stop the investigation because she'd solved the mystery.

Although glad to have got to the bottom of the whole ghost thing, her victory wasn't as sweet as she'd hoped. Her heart ached for Miss H. Fifty years she'd lived alone, stuck in a prison of bitterness and anger, unable to recover from her loss. Nothing but her painting to console her.

The skeleton brides Zoe had admired now seemed a symbol of an even bigger tragedy and she wasn't sure she'd ever be able to look at them the same way again.

Sirens jolted her from her thoughts as she left the cemetery and looked up to see a fire engine zoom by, cars pulling to the side of the road to make way. She smelled smoke in the air as she watched it slow near the Commander's Palace. Was the *restaurant* on fire? Thank God Jack was safe at the library.

But no, Zoe watched as the fire engine swung around the corner and headed down the road in the direction of Miss H's place.

No. It couldn't be.

The smoke could be coming from any one of many houses in the area but Zoe started to run anyway, almost flying arse over tit as her sandal caught in a crevice. 'Bloody trees.'

She corrected herself and kept on. Her heart flew up to her throat as she witnessed the chaos ahead. People and emergency vehicles clogged the street. Not one, but two fire engines were parked diagonally in front of the old pink house as firefighters aimed hoses like machine-guns, raining water down all over it. Policemen were shouting at crowds to keep back as nosy parkers tried to capture the drama on their phones.

Zoe couldn't have been gone for more than an hour. How had this happened so quickly?

'Miss H!' she screamed as she fought her way to the front of the crowd.

'Sorry, ma'am,' said a burly cop, blocking her way. 'I can't let you go any further.'

'I live there,' she sobbed, struggling against his hold as she stared in horror at the blaze. 'My boss. My *friend*. She's in there. You have to get her out!'

'The fire department are doing all they can.' He put an arm around her and despite herself she sagged against him, silently praying Miss H would be okay.

Seconds later, cheers erupted and Zoe straightened to see a man stumbling down the front steps, a figure slumped in his arms. As the paramedics swarmed in to assist, the man handed her over. It was only when he turned and tried to run back into the building that Zoe registered he wasn't wearing the bright yellow protective clothing of the firefighters.

'Oh my God! Jack!' she gasped as emergency workers launched at him, refusing to allow him back inside.

What was he even doing here?

It looked like he was screaming something, but Zoe couldn't hear what over the noise of the hoses or the roar of the fire.

She struggled against the grip of the officer. 'I have to go to him.'

'You need to let the EMTs do their job,' he said, holding her even tighter. 'Once the danger is gone and they've treated them, I'll take you to them myself.'

'Okay.' *Not*.

Using a strength she didn't know she had, Zoe broke free of the policeman and dashed over to where Jack was also being manhandled, shouting something about someone still being inside.

'Jack!' she screamed, as the intense heat of the fire hit her.

He stopped fighting and his eyes widened as if he couldn't believe it was her. 'Zoe? Thank God.' His voice was scratchy, but she could read his lips.

She threw her arms around him, only thinking as she felt his boiling hot skin that maybe her touch might be hurting. She pulled back and scrutinised him. His clothes were dirty but not burned, his face tainted by a few dark marks and he appeared to have lost his glasses, but aside from that he looked miraculously unscathed.

'What were you doing in there? Shh, don't answer that,' she gushed when he attempted to. She desperately wanted to run her hands over his face and through his hair, to kiss his cracked lips, but he looked in dire need of a drink.

'You okay, buddy?' asked one of the paramedics. 'Let's sit you down and check you over.'

While they checked Jack's vital signs, examined him for burns and offered him oxygen and water, Zoe glanced over to where another team were working on Miss H. She felt torn between going to check on her and staying with Jack, but in the end stayed where she was for fear of what she might see.

Questions whirled through her mind—how had the fire started? Had she left her hair straightener on upstairs? How long was Miss H in there before Jack turned up? *Why* was Jack even here?

She felt Jack's touch on her arm and turned back to look at him. 'What is it? You okay?'

'She was burning her paintings,' he said, his voice still raspy. 'In the fireplace. Screaming something about wasting her life.'

'Oh God.' Zoe felt sick. She might not have left an appliance on, but she'd left something much more dangerous where Miss H must have found it. 'What were you doing here?'

'I found out how Remy died and tried to call you a few times, but ...' He coughed. 'When you didn't pick up, I decided to come tell you myself and when I arrived, I saw the smoke. A neighbour said she'd already called 911 so I just went inside.' He reached for Zoe's hand and held it tight. 'I thought you were in there.'

'I'm fine,' she breathed, tears filling her eyes. 'And you got Miss H out. Thank you.'

'Was there someone else there? She kept saying something about Charlotte or somebody.'

'The cat!' Until that moment, Zoe hadn't given a second thought to Miss H's beloved pet.

'Ah, I see.' Jack sighed as they both glanced quickly at the house behind them. 'Hopefully she escaped.'

'She's already lost Edward, she's going to be devastated if she loses Charlotte as well. That's if ...' Zoe couldn't bring herself to verbalise the worst.

When he could, she and Jack walked over to where Miss H was being loaded onto a stretcher. There was a blanket over her and a mask on her face. She wasn't dead, but she didn't look conscious either.

'She's suffered serious smoke inhalation and burns to her hands. We're taking her to Tulane,' said one of the paramedics. 'And you should really come with us to get properly checked out as well.'

'I'm fine,' said Jack. 'Honestly. There's barely even a scratch on me.'

He sounded almost proud of his heroics, but Zoe shook her head, thinking of Remy. She did not want history to repeat itself on this very spot.

'You're going, and I won't hear otherwise. Can I come in the ambulance too?' she asked, not wanting to leave either of them. This was the second time Miss H had needed to go to hospital in a matter of weeks and both times had been Zoe's fault.

When the doors at the back of the first ambulance closed, she and Jack were ushered into the second. A cop mentioned something about talking to the both of them soon, and finally they were being driven away, leaving the chaos and the smouldering house behind them.

Zoe was supposed to be here supporting Jack, but it was he who reached out his hand and squeezed hers. 'She'll be okay,' he said, 'I promise.'

And although he had no authority to be giving such guarantees, Zoe found she did feel a little better.

39

Felicity

When Theo strode into the shop just before noon, Flick ignored the way her heart skipped a beat and opened her mouth to tell him to stop wasting both their time, but his voice rode right over the top of hers.

'Have you heard from Zoe?'

'What? I spoke to her about an hour ago. Why?'

'I just saw on Facebook there's been a house fire in the Garden District. It's Miss H's. Emergency services are on the scene now.'

'Oh my God!' Cold flooded her body. 'Are you sure?'

'Unfortunately.'

'How did it start? Is it still going? Is anyone inside? I should call her.'

Flick snatched her phone from under the desk before he could attempt to answer any of her questions. As she stabbed her finger against Zoe's name, Theo swiftly cleared the shop of customers.

'She's not answering,' Flick cried, a lump clogging her throat. 'Oh my God. What if she's in the house?' If something had happened to Zoe … *no*, that wasn't worth thinking about.

'Do you want me to drive you there?' Theo asked and she was thankful he didn't try to tell her everything was going to be okay.

'Yes. Please.' Her hands trembling, Flick grabbed her purse and keys from under the desk.

'Come on.' He wrapped an arm around her as they headed outside.

A little voice told her she shouldn't be leaning so heavily on him, but what else was she supposed to do? He knew the roads and the way to Aurelia's place much better than she did.

'What are you doing?' Theo asked a few minutes later when they were in the car and navigating traffic.

'I'm watching videos of the fire.' A quick search of 'Garden District house fire' on Facebook and she'd come across lots of them. People with smartphones were much quicker than the news channels these days.

'Do you think that's a good idea?'

Flick didn't reply, her gut churning as she watched the old pink house going up in flames, all the artistic detail and beauty crumbling before her eyes. How on earth did it start? Had Zoe confronted Aurelia about the wedding certificate? She wasn't sure how that could have resulted in this, but it seemed a mighty big coincidence that just when they'd discovered the truth, this happened.

'That looks like Jack,' she shrieked at the screen as she watched a man emerge from the burning house, carrying a woman that Flick immediately identified as Aurelia. 'But where's Zoe? Oh God, please don't let her still be inside.'

Theo reached across and put his hand on her knee. He didn't say anything and for that she was grateful, but his small gesture went a tiny way to calming her. Zoe was young and fit. If Jack had managed to carry Aurelia out, surely Zoe would have been able to escape as well.

'Did you know that Aurelia's husband didn't really leave her at the altar?' Flick said, trying to distract herself from thinking the worst.

Theo frowned but kept his eyes on the road. 'What do you mean?'

'He died just after their wedding—complications following a fire actually.'

'But …' He shook his head.

'When did you first hear about her?'

'Long before Rachel and I moved in next door. Neither of us grew up in the Garden District but the story of Miss H was a local legend.'

'Apparently it really was.' She told him what Harvey had told her about Aurelia never properly recovering from Remy's death. 'Somewhere along the line, Aurelia truly started to believe that he left her and as that's what she told people, eventually fiction became truth among the locals as well.'

'That's insane,' Theo said. 'Although I had a colleague once who suffered from something called complicated grief disorder after her child died. The doctors also called it "stuck grief" if I remember right.'

'What happened?'

'She suffered the normal signs of grief that anyone who's lost someone close does, but they became so debilitating and didn't improve at all with time.'

'Sounds understandable after losing a child,' Flick said, her heart squeezing as she thought of Zoe. *Please God, let her be okay.* 'I can't imagine ever being the same again after such a loss.'

'Yes, that's true, but most people eventually accept the loss, they never completely forget or recover, but they learn how to live again in a world without their loved one. They can move on and continue to love those still in their lives. My colleague wasn't moving on. She started carrying a doll around and calling it by her son's name. And she got angry with anyone who tried to bring her back to reality.'

'What happened to her?'

'Her husband convinced her to see a doctor and they put her in a mental health facility so she could get treatment. That was maybe a decade ago? Last I heard she's doing well—they had two more kids and she regularly takes them to visit their big brother's grave. But I can only imagine how much worse she might have become if she didn't get the help she needed. I guess maybe Miss H had something similar.'

'That makes an awful lot of sense,' Flick said with a sigh. 'And instead of helping her, people just started to go along with her version of reality, until it became local lore.'

They were just turning into Aurelia's street when Flick's phone started ringing. She glanced down at the screen to see a number she didn't recognise. Fear gripped her and she almost didn't want to answer it, not wanting to hear bad news.

'Do you want me to pull over and take that for you?' Theo asked.

Somehow his offer gave her strength, and she pressed accept and lifted the phone to her ear. 'Hello? Felicity Bell speaking.'

'Mum. It's me.'

'Oh my God, Zoe.' A rush of relief flushed through her at the sound of her daughter's voice. 'You're okay?'

'Yes, but something terrible has happened,' Zoe sobbed.

'I know. The house?'

'Yes.'

'Is Miss—'

'She's on her way to the hospital. So am I.'

'I thought you said you were okay?'

'Relax, Mum. I'm fine. I'm in the ambulance with Jack.'

'Oh God, is he okay?'

'Yes. They're just taking him as a precaution.'

She breathed another sigh of relief. 'So, what happened? How did the fire start?'

'I wasn't even at the house. I'd gone down the road to look for Remy's grave. I think Miss H found the wedding certificate and it jolted her memory. Jack arrived while I was out, and he rushed inside to find her trying to burn her paintings in the old fireplace. It probably hadn't been used in years—maybe decades—and he reckons it must have been blocked or something. I guess the police and the fire brigade will be able to determine that for sure, but it doesn't really matter how it started, the house is ruined.'

'Oh, Zo-Zo,' Flick said, hearing the hopelessness in her daughter's voice. 'It's people that are more important. How's Aurelia?'

'I don't know. Jack got her out but ...'

As Zoe's voice drifted off, Flick glanced out the window and realised they'd just passed Aurelia's street. She looked back to see smoke in the air.

'Where are you going?' she said to Theo.

'I assumed you'd want to get to the hospital,' he replied, clearly having overheard her conversation. 'But I can turn back if you want.'

'No. Of course not. Thank you.' Flick didn't need to see what was left of the house, she needed to see Zoe. She pressed the phone back against her ear. 'I'm on my way, sweetheart. I'll be there soon.'

When they arrived at Tulane Medical Center, Theo pulled up as close to the entrance as he could. 'Say hi to Zoe for me. Hope she's okay, and Jack and Miss H too.'

Her hand on the door, Flick frowned. 'You're not coming in?'

'I didn't think you'd want me to. But call me when you need to head home, I can come back and get you and Zoe.'

Flick thought for a moment. 'No. Thanks though. And thank you for driving me here—I really appreciate it. But we'll just get an Uber or something.' As much as she craved his company right now, she wasn't going to use him or play games.

'You're welcome,' he said, sad resignation in his eyes. 'Bye, Felicity.'

'Bye, Theo.' Without allowing herself to look back, Flick strode into the building and went to look for Zoe.

She found her in the same place she'd been only a few weeks ago, with the rows of plastic chairs, vending machines and TV mumbling in the corner. Talk about deja vu.

'Mum!' Zoe exclaimed as Flick approached.

They embraced long and hard and then both spoke at once.

'I've never been so happy to see you in my life.'

'How'd you get here so fast?'

Flick laughed. 'I was already on my way when you rang. Theo saw the fire on Facebook and came and got me.'

'See?' Zoe said with a half-smile. 'Whether you love or hate social media, you have to admit it has its uses.'

Arms still wrapped around each other, they grabbed two cups of coffee from one of the machines, then sat on chairs as far from other people as they could get. They passed the time rehashing what they'd both discovered about Aurelia and then googling the disorder Theo had mentioned.

'A small minority of bereaved people find themselves stalled in acute grief that can persist without respite, lasting years, or in rare cases, even decades, after a particularly difficult loss,' Flick read aloud off her phone screen.

'Losing Remy would have been very hard on Miss H,' Zoe mused. 'She'd already lost her parents, so he was all she had. And maybe she blamed herself for causing the fire that led to his death.'

Flick nodded.

'So,' Zoe said after reading more articles, 'in order to get over the pain of losing Remy, Miss H must have tricked her mind into believing that he left her, and then directed all her energies into being angry.'

'Yes. I guess there was also a kind of hope in this belief because she could cling to the possibility that he might see the error of his ways and come back to her.'

Zoe sighed. 'What happens now? Surely while she's here, we can ask someone to do some kind of psychiatric assessment on her? But is it even possible to help her after such a long time?'

Flick had no idea, but she reached out and squeezed her daughter's hand. 'One step at a time, darling. Let's just get through the next few hours.'

'Hours?' Zoe sighed and glanced at her watch. 'Feels like we've already been here days. Do you think I should go and ask someone what's happening? At least Jack should be out by now.'

'If that would make you feel better,' Flick said, knowing that telling her to be patient in this situation would be futile.

Zoe stood, but as she went across to the desk, the doors that led into the ER opened and out strode Jack.

He looked a little worse for wear, but even from a distance Flick saw the way his eyes lit up when he spotted Zoe. She watched as they hurried across the large space and threw their arms around each other. Their embrace looked a lot more than friendly, but then again, trauma had a way of making people closer.

Just when she was starting to feel a little awkward, they pulled apart and Zoe led him towards her.

'Hello, Jack.' Flick smiled. 'Sounds like you've been quite the hero today.'

He shrugged and blushed.

'How are you anyway?'

'I'm fine. Nothing more than a few scratches. No internal damage, although they said it might take a few days for my voice to return to normal.'

'Can I get you anything? Something to eat maybe?' Zoe asked.

He held up a bottle of water. 'This is all I really feel up to right now.'

'Any sign of Miss H in there?'

He shook his head. 'Sorry, Zoe. I did ask but they said they didn't have any news yet.'

The three of them stood in silence for a moment.

'Are you going to go home, or ...' Zoe's voice drifted off.

'I thought I might hang here for a bit and wait for news,' Jack said, 'if that's okay with you?'

'Of course.' Sounding ridiculously pleased by this idea, Zoe sat down next to Flick and Jack took the seat beside her.

For the next little while they chatted about the ghost—speculating as to why Zoe had seen him and why Miss H never had. Zoe had so many questions and Flick felt a little sorry for Jack, but despite being clearly exhausted, he answered as best he could.

'What do you think Remy wanted to achieve by appearing to me?'

He shrugged. 'My guess is he didn't like seeing the love of his life suffer so much without him. He couldn't move on when she was so clearly unable to herself.'

Flick couldn't believe they were actually having this conversation, but at the same time, nothing felt impossible anymore.

'I'm just going to the bathroom,' Jack said, touching Zoe's knee before pushing to his feet. 'Back soon.'

Zoe watched him go, smiling wistfully.

'Is something more going on between you two than ghost-hunting?'

'What?' Zoe blinked and looked as if she were about to deny any such thing but at the last moment, she sighed. 'I don't know. No. Maybe? I think I like him, and I'm pretty sure he feels the same way, but I have no idea how to feel about that. Just over a month ago I was married to someone else and never even contemplated *looking* at another guy, never mind having feelings and acting on them. I actually feel guilty thinking about Jack in that way. Can you believe that? After what Beau did, *I'm* the one who feels guilty?'

'You have nothing to feel guilty about, but you have been through a lot of emotional turmoil lately, so it's not surprising to feel a little confused.'

Zoe nodded. 'I know, and everything that's happened made me a little crazy for a while, but one thing I've realised over the last few days is that not all men are bad. Remy wasn't bad—he loved Miss H so much, he never really left her. And Jack isn't bad either. I think he's actually one of the good guys.'

'What does that mean for you two?'

'It means I'm not going to close off the possibility of something happening in the future, but I value his friendship too much to ruin it by starting something on the rebound. I need to talk to Beau properly, finalise things between us, and then find myself first.'

Flick smiled and drew Zoe close. 'That sounds like a very sensible decision, my darling. I'm so proud of you.'

'What about you and Theo?'

She stiffened. 'What about us?'

'I think he's one of the good guys too, Mum. Are you sure you really want things to be over between you?'

When she didn't answer straightaway, Zoe added, 'Look at Miss H. She's spent her whole life being bitter about her past, never allowing herself to open up to the possibility of a future. I know you're scared of getting hurt again, but do you really want to end up like that?'

Jack strode towards them, saving Flick from the need to reply, but Zoe's question hit her hard. She thought about nothing else for the next hour or so as they waited for news of Aurelia.

Had she been too hasty in her decision to cut Theo out of her life?

Once again, her mind drifted to Luna. Flick remembered her talking about fear. The woman was right, Flick was scared—so desperately scared of moving on and getting hurt again.

A couple of hours after they'd arrived, the emergency doors opened again and a man wearing green scrubs and a stethoscope appeared, saw Jack and headed towards them.

They all stood.

'How is she?' Zoe asked, grabbing hold of Flick's hand. She reached for Jack's with her other.

'I'm not going to lie to you,' said the doctor, 'it's not good. Aurelia has suffered severe smoke inhalation that has damaged her lungs, and she has third degree burns to her hands and arms as well. Although we've stabilised her, the next twenty-four to forty-eight hours are critical.'

'Can I see her?' Zoe asked.

The doctor nodded. 'But I'm afraid there's only room for one visitor at a time. She's not conscious at the moment, so although you can talk to her, don't expect her to respond.'

'Are you sure you're up to it?' Flick asked.

Zoe sniffed. 'Yes. I'll be fine. I want to see her. I want her to know she's no longer alone.'

Flick gave Zoe a quick hug before she headed off with the doctor. 'Do you mind staying with Zoe a little longer?' she asked Jack. 'There's something I have to do.'

'Of course not. Take your time. I'll take care of her, I promise.'

And, looking into his eyes, Flick wholeheartedly believed that he would.

'Thank you,' she whispered. 'You *are* a good man.'

416

40

Zoe

Zoe held her breath as she followed the doctor down a corridor into a large room with six beds around the perimeter. Three of the other beds were occupied but she only had eyes for one patient.

'I'll leave you with her,' said the doctor.

'Thanks.'

Miss H looked weirdly peaceful reclined slightly in the bed, but Zoe still struggled to hold back her tears. The mask on her face was attached to a machine beside her, and both her arms were wrapped in bandages from her fingertips all the way up to her armpits. Zoe wanted to hold her hand, but since that was impossible, she sat in the plastic chair beside her and spoke softly instead.

'Hello, Miss H. It's Zoe. I'm not sure if you can hear me, but I just wanted to say I'm so sorry for what happened today. I know you must be in a lot of pain right now, but I want you to know that I care about you and I want you to get better.'

But was that what Miss H would want?

She swallowed. This wasn't about making herself feel better or alleviating her guilt, it was about what was best for her friend. With no family and now probably no house, maybe she'd prefer to slip away peacefully, to finally be reunited with her beloved Remy. Even if she did recover from this physical setback, the journey to emotional recovery was going to be much longer. Zoe didn't know anything more than what she'd read on the internet about Miss H's condition—if that's even what she had—but she had a feeling remembering that Remy had died would be like experiencing that loss all over again. She'd have to go through all the stages of grief. Sure, this time she'd have proper support—Zoe would make certain of that—but it still wouldn't be easy.

At this thought, the tears she'd been managing to keep inside burst free and streamed down her face.

Eventually she spoke to Miss H again. 'I'm still here. And I'll be here as long as you need. I know this is partly my fault, so if you don't want me to work for you anymore, I understand. But if you do, I'll help you deal with insurance and everything else. You can get through this.'

About half an hour later, a nurse came over to check on Miss H. 'Is she your grandmother?'

'No … just a friend. But a close one,' she added, for fear the nurse might throw her out, but also because it was true. They might have only known each other a short while, but Zoe felt as if she'd matured and grown as a person so much during their time together. 'If … if she does wake up, when do you think it might be?'

The nurse gave her a sympathetic smile. 'I'm no fortune teller, but due to her medication, this lovely lady won't be with us again until tomorrow at the earliest. If I were you, I'd go home and get some rest, because it's when she wakes up that she's going to need you the most.'

'Okay. Thanks.' Zoe told Miss H she'd see her tomorrow and stood reluctantly.

'Where's Mum?' she asked when she emerged into the waiting room to find only Jack.

'She just popped out for a while. Said she had something she had to do. Sounded pretty important.'

Zoe frowned a moment, but then she smiled. At the end of what had been one of the hardest days of her life—and considering the last few weeks that was quite a feat—this was very welcome news. Flick deserved to be happy more than anyone.

'How's Miss H?' Jack asked.

'She's ...' Zoe shrugged. 'I honestly don't know, but she's in good hands for now. So ... do you wanna get out of this place for a bit?'

'That, Zoe Bell, is the best offer I've had in a long while.'

She chuckled and linked her arm through his as they left the hospital.

41

Felicity

Flick heard the piano and Theo's voice drifting out onto Bourbon Street before she entered the Blue Cat. It was like he was playing a funeral march or something. Gone was the usual spark in his voice and her heart clenched.

With a deep breath she walked into the bar, which looked much quieter than usual for midafternoon. Perhaps Theo's sombre tunes were scaring off the punters.

'Well, hello there,' said Lauri-Ann. She didn't look too pleased to see Flick. Theo had clearly told her they'd broken up. 'Is your daughter okay?'

He must have told her about the fire as well. 'Yes. She's fine, thank you.'

Flick glanced over to the piano where Theo sat, still playing. She couldn't help wincing at the sound.

'That's your fault, you know.' Lauri-Ann glared. 'So I hope you're here to fix things, because Lord knows I love that boy like a son, but if he keeps up with that caterwauling, I'm outta here.'

'I'm going to do my best,' Flick promised, then walked over to the stage.

The music stopped as her shadow fell over the piano. Slowly, Theo turned.

'Felicity?' Even melancholic, he was gorgeous.

'Do you have a moment?'

He nodded and stepped down to join her. 'How's Zoe?'

'She's fine. A little shaken, but physically okay.'

'That's good.' He shoved his hands in his pockets. 'And Miss H? Any news on her?'

'Not as good I'm afraid.' Flick told him what the doctor had said. 'But … I'm not here about all that.'

'Oh?'

She shook her head. 'I …'

All the way here she'd been rehearsing exactly what she was going to say. How she'd been miserable the last couple of days, how finding out the truth about Miss H had shown her there were two ways to live—in the past or in the present—and that she'd realised which one she wanted. But now that he stood only inches in front of her, the words got stuck in her throat. None were big or powerful enough to profess just how crazy she was about this man.

'I needed to do this,' she declared, then reached up on tiptoes, wrapped her arms around his neck and kissed him on the lips.

And *man*, he tasted so good. He felt so good. Kissing Theo, feeling his warm body up close to hers, *smelling* him, felt like home. It scared her how close she'd come to throwing it all away. How her fear had almost robbed her of another chance at happiness.

'Does this mean you've forgiven me?' he asked, when she reluctantly tore her lips from his to take a breath.

'There's nothing to forgive,' she gushed, blinking back tears. 'I overreacted because the intensity of my feelings for you scared me, but I love you and I'm sorry. Will *you* forgive me, please?'

He stared down at her and took her face in his hands. 'I love you too. So much,' he said, before bringing his mouth to hers in the slowest, most tender but enticing kiss she'd ever experienced. Like an earthquake whose aftershocks are felt far from the epicentre, she felt the effects right down to her toes.

'Would you two get a room?' called Lauri-Ann, but Flick could hear the joy and relief in her voice.

Theo laughed as he pulled back. 'Do you want to do just that? Or do you need to be getting back to the hospital?'

She glanced at her wrist, pretending to read a watch she didn't wear. 'It'll have to be a quick one.'

Theo grinned. 'Your wish is my command.' Then he took Flick by the hand and led her upstairs.

'Thank you for mending my heart,' she said moments later when he lay her down on his bed and began to peel off her clothes.

'No, thank *you* for mending mine.'

Flick was still smiling half an hour later when her phone beeped with a text message from Zoe: *If you're not otherwise occupied, would you and Theo like to have dinner with me and Jack?*

That would be absolutely lovely, she typed back.

Epilogue

Six months later

It was a balmy afternoon in the French Quarter. Music of all sorts and tastebud-teasing aromas wafted out from the restaurants and bars. Revellers filled the streets, many sipping cocktails from large plastic cups and snapping selfies with the beautiful buildings in the background. The vibe was happy, carefree and hopeful, which was exactly how Zoe felt as she danced down the street, a brass band behind her, friends and family surrounding her, and Flick and Theo front and centre.

Her mum looked divine in a figure-hugging white gown that Zoe had designed and made herself. Her long dark hair had been intricately styled in an up-do by her friend Neve that morning. Both Neve and Emma and their partners had made the journey for this special day and were a few steps behind Zoe now, enjoying the celebrations as much as everyone else. Flick carried a pretty white parasol in one hand, the other clasping Theo's as he walked beside her in a stylish black suit, looking like the proudest man on earth.

The happy couple had tied the knot less than an hour ago in an intimate ceremony at the cutest little pink chapel on Burgundy Street and Zoe still couldn't wipe the smile from her face. There was something special about being able to witness a parent getting married. It made her realise that, although they were a big part of her and her them, they were also their own person with separate, equally valid dreams and desires.

As they made their way towards Jackson Square to a soundtrack played by his jazz musician friends, Theo looked at Flick in a way that made it impossible for Zoe not to believe in love. And she was so damn happy that all her mum's dreams—dreams she perhaps hadn't even dared to realise she held—had finally come true. Flick had been so lost and broken when she and Sofia had parted ways and the last thing she'd been looking for when she fled to New Orleans was another relationship, but fate had had its own plans for her. And they were even better than she could ever have imagined.

Flick now lived with Theo above the Blue Cat and worked next door with Harvey. He was pleased to have the company and Flick was grateful she could still practise what she loved. She'd finished Edward for Miss H and then moved on to some projects of her own, focusing on local fauna. She'd also begun to do a little taxi-jewellery, which was something she'd always wanted to try. Zoe still didn't understand why anyone would want to wear any part of a dead animal on their person, but as long as Flick enjoyed her work, what concern was it of hers?

'So, this Theo bloke is a good guy?' Toby asked, jolting Zoe from her thoughts.

She smiled at her brother who was holding a massive cocktail and had been wearing a bamboozled expression on his face since he'd arrived yesterday afternoon. 'Yes, he's the best. How's your jet lag?'

'Okay, I think.'

'Good. Because Jack and I are gonna take you out tonight and show you a New Orleans good time. He'll give you your own personal ghost tour and then we'll have dinner and go dancing.'

Toby screwed up his face and Zoe laughed. 'Don't worry—Jack doesn't like to dance either, but it's the company that matters.'

'Are you and Jack like … you know?' Toby asked as he leaned in close so no one else could hear—as if they could over the band anyway.

She glanced across at Jack, who was bopping down the street on her other side, Miss H and Harvey next to him. 'No, we're just friends, but … never say never.'

'He's seems like a good bloke too, although not really your type.'

Zoe raised an eyebrow at her brother. 'I've dated a grand total of one man before in my life. I'm not sure I have a type. What about you? Any romance I should know about?'

'Nah.' Toby shook his head. 'Too busy working.'

'All work and no play makes Toby a dull boy,' Zoe said with a wink. 'You'll definitely have to let your hair down while you're here. I'll introduce you to Roxy—she works for Theo and is a hoot. She'll show you a good time.'

He chuckled. 'We'll see. How long till you leave?'

'Just a couple of weeks. I'm looking forward to playing tourist in my own country and I can't wait to visit Uluru.'

'You won't mind travelling with an old woman?'

'Be careful who you are calling old!' Miss H barked from a few feet away.

Zoe laughed. Her friend's hearing was better than anyone's and it was often a case of Zoe having to keep up with *her*. Miss H had

425

grabbed her second chance at life and, after recovering from her physical injuries and beginning treatment for her emotional ones, had been planning the round the world trip she'd always wanted to do, and had asked Zoe to accompany her. Their first stop would be Australia.

After the insurance company had paid Miss H out for her house, she'd put the land up for sale and sold it to a couple from Colorado who'd always wanted a summer home in the Garden District. Miss H had bought an apartment in a converted mansion, where she, Zoe and Charlotte—who'd been found two weeks after the fire, sheltering in Rachel's garden shed—were settling in well. She'd recently started painting again, but—much to the disappointment of many gallery owners—gone were the days of the skeleton brides. She'd turned her artistic skills to cats instead, but Zoe had no doubt that, in time, they would be just as sought after.

Zoe had also been painting more than ever and now had art hanging in local galleries as well. She and Miss H had floated the possibility of renting a studio and offering art classes for locals and tourists, but that would all depend on how they were feeling when they returned from their trip.

Zoe was still undecided on whether she would stay here— although to be honest it was hard to imagine living anywhere else. New Orleans definitely had a way of getting under your skin. You either loved or hated the place, and Zoe, along with Flick, Theo, Jack, Miss H and Harvey, was most definitely in the first camp.

'Congratulations,' continued the shouts from both sides of the road as the second line wedding parade continued on its way.

Zoe waved and smiled, feeling like someone famous, having the time of her life. As they neared the end of their journey through the streets, she felt a hand slip into hers and turned to Jack.

'Have I told you how hot you're looking today, friend?' he asked with the smirky-smile she'd grown to adore.

She grinned back. 'Once or twice. You're not looking so bad yourself, *friend*.'

And maybe, she thought with a thrill of anticipation, tonight was the night they'd finally cross the line from friendship into something just a bit more.

A Note From Rachael Johns

There are so many wonderful things about being an author—working
from home in your PJs with the fridge in close proximity, being able
to travel to interesting places in the name of research, walking into
a bookshop and seeing a book with your name on the cover ... the
list is endless. But one of my absolute favourite things is hearing
from readers. I'm constantly surprised, touched and delighted by the
correspondence I get from you wonderful people telling me how one
of my books or something in it has touched your heart.

Another thing that always leaves me pretty chuffed is readers
wanting a sequel.

Although readers have asked for a sequel to most of my books,
one book continues to get more requests than the others. That book
is *The Art of Keeping Secrets* and it is because of these readers that I
wrote this book (well, that and my love affair with New Orleans—
but more on that later). It took me a while to come around to the
idea because usually when I finish writing a book I've had enough

of the characters and I'm ready to say goodbye for good. However, I never say never, and some of my characters refuse to leave me alone.

Felicity Bell, Flick, is one of those characters. While her friends' stories felt complete to me at the end of *The Art of Keeping Secrets*, I had to concede that her ending was a little bit ambiguous and maybe that's why she never completely left me either. Over the last few years, I thought a lot about Flick and wondered what she was doing. It got to the point where I couldn't *stop* thinking about her and I knew then that it was time to go back and visit her, to check in and see what she was up to now.

How to Mend a Broken Heart is not a sequel in the truest form— you do not need to have read *The Art of Keeping Secrets* to read this story; I consider it more of a linked book.

Now anyone who has been following me on social media for a while will know I have a fascination with New Orleans. I went there in 2015 for a writing conference and fell in love with the French Quarter. I knew then that I wanted to go back and explore further afield one day, and, more importantly, write a book set there. It's a special place filled with a distinct culture, vibrant history, beautiful buildings, fabulous food, eclectic art and of course jazz music.

The moment I started thinking seriously about continuing Flick's story, I knew I wanted it to be set here and that she deserved a fabulous getaway to such a unique place. So, last year my friend and fellow author Anthea Hodgson and I went back to New Orleans, and this time as I strolled the markets in Jackson Square, went on ghost tours in the French Quarter, visited plantations, held a baby alligator on a trip to the Bayou and dined in the famous Commander's Palace in the gorgeous Garden District, I took Flick with me.

And we both had the time of our lives.

In Year Twelve English Lit I read Charles Dickens's *Great Expectations* and fell in love with the tragically romantic Miss

Havisham. Ever since then I've wanted to write a modern-day tribute to her with a bit of a twist. New Orleans, with its gothic atmosphere, seemed like the perfect setting for me to finally do this and I hope that you enjoyed reading about Aurelia Harranibar as much as I loved writing her.

I feel it needs to be noted that I was writing this book when the pandemic first hit and we didn't know how it would change the world. (I guess we still don't entirely.) I chose to continue to write a COVID-free world because I believe sometimes fiction is there to provide us with a reprieve from the stress of real life and also because this book would not have worked with current travel restrictions, business closures and social distancing. As *How to Mend a Broken Heart* isn't set in a specific year, I'll leave it up to you to decide whether it is pre-pandemic times or post, in a world where once again we are safe to travel freely and enjoy eating and drinking in restaurants and pubs.

Whether you were new to Felicity Bell or have been wanting more of her story, I thank you from the bottom of *my* heart for picking up *How to Mend a Broken Heart*.

I hope you enjoyed your visit to New Orleans, and don't forget, I always love to hear from readers!

Love, Rach!

Acknowledgements

I'd like to thank my agent, Helen Breitwieser, for believing in this book from the moment I sent you a few sample pages, and my publisher, Sue Brockhoff, for allowing me to write it and being so enthusiastic when you finally got to read it. It's so important to write what you love, but it really helps when you have a wonderful team cheering you on and helping you along the way. I'm so blessed to have both of you in my corner and I hope we can keep producing books together for many years to come.

Thanks must also go to the rest of the amazing and passionate team at HQ (HarperCollins)—it truly does take a village to produce a book. Much love and gratitude to (in no particular order) Annabel Blay, Natika Palka, Christine Armstrong and Johanna Baker for the hard work they put into the production, design and publicity of *How to Mend a Broken Heart*. Thanks to Theresa Anns, who holds the fort for HarperCollins in WA, but most importantly brings me Diet Coke when we visit bookstores, and to the rest of the sales team who also work tirelessly to get my books on shelves.

RACHAEL JOHNS

To the super-talented Alice Lindstrom for her awesome cover art, thank you!

I would also like to thank my brilliant editor, Dianne Blacklock, who once again saw exactly what I was trying to do and then helped make sure I got there. I know I always say it, but thanks too for your pruning skills. And I'm sorry that I can sometimes be a little stubborn!

A special shout out to Parrish Turner who did a final read on the manuscript. I am grateful for their insight and feedback and also for their knowledge on catfish and alligators!

A massive thanks to my writing friends, who are always at the end of an email (or Vox) to brainstorm, celebrate and commiserate. There are too many to name but special thanks to Beck Nicholas for reading every first draft and telling me not to throw it out the window, to Brooke Testa for reading the second draft and telling me the same, and to Anthea Hodgson who accompanied me on my research trip to New Orleans. It was a hard slog drinking all those twenty-five cent martinis, but someone had to do it! To Catherine McKinnon who went above and beyond, breaking her wrist specifically so I knew what a certain character would or wouldn't be able to do in the same predicament. Haven't I just got the best friends?

A big shout out to all the readers who pick up my books. THANK YOU! Thanks for posting on social media, for writing reviews and for messaging me to tell me how much you loved them. Also thanks to my fabulous online community—the Rachael Johns Online Book Club (find us on Facebook)—who are not only super enthusiastic about my books, but provide lots of fun and discussion during our monthly reads.

None of this would be possible without the support of booksellers and librarians—you all rock, thank you.

432

And finally, the biggest thanks goes to my family who I'm sure would much rather a wife, mother and daughter with a 'normal' career. And maybe one that didn't require me to spend so much time in my own head. I'm sorry I sometimes vague out when you're trying to tell me something—I really do love you all so very much. xx

talk about it

Let's talk about books.

Join the conversation:

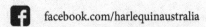 facebook.com/harlequinaustralia

 @harlequinaus

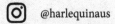 @harlequinaus

harpercollins.com.au/hq

If you love reading and want to know about our
authors and titles, then let's talk about it.

Don't miss ...

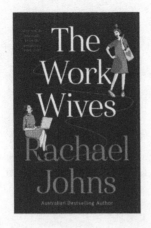

The Work Wives

by

Rachael Johns

Available Now